# Climbing Out of the Ruins

# David Spell

Volume Five of the Zombie
Terror War Series

Cover photo by Ahmadreza Heidaripoor. Used through Creative Commons CCO.

**ISBN:** 9781731299871
**Imprint:** Independently published

To Charlie and Pat.

Thank you for being great examples.

I don't say it enough but I love you!

"Ruins, for me, are the beginning. With the debris, you can construct new ideas. They are symbols of a beginning." Anselm Kiefer

"And your ancient ruins shall be rebuilt; you shall raise up the foundations of many generations; you shall be called the repairer of the breach, the restorer of streets to dwell in." (Isaiah 58:12)

"They shall build up the ancient ruins; they shall raise up the former devastations; they shall repair the ruined cities, the devastations of many generations." (Isaiah 61:4)

"When we rebuild a house, we are rebuilding a home. When we recover from disaster, we are rebuilding lives and livelihoods." Sri Mulyani Indrawati

# Chapter One

A group of thirty-five decaying, rotting zombies heard and then saw the silver four-door Toyota Tundra pickup as it rounded the curve, stopping seventy-five yards away from where they congregated in the roadway halfway between the truck and a rundown apartment building. As one, the group began growling and snapping their teeth together, shuffling towards the vehicle. Three figures quickly exited the truck and began engaging the infected. The driver, a muscular man clad in black, used the door as a barricade, firing his suppressed Colt M4 rifle over the top of it, making a head shot with almost every pull of the trigger.

The front passenger was a young, fit, African-American male carrying a camo-painted, scoped AR-15 rifle. A young white male exited from behind the passenger seat and brought his AK-47 to bear on the Zs who were intent on killing and eating them. In less than a minute, eighteen of the creatures were sprawled on the pavement, bullet holes in their heads.

The remaining seventeen zombies did not care or even notice that their companions had been shot, the crack of the gunshots only stirring them to a greater frenzy to get to their three victims.

"Reloading," Anthony Robertson, the black Marine corporal said, dropping the empty thirty-round magazine from his rifle and smoothly slamming in a fresh one from the web gear on his chest.

The other man who was firing beside Anthony, Travis Thompson, was not as effective at making head shots as the other two men. His AK soon ran empty as well, and he let his companions know that he was reloading. He dropped the empty magazine to the pavement and jerked a full one from a side cargo pocket on his pants, promptly dropping it, too.

Travis cursed out loud, made sure his muzzle didn't sweep his friends, then bent down to recover the loaded mag, finally managing to get it into his weapon. The Zs were now twenty yards away, only eight of them still standing.

Chuck McCain sighted over the driver's door, his six foot-two inch height making it easy for him to brace his rifle on the metal of the door. The two hundred and twenty pound former SWAT officer was deadly efficient, taking his time and missing few shots. When his rifle finally locked open, the remaining three infected were inside of ten yards. McCain's reload was a blur, his right thumb hitting the eject button to drop the spent mag, his right hand then grabbing a full one from the pouches on his armor plate carrier and inserting it into the firearm, his left hand hitting the slide release to send the bolt forward chambering a fresh 5.56mm round. In less than two seconds the rifle was back at his shoulder, pointing towards the threats.

McCain held his fire, though, letting Anthony and Travis make the last shots. "Scan the area," Chuck told the two younger men.

As the supervisor for the Centers for Disease Control Enforcement Unit in Atlanta, the big man had been involved from the very beginning when the zombie virus had been deployed by Iranian terrorists in the United States. He knew that the infected's strongest two senses were their smell and their hearing. Chuck's rifle was suppressed but the other two men's weapons were not. If there were any more Zs in the area, they would soon come running.

The low-income apartment complex was in front of them on the left side of the road, around a hundred and fifty yards away. McCain saw movement in the parking lot and seven more infected were coming their way, these moving much faster than the group they had just taken out. Chuck pushed the magnifier into place in front of his EOTech site, allowing him to make long distance shots.

These Zs looked mostly Hispanic, and were not as decayed as the first group, Chuck observed. In fact, McCain realized, the two fat zombies in the new group had been standing in the middle of the street two days earlier when he and Elizabeth had arrived. One of them still had on his cowboy hat, the other hefty Z wearing a belt buckle as a big as a normal dinner plate.

"Travis, cover our sides and our rear. Don't let anything sneak up behind us. Anthony, you feel up to making some long-distance head shots?" McCain challenged the young Marine with a slight grin.

The corporal looked at the man in black, easily twenty years his senior, and smiled. "I think the question is, are *you* up to it, sir?"

The forty-four year old federal law enforcement officer shrugged. "Let's see who can take down the most. I'm sure a young Devil Dog like you won't have any trouble out-shooting an old street cop like me."

Travis did what Chuck said, looking behind the truck and scanning the woods on both sides of the road, making sure that no infected got behind them. He had heard the conversation between his two companions, though, and couldn't help but smile.

Travis remembered a men's retreat at his dad's church a few years before. The guest speaker was a retired Green Beret who had brought the Bible to life for the fifty men in attendance, but who had also organized pushup contests and relay races in the parking lot between sessions. After the conference, Travis' father, Pastor Ben Thompson, thanked the speaker for his ministry but had questioned him on the PT contests.

The old soldier had laughed. "Pastor, you know that when you have two or more men together, they're going to want some competition. Men are competitive by nature and the pushups and sprints were just a small way to engage them on a physical level so that they could engage on a spiritual level."

Now, Chuck and Anthony are going to have a competition to see who can kill the most zombies, Travis thought with a grin.

The Zs had closed to a hundred and twenty yards, rushing towards what they hoped would be an easy meal.

"I'll start on the left; you start on the right," McCain said, raising his rifle.

His first shot hit one of the obese Zs just under the cowboy hat, puncturing his forehead. Anthony rushed his first shot and missed. His next round took one down, but his third round went wide of the mark.

Chuck's first three pulls of the trigger exploded zombie heads before he missed one of the moving creatures. McCain adjusted, however, and quickly dropped two more. The corporal made a good shot on a fast-moving zombie and all was quiet again.

"Sorry, Marine," Chuck grinned broadly. "Five to two. I think the old guy just took you to school."

Anthony just shook his head in disgust. Every Marine is a rifleman and none of them take getting outshot gracefully.

"Okay, that was good shooting, but those things weren't firing back at us, either. That changes the dynamics of any gunfight. I'd like to see how good you shoot when there's lead coming at you from the other direction."

Chuck nodded, unsnapping and removing the black kevlar helmet from his head. "You're right. I did two tours with a Special Forces A Team in Afghanistan as a police liaison. I saw my share of return fire and it does change everything."

The young corporal nodded at the big man with new respect. "Nice work, Chuck."

The three men watched their surroundings for another ten minutes but no other zombies appeared. "Let's head back," McCain told them. "Elizabeth and I need to hit the road."

### Hartwell, Georgia, Wednesday, 0830 hours

McCain stopped the pickup in front of two beautiful brick homes. Ridge Road was an isthmus that dead-ended into Lake Hartwell, a quarter of a mile further down. The two-story structure on the left was less than fifty yards from the lake and was where Anthony lived with his parents, Leroy and Betsy. Betsy was in the last stages of her fight with ovarian cancer. The zombie infestation and subsequent evacuation of much of the east coast had eliminated any possibility of Anthony's mom receiving medical treatment for her disease.

When Iranian terrorists had unleashed the bio-terror virus on the United States eight months earlier, the American President had declared war on Iran and unleashed the full fury of the US military on that rogue nation. The war was over within weeks, with Corporal Anthony Robertson seeing significant combat as Tehran was leveled. When it was clear that the fighting was over and Iran would never be a threat again, Robertson had requested emergency leave to return to Georgia to be with his parents before his mom died.

Right after the corporal had gotten home, however, the last three big terror strikes had been launched. Atlanta, Washington, D.C., and New York City were hit by simultaneous car bombs and suicide bombers. The explosive devices had all been packed with the normal shrapnel of screws and ball bearings, but these bombs had also been loaded with the zombie virus and radioactive waste.

The attacks had killed thousands and created thousands of new zombies that swept up and down the east coast and westward, deeper into America. The communications and power grids went down a few weeks later, increasing the chaos as survivors tried to flee to safer areas. Police officers quickly abandoned their posts, choosing to get their own loved ones to safety. With no one to stop them, packs of zombies and bands of robbers now roamed the countryside, looking for victims to prey on.

With the loss of communications, Anthony was unable to contact the Marine chain-of-command to find out where he should report. Along with his father, Leroy, his friend, Travis, and Travis' dad, Ben, the four men had kept watch on their neighbors' homes, protecting them from both zombies and looters.

Travis had served as his father's youth pastor at the Hartwell Community Church. The younger Thompson also ran one of the largest lawn care businesses in the area. Travis still lived with his parents across the street from the Robertsons. The Thompson's home was also on the water on the opposite side of the narrow isthmus. His mother, Angela, helped care for Leroy's wife, trying to make her last days as comfortable as possible.

Anthony and Travis opened the truck doors to exit the Tundra. The Marine held out his hand to Chuck. "Good luck, Mr. McCain. And congratulations on getting married."

McCain smiled, shaking the young man's hand. "Thanks Anthony. It was good meeting you. I'll be praying for your mom. And for what it's worth, I got lucky back there. I know that no one outshoots a Marine."

Robertson laughed. "You sure did!"

Chuck and Travis shook hands, but Thompson lingered for a moment in the truck. "I'm sorry I missed a lot of shots back there, Mr. McCain. I got flustered and dropped a magazine while I was trying to reload. You and Anthony were both so smooth."

McCain shook his head. "Nothing to apologize for, Travis. You did fine. Making head shots with an AK at that distance is tough for anyone, even with good optics. And remember, Anthony and I do this stuff for a living. The only advice I'd give is to practice, practice, practice. Use empty mags and work those reloads. It'll get smoother, I promise."

A hundred yards further up the road on the left was the Mitchell home where Chuck and Elizabeth had spent the previous two days. McCain pulled into the driveway, stopping in front of the house. The front door opened and Elizabeth rushed out, a concerned look on her face. She was dressed and ready to go in her gray cargo pants and black combat boots, with soft body armor over the outside of a green long-sleeve hoodie, bearing the logo of the Northeast Georgia Technical College where she had lived and worked as a guidance counselor and administrator.

Beth was wearing a 9mm Glock 19 pistol in a hip holster and her web gear, containing magazine pouches, a first-aid kit, and a flashlight, was strapped on over the body armor. A Smith & Wesson M&P AR-15 completed the package, hanging from a sling across the young woman's chest.

Chuck's wife of thirty-six hours had shoulder length light-brown hair, pulled back in a ponytail. She was a petite twenty-eight year old that McCain had rescued from kidnappers over a month before. After Chuck had killed the four murderers and would-be rapists and saved the young woman, they had sought cover in an abandoned house for almost three days as a vicious snow and ice storm blanketed the area. Elizabeth and Chuck had had a lot of time to talk as they waited for the storm to break. By the time McCain had finally gotten her back to the Northeast Georgia Technical College, where she lived with over eighty other survivors, the couple realized that they had fallen in love.

When Chuck had rescued Beth, he had been on his way to look for a clue as to where his daughter, Melanie, might be. She was dating Brian Mitchell, the young couple having met at the University of Georgia in Athens, where they were both students. When the zombie virus had been released on that school some months before, McCain was able to make sure that the couple fled before the campus fell to the infected.

Brian had driven Melanie to his parent's beautiful lakeside home northeast of the small town of Hartwell. Chuck had last spoken to his daughter over three months earlier. As thousands of zombies were surging in every direction on the interstate system, McCain had urged Brian's father, Tommy, to flee the area. Tommy had assured Chuck that they would be packing up and heading for his parent's farm near Hendersonville, North Carolina. Melanie was supposed to have called her dad back with the address of where they were going, but the communication grid had failed.

Chuck and Elizabeth had found the Mitchell's home on Monday, meeting Ben and Travis Thompson and Leroy and Anthony Roberts as they were manning a roadblock in front of their own residences. When McCain identified himself, Pastor Ben had given him an envelope with the address and a hand drawn map of where the Mitchells were going. Tommy Mitchell had also enclosed a key to his home in the envelope, as well.

As Beth and Chuck had sat in the sunroom, overlooking Lake Hartwell on Monday afternoon, McCain had gotten the courage to ask Elizabeth to marry him. Thankfully, she had enthusiastically said, "Yes!" Pastor Ben had performed the wedding on Monday evening in a candlelit service in the Thompson's living room.

"How'd it go?" Beth asked, opening the driver's door of the pickup.

"We got 'em all," Chuck answered, exiting the vehicle. "At least, all that we saw. There were a lot more than the group you and I encountered driving up here on Monday. Remember those two really big Mexican zombies near that apartment complex?"

She shook her head. "I only remember there was a big one in a cowboy hat. I was kind of focused on getting us out of there."

"That was one of them. I'm guessing we took out over forty Zs. Thankfully, when we leave, we'll turn off before we get to that apartment complex. I mapped out a route where we'll just skirt the downtown area of Hartwell. Then you'll drive us around the east side of the lake into South Carolina on Highway 29."

Beth nodded thoughtfully. "That seems like a long detour out of the way. Wouldn't it be better to head back towards Lavonia and just jump on the interstate over there?"

"Yeah, you're right, it's longer, but I think it's gonna be safer. We know Lavonia was completely overrun when those thousands of Zs swept through. We only saw a few on Monday when we got to Hartwell, except for that group near those crappy apartments down the road."

Elizabeth accepted her new husband's reasoning without a second thought. She was learning that in tactical matters, he was rarely wrong.

"Our packs are ready to go," the young woman said, tugging a black stocking cap over her head. "They're just inside the front door. I gathered up all the food that would fit in them and there was a pack of bottled water in the pantry that we can take with us."

Chuck smiled, following Beth into the house. "Excellent. I guess that's it then. It was nice of the Mitchells to let us use their home for our very short honeymoon. Hopefully, it won't be long before I can take you on a extended vacation."

The young woman turned and put her arms around the big man's neck, looking deep into his eyes. "That will be nice! Thank you for letting us stay the extra day. I know you had really wanted to leave yesterday but I'd have to say, lying in bed with you all day was one of the highlights of my life."

McCain pulled her close and kissed her. "I would have to agree with you, Mrs. McCain. I look forward to a lifetime of those."

**Hartwell, Georgia, Wednesday, 0940 hours**

The newlyweds stopped to say their good-byes to Pastor Ben and Angela Thompson. As the women were talking, Ben pulled McCain aside and shared some disturbing news.

"Chuck, I don't know if you've heard this or not, but I turn on my ham radio anytime I fire up the generator. It's a great way to get news about what's going on in the outside world. Most of the time, there's just static but this morning, someone was transmitting from down near Atlanta, saying that the city has fallen to a Mexican gang, a cartel or something."

"What? That's crazy!" said Chuck. "I know it fell to the zombies. I was in the middle of it, fighting them right after that car bomb and suicide bomber were detonated. Before we had a clue how bad it was, there were already thousands of Zs roaming the city. I lost one of my men and almost got killed myself."

Ben nodded. "It does sound crazy. This guy transmits every now and then and sounds legit. He said a big Mexican group has set up shop in Buckhead. This cartel leader has supposedly hooked up with a couple of the other gangs in town and they've formed some kind of alliance. They've cleaned out a lot of the zombies and have a safe zone where they live. The worst of it, though, is that these Mexicans have managed to find a bunch of survivors in the area, but have killed the men and kept the women as slaves."

Chuck shook his head. "Wow. I hope that's all bogus. I'd hate to think that could be true."

As they started their journey, Beth drove the big pickup with Chuck riding behind her in the backseat, cradling his M4, looking for threats. McCain chose the rear compartment so that he could fire out either side if they were attacked. Before the couple had left the technical college on Monday morning, Jake Nicholson, one of the faculty members, had some of the automotive students weld armor plating to the outside of the vehicle's doors, hood, and engine compartment. They had also replaced the plastic front bumper with a heavy metal one to allow the vehicle to plow through packs of infected.

Elizabeth retraced their route back towards the small town of Hartwell until Chuck had her make a couple of turns to get onto Old Highway 29 heading south. They were able to bypass the downtown area, heading for Anderson Highway, a major five-lane thoroughfare. So far, the roads had been clear of both the living and the dead.

As they made their left turn onto the highway, Chuck saw a Walmart Super Center, a Home Depot, and several restaurants just up ahead on their right. After they got past these, they would be out of the city, heading northeast towards South Carolina. There was no other traffic on the road and only a few abandoned vehicles littering the street.

"Movement in the Walmart parking lot," Chuck called out as they neared the store. "We're good. They're at least two hundred yards away."

There were cars scattered over the large parking area. The doors of the huge store were standing open and the windows were smashed out, with a group of over twenty zombies congregating near the front entrance. The sound of the Tundra got their attention, however, and they began shuffling towards the street. Chuck used the optics on his rifle to scan the crowd as they drove past. It was a mixed group: men and women, black and white, the virus had played no favorites. These infected were all well into the decaying process, their skin gray and hanging off of their bloody bodies. The bio-terror virus was the only thing that kept them moving.

Another group, this one closer to the street, was loitering in the Home Depot lot. Like the ones at Walmart, however, these had been infected for a while, their bodies rotting away and keeping them from moving quickly in pursuit of their prey.

"More at the Home Depot," Beth said, glancing to her right and shaking her head. "They look rough!"

"Yeah, other than that one young Z I shot on our way into town on Monday, and a couple of the ones we killed this morning, these all look like they turned months ago," Chuck commented. "This was a small town to begin with, maybe five thousand people, but with the few zombies we've seen, that tells me most of the residents were smart and got out of Dodge before it got bad."

They were soon out of Hartwell, moving into rural east Georgia. Beth drove straddling the centerline. With no other traffic to contend with, staying in the middle of the road would give them more options for escape if they faced an emergency.

They passed homes set hundreds of feet off of the highway, a few businesses, and several churches, but there were no signs of life. Fifteen minutes later, McCain knew they were approaching the bridge that would lead into South Carolina. Rounding a bend in the roadway, the overpass was just a half-mile in front of them.

"Can you stop and let me scope out that bridge? This was one of the areas I was concerned about when I was looking at the maps. It's a natural choke point and perfect for an ambush."

Elizabeth stopped in the middle of the road and Chuck climbed up into the back of the pickup, leaning over the cab, studying the area in front of him with his binoculars. The bridge crossing the Savannah River was more than two hundred yards long with a dense forest leading up to the overpass and continuing into South Carolina. There on the left, he thought. Just past the bridge was a driveway or a parking lot. From his vantage point, he couldn't see anything because the vegetation was too thick. That would be the spot if someone wanted to ambush unsuspecting motorists.

"What do you think?" Beth inquired as McCain got back into the pickup.

Chuck smiled, covering his anxiety. "I think I'm the luckiest man on the planet."

Elizabeth smiled back. "You're sweet. So, you want me to keep going?"

Chuck nodded. "After you cross the bridge, get into the right lane and floor it. There's something just inside South Carolina on the left, maybe a driveway or a park, but it would be a good place for bad guys to hide."

As they started forward, Chuck swung his rifle around so that he could shoot out of the left side of the vehicle, pushing the selector on the side of the gun to "Auto." The cold air blew through the open windows as Beth accelerated, her hands gripping the steering wheel tightly. McCain glanced over, seeing that their speed was at eighty-five miles an hour as they burst across the bridge. Chuck's eyes scanned over the top of his rifle as he pointed it out the window, waiting to be attacked. Half way to the other side, the sun reflected off of something chrome hidden behind the trees in that parking area.

Chuck didn't want to panic Beth and it was too late to turn around. The police officer tensed for contact, his finger on the trigger of the M4. As they raced past the potential ambush site, McCain saw that it was a recreation area where people could access the river. It was devoid of vehicles, except for one. He just got a glimpse of a wrecked silver Toyota 4Runner sitting inside the entrance as the Tundra sped by. There were no signs of people or of an attack.

The big man exhaled audibly in relief and after a half mile, Chuck tapped Elizabeth on the shoulder.

"We're good now, you can slow down. Good driving."

She relaxed, backing off of the accelerator but kept their speed at around fifty miles an hour, continuing their journey towards finding her husband's daughter. Elizabeth could see Chuck in her rear view mirror watching the forest on either side of them, determined not to be taken by surprise. He's so handsome, she smiled to herself, remembering the morning after he had rescued her. Her head had throbbed in pain from the beating she had taken at the hands' of her attackers, but she still had thought that Mr. Chuck McCain was one good-looking man.

"What's that up there?" she wondered out loud, movement ahead of them bringing her eyes and thoughts back to the road.

Another parking area was just ahead of them on the left, next to the lake. Suddenly, a black Cadillac Escalade burst out from the driveway into their path, blocking the road.

"Chuck! Look out!" Beth slammed on the brakes, skidding to a stop just as a bullet struck the armored hood of their Tundra and ricocheted into the far edge of the passenger side of the windshield, cracking it. Another shot slammed into the front of the pickup.

"Duck down and cut the wheels to the left," Chuck ordered.

She jerked the steering wheel in a counter-clockwise direction putting the Tundra length-wise to their attackers, the Cadillac SUV just a hundred and fifty feet away. Two black males were shooting at them with pistols and a third was firing a shotgun.

"Stay low and be ready to get us out of here," McCain said, diving out of his door and going prone on the pavement, aiming his rifle underneath the pickup.

He placed the red cross in his EOTech site on the leg of an attacker who was standing on the opposite side of the Escalade, firing a pistol at them through the open windows. McCain's 5.56mm round hit the thug in the center of his right shin, shattering it and sending the man screaming to the pavement.

Chuck quickly moved to the front of the Tundra and crouched, waiting until he saw a head poke around the back of the Cadillac. The gunman saw McCain at the same time, triggering his shotgun. Chuck heard a few pellets sing as they hit the armor plating on the side of the truck. The big man instinctively placed the site of his rifle scope over the young man's face and pulled the trigger. A red mist hung in the air as the dead shooter joined his wounded companion on the ground.

The Escalade started rolling forward, the third gunman having had enough after seeing his two friends bleeding on the pavement. He'd jumped into the driver's seat of the SUV, attempting to make a fast getaway. McCain was already on the move to the rear of the Tundra, never staying in one shooting position for too long.

He was startled by the explosion of three unsuppressed gunshots from inside their vehicle. McCain swiveled his head to see Elizabeth with her AR-15 braced against the open passenger window, looking through her Aimpoint optics. When he looked back up the street, the Cadillac lurched across the road and slammed into the guardrail. Beth turned and made eye contact with Chuck, bursting out in a huge grin.

"I got him!" she exclaimed.

The gunman that Chuck had shot in the leg was still writhing in the roadway, now exposed to view. The second shooter wasn't moving, lying facedown on the pavement. The Cadillac SUV sat motionless against the guardrail, the driver slumped over the steering wheel.

"Okay, let's pull up and secure the scene," McCain said, getting into the truck. "Stop in the middle of the road about twenty feet from the wounded one. I just put a bullet through his leg so he's still a threat. When we get out, your job is to watch behind us and watch our sides. Let me deal with the bad guys and then we'll see what they have."

"Got it," Beth nodded, her expression tense, driving them up the road.

Chuck's door was open and he was out of the vehicle before she could put it in park. His rifle was up as he slowly walked towards the wounded man. When McCain was ten feet away, the groaning gunman opened his eyes and saw the man in black approaching him. The thug still held his Hi-Point 9mm pistol in his left hand, his right clasped around his bleeding, shattered shin. The pistol started to swing towards Chuck, but the suppressed rifle barked twice, one 5.56mm bullet slamming into his chest, the second round hitting him in the forehead. The pistol fell from the would-be ambusher's hand and he lay still, blood pooling around his head.

"Watch the Escalade while I check this guy," Chuck told Elizabeth.

She covered the vehicle as McCain slowly approached the second man lying facedown in the roadway. His shotgun lay a few feet away. Chuck used his foot to roll him over, observing that the bullet had struck him just below the right eye. McCain could see that, like his companion, he wasn't going anywhere.

Chuck slowly eased over to the Escalade, his rifle up, finger on the trigger. Elizabeth was trailing him now, watching behind them. The driver was a very young black male, maybe sixteen, the CDC officer realized. One of Beth's shots had caught him behind the right ear, killing him instantly. A second bullet had passed through the top of the driver's seat, hitting the young criminal in the right shoulder.

"That was really good shooting, Beth. I'm impressed," Chuck commented.

As the adrenaline started to wear off and as she was able to see the results of her marksmanship, she didn't look so sure of herself. McCain opened the driver's door of the Cadillac and yanked the body out, dropping it unceremoniously to the pavement. Chuck searched the corpse for anything useful that he might have been carrying.

"Maybe I should've let him go," Elizabeth said, softly, uncertainty in her voice. "He's just a kid and he was running away. I didn't have to kill him."

Chuck glanced at his wife. "We'll talk about it later. Please keep watch while I go through the car."

The young woman turned away from the dead body lying at her feet and stepped to the rear of the SUV, scanning their surroundings, holding her AR-15 in a low ready stance. Should I have killed him? she asked herself. A wave of remorse washed over her.

McCain found another 9mm Hi-Point pistol laying on the passenger seat. This one was jammed, an empty casing sticking out of the ejection port. No surprise there, he thought, ejecting the magazine and checking the ammo. The 9mm bullets were full metal jacket and not Chuck's preferred hollow points, but the rounds looked to be new so he slipped the mag into his pocket. With ammo having become a limited commodity, he wasn't about to throw bullets away.

As a police officer, McCain had always been amazed at the number of criminals who chose the Hi-Point for their illegal activities. The guns were inexpensive but also bulky, ugly, and more importantly, quick to jam in a firefight. Maybe they were a step up from the proverbial "Saturday night special" but not by much.

The effective range of most handguns is twenty-five yards and closer. These dead thugs, whose only firearms training had probably come from playing video games, had engaged him and Elizabeth at twice that distance, only managing a couple of hits on the Toyota Tundra.

There was nothing of use on the body of the driver or inside the car. As Beth continued to watch their surroundings, Chuck searched the other two corpses. The one whom he had initially shot in the leg had nothing in his pockets. Surprisingly, his Hi-Point had not malfunctioned, but McCain still didn't want it. He removed the magazine of ammo and flung the pistol to the side of the road.

A Mossberg Maverick .12 gauge shotgun lay near the last attacker. The gun had a black polymer stock and forearm and looked to be in good shape. The dead man had eight extra shotgun shells in his pocket and another Hi-Point pistol tucked into his waistband. Chuck pocketed the shotgun shells, kept the loaded magazine of 9mm rounds, flung the pistol aside, and picked up the shotgun.

"See anything?" he asked Elizabeth.

"No, should we go check over there?" She nodded across the street to where the Escalade had made its appearance.

It was a small park that jutted out onto Lake Hartwell. A single driveway provided access, circling an island of trees in the middle of a parking lot. Since it was still winter, they could see past the stark vegetation to a small pavilion containing several picnic tables and brick grills scattered around the area. The parking lot continued past the picnic area, the back side of the recreation area concealed behind the island of trees.

Chuck shrugged. "Might as well. Maybe these clowns have a campsite back there we can scope out. Let's check the Tundra for damage first."

The armor had done its job. A round had impacted the metal bumper on the front of the truck, barely putting a dent in it. A bullet had ricocheted off the hood, leaving a crack in the windshield but not shattering it. They found a few other dings where 9mm bullets or .12 gauge 00 pellets had bounced off the side armor.

Before they got back into the Toyota, Chuck showed Beth how to swap out the mag in her rifle for a full one. He did the same with his M4 even though he had only fired four rounds. One of the things that the Green Berets had taught him was to use a lull in the fighting to make sure your weapon was fully loaded.

Elizabeth drove slowly into the park. With the leaves down, they could see almost the entire picnic area in the middle of the parking lot. As they pulled behind it however, they saw two vehicles sitting side-by-side against the curb, facing the lake.

A white Chevrolet Silverado pickup and a gray Ford Fusion both appeared unoccupied but they would need to check to be certain. Chuck had Beth stop ten feet behind the Chevrolet. He approached cautiously, his rifle up and ready, Elizabeth standing in the doorway of their truck covering him with her AR.

He started on the driver's side, visually clearing the bed of the pickup and then the passenger compartment. Empty. His nose, however, alerted him that there was something dead nearby. He glanced at Beth and touched his nose. She sniffed the air and nodded at him, bringing her rifle to eye level as she scanned the area for zombies. Her husband had taught her that that smell usually meant there were infected close by.

A quick check confirmed that the Fusion was also unoccupied. A flat grassy area to the right contained two tents, thirty yards away. McCain pointed at the tents and motioned for Elizabeth to follow him, the lake now to their left. The smell of death got stronger as they got closer to the camping area. Were there Zs in the tents? he wondered.

They were halfway there when a slight breeze brought the scent of death to Chuck's nostrils again. They were really close, he realized, fear making his heart pound. He stopped walking, spinning completely around in the parking lot, looking for the zombies. Where were they?

Beth smelled it too, but neither of them could see any Zs. Chuck raised his nose again, the strong odor of decay coming from the lake just a few feet to his left. He slowly moved in that direction. There was a four-foot drop off to the rocks below, the water just a few feet away. Five dead and decomposing bodies were sprawled on the rocks where they had been tossed.

Elizabeth was still standing in the parking lot, twenty feet away, watching their surroundings. She glanced at Chuck and saw a look of relief on his face as he looked down from the edge of the overlook.

"What do you see?" she asked quietly.

He shook his head and motioned towards the tents. "Let's clear the camping area first."

The flaps of both tents were open, Chuck shining his flashlight around the inside. The first tent was empty except for an air mattress in the middle of the floor with handmade restraints attached to the poles running alongside the canvas walls. There was blood splatter on the sides of the tent and on the pink sheet that covered the air mattress.

Elizabeth saw the anger in Chuck's eyes after he pulled his head out of the first tent. She had a sudden flashback to the morning after he had saved her life, how she had looked into his eyes and seen danger. Not that she had ever worried about him hurting her. He had risked his life to rescue her, getting shot in the process. While they had been trapped in the abandoned house, he had been the perfect gentleman, even turning down an offer of sex after Beth had had a little too much to drink.

She had seen, however, how dangerous her husband could be to those who threatened him or those he loved, and in her case at the time, even a complete stranger.

"What's wrong?" she whispered.

He held up a finger and motioned at the other tent. A quick check verified that it was also empty. McCain saw some supplies that he would investigate further but he needed to let his wife know what he had observed now that the scene was secure.

He pointed at the first tent and said, "Take a look."

Elizabeth knelt, shining her light inside. "No! Were these guys doing what I think they were doing?"

"Shhh. Not so loud," Chuck said, leading her back over to where he'd observed the bodies. "Let me show you what I saw over here.

It's pretty rough, but I think you need to see it."

As Beth looked down on the tangle of bodies on the rocks below, she felt a wave of nausea sweep over her. That was what they had smelled. It was the scent of death, but it was actual corpses and not zombies. McCain guessed that the bodies had been there for at least a week.

She saw the bodies of three men, one black, two white, all fully clothed, with gunshot wounds to the head. The nude corpses of a black female and a white female were tossed onto the rocks, as well. The women's bodies were covered with bruises, abrasions, and cuts. Their faces were battered and it took no imagination to figure out that they had died horrible deaths.

Unable to fight it, Elizabeth turned, vomiting off to the side. When she had emptied her stomach out, Beth realized Chuck was standing next to her, a concerned look on his face. When she stood upright, he handed her a bottle of water.

"I'm sorry," she stammered. "It's just…I mean, I can't understand. Why?"

"Let's go sit over there for a minute," McCain pointed over to the pavilion near where their vehicle was.

They sat at a picnic table sipping water. Late February in South Carolina meant cold temperatures at night and comfortable weather during the day. Currently, the sun was out, the temperatures felt like they were in the mid-fifties, and the slight breeze let them know that spring was just around the corner. It was a beautiful day.

"What do you think happened?"

"There are two vehicles there," Chuck shrugged, pointing at the Silverado and the Fusion. "Probably the black couple was together and the other two guys and girl were together. Those losers that tried to ambush us got those poor people to stop. They killed the guys outright and kept the girls around and used them until they got tired of them. That's why you don't need to feel bad about shooting the punk who was trying to get away. Remember, the rules have changed. Until the government starts functioning again, there are no police to protect you. There's no Thin Blue Line to keep us safe."

Beth nodded and took a deep breath. The young man in the Cadillac wasn't the first person whom she had killed. Over a month earlier, the Northeast Georgia Technical College was attacked by a gang connected with the men who had kidnapped Elizabeth. They had managed to trace Chuck and Beth back to the school and came seeking revenge for the four gang members McCain had killed.

Elizabeth had shot three of the intruders as a firefight broke out involving the rest of the gang, Chuck, and the campus security team. Thirteen attackers had been killed in the confrontation. Unfortunately, three of the campus residents had died with another five wounded, including McCain. Thankfully, his wound wasn't serious and after a month of healing, he and Beth were able to continue on Chuck's original quest to find his daughter, Melanie.

Chuck put his hand over Elizabeth's. "I know it doesn't seem right to shoot someone who's running away and isn't a threat anymore. I'm a police officer; I understand. You're a good person. I like to think I'm a good person. Something I learned from the Special Forces, though, is that you never let a threat walk away. If you can take them into custody, take them into custody. If you can't do that, you kill them. Whether you realize it or not, by shooting that guy in the car, you may have saved someone else's life tomorrow."

Beth looked into her husband's eyes. Originally, he wasn't going to take her on this trip up north, telling her it was too dangerous. After the attack on the campus, however, he realized that there were no safe places and she would be better off with him than she would be at the school. Chuck had spent two weeks training the young woman on weapons skills and tactics. Clearly, the training was paying off.

A grin broke out on her husband's face. "I'm proud of you," he said. "You really are becoming a deadly weapon."

She smiled back, his words making her feel better. "I've got a really good teacher."

McCain leaned in, kissing his pretty wife, his lips lingering, teasing. After a few minutes, the couple stood and walked hand-in-hand back to their armored truck to continue their dangerous journey.

# Chapter Two

## Buckhead, Atlanta, Wednesday, 1100 hours

Antonio, "Tony el Tigre," Fernando Corona stood in his red silk bathrobe on the balcony of the top floor of the fifty story apartment building that he had claimed for himself and his men. He was of average height but obese, his stomach protruding and making more than one of his soldiers think that their boss looked pregnant. In truth, however, he had lost at least twenty pounds since coming to Atlanta, the quantity of food that he was used to consuming every day, not being available. He wore his black hair long and slicked back, his idea of a cross between a ladies' man and a gangster.

The Peachtree Summit Luxury Condominiums was the name on the sign out front. Corona had already decided to rename it after himself. Casa de Corona or El Palacio de Corona? No rush. He had plenty of time and many more important things to concern himself with than naming his headquarters.

Two nude women slept in the large bed behind him. The light-skinned black girl and the blonde had been found hiding in an office building nearby, three weeks earlier. His lieutenant, Jorge Quintero, knowing his boss' taste in women, had not let the cartel soldiers harm these two. Quintero did make sure the two survivors watched his men execute their three male coworkers found in the office with them. Seeing their friends shot in the head had left the two ladies in a state of shock but ensured that they understood the gravity of their own situation.

Jorge let them know that he was taking them to his boss and that their lives were dependent on how happy they made him. Tiffany, the blonde, and Alissa, the African-American, both nodded, unable to speak as they remembered their friends' bodies left to bleed out in the Atlanta street. Quintero knew that he had done well as he saw Corona's eyes light up when presented with the pair of lovely captives.

Antonio considered himself a sophisticated man and had not harmed the women. He had slapped them around a little the first few days that he had them, but that was just to get their attention. They had quickly understood what was required of them, and had worked hard to please the cartel leader.

Corona scanned the skyline of the once beautiful city. Smoke rose from various locations throughout Atlanta. The smell of death and decay was still in the air but some of the recent death and destruction had been caused by him and his men. And he was just getting started.

Four months earlier, Antonio had been contentedly helping his uncle run the Tijuana Cartel. Even though they were located in Mexico, their cartel ran much of the drug and sex trafficking business in the Southern United States. Corona had visited Atlanta on many occasions, making sure their operations were running smoothly. On his last trip, he had personally executed two of his subordinates, one of whom had gotten greedy, while the other had become careless.

The greedy one thought that no one would notice if he skimmed a little money off the top for himself. It was the last mistake that he ever made. Corona's obesity did not take away from his physical strength. He was a dangerous man, having beaten more than one enemy to death. Tony the Tiger had made the thief's death as painful as he could, using his knife first, carving him up, before eventually shooting him in the stomach and letting him die slowly.

The careless cartel member had lost a shipment of ten kilos of cocaine to the police on a traffic stop. The drug runner had abandoned the car and fled on foot, managing to elude the officers and even their dog and helicopter.

No matter. The cartel would have killed him in prison if he had been arrested. He should have kept running and tried to disappear. By returning to his apartment, the subordinate just made Antonio's job easier. In Corona's mind, however, carelessness was not as great a sin as stealing from your employer, so this man received a quick death: a bullet to the back of the head.

In Tijuana, the senior leadership of the cartel had been following the events in America and especially the east coast closely. The cartel had even helped smuggle many of the Islamic soldiers and suicide bombers into the United States. The Muslims had paid the Mexicans very well.

Now, Antonio's uncle, Jose "Pepe" Corona, saw a chance to regain some of his cartel's lost glory. The Mexican Federal Police, at least those who weren't on his payroll, and the American Drug Enforcement Agency had killed or imprisoned many of his best people. Jose's brother, Antonio's father, Juan, had been killed in a shootout with the federales just two years earlier. Now was the perfect time to strike back against the arrogant gringos and reclaim some of what they had lost.

With the American east coast in shambles, and thousands of zombies still roaming around unchecked, this was the opportunity of a lifetime. Pepe called his nephew, Tony the Tiger, into his office and outlined his plan. At first, the younger man was shocked by the boldness of the idea. As his uncle talked, however, Antonio began to see that this was his chance to do everything that he had ever wanted to do. He could build his own criminal empire with his uncle's blessing.

Antonio brought his lieutenant, Jorge, twenty of the cartel's best soldiers, and his ever-present, four man security detail. A caravan of forty vehicles contained close to a hundred and thirty additional enforcers, many of whom had been serving life sentences in various prisons throughout Mexico. Most of the prison recruits were members of the vicious Sureños 13 gang, which had a strong presence in Mexico's maximum security facilities. Pepe's money and threats were able to secure their release, along with his promise that these notorious criminals would be crossing the unprotected border into the United States.

As the caravan drove towards Georgia, they stopped at every one of their operations across the south and drafted more soldiers to join them. It had not been an easy sell and Corona knew that he needed the men to buy into what he was asking them to do.

The idea of going into a city that was, for all practical purposes, under the control of thousands of zombies was not something that the American-based cartel members wanted to be involved in. They had a good life in their own cities spread across the American southeast and southwest. They were paid well to sell drugs and to run brothels. Why would they want to go to a place where someone wanted to rip their throats out and eat them?

Tony the Tiger became Tony the Politician. He promised them more than he ever would have under normal circumstances. These were clearly abnormal circumstances and he was ready to offer those who came with him a much larger piece of the pie. A total of thirty-seven more Mexican hombres malos volunteered to join him.

The journey to Atlanta was no picnic. They had to shoot their way through several groups of zombies, losing three of his men near Birmingham, Alabama. As they approached their target city, Antonio knew that getting into the urban center was going to be the most difficult part of the plan. The fight into the heart of Atlanta was brutal, and the cartel leader lost twelve more soldiers to the infected.

Two months later, things were finally looking up. The area around Corona's building had been purged of zombies. He had lost a few more men to the infected but other Hispanics, including a dozen members of the notorious street gang MS-13, had shown up wanting to work for him. This gang, composed primarily of El Salvadorans, was usually at odds with the Mexican cartels and street gangs. These twelve, however, pledged their loyalty to the cartel boss and he was willing to give them a chance in his ever-growing operation. Twenty gangbangers from former rival clans had also approached the cartel offering their services with additional recruits showing up daily.

Early on, there had been some conflict and a few fistfights between some of the gang members. Jorge Quintero had kept the tensions from escalating into gunfights by forcing the gangsters to work together. Work details and patrols had members of various groups mixed together.

Quintero had also threatened severe repercussions to any gang members who started a conflict. None of them were allowed to wear their respective colors. The only colors Jorge authorized were the red, white and green of the Mexican flag. All of the Latino gangsters were coming to understand that their survival depended on working together and that Atlanta was ripe for the taking if they stayed unified.

Antonio knew enough about the city to know that Buckhead was the most affluent area in Atlanta. After picking out the large high-rise condominium building for his headquarters, his men cleared it, floor by floor, until it was secure. The building was relatively new, with most of the apartments empty, waiting to be sold or rented out. The few survivors his men found in occupied apartments were dealt with harshly. The men were thrown from the balconies of the higher floors by laughing cartel members, the women raped or executed if they resisted. The pretty ones had been kept as slaves.

After the Peachtree Summit was secured Antonio had his soldiers begin clearing the surrounding area starting with their block. Barricades of abandoned vehicles were set up to block off the roads and to keep the infected out. That was going to be the biggest battle, keeping the zombies from returning to areas that had been cleared.

There were still plenty of survivors hiding out in the many other upscale apartments or seeking shelter in office buildings surrounding the cartel HQ. At first, they were excited to see Antonio's men coming to rescue them. Their joy was short-lived, however, as most of the male survivors were taken into the street and shot. The women were bound, and taken back to Corona's headquarters.

Some of the smaller, weaker men were kept alive, as Antonio considered himself a businessman who supplied the right product or service for every paying customer. He didn't think that many of his soldiers were gay, but these male sex slaves could eventually be sold, along with some of the women whom he had captured.

Within two weeks of the clan's arrival, former inner-city gang members began approaching his soldiers at their barricades, wanting to offer their services to the Tijuana Cartel. Tony the Tiger wished that he could staff his army with only Mexican fighters, but he knew that wasn't realistic. All of the Mexicans in the United States, both legal and illegal, weren't cut out to be cartel soldiers, but there were plenty of other roles in which his countrymen could serve. These African-American thugs looked tough and came from the same background as him and his cartel members.

Jorge handled the initial interview, giving the group of eight dark-skinned, unsmiling men some tasks to prove themselves. The first one was to bring back weapons. The cartel soldiers were well armed but they would always need more guns and ammo to equip their ever growing army.

Two days later, three military humvees showed up, all packed with weapons. There were M-16s, 9mm Berettas, some shotguns, and a few other assorted handguns. Just as important as the weapons, though, were the spare magazines and hundreds of rounds of ammunition. Each hummer also sported an M249 light machine gun in its turret. The group of eight black gangsters had also grown to thirteen as they had recruited a few of their friends.

Antonio joined his lieutenant at the barricade, smiling at the haul. Maybe these guys would work out after all, he thought.

"Bueno, amigos. Where you find all of this?"

A tall muscular man with a shaved head and a black, bushy beard answered, "We've had the hummers for a while. We took out a National Guard Patrol when they first showed up. The M-16s and a few Berettas came from them. Those weekend warriors can't shoot for anything. The zombies did a lot of the work for us, overrunning some the guard's checkpoints. We just had to go in, load up everything they left behind, and shoot some zombie soldiers.

"The police were also kind enough to give us some guns. A few of the pigs made the mistake of not watching their backs. We took care of them and relieved them of their stuff."

"What's your name, amigo?"

"Derrick, but you can call me 'DC.'"

Corona extended his hand. "DC, bienvenido for the Tijuana cartel. Welcome!"

Antonio was impressed. This weapons haul might not prove the loyalty of the new guys but it was a good start. He let the African-Americans each keep a long gun and a sidearm and the rest he had secured in the armory his men had set up in their headquarters.

Week by week, the cartel soldiers worked together, clearing the ever-widening area around their headquarters of zombies, seeking out human survivors, and looking for food, clothes, and supplies for the gang members. The fifty story apartment building housed the entire army for the moment, with a secure area around the intersection of Peachtree Road and Piedmont Road. Antonio found himself in control of one of the richest areas of the city.

He knew that eventually someone would come for him and his men. The question was, "Who?" The Atlanta Police Department didn't appear to be a threat. A couple of police cars had approached their barricade the first week the cartel was in town. His guards had opened fire, killing the two officers in the first police car. The second cruiser turned and fled. There had been no more police sightings after that.

The National Guard had shown that they were not up to the job. In so many cases the citizen-soldiers just had not had the training they needed to keep them alive in a city full of zombies and roving bands of heavily armed criminals. Patrol after patrol had been overrun by zombies. The soldiers had either been devoured or infected. In reality, they had had little or no effect on eliminating Zs from the city. In other cases, like DC had described for Tony the Tiger, gang members had ambushed the National Guard troops, killing them and stealing their equipment.

Corona suspected that eventually the government would send federal police officers after he and his men. He didn't fear the FBI or the DEA or any of their tactical teams. They just did not have enough men to arrest the Atlanta chapter of the Tijuana Cartel.

No, the only force capable of taking down Antonio and his soldiers was the American Special Forces, and he was gambling that that wasn't going to happen. The Americans didn't like to use their military on their own soil. That was good for him and his cartel but bad for the women and men who were already servicing his soldiers.

Corona's next goal was to begin expanding his empire further out into the state. Even as he established his foothold in the city, he wanted to begin moving out into the suburbs with his patrols. As word of his conquest got around, the cartel boss expected Mexicans from all over America to join him. Why wouldn't they? The selfish Americans hoarded all of their wealth, refusing to share it with their southern neighbors. As his army grew, Tony the Tiger was going to expand his empire as far as he could.

Antonio was not only a conqueror, though. He was also a businessman. The drug trade was still lucrative, even in the midst of a bonafide zombie apocalypse. People still wanted their cocaine, meth, weed, and the occasional prostitute. The Tijuana Cartel had it all and Antonio "Tony el Tigre" Fernando Corona was not going to stop until he controlled the entire east coast of the United States of America.

A knock on his door caused the two women to stir and brought Antonio back inside from the balcony. He opened the door, admitting Jorge Quintero who was holding two paper cups of steaming coffee.

"Gracias, amigo," the cartel leader said, taking one of the cups.

"De nada, señor."

Corona and Quintero met almost daily, discussing their progress and their operations. Jorge was one of the few men that Antonio trusted completely, having grown up together on the streets of Tijuana. They walked through the master bedroom out onto the balcony, Jorge glancing appreciatively at the two beauties in his boss' bed. The men seated themselves in patio chairs, sipping their coffee, gazing out over the city.

"So, how are we progressing?" Antonio asked in Spanish.

"We've cleared four of the surrounding blocks and our barricades are keeping the zombies out. We've killed hundreds, maybe more than a thousand of them. I know they're still out there, but we haven't seen any big groups in a couple of weeks.

"The challenge now is keeping our people fed. We're sending out teams every couple of days to find supplies. We've got a lot of mouths to feed."

Corona nodded. "How many women do we have?"

"I think maybe around forty, jefe. And ten men. Our soldados found a few survivors yesterday, but none that we wanted to keep."

"Are any of our people using the men?" asked Tony the Tiger.

"No, señor. We probably have some homosexuals in the ranks but they're too embarrassed to be seen using one of the male prisoners."

"Si, yo entiendo. Why don't we get rid of the men? That'll be ten fewer mouths to feed. We can even get rid of some of the women if they aren't doing a good job."

Jorge nodded. "Señor, I have an idea. Do you know Israel Ramirez? He's our maintenance man and a mechanic. He's the one who fixed the generators and got them running."

"He's that little guy, right? Not a soldier, but good to have around. He can fix anything."

"Si, señor, that's him. When he joined us a couple of months ago, I found out that he'd worked for the CDC, the American Centers for Disease Control. He was in the maintenance department there. He had a car when he showed up, and of course, we confiscated it. Ramirez got his stuff out of the car and had two black bags.

"I told him that we searched everybody and every bag. He was real nervous when I looked in the bags. One just had a fancy Apple computer, but the other one had some test tubes and chemicals and was maybe a scientist's bag. It had a tag with a woman's name on it saying she worked at the CDC. I asked Israel what this was. He said he wasn't really sure but he thinks it had something to do with the zombie virus."

"Why am I just now hearing about this?" Antonio asked, anger in his voice.

"I'm sorry, Jefe. I locked the bags in the armory and forgot about them. We had so much going on, fighting zombies, searching buildings. I apologize, but like I said, I have an idea if you want to hear it."

Corona waved his hand, indicating for his subordinate to continue.

"Gracias, señor. I wondered if we should do an experiment and see what happens if we stick one of the prisoners with some of the chemicals? If they turn into a zombie, we'll know that we have a powerful weapon in our hands."

Antonio's eyes bore into Quintero. Finally, after a full minute, the cartel leader smiled and spoke. "Un gran idea, hacer que suceda."

**Buckhead, Atlanta, Wednesday, 1300 hours**

Israel Ramirez was scared. No, he was beyond scared, he was truly terrified. The last eight weeks had seared images into his brain from which he would never recover. He had seen and done things of which he was terribly ashamed. Israel knew that his mother was praying for him back in Mexico. The young man wondered, however, if those prayers would ever be answered. Have I doomed myself to Hell?

The large generators hummed in the basement of the Peachtree Summit building as the small man checked to make sure they were functioning properly. Ramirez had earned the trust, as much as they trusted anyone, of Antonio Corona and his deputy Jorge Quintero by making sure the generators kept running. When Israel and Carlos and the four other gangsters had shown up in Buckhead two months ago, Jorge immediately offered Carlos and the others jobs as soldiers after hearing of their involvement with the Mexican street gang, the Brownside Locos. Quintero even let Carlos keep his street name, 'Boxer,' from his days as an amateur pugilist in Los Angeles.

The deputy cartel leader then looked over at the slight frame of Israel and asked, "What can you do?"

Ramirez was already questioning the wisdom of following his neighbor Carlos down here. Israel lowered his eyes, showing respect, and stammered, "Jefe, I'm a maintenance man. I repair things. Forgive me, but that is my skill. I'm not a fighter or a soldier. I know nothing about guns, but I'm willing to learn."

Quintero's hard stare finally softened. "Can you repair generators, the big ones? The two at our headquarters are broken and Señor Corona is angry. He lives on the top floor and he's very pissed that the elevator isn't working."

Ramirez glanced up at the big man with the shaved and tattooed head. "Si, señor. If it doesn't require new parts or some kind of major repair, I can fix."

Jorge had one of his men take Israel into the basement of the high-rise apartment building. The two large, commercial generators were new and should be running, the young man thought. He borrowed a flashlight from his escort and after ten minutes of removing panels and examining the machines, Ramirez stood in front of Quintero again.

"I can repair, señor. Someone has put the wrong fuel in both of them. These are diesel but somebody put regular gasoline in. I'll need to drain the tanks and the fuel line, and clean the filters. Then we can put in some diesel and they should be ready to go."

"Bueno, bueno. That will be your job," Quintero said, the relief evident in his voice. "How long will it take?"

"Maybe a day, a day and a half at the most. I'll need a lot of containers to hold the gasoline inside. We don't want to waste it. Do we have some diesel fuel stored here, Jefe?"

"I'll work on getting you the diesel and we'll find plenty of containers to put the gas in. I need you to start now."

"Si, señor."

Twenty-four hours later, the generators were humming, providing power to the apartment building. Jorge actually smiled and shook Israel's hand. "Amigo, you're now in charge of all our maintenance in this building and the others that we've taken over."

Now, Israel knew that he had to somehow get out of this nightmare. His fear came from knowing that, in all likelihood, there was no escape. If the cartel caught him trying to leave, they would kill him. If he somehow managed to get away, where would he go? The zombies were everywhere and the chance of evading the hordes of flesh-eating creatures roaming the city seemed slim.

Even though Ramirez had entered the United States illegally four years earlier at the age of twenty-one, he didn't consider himself a criminal. He had obtained a forged Social Security Card for five hundred dollars. This had allowed him to get a driver's license and a good job in the maintenance department at the Centers for Disease Control. Israel's illegal status should have prevented him from working for the government, but his purchased documents had never been questioned. He hoped to marry one day and raise a family in America. He loved the United States and desperately wanted to experience the American Dream.

Israel had learned English and had worked hard to be a model employee at the CDC. His salary, while low by American standards, was a fortune compared to what he could have made in his home of Ciudad Juarez, Mexico. He was able to afford a small, one-bedroom apartment in the suburb of Chamblee, just north of Atlanta, and was the owner of a six-year old Toyota Corolla.

Ramirez had been working the second shift at the CDC on the evening when the last attacks took place in Atlanta. He was shocked when he and his workmates gathered around the TV to see the video footage of the aftermath of a car bomb and a suicide bomber, both of which had blown up near Atlantic Station, an upscale outdoor mall, just off of the interstate near downtown.

Israel normally finished his shift at 11:00pm. He had gotten caught up, however, watching the news coverage of the attacks in one of the break rooms, not sure if he should leave or not with hundreds or thousands of infected reported to be spreading out through the city. At 1:00am, though, the decision was made for him. The director of the CDC had given the order for the facility to be evacuated, telling the third shift workers to leave immediately. Ramirez did not need to be told twice.

He hurried out to his gold Toyota and was just about to turn the key when he saw his first zombies moving across the well-lit parking deck. Israel quickly laid over in the seat, praying that they wouldn't see him, terror settling into the pit of his stomach as he watched infected people for the first time, up close and personal. His back and legs cramped from lying in the uncomfortable position for over ten minutes. How long should he wait? he wondered. Could they get to him inside of his car?

After what seemed like an eternity, Israel heard the building door open and close, then excited voices close by. Immediately, the sound of growling and snarling filled the air as the creatures rushed past his car in the direction of the people. Ramirez chanced to raise his head to peek out his window, watching the drama unfold around him.

A black man, one of the CDC security guards, and a beautiful white woman with long, wavy brown hair, wearing a lab coat, were standing near the exit door. Israel recognized both people, remembering that each had always been kind to him, smiling and thanking him whenever he had performed some maintenance task for them.

Suddenly, the security guard began shooting, the loud explosions echoing all around the parking deck. Israel watched several of the zombies collapse to the pavement. The couple eventually managed to get the door open again, rushing back inside.

The officer hadn't killed all of the zombies. The two remaining ones were banging on the metal door that had just been slammed shut in their growling faces. Ramirez saw two black briefcase type bags sitting in the parking lot. The couple must've dropped them, he realized. Now that the majority of the creatures had been eliminated, Israel knew that this was his chance to flee.

Those two bags looked very inviting, though. Maybe they held something important or valuable? His conscience smote him with guilt. No, those aren't my property. But at least I could hold them for those nice people, Israel thought to himself. We'll be back at work in a few days and I can bring them to that pretty woman. That idea made the maintenance man smile.

Ramirez started his car, the new noise causing the zombies to turn and begin shuffling his way. He drove toward the exit, stopping several yards away with room to turn around. The creatures kept advancing towards him, now a safe distance from the bags. He quickly turned the steering wheel and accelerated back toward the building.

The Corolla skidded to a stop next to the items. Israel threw open his door, tossed a leather briefcase and a canvas bag into the passenger seat and took off as the zombies lurched back toward him, just twenty feet away. He jerked the steering wheel to the right and blasted towards the exit, speeding past the two snarling Zs.

After three harrowing hours, Ramirez had finally managed to get back to his apartment. Several times he'd had to reverse his course to avoid packs of the creatures. Of course everyone else in Atlanta, it seemed, was trying to either get home or flee the city, so the gridlock had been maddening. Traffic was heavier than Israel had ever seen it before, even in the middle of the night.

The young man locked himself in his apartment, watching the news coverage of the incident on his small television. He heard the evacuation order given for the city of Atlanta, but where would he go? He had briefly considered driving back to Mexico, but that was a long way to go on interstates packed with other fleeing vehicles and large groups of zombies surging west looking for fresh victims to eat.

It wasn't long, though, before Israel realized that he had made a mistake in not leaving the city right away. His apartment was less than two miles from Interstate 85 and by the second day, Ramirez was seeing zombies regularly as he peered out his window. These used to be people, he thought, watching an older Hispanic man, covered in blood, his throat ripped open and a chunk of his face missing, stumble around in the parking lot below Israel's second floor room. An Asian woman followed behind the first zombie, large open wounds visible on both of her arms. One of her eye sockets was a bloody mess where the eyeball had been ripped out.

A wave of nausea swept over Israel forcing him to turn away from the window. Surprisingly, he felt safe in the upstairs apartment. So far, no infected had come up the steps. His other pressing problem, though, was the lack of food in his kitchen; his stomach already growling. Ramirez knew that he was going to have to find some groceries soon or he would starve to death.

Later in the evening of that second day, there was a soft knock at his door. His neighbor from across the hall, Carlos, slipped in, the butt of a pistol sticking out of his waistband, Ramirez noted. The two men weren't close friends but they had stopped to chat in the hallway from time-to-time and had even drank a few beers together the previous Cinco de Mayo.

The two Mexicanos had talked late into the night, glad to have each other's company. Israel learned that Carlos 'Boxer' Romero

---

**44**

was a construction worker, but was heavily involved in the Brownside Locos street gang. Boxer didn't have any ideas about what they should do, either, but he did invite Ramirez to share his own meager food supply across the hall.

"And amigo, we can take what we need if we have to," the gang member said, tapping the pistol sticking out of his pants.

Israel had stayed closed to Carlos, hoping that his new friend could keep him safe. They survived over the next couple of months, but just barely. The men went out on two foraging missions to the Hispanic grocery store and to the convenience store, both adjacent to their apartment complex. Each trip had terrified Israel and both times they had had to run from growling zombies, carrying as many supplies as they could stuff inside their duffel bags.

On their last expedition, they had rushed back inside their building, Carlos slamming the door shut just before the hungry Zs got there. Ironically, because their apartment complex wasn't in the best part of town, the doors were metal with reinforced frames, providing extra security against the ravenous creatures just outside. The men carried their looted supplies upstairs, as the sound of the Zs banging on the entrance echoed throughout the building.

A month later, their food was almost exhausted again and the number of infected had only seemed to increase. The two friends sat on Israel's battered sofa, trying to talk themselves into making another foray out to find some more food. Carlos was almost out of ammunition for his 9mm Taurus pistol, however, having had to shoot zombies each time they had gone out. The remaining seven bullets would not last long if they were attacked.

A full size brown Ford Econoline van suddenly roared into the parking lot and four of Carlos' friends jumped out, shooting the group of loitering Zs, and calling out for their amigo. The gang member welcomed them inside, introducing them to Israel as fellow Brownside Locos members. The guests excitedly told the two men of the arrival of the cartel in Atlanta and how they were setting up shop in Buckhead, just ten miles down the road.

"Come on, Boxer! You come with us. They need soldiers and they've got it all. Food, women, guns. Man, we're going to take over this city."

A chubby gang member introduced as "Gordo" looked disdainfully at Israel. Ramirez wondered how the man could still live up to that nickname, with food so hard to come by these days.

"What about him?" the hefty Mexican asked, nodding toward Israel. "He don't look like much of a soldier."

The apparent leader of the group, a tough looking, mustachioed with a large scar down his cheek spoke up. His street name, not surprisingly, was "Scarface."

"The cartel hombre we talked to said they need people to do other things besides fight. They've already taken over an entire city block and they need a lot of people to work."

Israel and Carlos packed up a few clothes and the six men rushed out to the parking lot. Ramirez did not want to abandon his car and dove behind the steering wheel as Boxer joined his friends in their stolen van. Quintero had given them the mission of tracking down and recruiting other soldiers. Carlos' apartment had been their first and only stop. No one wanted to chance getting overrun by the flesh-eating creatures so they decided to head back to the cartel occupied area of Atlanta with their two newest recruits.

For the past two months, Israel had worked hard to keep the machinery working and to keep a low profile, trying to to stay out of sight as much as possible. The electrical grid was still down and only a few of the captured locations had generators. He was in the middle of adding more diesel fuel to the two units in the basement of the big apartment building when Jorge had sent for him. This wasn't unusual; the deputy cartel leader had often called for him to give him various assignments over the last eight weeks.

What was unusual about this request, however, was that the escorting cartel soldier pushed the fiftieth floor button inside the elevator. That was where the big boss, Antonio Corona, lived. Ramirez had only met Tony the Tiger a few times so he was understandably nervous as to what this meeting might mean. His escort knocked on the door, which was quickly opened by Quintero. He dismissed the soldier, ushering Israel inside the plush apartment.

"Our maintenance man!" the pudgy gang leader greeted him with a smile.

"Hola, señor," Israel answered timidly, his brown eyes looking down, waiting for further instructions.

"Please come in and sit with us," Antonio gestured towards the two large, expensive black leather couches.

Jorge seated himself on the couch with his boss. After a moment's hesitation, Ramirez sat on the other sofa, on the edge of his seat, across from the other two men. That was when he noticed the black leather computer bag and the black padded nylon bag, laying on the coffee table between him and his bosses. Those are the ones I picked up on that parking deck at the CDC, he realized.

"I see that you recognize those," Corona said, motioning to the objects on the table.

"Si, señor."

"What can you tell me about them? I'm very curious to hear what you have to say."

Israel knew that he was a terrible liar, so he didn't even try. He told them exactly what had happened and how he'd planned on giving the bags back when the CDC had reopened. But, of course, he hadn't gone back to work and it didn't look like he would any time soon. Both Tony the Tiger and Jorge sensed that the simple man in front of them was telling the truth.

"And what about the ten vials in the padded bag? Do you have

---

**47**

any idea what's in them, or what the writing on them means, Israel?" Corona queried.

"No, Jefe," he shook his head, "but I think maybe the lady who dropped them was working on the zombie virus. She always wore a white coat and was some kind of scientist."

Upon being dismissed, Israel returned to the basement to complete his task, his mind on the meeting with the cartel leaders, wondering what it all meant. After finishing up, he climbed the stairs to the lobby as the elevator doors opened. Seven men exited: Tony the Tiger, Jorge, four soldiers, and a young, small-framed black man, his wrists secured behind him with handcuffs, a blindfold over his eyes. Jorge was carrying the nylon bag, the one that contained the ten glass vials of liquid. An uneasiness settled upon Ramirez as the men descended the outside stairs and turned right, stopping a few feet down the sidewalk in front of the Peachtree Summit.

Israel watched through a window in the lobby as a soldier unlocked one of the handcuffs on the prisoner and attached it to a rail of the tall fence that ran around the high-rise building. The young man reached up and pulled off the blindfold, a questioning look on his face. Jorge sat the bag down, pulled on a pair of rubber gloves, and withdrew a syringe from his pocket.

The deputy cartel leader reached into the satchel, withdrawing a random test tube. He inserted the needle of the syringe, pulling back the plunger, loading it. The prisoner saw what was about to happen and backed up against the fence, screaming at the men. Antonio stood off to the side, watching, letting Jorge handle this. The big boss held a gold-plated pistol just in case things got out of hand. Several other armed gang members had gathered outside to watch the spectacle.

Quintero issued several commands that Ramirez couldn't hear. Three of the cartel soldiers grabbed the man, restraining him, while the fourth pulled out a knife and slashed the sleeve of the prisoner's shirt open exposing his upper arm. The prisoner tried to pull away but was no match for the three cartel soldiers holding him in place. Without hesitation, Jorge stepped over and jabbed the man with the syringe and then quickly backed away. Jorge's men let go of the prisoner and jumped out of his reach.

After recapping the needle, Quintero carefully removed the rubber gloves, dropping them to the sidewalk. The now infected black man screamed at, pleaded with, and cursed his captors for three full minutes. As the bio-terror virus did its work, the young man's heart rate began to slow and his breathing became labored. He was sweating profusely, his body trying in vain to stop the inevitable.

Six minutes after getting injected, the prisoner lost consciousness, falling backwards, coming to rest against the base of the fence. Two minutes later he appeared to be dead. None of the Mexicans were going to get close enough to verify that fact, but Antonio and Jorge nodded at each other, clearly impressed. Corona's four bodyguards took another step backwards, anticipating what was about to happen, each of them drawing their own pistols.

Israel felt the hot tears running down his cheeks. It's my fault! If I hadn't picked up those bags, if I hadn't come here, this wouldn't have happened. I'm going to Hell, he thought, still unable to pull his eyes away from the scene in front of him.

Suddenly, infected man's eyes popped open, bloodshot and glazed over, a deep guttural growl sounding from inside of him, his teeth snapping together. The large group of spectators around him smelled like food and he lunged for them. One of his arms was handcuffed to the fence, however, and he was jerked backwards.

The new zombie leapt forward again, snarling loudly at the people just out of his reach. He was again stopped violently by the handcuff, this time popping his shoulder out of joint. The dead but infected body didn't feel any pain, however, continuing to throw himself forward towards his meal.

A gunshot silenced the zombie's growls, blood spurting from the side of his head. Tony the Tiger watched the corpse collapse to the pavement, making sure that it was really dead. After staring at the body for a full minute, Corona slid the pistol back into his waistline.

Antonio looked at his subordinates and smiled broadly, clapping his hands together. "Excelente, amigos! That's amazing! He'd have kept coming until he ripped his arm off. This was a brilliant idea, Jorge. We control the zombie virus now and you and I will discuss the best way to deploy it. Have some men dispose of the body. Make sure they are careful not to get any blood on them."

When Tony the Tiger and his four guards disappeared back inside their headquarters, Israel made his move, deciding that he had to escape and tell someone what was happening here. He had an idea that just might work. He doubted that God would answer his prayers, but maybe, if God was still listening to his mother's prayers, his plan might succeed.

### North of Buckhead, Atlanta, Wednesday, 1400 hours

Lieutenant Colonel Kevin Clark was riding shotgun in the lead humvee. This was the furthest south that he had taken any of his patrols and he was nervous. Corporal Corey Whitmer stood behind the colonel, manning the Browning M2 .50 caliber machine gun as the driver, Private Joe Ellison, led the three vehicle convoy down Peachtree Road towards their destination in the community of Brookhaven, between Chamblee and Buckhead.

The National Guard vehicles were all heavily armed. Besides the .50 cal in the colonel's vehicle, the middle hummer carried an MK 19 grenade launcher and the rear vehicle packed a light machine gun, the M249. Three soldiers rode in each hummer.

---

All the troops scanned the surrounding businesses and terrain, looking for threats. In the lead vehicle, the muzzle of Clark's M4 rifle rested against the open window frame, the muzzle pointing outwards. Private Ellison's M-16 sat next to him, pointing towards the floor of the vehicle, but his 9mm Beretta Model 92 pistol was out of the holster, wedged under his right leg where he could grab it. The colonel alternated between looking out the window and glancing at the GPS unit mounted on the dash.

"How much farther, Boss?" Thompson asked.

"We take a right in about half a mile. The house is on that street."

"Roger that."

The National Guard troops had been released into the fight against the zombies weeks after the last major attacks in Atlanta, Washington, D.C., and New York City. The President had hoped that federal and local police would have been able to stem the tide of the thousands of infected who took over and subsequently poured out of those three key East Coast cities. Law enforcement had put up a valiant fight but there were just too many zombies and not enough police.

When the guard troops were finally allowed into the conflict, they found themselves unprepared, resulting in the devastation of dozens of units from both zombie and gang attacks. Clark and his soldiers had come into contact with many of their brothers and sisters in uniform who had been infected and turned into zombies, often with tears in their eyes as they pulled the trigger to put them down.

Kevin Clark was not your typical National Guard officer, having risen to the rank of major in the regular army as an Airborne Ranger. As he was contemplating retirement after twenty years of service, he was offered a new commission, this one as a lieutenant colonel, if he would come to work as one of the commanders of the Georgia National Guard.

Even though Clark had been looking forward to retirement and spending more time with his wife, he knew that he had to take this position. As former member of the elite Ranger Battalion, Kevin felt an obligation to pass along the knowledge that he had gained during his many deployments to the citizen-soldiers serving under him. Being a part of the guard allowed him to sleep in his own bed at night, but it also provided him with the opportunity to impart his training and skills to the part-time warriors that he was responsible for.

Ironically, the colonel and Mrs. Clark had seen the zombie virus first-hand months earlier when it was released on the University of Georgia campus. Both of the Clarks were UGA alumni and tried to attend at least one football game a season. Just minutes before the kickoff of the home opener, infected people inside the packed Sanford Stadium began attacking anyone they could get their hands on. Kevin found out later that one of the terrorists had had a job in a stadium concession booth, using his position to infect pizzas with the bio-terror chemical. Within minutes of purchasing and consuming the tainted pizza, the fans had collapsed and died. Moments later, however, their bodies were awakened as flesh-eating zombies.

Three infected band members had gotten into the stands below where the Clarks were seated, attacking fans and creating a panicked rush to get out of the stadium. Kevin grabbed his wife's hand, rushing up the stairs from their lower level seats. A growling, infected woman lunged down the stairs towards them, blood covering her face and the front of her Bulldogs jersey. The former Ranger sidestepped the zombie, kicking her in the butt as she went by, sending her flying down the concrete steps, conveniently tripping up one of the zombie band members who had just started running up the stairs.

Gunshots rang out from both inside and outside the stadium as campus police officers confronted the rapidly increasing groups of Zs. The zombie virus had also been released inside the Tate Student Center, located just across the street from the stadium, sending many more infected into the surrounding streets, where over ninety thousand people had gathered for the game.

When the Clarks got to the landing where the exits were located, Kevin realized that they were trapped. Everywhere he looked, the infected were attacking people. How does this thing spread so fast? he wondered.

A young, African-American policewoman was leading a group of people towards a women's restroom, her pistol out but pointed at the ground. Kevin took his wife's arm, quickly falling in with the group of survivors. Clark was unarmed and he figured their chances would be much better being with an armed police officer. Officer Grace Cunningham had protected the twenty-seven survivors by keeping them locked safely in the restroom for several hours.

After Cunningham discovered that Clark was a military man, she gave him her backup pistol and asked him to help her lead the big group to safety. Officer Cunningham's dispatcher had eventually directed her to take the survivors to meet up with CDC officers who were already in the fight on campus and who would escort the group to an extraction point. The police officer and the soldier killed multiple zombies, but they had managed to get to the federal officers, led by Chuck McCain. The CDC team got the entire band of survivors safely across campus where a Department of Homeland Security helicopter had flown them all away from the infected campus.

For the last three months, Colonel Clark and his group of twelve other National Guard soldiers had acted as an independent force, eliminating zombies, and in several cases, taking out gangs of human predators, as well. The first thing that he had done was to establish a safe location in which his soldiers could bring their loved ones. Corporal Whitmer had actually been the one to suggest the location to the colonel. Corey's parents ran a Methodist retreat center on the Chattahoochee River, north of Atlanta.

The Wesleyan Center for Solitude had been a place for pastors and Christian leaders to get away and disconnect before the terrorist attacks that had brought the east coast to its knees. Now the center was home to the National Guard troops and their families. It was a secluded and a safe location. Whenever a patrol was sent out, three of the soldiers stayed behind with their fourth armed humvee, providing security for their families.

With no clear chain-of-command and with the communications grid down, Colonel Clark had done what any good Ranger officer would do: improvise, adapt, and overcome. He had gathered the remnants of three squads of troopers together, placing them under his command. After helping his soldiers get their families to the Center for Solitude, he decided that eliminating the infected would be their primary mission, understanding that the zombies would have to be destroyed before there could be any chance of society returning to normal. Clark estimated that his men and women had killed over two thousand Zs.

The National Guard troops had also been involved in several firefights with criminal gangs. Thankfully, only one soldier had been wounded and it had been minor. They had killed thirty-seven criminals. They took no prisoners, per the colonel's orders. He'd made it clear to his soldiers that he would accept full responsibility for his orders if they were questioned later. The soldiers had no facility in which to keep prisoners and no medical staff to look after those criminals whom they had wounded.

The colonel was proud of his warriors. They had stepped up and were committed to doing their duty to the best of their ability. He and his non-commissioned officers had set the bar high even before the zombie virus had been unleashed and his remaining National Guard troops were some of the best trained in America. Now, Clark was the only Georgia National Guard officer who was still alive, at least as far as he knew. The last three months of fighting had forged his team into some of the finest soldiers whom the colonel had ever commanded.

Today's mission was a strange one. It had started when he'd received a call on his satellite phone. It had laid silent for months, but had beeped yesterday afternoon with an incoming call. Someone identifying himself as the Director of Operations for the CIA, a retired Navy admiral, had somehow gotten Clark's name and satellite phone number and had dialed him up, asking (not ordering, Clark had noted) for him and his soldiers to check an address in Brookhaven for items that were important to the bio-terror virus research.

During the conversation, the retired admiral, Jonathan Williams, had given Clark the first news of what was happening in the rest of the country that he had heard in a long time. The admiral had let the colonel know that they were making progress in getting the infrastructure reestablished. One of the key components of that was exactly what Kevin's soldiers were already doing: eliminating the infected. This was happening in other areas of the affected areas as National Guard and law enforcement units had started to get their feet under them again. Williams had been impressed by Clark's initiative and asked him to personally thank his soldiers for their sacrifice and commitment.

The colonel understood that one never said "no" to an admiral, retired or not, and he and his troops were about to pull up in front of the address on Brookhaven Road, just off of Peachtree Road. The three humvees stopped twenty-five yards apart and offset, the spacing giving them a reaction gap in case they were attacked. Clark led Corporal Whitmer, Sergeant Thomas Jackson, and Private Dan Merchant across the wide front yard up to the large, classic two-story redbrick home. First Sergeant Ricardo Gonzalez was the second-in-command, monitoring the team's radio traffic while protecting their vehicles along with the other four National Guard troops.

Each soldier knew their job but the colonel still took point. Ranger officers were taught to lead by example and even as a field grade officer, Kevin led the way. The house was on a slight hill, sixty yards off of Brookhaven Drive. The neighborhood was quiet and Clark and his three soldiers were almost to the front door.

A shot rang out behind them and then another. "Contact!" First Sergeant Gonzalez's voice came through the earpiece in Clark's ear. "We got Zs coming down the street, an estimated group of fifteen, inside a hundred yards."

"Roger," the colonel acknowledged. "We'll make this quick.

More gunfire erupted from behind them as the soldiers in the hummers took down the infected walking towards them. All of the troops understood that the gunshots would draw in more zombies so time was of the essence. Within seconds the upscale residential area was quiet again.

The front door was standing open at the top of five concrete stairs. Clark had just reached the small porch when a decomposing, bloody, Asian male zombie, clad only in his boxers, burst outside, growling at the four men in front of him. The colonel's 5.56mm bullet punched through the bridge of his nose, sending him facedown on the landing.

The soldiers waited, weapons raised, to see if any other surprises were going to come out the door. Thirty seconds later, they heard footsteps and more growling approaching them from inside the house.

"I got this one," Sergeant Jackson said. The tall, muscular, dark-skinned African-American soldier raised his rifle just as an infected

Asian girl, probably no more than ten years of age, stepped through the doorway, her Minnie Mouse nightgown covered with gore, snarling and reaching for the men. The sergeant's round exploded the zombie child's small head, dropping her next to the man they presumed was her father.

"You guys OK?" Gonzalez asked over the radio.

"Roger," Clark answered. "We just took down two."

"Man, if I'd have known it was kid, I'd have let somebody else shoot her," Jackson said, disgusted. "I hate popping zombie kids."

"Yeah, Sarge, but she would've loved to have taken a bite out of your knee," Private Merchant noted.

The street behind them was still quiet, and they had not detected any other sounds from inside the home.

"Okay, let's do it," Clark commanded. "The office is upstairs. The safe is supposedly hidden behind some book shelves."

In their briefing earlier that morning, Lieutenant Colonel Clark had let his team know that they were tasked with recovering a hard drive and a notebook connected to the zombie virus vaccine research. Normally, they would also take the time to search for anything else of value inside the house. Food, bottled water, medicines, guns, and ammunition were things that they never had too much of.

Today, however, the colonel had told them that this mission was get in and get out. They were a long way from home and he didn't want to take any unnecessary chances. Clark knew that the closer they got to Atlanta, the more zombies they would encounter.

All of soldiers were experts at clearing buildings, having trained and drilled both before and after the zombie virus was released. When they reached the staircase inside the house, Merchant stayed at the bottom as his three companions went upstairs. He was responsible for making sure nothing came up the stairs after his friends.

Whitmer staged at the top of the stairs, watching the hallway but also able to see downstairs and cover Merchant. Normally, they would clear every room, but they knew if there were any more infected in the house, the noise would have brought them out already. Jackson followed Clark to the home office, stopping at the doorway, covering his boss as he entered the room to look for the wall safe.

This home, unlike so many others, had not been ransacked, the presence of the infected inside probably enough to send potential looters looking for an easier location. The office had three large bookcases against the walls, all stuffed with books, plaques, and photos. Kevin couldn't help but noticing the framed family photo of a handsome Asian man, a beautiful Asian woman, and their cute preadolescent daughter, all smiling brightly for the picture. He shook his head at the loss. He knew where dad and the little girl were, but where was mom?

The second bookshelf was the one that hid the small vault. The heavy wooden piece of furniture rolled when he pushed it, exposing the secret compartment mounted in the wall. Clark quickly pulled a pocket notebook out of his breast pocket, flipping it open to where he had written the combination during his chat with Admiral Williams.

"How much longer, Boss?" Gonzalez asked calmly over the radio. "We've got Zs coming from both directions. Probably twenty total."

"We're almost done. Take 'em out and get the vehicles started. We'll be right there."

Gunshots erupted from outside as the National Guard soldiers took down the zombies coming towards them.

A minute later, the safe was open. The hard drive and notebook were there, along with two pistols, a Glock Model 21 and a Sig Sauer Model P220. Interesting that these guns were in the safe, Clark mused. Maybe if the male zombie he'd shot had been armed, he might've been able to protect himself and his little girl.

Kevin didn't see anything else of value in the safe. The hard drive, notebook, and guns went into a nylon bag that he pulled out of his cargo pocket. He paused, but then on a whim, grabbed the family photo off of the shelf and slipped it in with the other items. The soldiers quickly retraced their steps out of the house.

On the return trip, Private Merchant had point with Sergeant Jackson bringing up the rear. As they started down the steps from the front porch, two Zs stepped into the view of the young soldier, having come from next door. The elderly white couple were both bloody, smelly, and had seen better days. The man was wearing red flannel pajamas and the woman, a floral flannel nightgown, her silver hair in rollers. Neither of the growling zombies had any teeth, their dentures evidently left inside their house. The private never stopped moving forward, firing two head shots that brought down both of the geriatric Zs, their brittle bones crackling as they fell to the grass.

All the infected had been cut down by the time the team regrouped around their vehicles. The only noise that could be heard were the rumble of the humvee's diesel engines and the metallic clicking of the troopers reloading their weapons. The colonel hesitated before getting into the hummer, checking to make sure that all of his soldiers were in and ready to go. Satisfied, he pulled open the passenger door of the big vehicle.

Suddenly, the unmistakable roar of automatic gunfire came from just south of their location on Peachtree Road. Clark jumped into his vehicle and motioned to Ellison to get going. Kevin punched the transmit button on the radio as the military convoy started moving.

"Gonz, did you hear that? Automatic weapons from close by?"

"Roger, we heard it. You want to check it out?"

The rattle of machine gun fire sounded like it was getting closer.

The soldiers could also hear squealing tires and racing engines heading their way.

"10-4. We haven't had a good firefight in what, two weeks or so?"

### Intersection of Piedmont Road and Peachtree Road, Buckhead, Atlanta, Wednesday, 1405 hours

Israel Ramirez had made his move. His adrenaline had shoved his fear onto the back burner of his sub-conscious. Someone needed to know what was going on. He had no idea who he was going to alert or how he would find any police or governmental authorities, but he knew he had to try.

After witnessing Corona and Quintero murder a man in their experiment with the virus, Israel had slipped out a side exit of the Peachtree Summit and made his way to the end of the block. The cartel headquarters was located on Piedmont Road a block south of Peachtree Road. At the corner of the two main thoroughfares was the gang's vehicle pool. A shopping center parking lot had been confiscated as the home for almost two hundred assorted vehicles.

Some of these had been driven from Mexico but most had been stolen from victims who no longer needed them. Often, when the criminals went out on looting missions, they would bring back any vehicles that appealed to them. In most cases, the owners were now zombies, anyway. Other times, the gangsters simply killed anyone foolish enough to still be hiding in the city with a nice car.

Several of the pickups had been rigged with machine guns taken from National Guard units. The two stolen military hummers in use by the cartel's security patrols were both out of the lot at the moment, driving around the four block area that was under their control.

Israel noted that the guards on duty were Juan and Rafael. They were seated in folding metal chairs at a small table at the entrance to the lot. The guards lived on the same floor that he did and they often took their meals together. A half-empty bottle of tequila and two glasses sat between the men, their rifles laying on the table, as well. All of the other entry points into the parking area had been blocked off.

"Hey, Chico," Juan greeted him, his speech slurred. For some reason, that was the nickname that he had given Ramirez. "What was the shooting about in front of HQ? We couldn't really see what was going on from here."

"Man, it was terrible!" Israel said, having mentally rehearsed his lines on the walk up. "One of the boy-toys turned into a zombie and they had to shoot him."

"Whoa!" Rafael exclaimed, also clearly enjoying the tequila. "Loco! How did he get infected?"

Ramirez shrugged. "I don't know," he lied, "but they managed to get him outside before they shot him in the head."

While the two inebriated sentries contemplated how someone inside their secure area had managed to turn into a zombie, Israel said, "Amigos, Señor Jorge wanted me to drive up to the gas station and get some more diesel."

Ramirez pointed to the QuikFill convenience store a block away. "I didn't have enough earlier to get the generators filled and Jorge wants to make sure they don't run out of fuel again. He doesn't want Señor Corona to have to use the stairs."

Both men chuckled, understanding the importance of keeping the chubby cartel leader happy. It was not unusual for Israel to ask for a vehicle since Jorge had him running errands and servicing equipment in some of the other buildings inside their secure quadrant. The large underground tanks at the QuikFill still contained fuel and Israel regularly went there for more diesel.

Juan pointed at a white Dodge Dakota pickup sitting twenty feet away. "Take that one, Chico. The keys are in it."

"Gracias, amigo."

Rafael got up to move one of the vans that was blocking the intersection so Israel could pull out. As the maintenance man drove out of the parking lot, he glanced back to his left and saw Jorge walking up the street towards the corner. He was still a half block away.

The brown Ford Econoline van pulled forward just far enough onto the sidewalk for the Dakota to get past. Ramirez glanced into the rear view mirror as he drove through the opening. Quintero was now sprinting towards them, yelling at the two sentries, and drawing his revolver. Thankfully for Israel, Juan and Rafael were both buzzed and their reaction times were slowed. The white pickup turned right onto Peachtree Road and accelerated north.

After the successful experiment, Jorge decided to walk over to the car lot and drive around the perimeter, which he did at least once a day. As the deputy cartel leader approached the corner, however, he saw his maintenance man, Israel Ramirez, in a pickup truck, driving out of the lot. Only higher ranking members of the gang were allowed to take vehicles without permission; all others had to have Quintero's approval.

Jorge started running, screaming at Israel to stop and for his two sentries not to let him leave. In moments, he reached the intersection, his chrome-plated .357 Colt Python in his hand. Quintero ran by his two men who still had not comprehended what was happening. Jorge rushed into the middle of the street, firing all six shots at the fleeing pickup, watching it speed out of sight.

Furious, Quintero threw the revolver to the pavement and stalked back to where Juan and Rafael stared at him, wide-mouthed. Without warning, Quintero punched Juan in the nose, knocking him onto his back. The deputy cartel leader pivoted and fired a kick into Rafael's groin, sending him to his knees. A short left hook put him all the way down.

In full rage mode now, Jorge alternated between kicking and screaming at the two downed sentries. He would have beaten them both to death or picked up one of their rifles and shot them, but he suddenly heard Antonio's voice inside his head from the last time he had killed one of his people for not doing their job. Tony the Tiger's own temper was legendary but he was doing much better controlling it since they had moved to Atlanta, knowing that he didn't have any men to spare.

The cartel leader had scolded his lieutenant, "Jorge, we can't kill any more of our men when they don't meet our expectations. Of course, they need to be disciplined from time-to-time, but try not to beat any more to death or shoot them."

Quintero stopped his attack, breathing heavily. Juan and Rafael writhed in pain at his feet, bloody, bruised, and probably with a few broken bones. He spat at them, still angry, when he realized that the two cartel humvees had stopped at the roadblock, watching the spectacle at the entrance to their carpool.

Jorge ran towards the vehicles, the four men in each one looking apprehensive as he approached. Everyone knew of Señor Jorge's temper. Two Mexicans and two black men were in each hummer, Antonio's way of trying to integrate the American gangsters with his cartel fighters.

The big, bearded black man, DC, was leading this patrol. He opened the passenger door of his lead hummer and stepped out, watching Jorge closely as he approached. DC kept his hand close to the 10mm Glock Model 20 in a cross draw holster on his web gear.

Quintero's English wasn't great, especially when he was agitated and he struggled to remember much of his English vocabulary. "DC, vai ahora y get that white pickup! Israel Ramirez quiere escapar! Catch him or kill him pronto!"

DC nodded at Jorge as one of the bilingual Mexicans translated the orders for everyone else. The black gangster swung back into the hummer. His driver, Melvin, aka, Melon, and he had known each other for years as members of the Black Mafia street gang in Atlanta. Melon accelerated and the two hummers went after the fleeing pickup.

### Peachtree Road, North of Buckhead, Atlanta, Wednesday, 1420 hours

Ramirez breathed a sigh of relief. He had actually managed to escape from the cartel. His meager plan was to drive by his apartment complex a few miles up the road. If the parking lot looked clear, he'd make a quick stop to grab some more of his things. All he had with him were the clothes that he was wearing.

After that, he had to try to find someone with the government. He hadn't seen any police in a long time and didn't know where to look. Maybe there were some soldiers around? That part of his plan was still a bit vague.

Sudden movement in his rear view mirror brought him back to reality. He had only managed to get four miles up Peachtree Road and the cartel's patrol already had sight of him. The two captured, armed humvees were closing fast. Something slammed into the back of the pickup, startling the small man. They were shooting at him, but were still at least a quarter of a mile back.

Thankfully, the road had some curves, making it harder for them to hit the Dakota. Israel considered turning off the main road and trying to lose them, but the gunshots had sent him into panic mode and he wasn't thinking clearly. More shots flew by him, hitting the asphalt with a spray of fragments and dust. The fleeing man held the accelerator to the floor, sending the pickup's speed to over ninety miles an hour.

The section of road in front of him now was a long straightaway. Ramirez jinked the steering wheel in both directions, trying to create a more difficult target. There in front of him! More humvees. Who were they and where did they come from? He glimpsed the American flags on them as these new military vehicles began firing their machine guns back towards his pursuers.

Suddenly, a long burst of bullets ripped into the Dodge Dakota from the cartel's weapons. The glass shattered behind Israel, and a heavy impact knocked him forward, against his seatbelt. One of the gang's rounds also found his left rear tire, bursting it and sending the pickup careening out of control. The Dakota veered to the left, back to the right, and then flipped, rolling over and over for fifty yards, finally coming to rest upside down, the tires still spinning.

When Israel regained consciousness, he found himself hanging upside down by his seatbelt. He tasted dust as he watched his blood dripping onto the ceiling below. Every part of him hurt as he felt his life leaving him. I hope my mother's prayers can save me, he thought. I don't want to go to Hell.

Ramirez heard footsteps and saw two sets of legs approaching him. They were wearing camo pants and combat boots. More gunshots rang out from the direction that he'd come, just as a young white soldier cautiously stuck his head inside the vehicle, pointing a gun at him. When the soldier saw that he wasn't a threat, Israel felt himself being released from the seatbelt and gently pulled out of the shattered pickup truck.

After hearing the automatic gunfire, Lieutenant Colonel Clark had led his three hummers to the corner of Brookhaven Road and Peachtree Road, where they could get a better view of what was happening. Less than a minute after getting in position, a white Dodge Pickup came racing into view, several hundred yards south of them.

"I'm guessing he's the rabbit," Sergeant Jackson commented over their headsets.

"I think you're right, Sarge," the colonel agreed. "I wonder who's chasing him?"

At that moment, the cartel's two military vehicles burst into view, their top-mounted machine guns blazing at the fleeing pickup. The nine National Guard soldiers did a double take. Were these comrades of theirs chasing a bad guy? In seconds, however, the fluttering Mexican flags attached to the captured humvees signed the gang members' death warrants.

"They're flying Mexican flags!" First Sergeant Gonzalez exclaimed over the intercom.

Clark had no idea of the cartel's presence in Buckhead but he knew that American soldiers would never fly the flag of a foreign nation on their vehicles. He also knew that many government vehicles and weapons had been lost during the bio-terror attacks.

"Light 'em up," the colonel ordered his two machine gunners.

Immediately, .50 caliber and 5.56mm rounds ripped into the two hummers. Clark's team also had a grenade launcher mounted on one of their vehicles, but its ammo was limited and it was only for use in the most extreme of situations. The machine gunner on the lead cartel vehicle managed to get off one last burst before a .50 caliber round blew his right arm off at the shoulder. The dying man collapsed back inside the hummer.

The colonel and his troops watched in horror as the fleeing Dakota pickup was struck and lost control, flipping and rolling over multiple times. The lead Mexican humvee had been targeted by Corporal Whitmer and his Browning .50 caliber machine gun. Besides taking out the machine gunner, one of the over two-inch long, half-inch wide projectiles had also struck the driver, Melon, in the head, exploding it and removing it from his shoulders, splattering DC and the Mexicans in the back seat with blood and brain matter.

Driverless, DC's hummer veered to the right, jumped the curb, and went airborne into the parking lot of the Brookhaven MARTA station. The parking lot of the Metro-Atlanta Transit Authority was half full of abandoned vehicles whose owners had been downtown after the bombs had infected the city weeks before. The out-of-control humvee slammed into a red Ford Mustang, knocking the sports car into a gray Volvo wagon parked next to it.

Private Jason Pearson, Sergeant Jackson's gunner in the third National Guard hummer focused the fire of his M249 light machine gun on the second cartel vehicle. The 5.56mm rounds tore through the unarmored body of the humvee, striking all four occupants. Their machine gunner was struck twice in the left leg, ripping open his femoral artery, and spraying the interior of the vehicle in red.

The Mexican driver of the stolen military vehicle tried to take evasive action to get out of the line of fire. He saw a driveway to his left, a Bank of America, and jerked the steering wheel in that direction, hoping to turn around and flee back to the safety of the cartel-controlled area.

The wounded man was going too fast, however, and his own wounds slowed his reaction time down. As he attempted the left turn into the bank parking lot, both right tires struck the curb, throwing the hummer into the air and onto its side. The vehicle slid to a stop directly in front of the bank.

"Gonz, set up your hummer in the middle of the street so Merchant can cover both directions with the grenade launcher," Clark ordered over the radio. "You and Long check on that pickup. See if there's anybody alive in there. Jackson and Pearson check the hummer by the bank, me and Whitmer will take the one across the street. After we secure the scene, let's police it up. We'll take all the guns and make sure no one else can use those humvees."

First Sergeant Gonzalez's driver, Private Lawrence Long, parked in the middle of Peachtree Road, allowing Private Merchant to swing his Mk 19 grenade launcher in either direction if they were attacked. Gonzalez and Long rushed over to the overturned Dodge Dakota. Lawrence carefully poked his head inside, his M-16 ready if needed.

"One male, First Sergeant, hanging from his seatbelt," the private said, as he pulled his head out of the pickup's cab. The young soldier lowered his voice. "He opened his eyes and looked at me but he's in bad shape."

It took both of the men to get the injured driver out of the truck. Gonzalez stood and called Sergeant Jackson's driver, Corporal Lisa Scott, on the radio and asked her to join them. She was the team's medic, having just earned her emergency medical technician certificate before things started falling apart.

"Sergeant Gonzalez, he wants to talk to you," Private Lawrence said, still kneeling beside the small Hispanic man.

Single gunshots echoed around the empty intersection as the rest of the National Guard troops secured the scene. Securing the scene meant that every criminal, even those who were clearly dead, received a bullet to the head. Clark's team was not taking any chances on any of their foes coming back as zombies.

Gonzalez bent down next to the dying man. He had a gaping wound where a machine gun bullet had hit him in the back and exited near his right shoulder. Blood was seeping out of the side of his mouth and there was no telling what type of internal injuries he had sustained in the crash.

A weak hand grabbed the first sergeant's sleeve and the young man's eyes opened. He began speaking rapidly in Spanish, with an intensity that surprised Gonzalez. After listening for thirty seconds, the sergeant realized that he was getting some very important intelligence information. Ricardo grabbed for the small notebook he kept in his cargo pocket and started writing, not wanting to miss what he was hearing.

Corporal Scott came running up, her medical kit slung over her shoulder. The young blonde soldier started assessing the injured man, even as he kept talking to Gonzalez. In the middle of a sentence, however, Israel grunted, exhaled, and was dead.

Sergeant Gonzalez sat back on his haunches, stunned by what he had just heard. Lisa started CPR, hoping to bring the dead man back. She had taken the time to put on rubber gloves and she only performed chest compressions on him, the zombie virus making the breathing component of CPR a scary task. After several minutes, however, he was still dead and the young corporal stopped her attempts to revive him. She sighed, dropping her bloody gloves on his chest.

In ten minutes, the two enemy humvees had been set on fire and the National Guard convoy was heading north, back to their home base. All of the enemies' weapons had been confiscated and the bodies left in the vehicles to be consumed by the fire. Clark's team had also quickly eliminated eighteen zombies, drawn by the noise of gunfire and car crashes.

### Buckhead, Atlanta, Wednesday, 1630 hours

Jorge Quintero had not seen Antonio "Tony el Tigre" Fernando Corona manifest that much anger in a long, long time. After hearing his lieutenant's report, the cartel leader cursed in Spanish and English for a full five minutes before flipping over the heavy glass coffee table, spilling a half-consumed plate of rice, beans, and tortillas onto the carpet, along with an open bottle of beer and two empties.

Corona walked towards the balcony, pausing in the dining room, breathing deeply. A cherry wood cabinet containing expensive china stood against the wall. The previous owners of this apartment had impeccable taste, Antonio had noted more than once. Without warning, he grabbed the side of the tall cabinet, wrenched it forward and released more of his stress as the glassware and china broke into a thousand pieces on the hardwood flooring.

Tony the Tiger spun around, eyes blazing, and pointed a finger at Jorge. "Kill them. Those two sentries failed you, me, all of us. Slowly, painfully, make them an example for the others."

Jorge paused before answering. "No, señor. We can't kill them."

The cartel leader crossed the room in two strides and stood eye-to-eye with his second-in-command, a furious expression on his face.

"What did you say?" he roared. "How dare you tell me 'No!'"

Quintero knew how far he could push, even as he smelled the beer and the spicy food on his boss' breath. He had earned the right to say "no" once and then try to explain his position. He also knew that if Antonio issued the order again to kill the two men, Jorge would go and have them executed immediately.

"Señor, you ordered me not to kill any more of our men because they did something stupid. You said we don't have any soldiers to spare. I beat them really bad already. I punished them. Juan's arm is broken and Rafael's jaw is dislocated and I knocked out some teeth. Plus, we lost an eight-man patrol. If we execute Rafael and Juan, we'll be down ten men.

"Forgive me, Jefe, but they didn't know any better. The little traitor, Ramirez, has borrowed vehicles before with my permission so this wasn't unusual. They shouldn't have been drinking while they were working, but most of our men are usually drunk or stoned so that's hard to enforce.

"My suggestion, señor, is that we tell everyone that you were going to have them executed, but after hearing the whole story you graciously decided to let them live. Everyone is expecting them to be put to death but we really do need every soldier. If you let them live, it'll inspire even more loyalty in the rest of the men."

Corona continued to stare into Jorge's eyes, processing what he had just heard. After a few minutes, he backed up and sat down heavily on the sofa, motioning for Quintero to sit, as well. Antonio exhaled and nodded at Jorge.

"Very well, I'll accept your recommendation. But you let them know that if they screw up again, I'll turn them into zombies."

"Gracias, señor," Quintero said.

"Tell me what you think happened up there," Antonio changed the subject. "You said our two humvees had been stripped and torched?"

"Sí, Jefe, I think the military did it."

"The military? The National Guard hasn't shown us anything. Those black gangsters who joined us said that they killed some of the soldiers and the zombies killed some more. The Americans don't want to use their regular military because it goes against some of their laws. That's just another reason why they're so stupid and we can't be stopped!"

Jorge shrugged. "We found .50 caliber machine gun casings and 5.56mm brass laying in the street. I know that the gringo citizens love their guns but I don't think too many people outside the army have .50 cals. Our vehicles were shot to pieces. Whoever hit us took everything. They carried away all of the guns and set the hummers on fire. The bodies were pretty messed up by the time we got there but it looks like the soldiers executed our people by shooting them in the head."

"And you said Ramirez was dead when you got there?" Corona asked.

"Sí, he was lying in the middle of the road. The truck he stole was upside down and he'd been shot in the back."

"So, he could've talked to the gringos and told them about the virus?"

"I suppose, señor," Quintero conceded, "but it really doesn't matter. We know that the Americans will come eventually. That's why you were wise when you said we needed every man. We're going to have to fight the gringo federales or maybe some SWAT teams but I think it'll be a while. They're still busy fighting the zombies. Maybe we should send back to Tijuana and ask for more men?"

Tony the Tiger looked thoughtful, his earlier fit of rage over. He currently had close to two hundred gang members with differing levels of skill and experience. In his heart of hearts, he knew that in a prolonged siege with the American law enforcement or their military machine, he would eventually be defeated. He was embarrassed to have to ask his uncle for more men, but he knew how to frame the request so that his Uncle Pepe would give him whatever he wanted.

"Put together a small team, maybe six or eight good soldiers. You handpick them and send them to Pepe. I'll write a letter for them to give him. When my uncle hears how much we've already accomplished and how this city is ours for the taking, he'll send us an army. Let's also send him ten of the women. Uncle Pepe has a soft spot for gringo women."

"Bueno," said Jorge, with a knowing smile. "We only have the one hummer left. Should we let them take it back to Tijuana?"

"No! That is my personal humvee," Antonio said. "Pack the girls into a van and send an SUV with them. The gringo police are still active in some states and it would be better not to attract attention."

The stolen hummer was the one that the black gangster, DC, had presented to the cartel leader. It was armored and had a light machine gun mounted in the turret. Corona would keep the military vehicle handy in case he needed to make a quick exit.

"No problem, señor. We have plenty of SUVs and vans to choose from. I'll go put a team together. When do you want them to leave?"

"First thing in the morning. Make sure that everybody you pick can drive. I don't want them to stop except to piss. If they drive hard, they'll be home by Friday afternoon. And if Uncle Pepe moves fast, we could have some reinforcements here by next week."

# Chapter Three

There had been no more surprises as Elizabeth and Chuck drove around the large man-made lake. McCain hoped to make it to the Foster's house before dark and to spend the night with them. Karen Foster was a nurse who taught Practical Nursing at the Northeast Georgia Technical College and was one of Elizabeth's best friends. Karen had asked Chuck if he would make a detour on his trip to check on her parents and let them know that she was OK.

McCain had no desire to make any unnecessary stops, but he also had trouble telling beautiful women, "no." Karen was attractive but, more importantly, she and Beth were close. And Chuck owed her. Karen had nursed the big man back to health several weeks before, after he had been shot in the hip during an attack on the technical college campus. This detour was the least McCain could do after Foster explained that she hadn't spoken to her folks in months. The Fosters had no idea if their daughter was even still alive, and Karen wasn't sure if her parents had survived, either. Chuck had a letter from the nurse which he and Elizabeth would hand-deliver.

If the Fosters were still alive and their home was secure, Beth and he would ask to spend the night there. If everything continued to go well, they would be at the Mitchell's farm and reunited with Melanie sometime tomorrow. But they still had a long way to go.

"We'll be coming to a big intersection in less than a mile,"

---

**74**

McCain let his wife know. "You'll be turning left onto Highway 187. It's a five-lane highway, running through whatever little town this is." He glanced down at the map pages laying on his lap. "West Gate. For about a mile we're going to be running the gauntlet of shopping centers, convenience stores, and restaurants."

Elizabeth made the turn and they were both surprised at the lack of looting damage, and seeing nothing to indicate that zombies had swept through. They saw no broken windows, abandoned cars, bodies, or anything else to let them know that there were infected in the area. Even more surprising, the homes they passed weren't boarded up and actually looked like people were still living in them.

"Now what?" Beth asked.

"Just ahead we'll cross part of the lake. It looks the bridge is about a mile long. If we get into any trouble on the bridge, we'll turn around and go back the way that we came, OK?"

Chuck made eye contact with Elizabeth in the rear view mirror. He could see the uncertainty in her eyes, but she nodded. "Got it."

Unlike the stretch of road that they had just traveled, there were several vehicles scattered across the bridge. They had to slow down and maneuver around them, Chuck suddenly realizing that they been parked in such a way to force approaching cars do exactly what they were doing: slow down as they were funneled into…what? he wondered. At least the vehicles all looked empty, he noticed gratefully.

Halfway over the bridge, he understood. A roadblock consisting of two police cars and two armed, uniformed officers awaited them.

"Not again!" Beth exclaimed. "What should I do?"

Maybe these were actual good guys, McCain hoped. Chuck and Beth were committed now. Backing up through the serpentine of cars would be difficult, especially if the two officers started shooting at them.

"You know the drill. Hands up, smile, and be prepared for fight or flight. I'll get out and introduce myself."

The Tundra stopped twenty-five yards from the two South Carolina State Patrol cruisers and the two young, fit men in their gray trooper uniforms, both holding rifles. One of them raised a bullhorn to his mouth.

"You in the truck, no sudden moves. Turn the vehicle off and step out with your hands up!"

McCain had already removed his rifle and helmet, but slipped his Glock back into the holster. He wasn't leaving his pistol in the car again.

"You wait here, I'll be right back," he said, with a confidence that he didn't really feel.

As he exited the pickup, he withdrew his badge and ID packet from his pocket, raised both hands, and stepped forward to meet the officers. These two didn't fit the stereotype of fat, rural troopers, McCain noted. One white, one black, both muscular, their AR-15s pointed at him and Beth.

"I'm a police officer," Chuck called towards the roadblock, walking slowly in that direction, his badge wallet open. "I'm the officer-in-charge of the Atlanta CDC Enforcement Unit."

The muzzles of both rifles lowered immediately. That's a good sign, Chuck thought. They were still pointed in his general direction, but pointed down was way better than being pointed at his chest.

McCain stopped ten yards in front of the barricade. "I've got my badge and ID card right here if you gentleman would like to see them."

The black trooper, a corporal, glanced at his partner, and then looked back at the big man in front of him, noting his holstered pistol.

"Come on forward, sir, but understand, we will use deadly force if you try anything foolish."

Chuck nodded and forced a smile, holding out his badge wallet as he reached the two silver State Patrol cars. Corporal Patterson and then Trooper Evans both examined the credentials carefully, finally handing them back.

"You can put your hands down, Agent McCain," the corporal said. "Sorry for the inconvenience. Who do you have with you in the vehicle?"

"That's my partner, Elizabeth," he lied. "We're on a mission related to the zombie virus, but as you can imagine, travel isn't easy."

Both troopers nodded and Evans asked, "Where are y'all going, sir?"

"We've got to get to Hendersonville, North Carolina. The plan was to take Highway 187 north. We've tried to stay off the interstates as much as possible. Can you let us through? Our turn off is just ahead, right?"

"We have orders not to let anyone cross the bridge," Patterson said. After a pause, however, he continued, "But, I'm not going to be the one to keep you from your mission, sir. I'll escort you down to your turn and speak to the officers manning the roadblock there."

McCain sighed with relief. "Thank you. Why are you blocking the bridge? The little town we just drove through looked clear and we didn't see any evidence of Zs having come through here."

The corporal waited a moment before answering. "We can't really talk about it, Agent McCain. I'm not asking you about your mission and I can't really give you any info on ours. The best I can tell you is that there is a marina on the other side of this bridge and there are some important people who've taken refuge on their houseboats. We're making sure that they stay safe."

"Fair enough," Chuck nodded. "What about zombies? Have you guys seen many out this way?"

"Oh, yeah!" Trooper Evans chuckled. "A few months ago, I thought the world was coming to an end. Now, the only ones we see are falling apart. They're decaying and can barely move. But, just so you know, we did get a report about two weeks ago of a big group up in the same area that you're passing through in the little town of Pendleton. The citizen told us that some came from the interstate near here and went north but some others came from Clemson. That's about fifteen or twenty miles north of here. Y'all be careful."

"Thanks for the info. Hopefully, we can keep eliminating those decomposing Zs to keep the virus from spreading. I haven't spoken to the home CDC office in a few weeks," McCain said, "but they're in a safe location outside of Atlanta, working around the clock on a vaccine."

A few minutes later, Chuck was back in the Tundra. "You're not my wife at the moment, you're my partner from the CDC," he told Elizabeth. "I'll explain later. Follow that police car; he's going to take us to our next turn. They've got a roadblock there, too. I think these guys are OK, but let me do the talking."

Three state troopers were manning the other location, one of them wearing sergeant's stripes. Corporal Patterson spoke with him for a few minutes. The other two officers couldn't help but gawk at the strange-looking vehicle. The half inch steel plating that had been welded to the doors, hood, and grill of the pickup was a conversation piece for the troopers. Elizabeth also got her share of stares from the police officers as they waited to be waved through.

The corporal and a beefy, red-haired man finally walked over to where Beth and Chuck waited, standing beside their pickup. They both smiled politely at Elizabeth and then looked at McCain.

"I'm Tim Robinson," the sergeant introduced himself, shaking hands with the couple. "You folks are free to go, but Corporal Patterson told me who you work for and I was hoping I could ask you a couple of questions."

"Of course," McCain answered. "I might even be able to answer them."

Robinson smiled. "Could I offer you a cup of coffee? We don't have much in the way of hospitality, but we do have a good supply of that."

Both Chuck and Beth nodded at the unexpected offer. "That would be great. Thanks."

The corporal asked how they took their coffee, walked over to the sergeant's police car, and withdrew a large thermos out of the backseat along with a pack of styrofoam cups. As he prepared coffee for their guests, Robinson dove in with his questions.

"Is there any progress on a vaccine for the virus?"

"When I left over a month ago, no, there wasn't. My team and I rescued one of the key scientists involved with that research a few days after the simultaneous attacks in Atlanta, DC, and New York. She was trapped inside the CDC headquarters. We managed to get her out, but in the process she lost most of her data. The samples she was working on, her computer, and her notebooks—all gone. The only bright side was that one of my agents retrieved a memory stick that he saw sticking out of a computer in her lab.

"It's a long story, but her assistant had gotten infected and tried to kill her. In all the confusion, Dr. Edwards left the memory stick behind but my guy grabbed it. So, at least she has that. But now she's having to recreate all that lost data. Dr. Edwards told me that she was just starting to see some real progress in her lab mice before all that happened. And now, with the power outages and communication grid down, it's a tough environment to work in."

"You left Atlanta a month ago?" the sergeant asked, surprise in his voice, as Patterson returned to hand Beth and Chuck cups of steaming coffee.

"Almost two now," Chuck answered, taking a sip of the hot liquid. "Thanks, Corporal. It's like the wild west between here and Atlanta. I'm starting to lose count of all the times that I've been ambushed. We were attacked this morning just inside South Carolina on Highway 29. Three guys tried to bushwhack us."

After it was clear that McCain wasn't going to give any more information on the incident, Corporal Patterson asked, "I guess those criminals aren't going to be causing any more problems?"

"No, they won't," Chuck conceded. "They had a camp set up in one of the little parks right on the lake. As we approached, they pulled their Escalade out to block the road and started shooting at us. After we dealt with them, we checked their camp. There were five bodies tossed nearby. Two of them were women who looked like they had suffered terribly. Three males had been shot in the back of the head. The scumbags had one of their tents set up as their rape pad."

These revelations of horrific criminal activity, less than an hour away, shocked both of the hardened state troopers.

After taking another drink of his coffee, McCain looked the corporal and the sergeant in the eye and said, "I've got a confession to make. Corporal, I lied to you over at the roadblock when I said that Elizabeth was my partner. She's actually my wife."

Chuck saw Beth smile as he came clean. A look of confusion crossed both of the police officers' faces.

"It's been a rough couple of months," McCain explained, nodding at his wife. "Beth was kidnapped after several of her friends were murdered by a nasty gang thirty or forty minutes inside Georgia off of I-85. They kidnapped her and, well, thankfully, I was in the area and was able to step in before they could rape and kill her. That was two months ago. We got married Monday."

Most state troopers are hard to surprise, having seen a little of everything in their law enforcement careers. The sergeant and the corporal, however, were both hanging on every word of McCain's, their mouths open.

Chuck paused to finish off his drink. "The leader of that gang was a dirty cop, he had credentials from the Franklin County SO. We found out later that he was running prostitutes, drugs, and stolen property. That particular officer and a large number of his gang won't be causing any more problems but, needless to say, Beth and I both have some trust issues."

Sergeant Robinson raised his eyebrows. "I can understand that. I'm glad you're OK, ma'am," he nodded at Elizabeth. "And congratulations on your wedding."

She gave him her sweetest smile. "Thank you, sir."

Corporal Patterson looked at Chuck. "Are you still working for the CDC, Mr. McCain?"

"I'm still the OIC of the Atlanta office, but my mission at the moment is finding my daughter. After the cell towers went down, I lost contact with her. When the chain-of-command fell apart at the CDC, and really, the entire government, I sent my agents home and told them to get their own families somewhere secure. Once I find Melanie and verify that she's safe, then I'll try to figure out how to get the Atlanta CDC office up and running again."

"One more question, please, Agent McCain. How bad is Atlanta?" Robinson asked. "I've got an aunt, an uncle, and several cousins there. They live up past Marietta. The zombies are bad enough, but we have a ham radio here and we keep hearing these crazy reports about a Mexican cartel setting up shop in Atlanta."

Chuck shook his head and shrugged. "I don't know anything about the Mexican cartel. The pastor that performed our wedding gave me the same info this morning as we were leaving Hartwell. He's got a ham radio, too.

"As for the Zs in Atlanta, it's bad. Me and my men, some local cops, and a few FBI agents were set up near the Braves stadium on I-75 after the car bomb and the suicide bomber detonated downtown. The President ordered us to make a stand and we killed hundreds of zombies but they steamrolled over us and just kept going. I lost a man, Atlanta lost a lot of officers, and all but two FBI agents were killed. Police were set up on every interstate around the city, but there just weren't enough cops to stop the thousands of Zs.

"Our roadblock was also unlucky enough to be the one where three Muslim terrorists attacked us from the rear while we were fighting the zombies. Two suicide bombers and a guy sniping at us with an AK. One of the bombers took out our Blackhawk just as it was landing. Most of us were wounded and lucky to have survived. It was a bad day.

"You know the rest. After that, the Zs began spreading out up and down the interstate system. Now, if those reports of a Mexican cartel moving in are accurate, that'll probably be my first order of business after they get communications restored."

"Wouldn't that be the FBI's jurisdiction, sir?" the sergeant queried.

"Normally, you'd be correct, and they may have a role to play. Let's just say that I have some insider information that the FBI has lost the confidence of the President because of some serious security breaches and leaks inside of the agency. Their failure to act was actually why the CDC Enforcement Unit was created in the first place."

The two South Carolina troopers were surprised at this revelation. The Federal Bureau of Investigation had long been considered the top law enforcement agency in America. If what McCain was telling them was true, that was about to change.

"It looks like you guys fared pretty well when the Zs swept through here?" Chuck asked, clearly impressed. "This part of South Carolina looks so normal."

Sergeant Robinson nodded. "Our governor gave the evacuation order pretty quickly. From the law enforcement perspective, we learned from watching how things were handled in Atlanta and the other cities. Instead of trying to make a stand, the state patrol, local cops, and even some armed citizens, we all kept up a fighting retreat, killing as many as we could and then retreating.

"The zombies kept chasing us and we kept putting them down, all the way across the state. When we got to North Carolina, we went east and west and let those Tar heel cops have their fun. Of course, there are still a lot of stragglers up and down the interstates and in the interior.

"We did receive a report two weeks ago of a big group north of here, in the direction that y'all are going. Highway 187 dead ends into Highway 76 about fifteen minutes up the road where you'll turn left. The town of Pendleton is maybe another two miles after that. Supposedly there were quite a few people there who didn't take the governor's evacuation order very seriously and now there's a big group of hungry zombies that want to eat them."

"How big is big?" Chuck asked.

Corporal Patterson answered. "The guy I talked to estimated around two hundred but it could be more than that by now. Clemson is only a few miles from Pendleton and that campus got hit pretty bad, kind of like that mess you guys had at the University of Georgia. And, I also heard that Hendersonville was overrun, sorry."

The corporal saw the federal police officer close his eyes at the mention of UGA and changed the subject. "Do y'all have maps of the area?"

"We do have maps," McCain answered, taking a deep breath and looking at Elizabeth. "Sounds like it's going to be an adventure."

She shrugged and gave a slight smile. "It looks like life with you is going to be one adventure after another."

This got a laugh from the two troopers. Patterson nodded. "Most of your route up to Pendleton should be clear, after you get under the interstate a mile from here. You'll see some abandoned cars and bodies lying around that haven't been removed. And, of course, we have straggler Zs that come through all the time even though we've worked hard to clear the area. Like I told you, we have some VIPs here that need to be kept safe at all costs."

"Thanks for your help and for your hospitality, Sergeant," Chuck said, extending his hand. "And I'd like to apologize for lying to you, Corporal. It's good to see that the thin blue line is still intact."

### South of Clemson, South Carolina, Wednesday, 1215 hours

The troopers had spoken the truth. The couple didn't see any infected as Beth drove them north on Highway 187. The state highway was a rural, two-lane, tree-lined road. The homes were spread out, most sitting well back from the street. After fifteen minutes, Chuck reached over the seat and touched Elizabeth's shoulder.

"Let's stop and eat?"

A redbrick, Baptist church appeared on their left. McCain directed his wife to pull around behind Mount Tabor Church where they would be hidden from view. The area looked safe and it felt good to be out of the vehicle again in the warm sunshine. Chuck lowered the tailgate of the pickup and they sat, legs dangling, sipping water and munching on protein bars.

"Those police officers were nice. I'm glad there are still some good ones out there," Beth commented.

"They really were good guys. In reality, most cops are. They get into that line of work because they have a desire to serve their communities. It's really a calling more than a job. The zombie virus changed everything, though. There were just too many infected for police departments to deal with.

"Then, when everything broke down, officers decided to abandon their posts and get their own loved ones to safety. Who could blame them? I did the same thing. We worked for weeks with no communications and no support before I finally pulled the plug.

---

A few of my guys chose to stick around and moved their families onto a remote CDC site outside of Atlanta in the suburbs."

Elizabeth remembered something she had been wanting to ask him and grabbed his arm excitedly. "You know what? You haven't told me about your house! Is that where we'll live after things return to normal?"

Chuck smiled. He had proposed to Beth on Monday. That night, he had asked Pastor Ben Thompson to perform the ceremony when he and Elizabeth went over for dinner. It was definitely an unusual set of circumstances, the couple only having known each other for a little over a month.

"Well, it's *our* house now, and bonus: it's paid off. When I was working my first contract with the military in Afghanistan, I saved almost every penny of my salary and paid off my mortgage. After my second contract, I bought a really nice pickup truck for cash and put the rest of the money in the bank. So we've also got a nice chunk of cash put away. I wonder if that money will still be there when all of this gets sorted out?"

"I haven't even thought about that," Elizabeth admitted. "I've got some money put away in a money market account. I was saving up to have a big down payment to buy my own place one day. I hope the banks are still solvent."

McCain shrugged. "We'll be fine, either way. But, back to your question: our house is nice. I think you'll be happy there. It really needs a woman's touch, that's for sure. It has three big bedrooms, a huge living room, and a basement where I have all my workout equipment. I just had the kitchen completely redone with new counters and appliances a couple of years ago.

"My favorite spot is the back deck. It overlooks the woods and the backyard has a small creek running through it. It's where I like to sit in the evening to unwind. A cigar, a glass of scotch, and now you sitting out there with me is something to look forward to."

"Do you think your…I mean our house is OK?" Elizabeth asked, still getting used to the idea of being married. "Did the zombies make it out that far?"

Chuck shrugged. "Who knows? I live about ten miles from the interstate just east of the little town of Dacula. When I left a couple of months ago, no Zs had been seen out there. I spoke to a couple of my neighbors and asked them to keep an eye on it. I think most of the people in my subdivision stayed. Thankfully, the folks on my street all got along and looked out for each other. I think it'll be OK."

Beth looked into Chuck's eyes and smiled. "I'm looking forward to playing house with you," she said shyly, leaning against him.

McCain was overwhelmed with love for this woman. She was leaving everything she knew to follow him. The path that she'd chosen was dangerous but Beth had not hesitated. Originally, he wasn't planning on taking her with him when he left the Northeast Georgia Technical College. The world as they knew it was just too dangerous, and he'd believed the secluded school would be a secure spot for the young woman.

The night before Chuck was scheduled to leave, however, thirteen heavily armed gang members infiltrated the campus, planning to kill McCain and kidnap Elizabeth in retaliation for the deaths of four of their friends at Chuck's hand, when he'd rescued Beth from those violent attackers. McCain had also cleaned out their safe house, taking a large amount of food and weapons that the criminals had stored there.

During the ensuing gunfight at the technical college, all thirteen of the intruders were killed by Chuck, Beth, and the campus security team. Sadly, three students were also killed, and five people wounded, including McCain. He had sustained a nasty wound when a .44 magnum bullet dug a deep trench down his left hip, requiring almost thirty stitches to close.

After the campus shootout, Chuck had changed his mind, asking Elizabeth if she wanted to accompany him when he left. With the attack on the college, the couple realized that no place was truly safe. McCain had already begun training the young woman, developing her tactics and weapons skills. In the two weeks before they started their journey, however, Chuck spent three hours a day helping Beth become proficient with her weapons.

They both enjoyed the brief respite, sitting on the back of the truck. He put his arm around her and held her tight.

"I'm looking forward to playing house with you, too," he said, softly. "But if you don't like it, or the neighborhood, no problem, we'll sell it and buy another one. I want you to be happy."

Chuck sensed there was more that Beth wanted to ask him but instead of talking anymore, their lips met and they sat in a comfortable silence until McCain said, "Let's get going?"

The drive through rural South Carolina was beautiful and they both had to work to stay focused on the fact that around any curve they could encounter danger. Four miles up the road, Elizabeth turned left onto the highway that would take them through Pendleton, where the large group of zombies had been reported. Chuck had checked the map for other routes but their options were limited.

As they continued north, they began to see clear evidence that the bio-terror virus had visited the area. Businesses with shattered windows, abandoned cars, their doors standing open, and the gruesome remains of what had once been people lying on the side of the road, in parking lots, or hanging out of vehicles attested to the presence of the undead.

"This doesn't look good," McCain commented, as he watched for threats.

Two, decomposing, nude zombies, a male and a female, rounded the corner of a gas station, drawn to the sound of the Toyota pickup driving by. The female Z was missing her left arm below the elbow. They shuffled towards the roadway as Beth passed them.

"I'll never get used to seeing that," Elizabeth said, shaking her head.

"Let's hope we don't have to. Half a mile up, we're going to turn right onto Highway 28," Chuck directed.

As they approached their turnoff, though, they could see a large group of infected in the parking lot of a small strip mall on their left, clustered around one business. McCain estimated at least fifty growling, snarling creatures were attempting to get into the Bombay Jewelers, according to the sign. The noise of the group carried to the couple as Beth slowed for their turn.

They were close enough now that they could see that the jewelry store had bars on the windows and door, but all the glass had been smashed out by the infected. At least twenty of them were reaching their arms through the bars trying to grab something. Or someone. The pickup truck came to a stop in the intersection.

"What are you doing?" Chuck asked, concern in his voice.

"There's someone in that store," Beth said. "Why else would those things be crowded around, reaching inside?"

"You're probably right. Let's go while they're are occupied."

"Chuck, we have to help them."

"No, we don't. Let's get out of here. We can't help everybody and that's a big group of zombies."

The Tundra continued to sit motionless in the middle of the road. The drama at the Bombay Jewelers was just two hundred yards away. McCain made eye contact with his wife as she looked at him in the rear view mirror. He saw a determination that he hadn't seen before in the short time that he'd known her.

"We have to help them," she repeated.

A few of the infected in the back of the crowd had seen the

pickup truck come to a stop and were already shuffling towards them.

"Elizabeth, please, we need to go. We really can't help everybody and there's just two of us."

"I know we can't help everybody, but if there's someone trapped in that store, we can help them. You know the Bible better than me but I think I read something to the effect of, 'Do unto others what you would want them to do unto you.' Did I quote that right?"

"Oh, yeah. You quoted it perfectly," he admitted, resignation in his voice.

Chuck quickly looked at the map pages in his lap, a plan starting to form. That's really not fair quoting the Bible, he thought. Not fair at all.

"Okay. Here's what we're going to do."

Two minutes later, after explaining the plan to his wife, Chuck exited the vehicle and assumed a kneeling position from which to pick off the infected. He raised the Colt M4 and began firing. After his first shot, Elizabeth began honking the horn, holding it down to get the attention of the Zs.

McCain shot thirteen of the infected but he couldn't take out the ones clustered around the windows. He didn't want to take a chance on hitting whoever was inside. The car horn and the gunshots did the trick, though. The rest of the horde, with the exception of five who were convinced that they were going to get to their victim inside the jewelry store, were now stumbling and lurching across the parking lot towards the Tundra.

Chuck was thrilled that these Zs had all been infected for a while, so that they weren't dealing with any of the sprinting zombies that he had encountered at other times. The federal police officer continued making head shots, dropping more of the creatures coming after them. Another eight had fallen by the time McCain stood, reloaded, and getting back into the safety of the vehicle.

"Drive towards that Firehouse Subs right up there on the left. I'm getting hungry again."

Elizabeth looked at her husband in the rear view mirror with disbelief. "You're hungry?"

"Bad joke," he laughed. "Stop in the middle of the road next to the sandwich shop and let me pick off a few more. I need you watching to make sure no others surprise us. We're making a lot of noise and zombies are going to come running, or even better, shuffling from every direction."

This was a slow moving group of Zs that were now pursuing and Chuck put bullets in the heads of eleven more. The others, oblivious to their companions' demise, continued towards fresh meat, growling and snapping their teeth together. McCain jumped back into the Tundra, swapping out the partial magazine of ammo for a full one, and slamming it into his M4.

"Turn into the sub shop and drive around behind it. Take a left on that road in the rear. It'll take us right back to the shopping center."

"Got it," Beth said, shoving the accelerator to the floor.

Three teenage zombies, drawn to the sound of the shots, stumbled out from the rear of the Firehouse Subs, directly into their path. Elizabeth never hesitated, slamming the heavy metal bumper into two of them, sending them flying head over heels across the parking lot. She knew that time was of the essence and the pickup skidded, tires squealing, as she made the left turn, driving them back towards the Bombay Jewelers.

"We'll be coming in from the other end of the shopping center," Chuck said. "Stop one store up from the jewelry store and let me take care of the ones that are still there. Then, we'll make contact with whoever's inside."

As the truck came to a halt in front of a nail salon, the five

---

zombies at the jewelers finally withdrew their arms from the smashed out windows, turning towards Beth and Chuck. McCain was out quickly and shooting, exploding their heads from less than twenty-five yards away. The five infected bodies made a bloody mess on the sidewalk and their stench was almost overwhelming. He did a rapid three hundred and sixty degree scan, making sure that they were safe for the moment.

"Pull up right in front and let's see what we've got."

Chuck used the sidewalk to approach the Bombay Jewelers, moving cautiously, not wanting to get shot by a survivor. When he peeked inside, however, he didn't see anyone. The jewelry cases were still full of jewelry, he noted with surprise. He motioned for Beth to join him. She's really cute, all decked out with web gear and guns, he thought, glancing at her getting out of the pickup.

Suddenly, a loud banging sound came from a metal interior door on the back wall of the store, startling McCain. He swung his rifle up in the direction of the noise. The door probably leads to storage or an office, he thought.

A low moan came from just inside the store. He moved further down the walkway, hoping to get a better view inside, and there she was. A small, preadolescent Indian girl was lying on the floor, curled up in a fetal position, next to one of the display counters. She groaned again, causing the banging from the rear to intensify.

"Hello? Are you OK? I'm a police officer and we want to help you."

Growling now accompanied the banging on the other side of the metal door. The girl on the floor made an effort to raise her head, trying to see who was speaking to her.

"Please, help me," the Indian girl whispered.

"We're going to try," McCain answered. "Have you been bitten?"

She managed to shake her head. "No, but I'm so weak. I don't think I can get up. I haven't had anything to eat or drink in so long."

"We'll get you out of there," he promised.

"What do you think?" Elizabeth asked.

Chuck shrugged. "Let's figure out a way to get in. These bars look pretty formidable."

"Why don't we try the rear?"

He shook his head. "We can hear the Zs in that back room, but there's no telling how many there are. I'd hate to force the rear door and get overrun. Let me check the truck and see if there's a crowbar or something. I'll be right back."

"Hang on," Elizabeth told the girl. "We've got to try and figure out a way to get in."

"I…have…the…keys…here," she said, weakly, holding up a set of keys.

Beth made eye contact with her. "I know it's hard but I need you to get up and bring me those keys. There's glass all over the floor but we want to get you out of there. What's your name?"

The girl on the floor took a deep breath. "Diya," she answered. "Diya Meena."

"I'm Elizabeth and the man you saw is my husband, Chuck."

McCain returned to Beth's side, holding a crowbar.

"She's got the keys," Beth said. "I'm trying to get her to bring them over."

Chuck nodded and looked back across the parking lot. The group from earlier was coming back, but it had grown, other Zs having been drawn to the noise. They were still three hundred yards away but there looked to be at least forty of them.

"Look," he motioned at the zombies, and then went to work trying to pry the door open.

Elizabeth turned and gave a slight gasp when she saw the Zs that were heading straight towards them. "Diya, there's a lot of zombies coming. We don't have much time."

The small girl pulled herself up to a sitting position, leaning back against one of the display cases. She appeared to be no older than twelve, maybe even younger. Her face was pale and drawn, her clothes hanging loosely from her tiny frame.

The burglar bars were designed to keep people from doing exactly what Chuck was trying to accomplish and he wasn't making any progress with the pry bar. The pounding on the door inside the jewelry store continued unabated, sounding as if multiple infected were trying to break through. I sure hope that door holds, he thought.

The girl summoned all of her strength and used the jewelry counter to pull herself to her feet. She leaned against the display, clearly unsteady as she tried to stand. Her eyes were focused on Elizabeth but Diya could now also see the parking lot beyond her new friends and the growling mob of flesh-eaters coming their way. Behind the door to her rear was more agitated grunting, snarling, and banging.

McCain watched the young girl walking slowly towards them. She was wearing jeans, a University of South Carolina hoodie, and pink Nikes. She had told them she hadn't eaten in a while and she looked like a skeleton. Chuck glanced behind him, checking the progress of the approaching Zs. A few of the faster-moving ones were inside two hundred yards now.

Meena stumbled as she got to them, reaching through the glassless door, grabbing the bars for balance. She extended the keys through the opening. McCain grabbed them but quickly saw that there were at least twenty keys on the ring.

He held them up and said, sharply, "Which one?"

The girls eyes were closed and she looked like she was about to pass out. Beth reached through the burglar bars and wrapped her hands around Diya's arms, helping hold her up.

Chuck began frantically working through the keys, one-by-one, trying them all. The eighth one was the charm and he carefully pulled the bars open. He and Beth grabbed the young girl and helped her outside.

The big man looked at his wife. "She can't stand up on her own. After we put her in the truck, can you check her for bites? We can't take any chances."

Beth nodded and they helped Meena into the front passenger seat of the Tundra. Elizabeth quickly pulled up the little girl's hoodie and a red long-sleeve t-shirt, checking her front and back, as well as her arms and legs, as McCain kept watch. The pack of Zs were only a hundred yards away.

"She's fine," Elizabeth told Chuck. "Just dehydrated and weak from not eating."

"Give her a few small sips of water and then let's move," Chuck instructed his wife.

As the precious water got inside of her, the girls eyes fluttered open. Beth held a plastic bottle to her mouth, speaking softly, "Just a little at a time. You're going to be fine. You're safe now."

"Let's go," McCain urged. "Give her another sip, strap her in and let's roll."

Diya locked eyes with Chuck. "Please, my family. They're the ones in the back room. They're sick."

The girl's gaze drifted to the rifle McCain was wearing. "Can you...I don't want them to make anyone else sick."

The snarling and teeth snapping open and shut carried across the sixty yards that separated them from the zombies in the parking lot. Chuck knew they were going to be cutting this close.

Beth saw the Zs getting ever closer, and now that they had rescued the little girl, she was ready to make their getaway. "Come on, we need to go."

McCain nodded but kept looking at Diya, understanding what she was asking him to do. "So, it's just your parents in that back room?"

"And my little brother and my uncle. My uncle was sick and he bit my dad and mom."

The police officer saw the fear on his wife's face. "Beth, get in and drive to the other side of the parking lot, honking the horn. Get that group to follow you. I'll take care of this and then you can come back and pick me up. Give me five minutes."

Elizabeth hesitated for a moment but then nodded, took a deep breath, and rushed around to the driver's door. In seconds, Chuck was hurrying back into the jewelry store as the Toyota Tundra was racing to the far end of the large parking area, horn blaring.

Inside the Bombay Jewelers, Chuck pushed the front door closed and plotted his best course of action. He decided to use his pistol since he needed one hand free to open the metal door. He pulled the suppressor from his belt and screwed it onto the threaded barrel of the Glock.

The banging had stopped and he quietly stepped over to the door, gently turning the knob, pulling the metal door towards him a few inches. He slowly backed away from the opening, raising the gun to eye level, circling around one of the jewelry counters, putting a barrier between him and the door.

"Here I am!" he called. "Come and eat me!"

Immediately, the office door flew open and the zombie version of Diya's dad rushed out, bloody and smelly, only to receive a 9mm bullet in the forehead. A female Z wearing a bright orange sari, covered in blood, tripped over the body of the man who had been her husband. As she attempted to get to her feet, Chuck shot her in the top of the head. Another bloody Indian, open wounds visible on both arms, rushed towards McCain growling and snapping his teeth together. The pistol round caught him in the nose and spun him around, his body landing on top of his brother and sister-in-law.

Chuck waited for the boy to come out but there was no more noise from the open door. McCain cautiously crept over to the opening and did a quick peek into the back room. The bloody remains of the child, Diya's brother, were scattered around the small storage room. After becoming infected, his parents and uncle had ripped him apart and eaten him. The stench of death was overwhelming.

Covering his nose, Chuck did an about face and quickly moved back into the store, avoiding Diya's unfortunate relatives. McCain glanced out the store window, noting with satisfaction that the parking lot zombies were shuffling after the armored pickup truck that was stopped, horn blaring, on the far side of shopping center. As Chuck scanned the inside of the store for anything useful, an idea suddenly came to him. He went behind the closest jewelry counter, opening drawers until he found what he was looking for.

When the Tundra stopped in front of the store two minutes later, Chuck dove into the backseat carrying a black container the size of a small suitcase. He saw the question in Beth's eyes in the rearview mirror but he also saw her relief that he was OK.

McCain directed his wife out of the parking lot, the group of Zs now shuffling back from other side of the shopping center. A mile up the road was a large convenience store, the doors and windows smashed out.

"Pull in there," Chuck directed. "If it hasn't all been looted, I'll see if I can pick up some Gatorade. That's what Diya needs."

Beth pulled cautiously into the parking lot. A few cars and trucks were scattered around the area, all appearing to be empty.

"Grab your rifle and hop out," McCain said. "Cover me and make sure nothing sneaks in behind me."

"I'll feel a lot better when we get out of this little town," Elizabeth said, a slight tremble in her voice.

Chuck smiled and pointed at the girl in the front passenger seat. "This was your idea and it was a good one. Your instincts were right on. This'll just take a minute."

McCain carefully entered the store after kicking the doorframe to see if any Zs were inside. The business had been ransacked and the Gatorade and PowerAde coolers were empty. He moved down another mostly empty aisle, locating the Gatorade powder.

Just as he grabbed the last two containers, a gunshot exploded outside. Chuck spun to see smoke curling out of the barrel of Beth's AR-15, a dead male zombie lying twenty feet away. As he rushed out to help, Elizabeth's muzzle tracked another one advancing towards her. She fired a second shot from fifteen feet, a 5.56mm bullet punching through the left eye of what had been a small, black-haired teenage girl, wearing a cheerleading outfit.

McCain stopped beside his wife, scanning the area for any further threats. He motioned for her to get into their vehicle and then followed. He was also ready to get out of the little town. They saw a few more infected as they made their way through the small business district of Pendleton but ten minutes later, they were cruising again on empty rural roads.

### North of Pendleton, South Carolina, Wednesday, 1340 hours

Ten miles later, McCain tapped Beth on the shoulder. "We need to find a place to stop and give Diya some Gatorade. It looks like there's another church just up on the right."

On his journey, he had found himself on more than one occasion, taking refuge in a house of worship. He couldn't really explain it but he just felt safe there. The added bonus was that most churches tended to be deserted during the week.

Elizabeth stopped in the roadway in front of Faith Fellowship, she and Chuck scanning the area for any signs of zombies or human predators. Beth pulled in, driving slowly around to the rear of the building, grateful not to see any cars in the parking lot. She stopped behind the church, out of sight from the street, under a metal awning by the back doors. All of the entrances and windows appeared to be intact.

Beth climbed out and walked around to check on their passenger. Diya opened her eyes and tried to smile, swallowing water from the bottle that was held up to her lips. Chuck handed Elizabeth the plastic container of Gatorade powder to mix for their patient.

As Elizabeth prepared the drink, Diya Meena looked up at Chuck. "Did you...?"

"I did," he said, softly. "I'm so sorry, but I took care of it."

Tears poured down the young girl's face. "They were sick for a long time. Thank you," she said, quietly.

Beth gave her a few sips of the Gatorade. "How long has it been since you've eaten or had anything to drink?"

"I'm not sure; I kind of lost track of time. I don't think I've eaten in over a week, and my water ran out two or three days ago."

After drinking some more of the replenishing liquid, Diya asked, "Where are you taking me?"

Beth glanced at her husband who shrugged, uncertainty etching his handsome face. "Do you have any family in the area?" Elizabeth asked, putting her hand on the young girl's arm.

Meena shook her head. "My aunt and two cousins live in Clemson but I think they're sick, too. My uncle came to the store and said that his wife had gone crazy and attacked him. It wasn't long before he started attacking my family."

The sobs began again, the small girl's body shaking as she cried. Beth leaned into the vehicle and held her tightly, knowing first-hand the pain of losing one's family.

Why does helping people have to be so complicated? McCain asked himself. What were they going to do with Diya? He touched his wife on the shoulder to get her attention.

"I'm going to walk around the church and see what I can see. If it looks secure, I think we'll stop here and spend the rest of the day and night. She needs to be taken care of and we can't do that on the road."

Beth nodded at him, watching him go. They both understood the dangers of stopping, knowing that there were zombies in the area.

McCain moved slowly around the building, staying close to the wall. He looked for signs of forced entry that might indicate someone else was lodging there. He didn't like the idea of spending the night, but Diya needed to be rehydrated as soon as possible. After that, they would try to get a little food in her. What she really needed was to be hospitalized with an IV in her arm. For now, Gatorade and chicken soup would have to do.

Chuck also realized that Elizabeth would be crashing physically very soon. He was surprised that she was still functioning as well as she was. They'd been in a shootout that morning and then taken on a pack of zombies to rescue the young Indian girl.

The normal physiological reactions after a strong adrenaline dump are physical weakness and exhaustion for those who aren't used to operating at a high level of intensity. That could be compensated for by intensive training, but in Beth's case, a good night's rest should take care of it.

As Chuck reached the front of the Faith Fellowship, the sound of an approaching vehicle made him slowly drop to the ground behind a large bush. A red Ford Expedition was driving north from Pendleton, where McCain and the ladies had just come from. As it went by, he counted four men, the two in the backseat pointing rifles out of their open windows. Leonard Skynard's "Sweet Home Alabama" blasted over their sound system, the occupants clearly not concerned with attracting infected people.

The SUV continued past the church without slowing down. Chuck waited for two minutes and then crouch-walked in front of the church building, making sure that the main doors and windows were secure. He completed his circuit, working his way down the opposite side of the facility, finally ending up back where he had started.

Beth stood beside the open passenger door of the Tundra, holding her rifle in a low ready position. She exhaled audibly when she saw Chuck.

"I heard a car."

He nodded. "I saw it. A red Ford Expedition coming from Pendleton. I counted four guys, two of them holding rifles."

Anxiety filled Beth's eyes. "So, what are we going to do?"

Chuck smiled, trying to put her at ease. "We're going to break into this church and take care of our patient."

"But what if those men come back?"

Her husband shrugged. "I'll kill them."

The crow bar hadn't been of much use on the burglar bars at Bombay Jewelers, but it made short work of the rear door of the Faith Fellowship. Chuck was able to pop the door open while only doing minimal damage. He asked Diya to wait in the Tundra, locked for her protection, while they cleared the interior of the building, making sure it was safe.

McCain then carried the weak girl inside and laid her on a row of four padded chairs inside the first room on the left. They had chosen a Sunday School room for children complete with a painting of Moses standing in front of the parted Red Sea on one wall and the shepherd boy, David, confronting a giant on another. The rear entrance of the church had brought them into a small lobby connected to the children's wing of the worship center, complete with multiple classrooms.

After finding a small kitchen on the other side of the church, Elizabeth located several tablecloths. Two of the black ones went over the window of their room while the others would be used for bedding. A white cloth covered Diya as she rested. As Elizabeth held the plastic water bottle containing Gatorade up to the girl's lips, Chuck worked on the back door, managing to re-secure it. After making sure they were as safe as they could be inside the building, he checked in on the two girls.

"You OK?" Chuck asked his wife.

Elizabeth gave him a weary smile. "All of a sudden I'm feeling really tired," she yawned.

"The adrenaline is finally wearing off," he told her. "We've had a pretty full day. I think you're entitled to have the afternoon off. I managed to get the rear door locked again. I'm gonna go check the rest of the building and see if there's anything that we can use."

"How're you feeling, Diya?" Elizabeth asked the young girl after Chuck left.

Beth had found a spoon in the kitchen and was sitting next to Meena, giving her some small bites of canned chicken soup, being careful not to let her eat too much in one sitting. It would be several days before she would be able to start eating normally again. Several cans of soup had been left behind in the Mitchell's pantry and Elizabeth had helped herself when she and Chuck had left.

"So much better," Diya answered with a smile, sitting up. "I feel so weak but the water, Gatorade, and that soup are bringing me back to life."

"How old are you?"

"I just turned thirteen. My brother was only eleven." The memory of her dead family brought another wave of sadness back and she closed her eyes.

"How long had you guys been in the store?" Beth asked, wanting to keep her talking. "Were y'all camping out in there?"

Diya nodded. "My father thought we would be safer there. He watched the news and said that our house was in path of the zombies. Papa was worried about our business, too. He said that people were going to be using the zombie crisis as an excuse to rob and steal and do other bad things. He and Mama set up the back room like an apartment. We've been there a few months.

"We had plenty of food and water and no one had bothered us. Papa had a shotgun but he'd never used it. I heard Mama ask him why we didn't leave, go somewhere safer. She was worried about me and Sunil, my brother.

"They thought I was asleep but I was just pretending. Papa told Mama that the jewelry store was all he had to give us. They wanted me to be a doctor. Papa was going to pay for me to go to medical school and for Sunil to go to law school. I don't know if my brother even understood what a lawyer was. Our parents wanted to help us, and we would do as they asked. That's our culture."

Elizabeth patted the grieving girl's shoulder. "Your parents sounded like good people. I'm sure they were very proud of you."

"But I couldn't help them, Miss Elizabeth. When my uncle came to the store he told my dad that my aunt had jumped on him and started biting him. He thought that she had hurt their two sons, too, but he couldn't get to them. Uncle rushed out of the house and drove over to get my father's shotgun.

"But then Uncle just stopped talking and collapsed onto the floor. Papa and Mama tried to help him; my bother and I just stood there, wondering if he was dead. Papa yelled for me to get the first-aid kit on the other side of the room.

"Just as I grabbed it, Mama started screaming, my brother was crying, and Papa was yelling. I rushed back across the room and saw Uncle biting my brother's leg. The blood was pouring out and he was pushing on his head, trying to make him let go. Papa started punching Uncle but he just kept biting Sunil.

"Uncle made a horrible growling noise as he chewed. I could even hear his teeth grinding. Then, he let go of Sunil and grabbed Mama and bit her on the face. Papa kept hitting him but Uncle wouldn't stop. I ran over and hit uncle in the head with the first-aid kit. It was plastic and it just broke open and everything flew out onto the floor. Papa grabbed me and shoved me towards the door. 'Go into the store! Get out of here and lock the door!'"

The tears were pouring down the young girl's face as she relived the horror of that day.

"Shh," Beth said, softly, pulling her new friend close and hugging her. "I'm so sorry. You don't have to say any more."

"But I feel so guilty, Miss Elizabeth. I ran away and left my parents and brother with my sick Uncle. I didn't even try and help, but I could hear everything. It was terrible and I was so scared. After my family got sick, they started trying to get to me, banging on that door.

"I didn't know what to do. All our food and water was in the back room. I found three granola bars in one of the drawers and four bottles of water.

"The zombies showed up a few days later. They smashed all the windows out as I tried to hide behind one of the counters but I think they could smell me. Every day I just laid there on the floor, trying to pray to one of our gods.

"All the days started running together and I hadn't eaten in so long, over a week, and I'd finished my water. I finally decided that I'd open the back door and join my family. I was going to die anyway, either by starving or getting sick with my family. My mind was telling me that's what I should do and my gods weren't helping me.

"I was trying to get my courage to open the door and die when I heard a car horn. When I managed to stand up, I saw Mr. Chuck across the street shooting the zombies. I must've fainted because the next thing I remember was Mr. Chuck and you standing in front of the store.

"You saved me but I don't know what to do now. My family is

dead. I have no other relatives in America. I have no money. I feel so empty, so lost, and so guilty."

Diya began weeping again and Elizabeth held her, letting her cry it out. After a few minutes, the girl's sobs finally subsided and Beth began speaking to her, very quietly, about how she had lost her own parents to the deadly bio-terror virus. Elizabeth didn't spare any of the details, describing how her mother had gotten infected and then attacked her father, ripping his throat out.

When Beth had tried to intervene, her mom had turned on her only daughter, wanting to devour and eat her, also. Elizabeth grabbed the first thing within reach that she could use as a weapon, a heavy crystal vase, and smashed it against her mother's skull, killing her instantly. By this time, the virus had worked its way through her father's body, reanimating him. He went after his daughter, as well, and Beth fled the house.

An ambulance and a police car had just pulled up to the residence in response to what Elizabeth had called in as a medical emergency. When the growling, bloody, infected man came charging towards the emergency personnel, the police officer fired several shots into the new zombie, a bullet to the head putting him down for good.

As Elizabeth continued to hold Diya's small frame, she shared how guilty she had felt in the aftermath of losing her own parents. She had been the one to strike down her precious mother and had made the 911 call which resulted in her father's death. Even though she hadn't fired the shots, she still carried guilt and remorse for months because she hadn't been able to help them. She even told Diya about the deep depression that she had sunk into, only coming out of her campus dorm room when she absolutely had to.

McCain returned after his search of the building. When he got to the doorway of the classroom, however, he saw his wife holding Diya, comforting her. It was clear that the Indian girl had been crying, and crying women always made the big man uncomfortable. Not wanting to intrude, Chuck backed out, seated himself in the hallway near the back door where he would have some light, and opened the Bible that he'd picked up from a seat in the auditorium.

Meena made no move to pull away from her new friend's embrace, finding comfort in her touch. After a few minutes of silence, Diya said, "You don't seem depressed to me, Miss Elizabeth. I think that you're a happy person."

Beth smiled. "That man out there, Mr. Chuck, helped me work through it. He helped me to see that there was nothing I could've done to save my parents. It was a terrible thing and I miss them so much, but it wasn't my fault.

"Something else that you should know is that Mr. Chuck saved my life, too. Some bad men had kidnapped me and were going to hurt me. Mr. Chuck showed up and rescued me. I'm telling you this because we want you to feel safe with us; we'll take care of you. None of us knows what the future holds but God was watching over you today and must have some special plans for your life."

Elizabeth's vulnerability struck a chord with Diya and the young girl began asking her questions about her life. She was surprised to learn that Beth and Chuck had only been married a few days. Meena instinctively looked at Elizabeth's left hand, not seeing an engagement or wedding ring.

Beth saw the look and shook her head. "Not yet. It happened kind of fast but I'm sure Mr. Chuck will get me something nice when things get back to normal."

Diya gave a wistful smile. "I could've given you something from the store. My father let me help him. I'd go with him to the trade shows and wholesalers to pick out what we would sell. He always let me pick out the wedding sets," she said, proudly.

Chuck couldn't hear what the two ladies were talking about but it was clear that Beth had made a friend. She's good, McCain realized.

Diya had just lost her entire family and she and Elizabeth were talking and even giggling. The question now was what do we do with the young girl? No problem, he told himself. It'll work itself out.

A few hours later, the sun had set, they had all eaten, and Diya Meena was tucked under the white tablecloth, sleeping on the four padded chairs that had become her bed. Chuck and Elizabeth walked around the inside of the worship facility holding hands and chatting quietly. Beth had supervised Meena as she had eaten some more soup, making sure she didn't overdo it. Now, the couple was enjoying a few minutes by themselves before they also tried to get some sleep.

McCain led his wife into the sanctuary and they sat alone in the big, open room. Chuck leaned over and kissed Elizabeth, holding her face in his hands.

"I'm so proud of you," he said, as they came up for breath.

"Why? I thought you were going to be mad at me for making us stop to rescue Diya. That was a scary situation."

"No, I'm not mad at you," he said, his arm draped over her shoulder. "You did good. I mean, it's been a day. You took out one of the bad guys who tried to ambush us this morning. And your instincts were spot-on about rescuing Diya. It was the right thing to do. When I get mission-focused, I don't let anything knock me off track. I'm glad we did it, now we just have to figure out what to do with her.

"Plus, you showed a lot of courage during that rescue. That was probably one of the biggest groups I'd ever taken on by myself, but we did it. And then when we stopped at that convenience store, you were like Annie Oakley or something taking out those two Zs."

Beth chuckled. "I didn't even think about it. You said to cover you and when they came out from behind the building, I just reacted.

More of the benefits of your good training."

After a few more minutes of kissing, they simply held each other. "You told me one time that God speaks to you in different ways," Elizabeth said, softly. "You said sometimes he would speak to you as you read the Bible or sometimes it was like a quiet voice deep inside of you."

"That's right," Chuck replied.

"That's why I wanted to rescue whoever was trapped in that store. It wasn't an audible voice, but I just knew that we were supposed to help them. Is that crazy?"

"No, not all. You told me a while back that you were trying to find your way back to God. I've always believed that we don't really have to find our way back to him. No matter how far away we might have fled, as soon as we turn around, he's standing there waiting on us with a big smile on his face. It sounds to me like you're back."

"That's really beautiful," Beth observed quietly. "I've never thought of it like that before."

McCain sat against the wall just inside the classroom, his rifle beside him. Elizabeth and Diya were both sound asleep on the comfortable chairs. He was dozing but couldn't give himself completely to sleep for fear that predators would sneak up on them. The two years that he had spent with the Green Berets in Afghanistan had, among other things, taught him the importance of being a light sleeper.

After the SF soldiers had accepted him as part of their team, the police liaison officer had pulled his share of sentry duty on those ops that required spending the night in the field. One of the Special Forces sergeants told Chuck that he was the first law enforcement contractor that they'd had who had volunteered to take a shift keeping watch over the team as they slept.

Movement in the classroom brought him fully awake. He

activated the small flashlight he wore on his belt. A red filter diffused the light but still allowed him to see Diya sitting up on her bed of chairs, rubbing the sleep out of her eyes.

"You alright?" Chuck asked quietly, not wanting to disturb Beth.

"I need to use the bathroom," the young girl answered shyly.

McCain stood. "Come on, I'll walk you over there and let you use my light."

Meena got unsteadily to her feet, still weak from her ordeal. "Here, hold my arm for support," Chuck offered.

He slowly guided Diya to the restroom, just two doors down from their temporary base. McCain handed her the flashlight and said, "I'll be waiting for you right here."

A few minutes later, the police officer led the girl back to her resting place and seated himself on the floor, the room again almost pitch black, the luminous dial on his watch showing 0225 hours.

"Thank you, Mr. Chuck."

"No problem."

"Really, thank you for everything. You saved my life. Miss Elizabeth told me you're trying to find your daughter but you stopped to help me."

"It's OK, Diya. I'm glad we were there for you. Plus, I have something for you in the truck. A present."

"A present? What kind of present, Mr. Chuck?"

"I found a black bag in the store, like a small suitcase."

"Oh, that was my father's jeweler bag."

"Well, I cleaned out all of the counters and put the jewelry in the bag. I figured you might need it when things get back to normal. You're going to need some money and that's a lot of beautiful jewelry that you can sell."

There was no response from Diya for several minutes. McCain realized that it was because she was sobbing quietly. She finally said, "Thank you very much, Mr. Chuck. That was very nice of you to do that for me. Thank you very, very much."

After another few moments of silence, Meena asked, "What will happen to me, Mr. Chuck?"

"We're going to visit some people tomorrow, if we can find them. They're the parents of Elizabeth's best friend. From what I've heard, they live in a really nice, safe place, on a small farm. We'll talk and see if you can stay with them."

"I…I think I'd rather be with you and Miss Elizabeth."

"I understand but after we leave there, we still have a tough journey ahead of us. It's going to take you a while to get your strength back. But, whether you stay with the Fosters or come with Beth and I, we'll do everything we can to protect you."

"Yes, Mr. Chuck," she answered, resignation in her voice.

### North of Pendleton, South Carolina, Thursday, 0800 hours

Diya had more cold soup and Gatorade for breakfast, while Chuck and Beth ate MREs from their backpacks. The Meals Ready to Eat contains a chemical warming pouch that allow the user to heat their food. McCain showed his wife how to use it and they both enjoyed a hot cup of instant coffee.

After eating, Chuck walked through the worship center, peering out all of the windows, making sure that there were no surprises waiting on them outside. After satisfying himself that it was safe, he led the two ladies to their vehicle. Meena reclined in the front passenger seat while Elizabeth drove. McCain took his backseat perch to better protect them as they traveled.

Beth turned left out of Faith Fellowship Church as the three continued their journey. The sky was overcast and it looked like rain was in the forecast. The temperatures had been unusually warm over the last few days. Today, however, felt like a cold front was moving through, especially as they drove north towards the higher elevations of the Blue Ridge Mountains. It didn't help that the police officer rode with his two side windows and rear window down to enable him to respond quickly in the case of an attack.

The road was empty and the rolling hills were beautiful. Twenty minutes after starting out, he heard his wife's voice calling him.

"Chuck! Turn around!"

McCain's head snapped up and he realized that he'd been dozing, the lack of sleep from the previous night catching up with him. His head snapped around, quickly seeing what Beth had seen: a red SUV was following them, several hundred yards to their rear.

"How long have they been behind us?"

"I don't know. I just saw them."

The optics on McCain's rifle confirmed that it was indeed the same Ford Expedition he'd seen drive by the church the previous day. He could make out four figures inside the vehicle. For the moment at least, they were maintaining a respectful distance.

"You'll turn left in about a half mile onto Highway 178," he told Elizabeth. "It's a few miles longer this way but it'll keep us from having to drive through a couple of these little towns. We'll see if our friends follow us."

The Expedition made the left turn also, continuing to follow, but making no move to overtake the Tundra. Less than a mile down on Highway 178 they passed through the small community of Shady Grove. The Red SUV stayed behind them, continuing to keep plenty of room between the two vehicles.

"What do you think they're doing?" Beth asked over her shoulder.

"They might be doing the same thing we are, trying to get some place safe. As long as they keep their distance, everything's fine."

In his heart, though, Chuck didn't believe that. He had seen the armed males in the Ford the previous day as they had driven by the church and it had looked to him like they were out hunting. The only question was, what kind of prey were they going after?

Shady Grove appeared to have had an encounter with the zombie virus. The telltale signs of smashed out windows, abandoned vehicles, and the remains of partially consumed bodies were scattered around a grocery store parking lot and a convenience store. In three minutes, however, Elizabeth had driven through the small town without seeing any Zs. The big SUV was still behind them, but now appeared to be slowly inching up and getting closer.

"Is everything alright, Miss Beth?" Diya asked, seeing the anxious look on Elizabeth's face as she kept glancing at the rear view mirror. "Is someone following us?"

Meena had her seat back, resting as they drove. Elizabeth glanced over and forced a smile.

"We're fine, Diya, Mr. Chuck will take care of us. How are you feeling? You're looking a lot better this morning."

"I'm feeling much better, but I'm so hungry! I'm ready to eat again."

Beth watched Chuck in the mirror watching the Expedition behind them. He definitely looks concerned, she thought. She had supreme confidence, however, that her husband would do whatever needed to be done to keep them safe.

The two-lane blacktop in front of them was now straight and empty. Suddenly, the Ford SUV accelerated, rapidly closing the distance between the two vehicles. McCain flipped the selector on the side of his M4 to "Auto" and braced it on the open rear window. The occupants of the Expedition were all white males in their twenties. With his right hand he waved the big vehicle off through the open window, hoping that they would take the hint.

Chuck had learned this tactic from the American Green Berets in Afghanistan. No soldier wanted to shoot an innocent civilian whose only crime was being too stupid to know that you shouldn't approach a military convoy. In most cases, the civilian quickly realized that having a rifle, machine gun, or grenade launcher pointed at you wasn't a good thing and would back off.

Here, though, the response of the front passenger was to lean out his window, pointing an AK-47 towards the Toyota pickup. McCain was already aiming and fired a short burst, one 5.56mm bullet catching the gunman in the side, a second slamming into the side of his head. The rifle clattered to the roadway at seventy miles an hour, the shooter collapsing, hanging halfway out of the vehicle. Blood and gore from the gunman's skull splattered the side of the Ford and into the open rear window, coating the two backseat passengers.

Chuck saw the bloody men trying to raise rifles of their own as he swung the muzzle of his Colt towards the driver. He fired two bursts into the windshield at the driver's head. Through his EOTech optics, McCain saw the man's head snap back as a hole appeared in his forehead. Another bullet caught the driver in the throat, sending a red spray into the air.

The SUV swerved violently to the left, now driverless. Chuck fired the remaining eighteen rounds of his thirty round magazine into the passenger compartment as the big vehicle careened across the center line into the oncoming lane. It continued onto the opposite shoulder, slamming into a utility pole in a cloud of smoke and dust.

"Problem solved," McCain said, inserting a fresh magazine into his rifle.

He glanced up front and saw Beth reach over, placing a comforting arm on Diya. The young girl was curled up in a ball, her hands over her ears. The suppressed rifle was still loud, especially in an enclosed environment, but Chuck had long since gotten used to it.

"How's it going, Diya?" he asked.

"Oh, Mr. Chuck, that was so loud and I was so scared," she answered, her voice trembling. "Are we OK?"

"We are now. There were some bad men in a truck that wanted to rob us. One of them was about to shoot at us but I got him first."

"But why would they want to hurt us?"

"I don't know," McCain answered, now wide-awake as he continued to scan the area, looking for additional threats. "There are some evil people in the world and they're taking advantage of the breakdown in society to do bad things."

Meena nodded. "My father said that people would use the zombie virus as an excuse to rob and steal."

"Your father was a smart man."

### Travelers Rest, South Carolina, Thursday, 1025 hours

The Fosters lived on Callahan Mountain Road, near the North Saluda Reservoir. Karen had given Chuck a Google map showing her parent's home, along with the address and directions. McCain had been impressed with what he saw from the aerial photos. There were no other homes within at least a one-mile radius and their house was almost six hundred feet off of the road, on a ridge surrounded by dense forest. The other attraction to the security-minded man was a reservoir only a few hundred yards away, providing them with a water source.

Chuck's biggest concern was how to safely make contact with the couple. Karen had told him that her dad, Jack, had served in the Army in Vietnam and was a prepper. McCain didn't care to think about coming this far out of his way to do a good deed just to get shot!

After dispatching the red Expedition, the three travelers had not seen any other living people. They did see zombies, including one large group congregating around the scene of a vehicle accident that appeared to have happened weeks earlier. Both of the northbound lanes of Highway 25 were completely blocked with multiple crashed cars, the area seething with hungry infected people. The grassy median looked passable and Chuck directed Beth to carefully cross it and then accelerate north in the southbound lanes.

A few miles later they turned off the highway onto another winding two-lane road. The houses were all situated hundreds of feet off the roadway, with plenty of land between them. They were now in the foothills of the Blue Ridge Mountains, the terrain rising all around. The temperatures had continued to drop and the dark gray clouds threatened rain, or worse.

As they turned onto the Foster's street, Chuck noticed that they were in a small valley, hills rising on both sides of Callahan Mountain Road. After two miles, they found the address, the street numbers hanging from a metal gate that blocked the gravel driveway with a chain link fence surrounding the property. The Fosters really had picked a great spot, McCain thought, even more impressed now that they were here in person. He couldn't see the house, the driveway climbing through the woods, disappearing around a curve. A small creek ran under the driveway providing another water source, while having the house hidden from view of the street was a brilliant tactical move.

"What do you think?" Beth wondered. "Honk the horn?"

"Let me check the gate," he answered, exiting the pickup.

Heavy chains secured the entrance, locked with the biggest padlock that McCain had ever seen. He climbed back into the Tundra.

"Let's pass on honking the horn. We don't know who or what else might be lurking in the area. Why don't you drive down the road a little further? Maybe we'll be able to see the house. They might even have another entrance."

Elizabeth drove slowly, all eyes peering up the wooded hill trying to catch a glimpse of the Foster's home. After a mile, however, they hadn't seen anything, the house concealed well behind the trees.

"Let's go back to the gate. I'll climb it and sneak in."

"Do you think that's safe?" his wife asked him.

"Not really, but I can't think of anything else. I can be pretty sneaky when I need to be. I'll slip in, make contact, and get Mr. Foster to come let us in."

McCain checked all of his equipment and was about to start climbing the metal barrier.

"You can just stop right there, fella!" a voice rang out from nearby, followed by the unmistakable sound of a round being chambered in a weapon. "You get your ass off of my property right now or I'm gonna start shooting."

"Mr. Foster?" Chuck asked, taking a step backwards and keeping his hands away from his rifle.

He still hadn't seen the man behind the voice. There were a couple of big hardwoods on the other side of the gate, next to the driveway. That's where it sounded like the voice was coming from.

"Who are you?"

"I'm a federal police officer. I've got my ID if you want to see it."

"I don't have much use for cops, especially federal ones."

In spite of himself, Chuck laughed out loud. "I hear you. I don't like most of 'em either. We're also friends of Karen's. My wife, Elizabeth, is in the truck and she and your daughter are close friends. Karen asked us to stop by."

There was a hesitation on the other side of the fence. After a moment, the voice spoke again, with much less hostility this time. "Karen sent you?"

"Yes, sir. We've got a letter for you from her that she asked us to deliver. She told me to ask you if you've been taking care of Tommy's grave."

Before he and Beth had left the Northeast Georgia Technical College, McCain had asked the nurse for something that he could tell her parents that no one else but their family would know. Karen had explained to them that her first pet was a big tomcat named "Tommy." He'd been bitten by a rattlesnake and had died when Karen was just nine, breaking the little girl's heart. Her father had no idea how to comfort the distraught child but he had created a beautiful grave marker and always kept the area around it clean. Mr. Foster had even organized a special memorial service for the kitty and had worn his Army dress uniform as he conducted the ceremony for Karen and a couple of her friends.

"I'm coming out," the voice said, quietly.

Chuck observed a wiry, gray-haired man in his late sixties, clad in camouflage clothing, step out from behind a large oak tree, and walk slowly towards the entrance. He was carrying a full-size Springfield Armory M1A rifle, the muzzle pointing towards the ground. The older man cautiously regarded the big, heavily-armed figure, clad in tactical clothing, standing on the other side of his gate.

"I'm Jack Foster." He made no offer to open the gate or to reach through and shake hands.

"I'm Chuck McCain. That's Elizabeth in the driver's seat. She and Karen work together. The other girl is Diya. We rescued her yesterday. We weren't in time to save her family, but were able to help her." McCain lowered his voice. "She's still in a bit of shock. Her entire family got infected. When we found her she was dehydrated and hadn't eaten in over a week."

The older man nodded, taking it all in. "You said you had a letter from my daughter. Is she alright?"

Chuck nodded. "She's doing fine, still at the technical college. We just left there on Monday. They've got a big group of survivors looking out for each other and I think they're going to weather this thing just fine. Elizabeth has the letter and she can give you the full update. Can we come in? Karen asked us to stop by and we came out of our way to deliver it. She told us that maybe we could get a home-cooked meal?"

The dark clouds finally gave way and a cold rain started to fall. Something clicked inside of Foster. He slung his rifle and reached into his pocket, withdrawing a key chain.

"I'm sorry for my lack of hospitality. It's been a long time since we've had any guests."

After opening the gate, he shook hands with Chuck and Beth and nodded at Diya. "I'll ride with you up to the house. The missus is waiting for me to come back and if you pull up without me, she'll probably start shooting."

The older man waved the Tundra through where Elizabeth stopped and waited.

"We wouldn't want that, Mr. Foster," McCain said, as Jack climbed into the backseat of the truck with him after resecuring the gate.

"How'd you know we were here?" Chuck asked. "Karen gave us your address and a Google map so I knew we were at the right place, but we weren't sure how to get your attention. That's why I was about to climb the gate."

"It's one of the great things about this spot," Jack nodded. "You can't see the house from the road, but from our sunroom up there," he motioned up the hill, "we have a pretty good view of everything down below us when the leaves are off the trees. Kim and I were sitting out there drinking a cup of coffee and I saw you folks pull up. We haven't had any problems to speak of but I have run off a few carloads of people who did the same thing you just tried. They'd pull up to the gate and start trying to climb it. Up to now, I've been able to persuade them to get back into their vehicles and leave.

"When y'all stopped, I grabbed my rifle and eased down towards the entrance. Then, when you came back, I thought I was going to have problems, especially when you got out dressed like you were ready to go to war."

Chuck smiled, removing his helmet and laying it in the seat. He ran a hand through his dark brown hair and said, "I can appreciate that. We've had a few run-ins with some rough characters, ourselves."

Jack picked up two pieces of empty 5.56mm brass from next to him on the car's seat. He held them up, a questioning look on his face.

"Like I said, we've had an interesting trip." McCain nodded at the brass Foster was holding. "We had an SUV with armed men try to run us off the road this morning."

The older man's eyes widened. "I guess we've been kind of sheltered out here. It makes sense, though. When law and order start breaking down, the criminals can prey on the weak and helpless. I guess the fellas who tried to mess with you learned the error of their ways?"

Chuck just shrugged and gave a slight nod. He was always hesitant to talk about his kills with people he didn't know. Elizabeth followed the winding gravel driveway which led to a single-story, sand-colored brick home. Jack was out before Beth had brought the Tundra to a complete stop. A small woman with long gray hair, pulled back in a ponytail, stood in the doorway pointing a Ruger Mini-14 rifle at the strange pickup.

"It's OK," Jack alerted her. "These are friends of Karen's."

Kim Foster lowered the rifle, her eyes widening at the news. She took a step outside, staying under the awning that covered the entranceway. A smiling young woman climbed out of the driver's seat and a big man wearing black got out of the rear compartment. A young Indian girl slowly pulled herself out of the front passenger seat, holding onto the door for support.

"Mrs. Foster? My name's Elizabeth," Beth said, approaching her friend's mother. "Karen and I work together; she's my best friend."

A sudden thought came to the older woman. "Oh, my God! Is Karen alright?"

"She's doing great, ma'am. I just saw her on Monday, but she asked us to stop by and let you know that she's fine and that she really misses you guys. She wrote you a letter. It's in my backpack."

The tears started flowing and Kim held her arms out, Beth letting her best friend's mom cry on her shoulder. Jack saw that Diya was walking very slowly and he gently offered her his arm, helping her inside. After Mrs. Foster regained her composure, Chuck approached. The rain was coming down harder now, mixed with ice.

"This is my husband, Chuck," Beth said.

"It's really nice to meet you, ma'am," McCain said, shaking Mrs. Foster's hand. "Karen is a very special lady. We'll tell you the whole story later, but I'm a police officer and your daughter took care of me recently after I got shot. She oversees all the medical care at the college and is doing an amazing job."

The woman's eyes glowed with pride. "It's nice to meet you, Chuck. Please come in. We haven't had any visitors in a long time."

McCain was surprised at how warm it was inside the Foster's home. The welcome heat was emanating from a large wood-burning stove, but Chuck had not noticed the telltale sign of smoke. He instinctively stepped over to it, warming his hands. This was the perfect set-up, Chuck realized. The stove had ample room on top for cooking, and a stainless steel coffee pot hissed slightly on the hot metal, letting him know that the morning was going to continue getting better.

Once everyone was inside, Mrs. Foster became the model southern hostess offering everyone coffee and making sure they were comfortable. Jack pointed to a recessed area in the wall near the entrance where Chuck and Elizabeth could put their equipment. The couple made sure that their rifles were set on "Safe," stood them against the wall, stripped off their web gear and body armor, and laid them on the floor. They both kept their sidearms on and seated themselves next to Diya on a comfortable leather couch near the hot stove.

"How long has it been since we've been this warm?" Chuck asked, looking at Beth.

"Too long. This feels so good. Thank you for letting us in," she said, smiling at the Fosters. Elizabeth had withdrawn Karen's letter from her pack and handed the sealed envelope to Mrs. Foster.

McCain turned to the older man. "Mr. Foster, I'm really curious. I didn't see any smoke pouring into the sky when we pulled up. We've been very hesitant about starting fires as we've traveled. Zombies have a powerful sense of smell but there are also a lot of criminals roaming around and smoke from a chimney is an easy way to let them know that there are potential victims nearby."

"Please, call me, 'Jack.' I upgraded our wood stove a few years ago and installed a smokeless chimney. I don't claim to understand the technology but it does a great job of dissipating the smoke. I've been concerned about zombies, too, but we haven't seen any out here. Maybe we're far enough off the beaten path that we'll be OK."

Kim finished reading the letter from her daughter and handed it to her husband, wiping her eyes. "Here, you'll want to read this."

After a lunch of venison chili and homemade biscuits, Chuck and Jack sat in the Foster's sunroom sipping tumblers of Macallan twelve-year single malt scotch. The two men got to know each other as they sat drinking and watching the freezing rain fall outside. According to the Foster's thermometer, the temperature was twenty-nine degrees.

Laughter overflowed from the living room where Elizabeth caught Kim up on her daughter's life. Diya had enjoyed some of Mrs. Foster's homemade chicken and vegetable soup, the older woman thinking the recently starved girl would be better able to handle that than the chili. Meena had devoured a bowl of the

---

delicious soup and a biscuit. Now, she was napping in a guest bedroom.

"So, what's your plan, Chuck?" Jack wondered. "I wouldn't recommend traveling any more today. Not with this weather. The temperatures are dropping and if something happened to your truck and y'all got stranded…"

Foster let the statement hang in the air. McCain took a drink of his scotch and nodded. He had been thinking the same thing.

"Would you mind if we spent the night?" Chuck asked. "I hate to be a burden. I'd planned on stopping by, delivering that letter, maybe having a bite to eat, and then heading out."

Jack waved his hand dismissively. "Y'all are no burden at all. We're set for food for at least another six months, plus we'll have our garden when it warms up. It's nice to have you guys and as you can hear," he nodded towards the living room, "Kim is enjoying having some company. My poor wife has just had me to talk to since this mess started and, well, as you can tell, I'm no conversationalist."

McCain chuckled. "Thanks, Jack. We'll see what the weather looks like tomorrow. This is killing me. My daughter is only about an hour away and now we're having another winter storm."

"Yeah, Kim and I were pretty sure that Karen was OK. She's smart and resourceful, like her mother, but the not knowing just gnawed at us."

"That's right," Chuck agreed. "We don't realize how much we take modern communications for granted until they're gone."

"What about Diya? Are y'all taking her with you? She seems so weak."

"She needs to be in a hospital," McCain said. He paused and took a deep breath. "I was going to ask if we could leave her with you guys? No pressure. If that's not a good idea, no problem, we'll take her with us."

Jack looked out the window, sipping his whiskey. He was silent for several minutes. The older man finally turned back towards his new friend.

"Let me talk to Kim. I think we can do that. In fact, I'd like to have her stay." Foster lowered his voice. "This isolation has been getting to my wife. Me, I love it. I'm happy being out here by myself. But Kim, she needs people. Before the zombies, she would drive to town once a day or go see one of the neighbors. Now, we're cut off from everyone and everything. I think having someone to nurse and to take care of would really help her."

McCain breathed a sigh of relief. "That would be great. Diya seems like a sweet girl and she's been through a lot. Now she needs some good people to look after her."

# Chapter Four

**Centers for Disease Control Compound, East of Atlanta, Thursday, 1400 hours**

Eddie Marshall, Andy Fleming, and Alejandro "Hollywood" Estrada strolled towards the front entrance of the rural compound to give their civilian security counterparts a break. The federal agents had just walked the perimeter of their hundred acre compound making sure that the fence was secure and checking for potential threats. The three CDC officers and just two of the civilian security team had chosen to stay and guard the scientists who were working around the clock, trying to find a breakthrough in developing a vaccine or a cure for the zombie virus.

"I hope Jimmy's OK," Hollywood commented, referring to his best friend in the unit.

Eddie grunted and Andy nodded. "If anybody can make it into Athens, find the girl, and get back out, it's Jimmy," Fleming commented, but not sure he believed it himself.

"I'm worried about all of them," Marshall admitted with a sigh. "Jimmy, Chuck, Scotty, Chris, Terrence. They're all badasses, but we know that it's a different world out there now."

Eddie and Andy had both been team leaders at the Atlanta office of the CDC Enforcement Unit, choosing to move their families into the safety of the rural complex in exchange for providing security. Originally, Eddie and Chuck McCain were the team leads, but after their officer-in-charge, Rebecca Johnson, had been killed in a shootout with one of the Iranian terrorists responsible for deploying the zombie virus, McCain had been promoted to head the Atlanta operation. Fleming had served as McCain's assistant team leader and had been quickly promoted to fill the team leader role on Chuck's former squad.

Before the CDC had called, Andy had been a Marine Staff Sergeant assigned to the United States Marine Corps Forces Special Operations Command (MARSOC). These highly trained special operators were the Corps' answer to the Army's Special Forces. After leaving the Marines because of a family crisis, Fleming had spent a year working in the private sector before being recruited for the new CDC Enforcement Unit.

Hollywood Estrada was a member of Eddie's team. He had joined the Army right out of high school, serving as an MP, military police officer. After five years, Estrada took an honorable discharge to pursue his lifelong dream of becoming a civilian police officer. He hoped to work for a federal agency but without a college degree he knew that his only chance was gaining some experience first with a large local department. He was hired by the Los Angeles Police Department and worked there for seven years before starting the application process to become an agent with the Drug Enforcement Administration. That was when Hollywood had been approached by Rebecca Johnson and offered a job with a new federal law enforcement agency.

Jimmy Jones was Marshall's assistant team leader and had originally joined his three teammates at the remote CDC location. Jones had attained the rank of captain in the Marine Corps, completing two combat tours in Iraq. When his mother was diagnosed with a terminal illness, however, he had resigned his commission to care for her before she passed away.

Jimmy had then become an Alabama State Trooper where he served for five years before also applying to the DEA. That was when he, too, had popped up on Rebecca Johnson's radar and been offered a job with the new CDC Enforcement Unit. Jones was a natural leader, on track to have a team of his own until terror attacks had crippled the government.

During the horrific attack on the University of Georgia campus in which Rebecca Johnson had been killed, the CDC officers were deployed to rescue as many civilians as they could. It took over two hours before the federal agents could get onscene. By then, over a thousand people had been killed with several thousand more infected with the zombie virus.

Two terrorists had deployed the bio-terror weapon at the home opener football game. Over the next few hours, most of the UGA campus police department was wiped out, along with about half of the Athens-Clarke County police agency. One of the few surviving campus police officers was a beautiful young black woman named Grace Cunningham.

Cunningham had been stationed inside the stadium when the virus was first released at the Tate Student Center just across the street. The police officer had rushed towards the packed student center to see if she could help. Zombies quickly chased her back inside Sanford Stadium where the campus police officer shot and killed a number of the infected attackers. Grace was able to herd a group of twenty-seven survivors into a restroom where they remained safe for several hours. Cunningham was eventually able to make contact with her dispatcher and learned that CDC officers had arrived on the campus.

Grace, along with the help of National Guard Lieutenant Colonel

Kevin Clark, led the group out of the stadium and connected with the federal agents. Chuck McCain and his men escorted the survivors across the zombie-infested campus to an extraction point. It took three trips to get them all away by helicopter, but Officer Cunningham had gone above and beyond, fulfilling her duty of protecting and serving that day.

The campus police officer had also caught the attention of Jimmy Jones. They had not seen each other since that fateful day, but had spoken on the phone regularly until the communications grid collapsed. Jimmy had fallen in love with the young woman, but found himself torn by the conflicting emotions of love and duty.

A month after the remaining CDC employees had found refuge and security on the compound, Jones had told Eddie and the others that he was going to Athens to find Grace. The other men understood and no one bothered to try to talk him out of it. If the roles were reversed Eddie, Andy, and Hollywood would all be doing the exact same thing. They had waved goodbye as he pulled away from them using the white Chevrolet Astrovan they had taken from terrorists whom they had killed in the gun battle near the Atlanta Braves stadium.

A month and a half later, however, Jimmy's teammates understood that he probably wasn't coming back. The National Guard and neighboring police departments had attempted to clear the infected from Athens to no avail. They had killed almost two thousand zombies but had lost over a hundred soldiers and police officers, most of whom, ironically, were now infected and continuing to spread the virus. While Fleming spoke with confidence of Jones' ability, each of the three men knew that all of their missing teammates were very likely dead by now, or worse, walking around as zombies.

Of the original two four-man teams working out of the Atlanta office, both Eddie and Chuck had lost agents killed in action. Marco

Connelly had been overpowered by a pack of zombies right after the virus had first been deployed. The saddest part of that incident was when the bio-terror virus had reanimated the officer, Rebecca Johnson had been the one to put a bullet into zombie Marco's head, putting him down for good.

Luis García had died from gunshot wounds sustained as the CDC agents, Atlanta police officers, and a few FBI agents attempted to stop a pack of several thousand zombies surging up Interstate 75 near the Atlanta Braves baseball stadium. Three Iranian terrorists, two wearing suicide vests, the third armed with an AK-47, had attacked the officers from behind as they were battling zombies in front of them. García's body armor had not been able to save him as one AK round struck him in the leg, with a second bullet penetrating his unprotected left shoulder, and digging into his chest.

"Hey, Darrell, you guys need a break?" Eddie asked Darrell Parker, when the CDC agents reached the guard shack.

Darrell was a retired City of Baltimore police sergeant. After sitting around the house for a year, he'd had gone to work for the Centers for Disease Control as part of their civilian security team, eventually becoming a supervisor.

The sixty-something, white-haired African-American man stood, and nodded at the CDC agent. "Thanks, Eddie, I believe we will."

Parker and his partner, Marcel Adams, spent their days manning the small guard shack at the entrance to the CDC location. Marcel, was a light-skinned, athletically built twenty-four year old. He had been a security forces member in the Air Force for four years before deciding to get out and become an Atlanta Police Officer. He took the job as a security officer with the CDC to bring in some money while he worked through the hiring process with APD.

When the zombie virus began to pop up around Atlanta and other big cities, it disrupted much of the police department's administrative functions, including hiring. Thankfully for the CDC,

Marcel had stuck around, offering to move into the rural compound. Despite the age difference, Parker and Adams had become good friends.

Even though no zombies had found their way to the temporary CDC base, both security officers were prepared, each packing a pistol and a long gun. Darrell had finally given up his trusty .38 Special revolver and was carrying a 9mm Smith & Wesson M&P. Marcel preferred the 9mm Beretta Model 92 pistol, just like the one that he'd used in the Air Force. Adams also had a Bushmaster AR-15 slung over his shoulder, while Parker carried a .12 gauge Remington Model 870 pump shotgun.

Marcel nodded at the CDC agents. He was still getting to know them, and if he was honest, a bit in awe of the three men. He had heard about all the zombies and terrorists that they and their other teammates had taken down. Darrell had even told him that Agent Marshall and his team had traveled to Virginia and located one of the terrorists who had launched the attacks on the University of Georgia campus. Terrell Hill had been arrested, while Marshall had shot and killed notorious Iranian bomb maker, Usama Zayad, on the same operation.

"Andy, your boy, Tyler, was out here earlier, keeping us company," Darrell said, with a smile, looking at the former Marine.

"He wasn't bothering you or getting in the way, was he?" Fleming asked, concern in his voice.

"Oh, no, sir! He's a fine young man. I just wanted to tell you that I think you and the missus have done a great job with him. He's smart, polite, and I like having him around. He had on his rifle and web gear and I know you've trained him well. I'm trustin' the good Lord that no zombies will ever wind up out here, but if they do, I think young Tyler will be a real asset."

"Thanks, Darrell. I'm sure proud of him. The poor kid is bored to death being the only teenager out here in the middle of nowhere."

"I imagine so. Well, you tell him he's always welcome to hang out with Darrell and Marcel."

The CDC compound was surrounded by a six-foot chain link fence with razor-sharp concertina wire running around the top. The massive gate was wide enough to admit the RVs and campers that Fleming, Estrada, Jones, and Marshall had "liberated" from the recreation vehicle dealership a few miles away. It had taken a several trips but there were now eight of the full-size vehicles and even four pop-up campers inside the compound, supplementing the already cramped living quarters.

The center had been stocked surprisingly well with canned goods and freeze-dried foods. Dr. Charles Martin told the enforcement agents that the remote site was originally set up for only the most sensitive research and experimentation, and was designed to house no more than twenty researchers and support staff. Now, there were close to sixty people crammed inside the living and work spaces, most of them epidemiologists and scientists working on developing a vaccine for the zombie virus.

Dr. Martin was the Assistant Director of the Office of Public Health Preparedness and Response. On paper, the CDC Enforcement Unit reported to him under the umbrella of the Department of Homeland Security, but the good doctor and all the team leaders knew that the Central Intelligence Agency was their true boss, at least until Chuck had lost the ability to communicate with them. Until the communications grid was restored, Martin was the acting Director of the CDC.

Dr. Martin had spoken to Eddie a couple of days before, letting him know that they would need more supplies within the next two weeks. Marshall and his teammates would put off leaving the compound for as long as they could. With just the three of them and only two security guards, they were woefully understaffed. Sending a team out to hunt for food would leave the research facility in a vulnerable state. They all rotated working night shifts so they were always tired. They kept two sentries at the front gate every night. Eddie had authorized one agent or security officer to sleep while the other kept watch.

The three federal agents sat on folding chairs in the guard shack, gazing out the big window and down the single lane driveway. Each of the men was grateful to be in a safe place. So many people had been lost to the virus. There was no price tag that Eddie or Andy could place on having their loved ones in a secure environment.

"How's Candice feeling?" Fleming asked Marshall.

"Man, she's been puking her guts out for the last three days. How long does morning sickness last?"

"Amy said her's lasted about a month."

"I can't imagine a month of that," the muscular man said, shaking his head.

Estrada laughed. "American women just aren't as tough as Mexican women. My mom had me in the morning and was back out picking grapefruits in the afternoon in the hot sun, with me strapped to her chest."

"That explains a lot," Eddie commented. "Your brain was fried from a young age. Do you guys mind if I go check on Candice?"

Andy waved his friend off. "Go, we've got this."

**Centers for Disease Control Compound, East of Atlanta, Thursday, 1430 hours**

Eddie and Candice's current home was a thirty-two foot long Winnebago. The RV was a far cry from their beautiful home in the upscale suburb of Alpharetta, but up to now, no zombies had found them and Eddie was grateful to be in a safe location with his pregnant wife. The Winnebago was parked on the far side of the compound, mixed with the other RVs, campers, and even a few tents. As he strode to check on Candice, Marshall reflected on the choices that had guided him to where he was today.

The former college football player was six foot three and a muscular two hundred and thirty pounds. He was dark skinned and kept his head shaved. He looked like he could still play linebacker for his alma mater, Notre Dame.

After graduating with a degree in Criminal Justice, but, surprisingly, not getting drafted by the NFL, Eddie had pursued his second dream of becoming a City of Chicago police officer. He'd spent fifteen years there and had loved every second of it. He eventually was able to land a position of working as an undercover narcotics detective. That assignment had provided one adrenaline rush after another.

After he had gotten promoted to sergeant and been back to the uniform division for a couple of years, Eddie started thinking about going federal. With his college degree, his years of law enforcement experience, including the last three as a supervisor, Marshall applied to and was hired by the United States Marshals Service.

Eddie found himself pursuing murderers, mafia hit men, cartel leaders, and many other fugitives. The adrenaline rush of tracking down and arresting some of the most dangerous people on the planet reinforced that Marshall had made the right career choice. And then Rebecca Johnson had come along.

He still had no idea how he had come to her attention. Eddie wasn't looking for another job, but the timing couldn't have been better. If he was honest, his marriage was unraveling due to the strain of his constant travel all over the country, and even abroad, to capture fugitives. Candice was an incredibly successful financial advisor in Chicago. The couple had never made time for having children, but when they finally did start trying, Eddie in his late-thirties, Candice a few years younger, nothing had happened.

Marshall knew that his wife wanted children and felt terrible that she hadn't been able to conceive. With him being gone for days and weeks at a time, however, there weren't a lot of opportunities for them to try and make a baby. Eddie sensed the distance growing between he and Candice, but told himself that one day he would slow down

Eddie had been working for the Marshals for two years and had just returned home from being gone for three weeks, locating and arresting a particularly slippery mafia boss. He was shocked to find that his wife had moved out, leaving a note on their bed that she needed some time to think. Eddie immediately called her cell but it went straight to voice mail. He left message after message, begging her to come home or to at least call him back.

Candice eventually texted him, saying that she had moved in with her mother until she could find her own apartment. When he finally got her on the phone, she had spoken the words that he didn't want to hear. She was done with him and wanted a divorce.

Eddie had some vacation time built up with the Marshals, and immediately called his boss, telling him that he needed to take two weeks off. For the first couple of days, he just sat around the apartment and drank, trying to ease the pain. He really did love Candice, but he could see now how he had taken her for granted and had, at least on a practical level, loved his job more than he had loved her.

His wife had made it very clear that she didn't want to talk to him and he had honored that, keeping his distance instead of driving across town to his mother-in-law's house. It was eating him up on the inside, though. Eddie Marshall was a man of action and he wanted to fight for and save his marriage. He just didn't know where to start.

The phone call from Rebecca Johnson had come as he sat on his couch sipping a glass of Coca Cola mixed with a liberal dose of Jack

Daniels and feeling sorry for himself. He didn't recognize the number and let the caller leave a message. When he listened to it later, however, he was intrigued. The woman wanted to talk to him about a job with the CDC. Since when did the Centers for Disease Control have an enforcement unit? And what did they do? Arrest people who didn't get an annual flu shot? And how had they even gotten his phone number?

Marshall was curious enough to return Johnson's call. She wouldn't tell him much over the phone but offered to fly to Chicago from Washington, D.C. in two days and meet him for coffee. He agreed to talk with her but couldn't imagine hearing anything that would pull him away from his current job.

Eddie was ten minutes early for the meeting as he walked into the upscale cafe near the O'Hare International Airport. A tall, very attractive blonde with an athletic build, stood up from her table and motioned him over. How did she recognize me? he wondered. Rebecca's handshake was firm as she handed Eddie her ID packet. It identified Rebecca Johnson as a Security Specialist with the Centers for Disease Control Enforcement Unit. A waitress took their coffee order and disappeared.

"Thank you for coming, Agent Marshall. I promise I won't waste your time," Johnson said, smiling.

"You definitely got my curiosity up. Since when does the CDC have an enforcement unit?"

"Since now," Rebecca answered. "We're just getting it started. You would be one of our first agents. The President recently signed an executive order calling for the CDC to create an enforcement branch. The reason for that order is classified, but if you decide to come work for us, you'll be given a security clearance that would authorize you to have the big picture of what's going on.

"What I can tell, though, is that there are significant bio-terror threats looming on the horizon. They are very dangerous, probably as dangerous as anything we've ever faced as a nation. The President has authorized us to move rapidly to get this thing up and running so that we can respond quickly and decisively."

A Presidential Executive Order? That sounds like a big deal, he thought. And that is some interesting terminology: "quickly and decisively?" Eddie worked for the federal government. He knew that they didn't do much of anything quickly and decisively.

Marshall nodded. "But, isn't that a job for the FBI? I thought they already had a terrorism division?"

Johnson gave a grim smile. "Yes, they do. Let's just say that the wheels turn very slowly at the Bureau and the President realizes that. Have you had many dealings with the FBI?"

Eddie chuckled. "Yeah, I have and you're right. The wheels do turn very slowly over there."

Rebecca nodded. "The FBI is good at what they do but we're being given the opportunity to create a small, quick-acting agency that will neutralize problems before the FBI even knows that there was one. We'll work under the umbrella of the Department of Homeland Security instead of the Justice Department."

Neutralize problems? That's unusual phrasing for a law enforcement agency, he pondered. Eddie wasn't sure what to think.

"Well, this all sounds very interesting, Ms. Johnson, but I'm not sure that I want to leave a really good job for a startup agency. But if I did, what would my position be?"

"You'd be a team leader. Our plan is to have at least two four-person teams at each office. You'd be assigned to the headquarters office in Atlanta."

"Atlanta? I don't want to live in Atlanta. I grew up here. Chicago's my home."

Rebecca didn't answer for a moment, looking into Eddie's eyes. He had the feeling that she was looking right through him and knew much more about his personal life than she was letting on.

"Sometimes a fresh start is a good thing," she finally said, quietly. "One of the things that I can promise you is that there will be very little travel with this position. I know that you marshals spend a lot of time away from home and that can be tough on one's personal life."

Eddie was sipping his coffee that had just arrived, but the woman's last comment caught him off guard and he burned his mouth. He gently set the cup down and wiped his mouth with the cloth napkin, looking at Johnson suspiciously. Her eyes didn't give anything away. Did she know about his separation from his wife?

"I know what your current salary is," Rebecca changed gears again. "You'd start at a hundred and fifty thousand dollars a year with us, plus a great benefits package. The cost of living in Atlanta is much lower than Chicago so that's a pretty significant raise."

Johnson stopped talking and waited for the giant of a man in front of her to say something. He had a stunned expression on his face after hearing that his paycheck would be more than double what he was currently making if he actually decided to change jobs.

"Well, that is definitely something to think about," Eddie finally said. "I'll need to think about your offer. And discuss it with my wife, of course."

Marshall watched her closely as he said that and saw her give him a slight nod. She knows, he thought. This was like no job interview that he'd ever had.

"I want to make sure I'm clear on what you're saying, Ms. Johnson. You're offering me a job? I don't need to go through a hiring process?"

Rebecca flashed her beautiful smile again. "That's correct. I usually take care of my background investigation before I interview someone. Of course, I've read your file and talked to previous supervisors with Chicago PD and with the Marshal's Service. I think that you'd be a great addition to our agency."

What Rebecca didn't tell Eddie was that he had also been screened through the CIA's proprietary software that evaluated an individual's intelligence, emotional makeup, and suitability for the job. He had passed with flying colors on every level.

"If you accept my offer," Johnson continued, "you'll start in six weeks. You'll attend a two-month training course at the Federal Law Enforcement Training Center in Charleston, South Carolina. If you come by yourself you can stay in the dorms on campus but if you want to bring your wife, we'll foot the bill for a hotel. If you've never been to Charleston before, I'd recommend bringing Mrs. Marshall with you. It's one of the most beautiful cities on the east coast."

Eddie took a deep breath. Why in the world would he want to leave the U.S. Marshal's Service to join a startup agency? What was it that she had said? That they were facing one of the biggest bio-terror threats in history?

"How long do I have to think about this?" he asked.

"Today is Wednesday. Could you let me know something by Monday?"

Marshall nodded. "Yes, ma'am. I'll let you know something by then."

By the time that Eddie got back to his apartment, he had made up his mind. He called Candice, knowing that she was at work and expecting to get her voice mail. She answered on the first ring.

"Hi, Eddie," she said, her voice flat.

"Hey, Baby. How you doing? I really miss you."

"Please don't 'baby' me. I told you that we're done."

Marshall took a deep breath. "Okay. Sorry. I was calling to see if you'd have dinner with me Friday? Maybe we can talk things out?"

There was a long pause on the other end of the call. "I'll meet you for coffee Friday after work. I have some things that I need to tell you, but it would be better if we talk face-to-face. But I want to make this very clear, Eddie, I want a divorce. I can't keep living like we've been living. I've put up with you never being home and putting your career before our family for too long."

Eddie heard her voice catch as she continued. "Because of your career we haven't even been able to have a family. I'll meet you, but my mind is made up."

Candice expected some push back but all she heard was, "You're right. I'm guilty of all that and I'm sorry. I've got some things to tell you, too. And I won't argue with you. I know once you've made your mind up that's the way it is."

Marshall made sure that he was early to the Starbucks on Friday afternoon, ordering for both of them. Candice had told him she would come there straight from her office. When she walked in, he stood and waved. She was just as beautiful now as when they had gotten married eleven years earlier. She was tall, full-figured, with cocoa colored skin. Her hair was pulled back and the diamond necklace that he had given her for their tenth anniversary sparkled around her neck.

Eddie wanted so badly to reach out and take her in his arms but he had to play it cool. If he had any chance at all of winning this woman back, he couldn't push her away in the first five minutes.

"Hi, Candice. You look beautiful, as usual," he smiled.

"Thanks, Eddie," she said, seating herself across from him and sipping her drink. "Thanks for ordering for me."

After a couple of minutes of uncomfortable small talk, Candice was clearly ready to get down to business.

"You first," she said. "You told me you had something to tell me."

The former linebacker-turned-Chicago-police-officer-turned-federal-marshal didn't get nervous about much, but he sure felt butterflies fluttering around in his stomach as he stared at the woman he loved. The only way he knew to deal with fear, though, was to punch it in the face.

"I'm turning in my resignation on Monday."

Candice had expected Eddie to promise to change, to beg for forgiveness, maybe even agree to go to marriage counseling. This wasn't even on the radar of what she had thought she might hear.

Marshall watched his wife's mouth drop open and her eyes get big.

He continued talking, hoping to take advantage of the surprise factor. "I've been offered a position at a new federal agency. I'll be moving to Atlanta and I was hoping you might consider going with me. I know I've been…"

"No, no, no," Candice said, putting a hand to her forehead, leaning back, and shaking her head.

This was definitely not the response that Eddie was looking for, so he paused, waiting for her to say something else.

"You talked to Kirby, didn't you?" Her eyes bored into him with anger.

"Kirby? Why would I have talked to Kirby? I haven't even seen him since I threatened, I mean since I spoke with him after he asked you out."

Kirby was Candice's boss. He'd made a pass at her right after she had started working there, four years earlier. Eddie had had a brief conversation with the man one day after work and since then, he had been the perfect gentleman and boss.

"I don't believe you, Eddie. You had to have talked to Kirby. That's the only way you could've known."

"Known what, Baby? I don't know what you're talking about."

"Don't call me 'baby,'" she hissed. "How did you know about Atlanta?"

"I told you. I was offered a job there on Wednesday, two days ago."

Candice shook her head, clearly still agitated. She stared into her estranged husband's eyes, looking for an answer.

"Are you telling me that you didn't know I was taking a transfer to Atlanta?" she asked, continuing to watch him closely.

Now it was Eddie's mouth that fell open. He started to smile but that might be misconstrued. Instead, he just shook his head.

"That's great!" he said, cautiously. "How did that come about?"

"There was a management position available at our branch in Georgia. It's a big pay raise and," she lowered her eyes, "it was going to get me away from you. I have an appointment with a divorce lawyer on Monday. I want to get it over with and start fresh in a new city."

That was a punch in the gut. She's planning to file for divorce next week, he thought. You better bring out your A game, Eddie.

"Congratulations on the promotion. You'll be a great manager. I'm really proud of you."

Candice looked back up and saw the sincerity on Eddie's face. Maybe he really didn't know, she thought. What an odd coincidence, though. What are the odds on both of them taking new jobs in the same city on the other side of the country?

It's now or never, Marshall thought. "I've been looking online. We've always talked about buying a house, living in a nice neighborhood, starting a family."

Mrs. Marshall started to protest but Mr. Marshall held up his hand. "Please," he said, softly. "Just let me say what I have to say."

Candice nodded at him and sat back.

"The cost of living in Atlanta is so much less than Chicago. Candice, we could buy a really nice house and live in a great part of town. I was also looking at some of the fertility clinics. There are a couple of good ones in Georgia. I'd really love to get serious about having kids with you.

"This new job that I'm taking doesn't have much travel. That was part of the reason that I accepted the position. I want to have a family with you. Now, if your heart is set on a divorce, I won't contest it. I won't bother you in Atlanta. I'll let you have the fresh start that you want.

"But I still love you and I have to ask: Would you be willing to give me and us a second chance?"

Eddie hoped the tears streaming down his wife's face were a good sign. He'd given it his best shot. What was she going to say?

Candice was silent for a long time. She finally reached across the table and grasped his massive hand.

"Can I go home with you tonight, Baby?" she asked.

It had taken them awhile, but they had finally conceived. At the worst possible time in history, Marshall realized, as he turned the handle on the RV door. Candice was lying on her side in the bed. Hearing him come in, she turned over to look at her husband.

"Why did you do this to me?" she asked weakly.

Eddie gave a slight smile. "At the time, I remember you saying, 'Yeah, Baby, keep doing it, don't stop!'"

Candice shook her head, trying to suppress a grin. "If only I had something to throw at you."

Marshall sat down next to his wife, wrapping his strong arms around her. "I'm sorry you're not feeling good, but I know that you're going to be such a great mom. And this craziness isn't going to last forever."

"Can we keep the RV after all the zombies go away?" she asked.

Eddie laughed. "I don't think so, but I'll buy you one for Christmas. Can I get you anything?"

"Just lie here with me for a few minutes?"

## Centers for Disease Control Compound, East of Atlanta, Thursday, 1515 hours

Andy, Hollywood, Darrell, and Marcel sat in the guard shack, speculating about how long it was going to be before the government came out of hiding and started repairing the infrastructure. The small building had large windows on each side, allowing them to keep an eye on their surroundings. None of the agents or security officers would admit it, that although they were thankful to be in a safe location, they were also bored from the inaction of the last two months.

Suddenly, the sound of an approaching car engine startled them to their feet. Fleming and Estrada recovered quickly, stepping out of the guard shack, rifles at the ready.

"Marcel, could you go ask Eddie to come back over here?" Andy said, over his shoulder.

"Yes, sir," he replied, sprinting for the Marshall's RV.

A purple Oldsmobile Cutlass, with a white top, roared around the curve a hundred yards away, driving straight towards the gate of the complex, but stopping well short of the entrance. The shiny chrome spinner rims kept rotating even after the car had stopped. Andy and Hollywood could make out two occupants through the heavily tinted windows.

Fleming raised his M4 and was about to yell for them to exit the car when the passenger door flew open and a familiar figure stepped out and threw his hands up in the air.

"What's the matter?" Jimmy Jones yelled. "You got a problem with a brother driving a purple car?"

The men inside the compound started laughing, each of them thrilled to see their teammate. "Amigo, you can drive anything you want," Estrada yelled back. "Get your ass in here."

---

**141**

They unlocked the gate and the car quickly pulled inside. Jones jumped out and hugged both of his fellow CDC agents and Darrell, everyone trying to talk at once. A few minutes later Eddie came sprinting up, leading Marcel by twenty feet, even though the older and bigger CDC agent was wearing almost thirty pounds of equipment. Marshall grabbed his assistant team leader and close friend in a bear hug.

"You've got some 'splaining to do," Eddie said, feigning anger. "And where did you find that car?"

Jones laughed. "I'll fill you in later, Boss. It'll take a while."

"Man, Jimmy, you look like crap," Andy commented with a grin. "Did you lose your razor?"

Jimmy smiled and nodded, running a hand over the growth on his face. Jones stood six feet tall and normally weighed about a hundred and eighty pounds. Before joining the Marines, he had attended the University of Alabama on a track and field scholarship as a sprinter. He looked like he had lost twenty pounds since his friends had last seen him.

The former Marine captain was wearing a camo National Guard field jacket over his plate carrier. A full-size M16 hung from a strap across his chest. A 9mm Beretta pistol was attached to his body armor to supplement his issued Glock 17 that he was wearing in a holster on his side.

Jones turned and motioned for the driver of the Oldsmobile to join them. A tall, attractive young African-American woman exited the vehicle slowly and approached the men.

Jones lowered his voice. "Grace is in a bad way. She lost her whole family; she had to kill her parents after they got infected. Then she got shot a couple of weeks ago and is still recovering."

The men parted and allowed Grace Cunningham into their circle. That poor girl, Eddie thought. He couldn't even imagine what she was feeling after having to put down her own parents. The expression on the girl's face was blank, her eyes sad. Jimmy wrapped an arm protectively around her.

Cunningham had on heavy body armor over a University of Georgia hoodie. A much-too-large camo jacket was keeping her warm. Her police issue pistol belt held her sidearm, extra ammunition, a taser, a collapsible baton, and handcuffs. A bandolier of shotgun shells was slung over her shoulder, her pump shotgun left in the vehicle. An embroidered UGA Campus Police stocking cap was pulled low on the young woman's head.

Jimmy smiled at his companion and spoke gently. "Grace, I know it's been a while since you've seen these three clowns so let me introduce you again. First of all, the big ugly one is Eddie, my boss. His wife is Candice and you'll meet her later. The ugly Latino is Hollywood, and this ugly guy," he said, pointing at Andy, "is another Marine. His wife, Amy, and his son, Tyler, are here, as well.

"Over here, we have Darrell and Marcel. They're part of the CDC's security team and have the distinct pleasure of working with us."

Grace forced a small smile. "It's nice to see everybody again. Where's Chuck?"

When no one answered, Cunningham's eyes got big. "Not Chuck? Please tell me he's alive!"

Jimmy looked at Eddie, not knowing if he had heard anything from their leader while he'd been gone retrieving Grace. Marshall spoke up and shrugged. "Grace, as far as we know, Chuck's still alive. He left a couple of months ago to find his daughter. We figured we would've seen him by now or heard something."

The young woman's shoulders slumped, a look of resignation on her face. She had been hoping to talk to Agent McCain. Cunningham knew that he would understand what was going on inside of her.

Grace had been there on the UGA campus that fateful day when the zombie virus had been deployed. Previous to meeting any of the CDC agents, she had witnessed the shootout that left Rebecca Johnson and the terrorist, Amir al-Razi dead. Later in the day, Jimmy had told her that Johnson had died in McCain's arms, breaking the big man's heart.

Even though she had only been with the CDC officers for a few hours, she had felt Chuck's pain. She'd seen the hurt in his eyes, even as he continued fighting and killing infected people and saving survivors. Grace felt a sense of connection with all the CDC agents who had risked their lives to rescue so many people. For some reason, she had expected McCain to be here when she and Jimmy arrived and was terribly disappointed when he wasn't. Cunningham felt that no one could really understand the pain she was feeling except for the big CDC agent, who had also lost someone who had meant everything to him. I hope he makes it to his daughter, she thought.

And, of course, she felt something for Jimmy. Grace had given him her phone number that day in Athens and had thoroughly enjoyed getting to know him over the phone. The zombie crisis had prevented them from seeing each other but they had talked and texted many times until the grid collapsed a month later.

The Georgia Bureau of Investigation had commandeered an empty hangar at the Athens airport, just a little over a mile from where the virus had been deployed. Both marked and unmarked police cars, fire trucks, and ambulances, along with a contingent of news vehicles, littered the parking area around the command post. After the CDC agents' Blackhawk had dropped her off at the CP, she and another surviving campus police officer, Jennifer Fletcher, were interviewed by the GBI and several members of the Athens-Clarke County Police Department. They were the first two officers to make it out of the center of the maelstrom whom the command staff had been able to talk to.

After a ninety minute debriefing of what they had seen and done, Grace was finally able to step out of the hangar and return her mother's thirteen phone calls.

"Mama, are you and Daddy OK? Is Hope with y'all?"

"We're all here, but what about you? Are you alright? We've been watching the news and I've been worried. It's been so long and you didn't return my calls."

Grace heard the concern in her mom's voice and breathed a sigh of relief. Her younger sister had been talking about trying to get tickets to the game that day. In the end, she had chosen to stay home and watch it on TV with her boyfriend, Darius.

"I'm alright, Mama, but…I don't even know how to describe it. People are sick and doing terrible things to each other. You guys need to leave, right now! Get in the car and get out of Athens."

There was a long pause on the other end of the phone. "Darlin', I don't think your daddy's going anywhere. He's been watching the news and praying all afternoon. Where are you?"

"I'm at the airport on the other side of town. They've set up a base to bring survivors to and the GBI's trying to coordinate a response. I was right in the middle of it when people started turning into zombies in the stadium. It was just the grace of God that I got out of there alive."

"Oh, Darlin', I'm so sorry!" Mrs. Cunningham exclaimed. "When are you coming home?"

"I don't know. There are just a few of us from the campus police department left. I think…," the emotion suddenly bursting inside the young officer, "I think most of our department is gone, Mama. I think Jennifer and I are the only two who made it out. Can I talk to Daddy?"

A few minutes later, Mrs. Cunningham came back to the phone. "I can't find your father, Grace. Hope said he was going to walk Darius out to his car but he hasn't come back in."

Grace remembered the feeling of fear when her mother had told her that. "Mama, he can't be outside! Those things are everywhere!"

Later in the evening, the officer had managed to get her father on the phone. He was unharmed, and Grace begged her father to get out of the city.

"Grace, you know I can't do that. I'm a pastor and people are depending on me. What kind of minister would I be if I ran away?"

"A living one," Grace said, quietly. "Daddy, the zombies will get to your neighborhood. There's no way to stop them. I was there. I saw it. There are thousands of them. Please, Daddy, pack up Mama and Hope and go somewhere safe."

"What about you, Sweetheart, are you going somewhere safe?"

"Daddy, I'm a police officer. This is what I do."

"And I'm a pastor. This is what I do."

The younger Cunningham knew then that the elder Cunningham's mind was made up. Reverend Samuel Cunningham had been the leader of the Athens AME Church for over twenty years. His congregation knew that they could come by his house or call at any time if they had a need. After that conversation, Grace never again mentioned leaving to her father.

After fighting zombies and rescuing survivors for over eighteen hours that terrible day and into the next, Grace had collapsed into the back of a police cruiser for a nap. She finally managed to go home two days later for a brief respite. Her parent's house was in the southern part of the city near the university's baseball field. Circling wide and coming in the from the south, Cunningham only saw a few Zs, one here, three there. Her neighborhood had thankfully been spared, but she knew that it was only a matter of time.

For the next month, Grace joined forces with several neighboring law enforcement agencies and eventually the National Guard in trying to take back the city of Athens and the UGA campus. They were still finding people hiding in dorms, homes or businesses, but not many. It was a lost cause, Cunningham realized. She had managed to visit home twice more during that time to check on her family. The rest of her waking moments had been spent fighting and killing zombies or sleeping at the command post.

Jimmy had called her two days after they had met and left a voicemail. She had returned his call, sitting outside against the metal wall of the aircraft hangar. They had talked for over an hour. After hanging up from another of their calls, Grace asked herself, how crazy is this? He's fighting zombies around Atlanta. I'm fighting zombies in Athens. When we have a break, we talk on the phone, getting to know each other.

At this rate, she knew that they would never see each other again. The odds of both of them surviving weren't very good, but their phone calls gave Cunningham something to look forward to. Talking to Jimmy was the one normal thing in her life that she could enjoy.

Four weeks after the attack on the UGA campus, they were no closer to eliminating the thousands of infected. The National Guard advised the GBI and local law enforcement that it was time to pull back. The guard had lost forty-two soldiers and the multi-police agencies had suffered a combined sixty-one more casualties. There were no replacements stepping in to fill the holes left by those who had been killed.

The National Guard was pulling out altogether until they could be reinforced. Without the heavy firepower of the military, the local police had no chance at all. Grace knew then that it was time to get back to her family. If they wouldn't leave, maybe she could at least protect them.

Jennifer Fletcher's family was in Virginia and that was where she was heading. The two friends hugged and Grace started across town to her parent's house. She hadn't been able to reach any of her family for several days, but the communications grid appeared to be dying, the signal on her phone going in and out.

As the police car got near its destination, Grace saw several groups of infected. They began following as she raced by them. When Officer Cunningham arrived and saw the front door standing open, she instinctively knew that it was too late. She had to know for sure, though, and Grace cautiously approached the residence, her well-used Remington .12 gauge pump shotgun at a low ready. There were no sounds coming from inside and she listened for several minutes at the open door.

Normally, she would call for a backup officer. One of the cardinal rules of law enforcement was that you never searched a building or residence by yourself. Of course, there was no backup available and this was her parent's home. Her home.

Grace moved inside, securing the heavy, wooden door behind her, then clearing the downstairs area. Suddenly, she heard a noise, a loud bump from upstairs. She took her time, working her way up to the second level, not sure what she was going to see, scared of what she would find, but knowing that she had to check.

At the top of the staircase, Cunningham could see down the hallway, noting that each door was closed. Another loud bump startled her, the noise coming from her parent's room located at the end of the corridor.

Slowly, she moved down the hallway until she was standing next to her mom and dad's bedroom door. Someone or something was moving around inside the room.

"Daddy? Mama? Hope?"

Suddenly, something big slammed into the flimsy door, cracking it and shaking the frame. Grace gasped and jumped backwards, raising the shotgun. A loud growling and the sound of teeth gnashing carried into the hallway. The police officer knew what those noises meant; she'd heard them continuously over the last several weeks. The only question now was who was growling and gnashing their teeth?

Grace backed down the hallway to give herself some space as someone continued to crash into the hollow wooden door. After the fourth time, the wood began to splinter. As they continued to assail the door, it finally gave way, with the now infected Reverend Samuel Cunningham falling into the corridor. When he saw Grace, he pushed himself to his feet and charged, snarling at his daughter.

Samuel had always been Grace's role model but she knew instantly that this was not her father. His spirit was already with God. This was just his body, she told herself, as she looked into the red eyes, the blood dripping out of his mouth and coating the white dress shirt he'd had on at the time of his infection.

"I'm sorry, Daddy," she said, tears streaming down her cheeks as she raised the shotgun. At a distance of ten feet, the blast of 00 buckshot caught Samuel full in the face, almost completely severing his head from his body. Blood and gore splattered the wall as the zombie pastor collapsed to the floor.

Grace instinctively worked the pump-action of the shotgun, ejecting the spent shell and loading a fresh round. Something else was moving in the bedroom. This sounded like someone was sliding over the hardwood floors. Cunningham waited, the sight of her father's body starting to make her nauseous. Another face appeared in the bedroom doorway. The head was at floor level, though, the body dragging itself along.

"Mama? Is that you?"

The head raised itself and Grace saw that this was, or at least had been, her mother. The woman's throat had been ripped out and so, minus her voice box, Mrs. Cunningham was unable to growl, her mouth wide in a silent snarl. Her eyes looked right through her first-born as she pulled herself across the floor.

A moment later, Grace saw why her mother couldn't stand. Her left leg was missing from the knee down. The police officer watched in horror as her beautiful mother came straight towards her, using her arms to pull herself down the hallway, intent on killing and eating her.

"I'll see you in Heaven, Mama. I love you." The shotgun roared again.

Grace didn't want to look in the bedroom. Hope had to be here somewhere. Was she going to have to shoot her sister, also? Suddenly, the sound of growling carried into the house from outside. The sound of my shots, she realized, told them that I'm here. The campus police officer fed two shotgun shells into the bottom of the gun, loading the magazine tube back to capacity.

Cunningham stepped over the bodies and reached her parent's door. She paused and listened. Nothing. Her nostrils, however, picked up the unmistakable stench of death. A quick peek inside let her know there was nothing standing in the room. Grace stepped in, stopping just inside the door. What was left of her sister was scattered and splattered across the bedroom, her parents having ripped Hope apart and devoured her. The older sister couldn't hold it in any longer and turning away from the carnage, she vomited onto the bedroom floor.

Grace had locked herself in her basement bedroom, crying for two days and not eating anything, a sense of emptiness growing inside of her. The pack of Zs outside, however, just wouldn't leave. After shooting her infected father and mother, zombies had tried to get into the house, the noise of their scratching and banging at the door terrifying the young woman.

Cunningham had finally left her bedroom, knowing that she needed to eat something and figure out what she was going to do. A peek out the living room windows revealed over a hundred of the nasty creatures in the street, shuffling in both directions, looking for victims. And those were just the ones that she could see. The good news was that they had lost interest in her house and had moved away from her front door.

Over the next few weeks, she lost any sense of time locked in her home, while hundreds of zombies continued roaming the area. She was glad to be away from the bodies of her poor family, but after a few days, the stench was awful, even in the basement. She would have left, but had no idea where to go, and the zombies would swarm her the minute she stepped outside.

Grace had no idea how her father had gotten infected. She suspected that he'd tried to help someone who already had the virus. That was who he was. Daddy would help anyone at any time, black, white, Hispanic, it didn't matter.

Cunningham tried to call Jimmy but it wouldn't go through, so she sent him a text detailing where she was and what she'd been forced to do. Grace had no idea if he was even still alive or if he had received her message. She had really enjoyed talking to him on the phone and even thought she might be falling in love with the handsome federal police officer.

The young woman had hoped that they could go on a on a date, which would have, of course, meant meeting her parents. Their first date would have been a dinner with Mama and Daddy. That was one of Daddy's ground rules: if you want to go out with one of my daughters, you first have to join us for a family dinner. The thought of her parents not meeting Jimmy made her eyes water. The uncertainty of not knowing if he was still alive started her crying all over again.

The water in the house was still running and the campus police officer had wisely filled every container that she could find. Mrs. Cunningham always kept a well-stocked pantry, so Grace figured she still had several weeks worth of food. A week after shooting her parents, the power had gone out. Five days after that, the water also stopped flowing.

Grace spent most of her days in her bedroom, trying to read her Bible or pray, wondering if God was even listening, because it sure

---

didn't seem like it anymore. Cunningham also spent time every day looking out the windows on the first floor of the house, checking to see if the Zs were still around. She estimated that there were over three hundred milling around her's and her neighbor's houses. Cunningham had no idea if there were any other survivors in the area, although the presence of so many zombies indicated that there had to be others like herself nearby, desperate to escape.

Grace considered taking a chance and sprinting for the police car parked in the driveway, but there were too many Zs, and she knew that, even if she made it, the Ford Crown Victoria couldn't plow through them all. For the moment, she would have to stay put, hoping the infected went somewhere else. Eventually, though, she knew that she would have to risk it. *I should've gotten the address to where Jennifer was going*, she thought.

After several weeks of living in uncertainty, she had lost track of time and didn't even know what day of the week it was. She had just come upstairs from the basement to peer out the windows and to get something to eat. Cunningham estimated that she only had about two week's worth of water left. The officer had a bandanna wrapped around her face to block out some of the scent from her family's decomposing bodies. Her watch indicated that it was 1330 hours.

Suddenly, a explosion sounded from up the street. Grace rushed to the front windows and watched the hundreds of bloody, growling zombies rushing in the direction of the loud noise. *What should I do?* she wondered. *Should I use that distraction to leave?*

Three minutes later, a light tapping came from the back door, the one that led out onto their large deck. Cunningham cautiously made her way to the rear of the residence, her shotgun up and ready. She heard the doorknob jiggle and then more knocking. Grace quietly pulled the French blind back slightly on the window, letting her see out onto the deck.

It was a black man wearing dark clothing, a helmet on his head, holding an M4 rifle. Grace felt a stab of fear. Who was this and why was he trying to get into her house?

"Grace," a voice called softly. "If you're in there, open up. It's me, Jimmy."

Cunningham gasped as she fumbled with the door locks. "Jimmy? Is that really you?" she asked as she jerked the door open.

"Were you expecting some other good-looking man to come rescue you?" he said, with a smile.

Grace fell into his arms and started crying. Jimmy pushed the door closed behind him and locked it while continuing to hold the young woman. She held him tightly, sobbing into his chest.

The stench of death hit Jones square in the face. He hadn't received Cunningham's last text so had no idea what she'd been through. Fortunately, Grace had given him her home address weeks ago, in the hopes that he could come have dinner with her and her parents when things got back to normal.

After her sobs subsided, Jimmy asked gently, "What's that smell?"

Cunningham started weeping again. "It's my family," she managed to get out. "They're all upstairs. Dead. I had to shoot my parents."

Jones held her tightly. "Oh, Grace, I'm so sorry! I wish I could've gotten here sooner, but I'm gonna to get you out of here."

After a few minutes, Grace pulled back wiping her face. "I'd pretty much given up. There are hundreds of those things wandering through the neighborhood. What was that explosion?"

Jimmy gave a slight smile. "I threw a flash bang grenade up the street and hurried over while they were distracted."

Cunningham took Jones' hand and led him down to her basement retreat. "My room's down here and the smell isn't as bad."

## Centers for Disease Control Compound, East of Atlanta, Thursday, 1600 hours

Jimmy and his three CDC companions sat around the metal table in their "headquarters." Dr. Martin had allotted the agents two small rooms to use as an office and as a storage area for their equipment. In reality, the men didn't spend a lot of time in the crowded office. The briefing table served its purpose whenever they needed to meet. At the moment, a bottle of Maker's Mark bourbon sat between them, each man holding a tumbler of the whiskey.

"I was saving that bottle for when the baby comes since I don't have any cigars to give out," Eddie said. "But, I figure Jimmy and Grace making it back was worthy of a celebration."

The four friends clinked glasses. Grace was resting in a popup camper that wasn't being used. It was parked near Eddie and Grace's RV, and Marshall had directed Jones and Cunningham to their new home. After they got their meager possessions unloaded, Grace told Jimmy that she needed to lay down for a little while. Jones had hugged the young woman and said he would be back to check on her later.

"So, you got to Athens without any problems?" Marshall asked, pouring a little more bourbon into Jones' glass.

"Yeah, that was the easy part. I didn't see any Zs until I got within ten miles of there. But once I started seeing 'em, they were everywhere, big groups of them. A lot of 'em were still wearing their Bulldog colors. I ain't no Dawgs fan," the former University of Alabama track star admitted, "but seeing all those rotting, decaying students and faculty members was sad. Not sad enough to keep me from shooting a bunch of them in the head, but, you know how it is.

"When I was approaching the big interchange, where Highway

78 runs into Highway 441, that was when the excitement started. Every lane and every exit or entry ramp was blocked. Cars and trucks were smashed into each other and the guardrails. Some of them were overturned and others had burned up.

"There were Zs swarming all over the place. I'm guessing that those roads got jammed up back when the virus was released on campus. Maybe some people who hadn't turned yet got to their cars and tried to flee. Or maybe they were just all scared and trying to get out of the city.

"Of course, when the zombies saw me stop a couple hundred yards back they came running. There was maybe two hundred of 'em coming from in front of me and another group coming up from behind me. I turned the radio up and put the windows down so they could enjoy some P. Diddy.

"I grabbed my pack, put the van in drive, jumped out, and started running. It hit a few of the suckers and the stereo kept a lot of 'em interested. Maybe thirty chased me but the woods were really thick and I finally lost them.

"Problem was, now I had to go the last three miles to Grace's house cross-country on foot. It only took me an hour to drive from here to where I had to dump the vehicle. Then, it took me two days to cover those three miles walking. There were Zs everywhere!

"The worst of it was that last mile. Her parents lived in the middle of this huge residential area near the baseball stadium and the Zs acted like they owned the place. Thankfully, all the houses I came to were empty or just had a zombie or two that I could pop and duck inside until the coast was clear.

"When I got close to Grace's place, I snuck over to the next block and lobbed a flash bang as far as I could. That distraction gave me enough time to get back to her house and knock on the door. Thankfully, she didn't shoot me as an intruder."

Jimmy had finished his bourbon and looked at Eddie, holding his glass up. Marshall poured them all another drink.

Jones paused before continuing, staring into his glass. "Man, Grace had it rough. She had to shoot her mom and dad. The parents had killed her sister, ripped her apart. Grace was trapped in that house for weeks with those smelly bodies decaying upstairs. She was glad to see me but hasn't said a whole lot about what happened with her family. She's still in shock.

"We stayed at her place for almost two weeks. I wanted to turn around and leave immediately but there were just too many Zs. The flash bang I had thrown backfired and brought more of the suckers from the surrounding areas into the neighborhood. After the first week, the pack had shrunk a little but then it started snowing before we could leave. I didn't want to chance trying to escape on icy roads. The problem was, we were just about out of water and we knew we going to have to make our move. We waited until the first day that the temps were over freezing and the sky was clear.

"I knew it was gonna be run and dive into her police car and haul ass. We loaded up our backpacks with what little food and water was left, jumped into the cruiser and took off. That drive out of there was some scary stuff. It wasn't quite as bad as that day we got overrun at the Braves stadium, but it sure was close! I kept thinking the Zs would thin out but I was running over them left and right. There were just too many to dodge. The front end of that cop car was taking a beating and I knew it wouldn't be long before we'd have to ditch it. I was just hoping to get south of the city first. And to make it even more interesting, there were still patches of ice on the road.

"My plan was to get out of Athens and then take back roads. We'd just crossed over Highway 78 when a mob of Zs charged at us from apartments on both sides of the street. Grace started shooting at the closest ones on her side and I was trying to get us around the ones in the street. We had just managed to get past most of them when this fat girl Z jumped right out in front of us. I ran over her, but she got stuck underneath the chassis and that was it for the car.

"Grace was still shooting her shotgun but I couldn't even look 'cuz I've got about ten nasties right on top of me on my side. So, I'm poppin' heads with my Glock, Grace is blasting away out her window. After a minute, all the Zs were down. There were some more heading towards us but they were about seventy yards away.

"We grabbed our packs, bailed out and started running. We didn't slow down for ten minutes. We knew we needed to create some distance. I shot a few stragglers as we ran through a neighborhood and we finally we got to a wooded area where I was hoping we could lose them."

Jimmy paused to sip his whiskey, reliving the tense moments.

"We climbed a hill and I took a look at the maps I'd taken with me. Bein' a Marine officer, I know a thing or two about land navigation."

Andy laughed and nodded at Eddie and Hollywood. "You guys know what the most dangerous thing is in the Marines?"

Marshall and Estrada shook their heads. Fleming continued, "It's an officer armed with a map and a compass."

"The enlisted Marine does speak the truth," the former Marine captain acknowledged with a grin as they all laughed.

"Anyway, after a few minutes of figuring out where we were and catching our breaths, I heard growling coming our way so we started running again. There was another neighborhood about a quarter of a mile away through the trees and we headed for it.

"This street had maybe ten or twelve houses on it. We came out of the woods into a backyard and, thankfully, nobody shot us as looters. The first house we saw turned out to be empty and pretty easy to break into. We got inside and watched out the windows.

"After about ten minutes a group of twenty Zs came stumblin' out of the woods. They had evidently lost our scent in the forest because they shuffled past where we were hiding and just huddled in the street growling at each other. A few more joined them, I'm guessing former residents of the subdivision we were in.

"So now, we're trapped inside another house, we got no transport, it's getting colder, and our water was running short. Thankfully, the good people whose house we were in had some bottled water in the pantry but we only had food enough for a few more days."

"How'd Grace get shot?" Eddie asked.

"After two days in that house, things got real interesting. A National Guard hummer came roaring down the street. They cut down the all the zombies with the M-249 mounted on top and then they started going house-to-house. Grace wanted to go out and make contact with them. She thought they'd help us get out of there, but I was gettin' a bad vibe off these troopers. There were three black guys and a black girl. I watched 'em kicking in front doors, then we'd hear some shooting inside the houses. Maybe they were capping Zs but something just didn't feel right.

"Grace still wanted to show ourselves and she was pissed at me when I told her 'no.' When they pulled up to our house, I grabbed her and we ducked out the back door and ran for the woods. Of course, when we got to the edge of the forest, some Zs were heading straight for us. I guess they were running to the sound of gunfire.

"This was a big group so I decided maybe we should take a chance with the guard, after all. We go running back to the house and those National Guard bastards came out the rear door shooting, not at the zombies, but at us! Two of 'em had M-16s, one of them had a shotgun, and the girl was shooting her Beretta.

"Thankfully, they weren't very well trained and stayed bunched together. I dropped one and then my rifle took a round, right in the center of the receiver. I heard Grace grunt and saw her stumble, but she kept moving left while I was moving right. Grace got the girl, hit her in the face with a blast of 00 buckshot. My M4 was out of the fight, bullets were whizzing around me, and now I'm hearing Zs growling, coming up behind us.

"I whipped out my Glock and killed the last two soldiers, but the Zs were less than twenty feet away, almost fifteen of them. I looked over and saw Grace was down on her knees and in pain. So now I'm running for her, shootin' Zs, and starting to get a little concerned. I know the Marines and Roy turned me into a deadly weapon but this wasn't looking good."

Roy had been the CDC agents' firearms instructor when they had gone through their initial training. While not speaking at all about his background, the common consensus was that he was a retired Navy SEAL turned contract instructor.

"I killed over half of them but then my pistol ran dry. Man, then things got real crazy. They were too close for me to reload so I dropped the Glock and whipped off that useless rifle and started swinging it. I crushed some skulls but then I felt one of the nasties grabbing my shoulder. Thank God, Grace managed to get up and put a shot into that Z's head. That was the last one but with all the shooting, we knew their buddies would be heading our way."

"Were those real National Guard troops or bad guys masquerading?" Hollywood asked.

Jimmy shrugged. "That's a good question. Grace was really hurting so I helped her back inside. She had been hit in the vest and was stable, so I went out and gathered up weapons and ammo from those idiots. I think one of 'em was still breathing but I didn't even bother to finish him off. I knew he didn't have long. I also snatched the dead girl's body armor for Grace and two of the guy's coats. If we were going to be stuck in that house, we needed to stay warm.

"But here's what really pissed me off. While I was grabbing their stuff, I saw tattoos on two of the dudes. 'BMF.' Black Mafia Family. That's a really hard-core street gang. I didn't take the time to look but I'd bet the other guy and the chick were marked as well. My guess is that these were legit National Guard troopers who decided to go rogue when everything fell apart. And as gangsters, they resorted to doing gangster stuff.

"Even in the Marine Corps, we had gang members make it through recruitment and boot camp. They usually didn't last long before they got caught doing something stupid and I've heard the same thing has happened in the other branches of the military, as well."

Hollywood spoke up, "Yeah, when I was in the Army, I was recruited by a couple of different Mexican gangs. As an MP, we even arrested some gang bangers when we could catch them selling drugs or trying to steal weapons to resell to their gangster buddies."

Jones nodded and continued, "After I got the doors barricaded and made sure the house was secure, I went to check on Grace. She'd taken two 9 mil rounds to the vest and a third grazed her left arm. Her vest saved her but I'm pretty sure her sternum was cracked. I'm just glad she didn't take an M-16 round. All she had on was her police pistol-rated vest. That's why I grabbed the heavy one the dead girl had been wearing. Grace needed stitches on her arm but the best I could do was clean it, bandage it, and tie it up real tight.

"The good news was that now we had a vehicle. When I went and checked it, the hummer only had a quarter tank of diesel but they also had a few boxes of MREs and some more water so we were OK for a while. There was a lot of stolen crap in the hummer, too. Jewelry, cash, and some other loot those goons had snatched from houses."

"You said your rifle got shot in the receiver? Were you able to fix it?" Andy asked.

"Not a chance. That bullet hit the ejection port and screwed the bolt up. It wouldn't shoot and I couldn't even get the action to cycle. But the scumbags gave us two M-16s, a Mossberg .12 gauge, and a Beretta," Jimmy said, pointing at the pistol attached to his plate carrier and an M-16 standing against the wall.

"All that shooting drew in the zombies and they surrounded us, just shuffling around our house and the neighborhood. We hunkered down in place and tried to be quiet. It was cold and Grace was in a lot of pain. I had a few pain pills in my IFAK but she burned through those in three days and then just had to grunt it out.

"After probably a week and a half, Grace was able to get around again. I remember from Marine Combat First Aid Training that a cracked sternum takes several weeks to heal fully. She wasn't a hundred percent but it looked like most of the Zs had moved on and there were just some stragglers hanging around the area. I told her that we needed to get out while the coast was clear. When I cranked up that humvee, though, a bunch came running so we played Frogger gettin' out of the neighborhood.

"We were close to Highway 78, but I knew the big interchange with Highway 441 was blocked. I drove south until we were out in the middle of nowhere. I stopped and gave Grace a crash course on how to use the machine gun.

"There's a little town over there, Watkinsville. It's maybe eight or ten miles from Athens. The Zs had swept through there like locusts. There were partially eaten bodies, body parts, and some decaying zombies still hanging around.

"It looked like the police had tried to make a stand. They had set up some barricades and had the road blocked. There were a couple of zombie cops who wanted a bite of us but the big bumper of that humvee put them out of their misery.

"Right after we got out of town, the hummer started sputtering and then died. The gas gauge still showed a quarter tank but that bitch was dead and there was no reviving her. We loaded up with as much ammo, food, and water as we could carry and started hiking.

"After a mile, Grace's chest was really hurting and I knew we needed to stop again. There was a business park just ahead, and being a highly trained Marine officer, I read the directory and saw just what we needed."

"A Marriott?" asked Eddie, grinning.

"That would've been OK, too. No, I broke into Dr. Lombardi's office. The sign said he was a general practitioner, and he had plenty of good drugs. I found some pain pills for Grace and some antibiotic cream for her wounded arm. She's gonna have a nasty scar but at least it didn't get infected.

"It wasn't as comfortable as a Marriott but we didn't see any Zs and it was a good place to let her heal up and rest for a few more days. Neither of us had gotten much sleep at her house or that other one with zombies just outside.

"We were only a couple of miles from Highway 78 so three days later we started walking. There was a big convenience store right next to the highway. I saw that purple Olds sitting next to the gas pumps and I knew that the good Lord was looking out for this brother and sister. There were a few chewed-up bodies lying around but when we made for the car, some Zs came pouring out from behind the building. There were about twenty of them but they were only fifty yards away from us.

"I had Grace check to see if the keys were in the car while I started popping heads with my National Guard issue M-16. She yelled that the keys were in the ignition, got it cranked up, and we were in business. We hauled ass out of there with the nasties shuffling after us. An hour later, we were home."

"Wow! That's enough excitement to last a lifetime," Eddie nodded thoughtfully. "Now, if we could just hear something from Chuck, Scotty, Chris, and Terrence."

The friends sat in silence for couple of minutes, glad to be back together. Andy finally broke the silence.

"No rush, but after Grace is feeling better, do you think she'd like to help with security here? It'd probably be good to give her something to do. She doesn't need to be sitting around thinking about things and we could really use her."

"Definitely," Jimmy said. "I told her the same thing on the drive over. We need everybody and she's proved that she's a badass. We all saw how she got that group of survivors out of the Sanford Stadium when the zombie virus was unleashed. And I got to see her taking out Zs and dirty National Guard troops. She's good. And speaking of the lovely young woman, I think I'll go check on her."

## Centers for Disease Control Compound, East of Atlanta, Thursday, 1715 hours

Dr. Nicole Edwards stood up from her desk, laying down the latest test results for the zombie virus vaccine her team was working on. She was one of the top epidemiologists in the world, but she hadn't been able to concentrate on anything for the last two hours.

"I'll be back in a few, I need some fresh air," she told her colleagues, three men and two women scientists, busy at different work stations in the small lab, and walked outside.

Earlier, on her way back to the lab after a late lunch, she had had heard the car pull up outside the gate. Her heart had leapt inside of her, hoping that he had finally returned. Nicole didn't approach the gate per the security protocol that the enforcement unit had in place. She did, however, watch from a distance, hoping and praying.

The purple Oldsmobile had indeed been occupied by a CDC enforcement officer, just not the one whom she had wanted to see. Of course, she was happy that Agent Jones had returned safely and that he had been able to rescue the young woman. That was great news.

At the same time, Edwards felt something die inside of her, realizing that he probably wasn't coming back. She couldn't explain her feelings. Chuck McCain had never said or done anything to indicate that he had any romantic notions towards her. Nicole, on the other hand, had fallen in love with the big man. It reminded her of the crush she'd had on the quarterback of the football team when she had been in high school. Johnny Masters hadn't even known that she existed but Nicole had fallen for him anyway.

Dr. Edwards had always admired McCain from a distance, especially while her friend, Rebecca Johnson, was still alive. Nicole knew the two had loved each other, even though they had downplayed their feelings in public. After Rebecca was murdered, the scientist had hoped that one day, after Chuck's heart had healed, the two of them might be able to get together.

Nicole unconsciously pulled her long, wavy brown hair forward and let it lay over her right shoulder, thinking back to that day, months earlier, when she had almost given up hope. She and the security supervisor, Darrell Parker, had gotten trapped inside the CDC security office while zombies roamed just outside. After several days of being locked in the dark office, Edwards had experienced a nightmare, waking up screaming and alerting the Zs that fresh meat was just on the other side of the metal door.

The creatures were just about to break through and she and Darrell knew that they were about to die. Suddenly, gunshots sounded from the other side of the door. Moments later, they heard McCain's voice, asking if anyone was inside. Darrell had opened the door and Nicole had thrown herself into Chuck's arms, embarrassing both of them.

In reality, they had never even had a conversation before that day, but she had fantasized about him coming to her rescue. Her feelings for McCain intensified over the next month. Chuck had very generously let Nicole share his guest room with Scotty Smith's girlfriend, Emily. Since the scientist's apartment was located near downtown, in the Buckhead community of Atlanta, she was grateful for his offer. Plus, it allowed her to stay close to Chuck. He'd been polite but had kept his distance as she shared his house. This, however, only increased Nicole's desire to get close to him.

McCain and the other two male roommates, Scotty Smith and Darnell Washington, Emily's paramedic partner, were all perfect gentleman. Chuck had made a point of checking with Nicole regularly to see if she needed anything and had loaned her a computer so that she could continue working. At the same time, it was obvious that he wasn't looking for female companionship.

Edwards had overheard McCain talking to Smith one evening about his plans to go find his daughter. Scotty had wanted to go with his boss but Chuck had gently turned him down, reminding his friend that Emily needed him. Nicole remembered the feeling of fear she'd felt when she had heard that Chuck was launching out on his own.

And now he's been gone for close to two months. What happened to you, Chuck? she wondered. A cold breeze blew over the CDC compound, Dr. Edwards wrapped her arms around her shoulders and turned to go back inside. She still had a lot of work to do.

# Chapter Five

**Buckhead, Atlanta, Friday, 1100 hours**

Antonio Corona stood on his balcony, which overlooked the area that his men had secured, but the cartel leader's gaze carried beyond, towards the skyline of Atlanta just a few miles away. He wanted the entire city, not just the ever-growing foothold that he was carving out in this exclusive neighborhood. He was torn between wanting to rush into action while simultaneously feeling a sense of caution, as well.

The loss of his patrol on Wednesday had rattled him. He knew that the Americans would eventually come after him, but was shocked to hear that his entire eight-man patrol of hardened soldiers had been taken out with no apparent casualties to their ambushers. Corona was pleased that the traitorous maintenance man had been killed, may he rot in Hell. I only wish I could've been the one to send him there, Corona thought.

Later in the afternoon, when the patrol never returned, Quintero had led a group of additional gangsters to the scene. After walking around the still smoking carnage, trying to figure out what had happened, the lieutenant returned to let his boss know that their patrol had been slaughtered. Each of the bodies of his men had received a shot to the head from close range to go along with whatever other wounds they had taken.

There was no way that the American police had done this. They were bound by so many rules, they would have never shot wounded criminals in the head. The military? Tony the Tiger didn't think so. They were also forced to follow stringent guidelines and were forbidden to even operate on their own soil.

So who killed his men? Antonio knew that the gringos loved their guns. Maybe it was a rival gang? If that was the case, they were clearly a force to be reckoned with. All the more reason for the team he had sent out to get to his uncle quickly and bring back more soldados.

The Nissan Armada containing four soldiers and the white Chevrolet full-size van with two more gunmen to guard the ten women they were taking to Uncle Pepe, left early Thursday morning. They should be in Tijuana later today or tonight. Hopefully, the old man would be in a good mood when he read his nephew's letter. The younger Corona had wondered several times over the last few months if his uncle had not been trying to get rid of him by sending Antonio to try and capture an American city.

It didn't matter. Corona and his men had made steady progress, securing a large area of prime real estate just a few miles outside of downtown Atlanta. More cartel soldiers would allow Tony the Tiger to continue pushing outward, enlarging their presence in the large American city.

Antonio knew it wouldn't hurt that he was sending his uncle some gifts. Jose Corona was already fabulously wealthy from his many criminal enterprises, but his nephew knew the way to Pepe's heart. Antonio had sent the blonde who had been keeping him entertained and nine other young gringo girls. Tony the Tiger had grown tired of the blonde girl anyway. He'd keep the black chick around a little longer and had told Jorge to keep his eyes out for someone fresh as their patrols continued slowly expanding their area of conquest.

Antonio's soldiers had been ordered not to touch the girls during the long road trip to Mexico, but the cartel leader was no fool. He just hoped the women survived the trip to spend some time in Pepe's bed. The girls would get Uncle Pepe's attention. And when he tired of them, he'd add them to the stable of one of his many brothels.

Corona's other gift, however, would earn the young man his uncle's affection forever. Two vials of the zombie virus from the black case the maintenance man had recovered would give Jose Corona a new weapon to use in Mexico and beyond. Antonio just hoped his uncle would respond to his request for more men sooner, rather than later.

### Centers for Disease Control Compound, East of Atlanta, Friday, 1115 hours

Darrell Parker, Marcel Adams, and Andy's son, fifteen-year-old Tyler Fleming sat in the guard hut at the entrance to the CDC compound. Marcel and Tyler chatted quietly while Darrell napped peacefully in his chair, snoring occasionally, eliciting chuckles from the other two men. The sudden rumble of diesel engines echoed up the driveway, waking the retired police officer and causing all of them to jump to their feet. Marcel's chair flipped over in his haste to grab the AR-15, leaning against the wall.

Three humvees roared into view down the long driveway. A soldier was standing in the open top hatch of each vehicle manning a heavy machine gun in the lead hummer, a grenade launcher in the second, and a light machine gun in the third.

"Tyler, run go get your daddy and the others," Parker ordered the teenager, concern evident in his voice.

The younger Fleming took off at a sprint to tell the CDC agents that they had company. The military vehicles were flying American flags, and Darrell noted that the three soldiers standing in the hatches had their weapons pointed away from the compound.

The hummers stopped about thirty yards short of the gate. The passenger door of the lead vehicle opened and a soldier in crisply pressed BDUs stepped out, his hands empty, but wearing a pistol in a cross-draw holster on his body armor. The soldier removed his helmet, set it inside the vehicle, and waved at Marcel and Darrell.

"Gentleman," he called out, "my name's Lieutenant Colonel Kevin Clark with the Georgia National Guard. I have orders to make contact with the CDC enforcement agents who might be here. Specifically, I was told to contact Eddie Marshall or Andy Fleming."

"Colonel, I've already sent for Agent Marshall and Agent Fleming," Darrell answered. "They'll be right with you."

Moments later, all four CDC officers came rushing to the gate, locked and loaded, unsure if they were about to be attacked. After getting the download from Parker, Marshall examined the soldier closely. He sure looks familiar, Eddie thought.

"I'm Eddie Marshall, Colonel," the CDC team leader called out. "How can we help you?"

"Agent Marshall, may I approach the gate? I've got my ID card right here. I believe we met a few months ago on the University of Georgia campus. You gentleman helped my wife and I get out of a sticky situation," the colonel said, with a smile.

That was where he'd seen him, Eddie realized. No surprise I didn't remember him, though, with Rebecca getting killed and the rest of us fighting for our lives, trying to rescue as many people as we could.

"Of course, Colonel. Now I recognize you. What can we do for you?"

Clark strode towards the entrance, handing Marshall his ID card through the fence. "I've got orders to report to you and to deliver something to whoever is in charge here at the CDC. Can you let us in?"

Five minutes later, Eddie and Andy were leading Kevin and First Sergeant Ricardo Gonzalez into Dr. Charles Martin's small workspace. Dr. Martin was a diminutive man wearing a white lab coat and wire-rimmed glasses. He was surprised at the sight of the camo-clad strangers.

Eddie made the introductions and the colonel handed Martin a small black canvas duffel bag. "Dr. Martin, I was told to give you this along with a message from Washington."

The duffle bag contained a computer hard drive, a small notebook, and several other items. Martin removed the hard drive and flipped through the notebook, clearly not recognizing it. He looked up at Clark.

"You said you also have a message for me, Colonel?"

"Yes, sir. I was told to tell you that those belong to Dr. Kim Bae-yong and that you should expect her to arrive here tomorrow."

Dr. Martin's eyes grew wide. "Where did you get this information? We haven't had any outside contact with anyone in weeks."

Kevin smiled. "Funny thing. I was issued a satellite phone back when I took the job with the National Guard. I didn't think it even worked until a few days ago when it started beeping at me. A retired navy admiral who identified himself as the Director of Operations for the CIA was on the other end. I think he said his name was Williams."

Eddie and Andy looked at each other, surprised. Other than

McCain, they were the only Atlanta agents to know of the CIA's involvement with the CDC. They had never met Admiral Jonathan Williams but had been given his contact information back before the communications grid collapsed.

McCain had told them that Williams was originally a Navy SEAL in Vietnam. He was wounded severely on his second tour and forced out of the elite unit. He chose stay in the navy, however, eventually attaining the rank of admiral. On his retirement, he accepted a job as the Assistant Director of Operations with the Central Intelligence Agency.

Clark continued. "Anyway, this Admiral Williams very politely asked me to take my soldiers to a house near Buckhead. He told me where the safe was located inside the residence and even gave me the combination. Those were inside the safe," he said, nodding at the hard drive and the notebook.

"And you say Dr. Bae-yong will be here tomorrow?"

"That was the message I was asked to convey," Kevin answered.

Dr. Martin nodded and laid the items on his desk. "Did you have any contact with Kim's family?" he asked softly, looking at the colonel.

The expression on Clark's face told the scientist everything.

"I'm sorry, sir," the soldier answered. "They were in the house, a man and a young girl. They were both infected."

Martin's eyes watered as he removed his glasses and wiped them with his sleeve. "I'm sorry, too. Our families were very close. Kim and my wife were roommates at Harvard. Dr. Bae-yong is probably the leading epidemiologist in the world, with Dr. Nicole Edwards, who's onsite here, being a very close second.

"Kim works for us but was on loan to the German version of the CDC when the last big attacks took place. The FAA immediately cancelled all flights so she's been stuck in Europe. We've had no contact with her for months. Before the phones and internet crashed,

Kim texted me, asking me to get her home. I promised that I would try."

The small man sighed deeply. "I failed her. No one in Washington would return my calls. They were having problems of their own there, of course. Clearly, there are still some people in our government who are working and somehow they've managed to get Kim back to America."

"Yes, sir," Kevin nodded. "I took the liberty of bringing a framed family photo from her home office. I had a feeling it might be important to someone. Also, there are two pistols in the bag that were in the safe. I didn't want to leave them for looters."

Charles withdrew the picture of the Bae-yong family, looking at his friends, two of whom were now dead. Martin started to get emotional again but Clark had something else to tell him and the CDC agents.

"There's something else that you all need to hear," Kevin said, looking at Eddie and Andy. When he was sure he had everyone's attention, he continued.

"Right after we left Dr. Bae-yong's house, we heard gunshots, automatic fire. Two stolen National Guard hummers were chasing a pickup from the direction of Buckhead. The humvees were flying Mexican flags. We took them out but they shot the truck up and it flipped over on Peachtree Road. First Sergeant Gonzalez spoke to the Hispanic driver before he died. Can you tell them what he told you, First Sergeant?"

Gonzalez cleared his throat. "Yes, sir. It was young Mexican male. He told me that the Tijuana Cartel has taken over a big chunk, maybe several blocks of Buckhead. He said that they're doing bad things, killing a lot of people, and have a big group of women and a few men whom they're using as sex slaves.

"This kid was starting to fade but he managed to say that the cartel also has a quantity of the zombie virus and he had just watched them inject someone they had captured to see what would happen. After the person died and turned into a Z the cartel boss shot him in the head.

"I asked him how a Mexican gang got ahold of the virus. He said that he used to work for the CDC and kept saying he was sorry. I tried to get more information out of him but he was too far gone. He didn't have any ID and I didn't get his name."

Martin, Marshall, and Fleming were stunned. The idea of a Mexican cartel taking over a large section of American real estate was bad enough. Being in possession of the most dangerous bio-terror weapon ever invented made the situation catastrophic.

A few minutes later, the CDC agents and the National Guard soldiers were all gathered around the humvees, the troopers describing their work over the last few months in eliminating infected around Atlanta. Even some of the CDC researchers had come out to listen, hungry for news.

As his soldiers told stories to an engrossed audience, Colonel Clark motioned for Andy and Eddie to step off to the side, wanting to speak to them privately.

"Where are Scotty Smith and Chuck McCain?" he asked.

Former Army Ranger Scotty Smith had served as a sergeant under then Major Clark in Iraq. They had reconnected that fateful day on the UGA campus when Scotty had recognized his former CO in the group of survivors they were escorting across campus for exfiltration. Clark and McCain had met, as well, and the colonel had been impressed with the big man's calm, steady leadership during one of the worst terrorist attacks in history.

Fleming spoke up. "When the communication grid went down, Chuck kept us working for a couple of weeks but finally pulled the plug because we had no chain-of-command and no support system. He gave everyone the option of moving here to this rural research site or taking our families somewhere else that was safe.

"Scotty was going to escort his girlfriend to her parent's home in Tennessee. Chuck left to try and find his daughter up near Hendersonville, North Carolina. Two of our other guys left together. Their families live out west of Atlanta, off I-20. We haven't heard from any of them in almost two months."

Kevin shook his head. "I don't know about your other two guys but I fought side-by-side with Smith in Iraq and McCain impressed the hell out of me that day in Athens. If any two men can hold their own, it's those guys."

### Travelers Rest, South Carolina, Friday, 2030 hours

Chuck and Beth lay intertwined in the warm bed in the Foster's guest room. Snow and ice had prevented them from leaving that morning. McCain was anxious to get to Melanie but he couldn't complain at all about his present company or position.

The sky had finally cleared after dark and the newlyweds had stepped outside to briefly gaze at the stars. It was still cold but the temperatures were above freezing now and McCain felt confident that they could leave on Saturday morning. The couple had chatted quietly, making plans, as they stared at the clearing sky.

They still weren't sure how Diya was going to take the idea of being left behind. The young girl had pretty much done nothing but eat and sleep since they had arrived, recovering from her severe dehydration and from not eating for a week. She was in no condition for another journey. The cold forced them back into the house and they told the Fosters goodnight.

"This feels so normal," Beth sighed, her head on Chuck's chest, the heavy blankets wrapped around them in the bed.

"Yeah, it really does."

"Do you think things will ever really be normal again?"

McCain hesitated before answering. "I do. Most of the zombies that we're coming across are decaying and almost falling apart. They won't last much longer. We haven't seen a lot of fresh Zs as we've traveled, which means the virus isn't spreading as much. It may take a while, but this will eventually pass and we'll get a chance to help rebuild what has been destroyed."

Elizabeth was silent, her hand rubbing Chuck's bare chest. The big man sensed that there was something on her mind.

"What do you think?" he asked. "What do you want to do after things get back to normal? Do you want to go back to work at the college? We could buy a house out that way if that's what you want to do."

"I just want to be with you. You said your house, our house, needs a woman's touch so I'm looking forward to doing some decorating. I've never had a house of my own. And maybe…maybe one day I could be a mommy?" she asked very quietly. "I know we haven't talked about that, Chuck, and if you don't want to have any more kids, I understand. I love you no matter what."

That was what she was hesitant to mention the other day, he thought, when she had asked him about his home. He stroked her hair as the idea of being a dad again ricocheted around inside his head. The idea of raising another child? Not his first choice, especially with the challenges they would be facing, rebuilding the broken society, but why not? If Beth wants a baby, I'm not going to deny her that joy, he told himself.

"I'd love to have a baby with you," he finally answered.

"You would? Really?" She sounded surprised and relieved.

"I think we need to wait a year or two but I know you'll be an incredible mother. We probably need to work on our technique for awhile though," he grinned, pulling her top of him.

"I didn't mean have a baby right now," she laughed, pressing herself against him. "But you're right. Practice makes perfect."

### Andrews Air Force Base, Maryland, Friday, 2200 hours

The black CIA-owned Lear jet rolled to a stop inside a large hanger while ground crew personnel hastily pushed the doors to as the pilot shut down the plane's engines. When the giant metal doors were secured, the lights inside were flipped on. Andrews had several generators that allowed the large base to continue functioning.

The side door of the jet opened and a stairway was rolled against the side of the plane. Four heavily armed men were waiting in the hangar, near the bottom or the stairs. An attractive Asian woman was the first one out of the aircraft, carrying a briefcase and a small suitcase.

One of the armed men stepped forward. "Dr. Bae-yong? I'm Tu Trang." He nodded at the other three men. "We're with CDC enforcement and we'll escort you to your quarters for tonight. We'll also be accompanying you to Georgia tomorrow."

Tu Trang Donaldson was the Supervisory Agent in Charge of the Washington, D.C. office. Trang had spent fifteen years in the Army Special Forces, wearing the coveted Green Beret. After his marriage, he'd left the military, joining the Secret Service. His close friend and fellow agent, Luis García, had been recruited away from the Secret Service by the CDC to come work for their new enforcement unit. Luis had been able to convince Tu to join him, Trang being stationed in DC, while his friend worked out of the Atlanta office. Unfortunately, García had been killed in the attack on Atlanta several months earlier.

The compact, muscular man standing next to Trang was Jay Walker, one of Tu's team leaders. Walker was a former SEAL Team Six member and had retired after twenty-two years of service in the elite unit. The former SEAL was quickly recruited to bring his expertise in fighting terrorists into the new federal law enforcement agency.

The two other CDC agents in the hangar were LeMarcus Wade and Terry Hunt. Wade was a tall, muscular African-American, former Recon Marine and Walker's assistant team leader. Hunt was a solid six foot, a hundred and eighty pound former Air Force parajumper, turned Virginia State Trooper, turned CDC agent.

Two men made their way off of the jet and stood behind Dr. Kim Bae-yong. They both wore black BDUs and sidearms. One was around thirty years of age, while the other appeared to be in his seventies.

An additional two men, both tall and muscular, stood at the top of the stairway watching the proceedings below carefully. Both sported bushy beards, combat clothing, including body armor, sidearms, and Heckler & Koch 416 rifles cradled in their arms. Jay and Tu glanced at each other, recognizing the bodyguards from a previous encounter. One of them was a former Delta Force operative, the other had served briefly with Walker in SEAL Team Six before leaving mysteriously. The rumor mill speculated that both had been recruited to work for the CIA.

"Gentleman, my name is Admiral Jonathan Williams," the older man said, approaching the CDC agents and extending his hand. "I'm the Director of Operations for the CIA. Mr. Trang and Mr. Walker, I believe you two have met my assistant here, Shaun Taylor," he said, nodding at the younger man. "I know that you two signed a confidentiality agreement with Chuck McCain. Things have changed, however, and nowadays I'm not too concerned about who knows what. You can brief these other two fine agents at your convenience on the CIA's role in supporting CDC's enforcement unit."

"Of course," Williams continued, with a twinkle in his eye, looking at Jay and Tu, "some things are better left unsaid."

Trang and Walker knew exactly what the admiral was referring to. After the last big attacks in New York, DC, and Atlanta, Shaun Taylor had met with the two agents and given them an off-the-books mission. The terrorist mastermind for all the east coast attacks had been located, hiding at a remote farm house in Pennsylvania.

Jay and Tu had accepted the mission and infiltrated the property in the middle of the night, killing both of Imam Ruhollah Ali Bukhari's bodyguards. The imam had then been subjected to a very thorough interrogation and then executed by lethal injection, zip-tied to a chair.

The result of that interrogation led to Chuck McCain and Andy Fleming capturing the main Iranian mole who had managed to get inside the Federal Bureau of Investigation. Special Agent Mir Turani had been turned over to the CIA and transported to a secret location where one of their special interrogation teams could work on him. Terrorist sympathizers in the FBI and other federal agencies had since been identified. Several had been captured, while others were still on the run.

In some cases, the agents were not Muslims or even sympathetic to Islam. They were just corrupt and were willing to take money to betray their country. Others, like the late Deputy Director of the Weapons of Mass Destruction Directorate, Charles E. Trimble, III, had been caught in compromising positions and were being blackmailed. When Trimble's indiscretions became public, he put his service weapon into his mouth and pulled the trigger while sitting at his desk.

Williams turned to Kim Bae-yong. "Dr. Bae-yong, I'll leave you in the hands of these very capable men. They will take care of you and get you to Georgia safely. I'm very sorry we couldn't get you home earlier, but I know that your presence at the CDC research site is going to be a blessing."

"Thank you, Admiral Williams. You don't need to apologize. The CIA seems to be the only federal agency right now that is getting anything done. Thank you for everything."

The scientist reached over, and to the admiral's surprise, gave him a hug. William's patted her back and turned towards Trang and the others.

"I have another mission that I'm involved in so I'm leaving right away. My hope is to join you in Georgia sometime next week to discuss a very important operation that I'd like for you four to be a part of."

Jay and Tu both snapped to attention and said in unison, "Yes, sir!"

Trang and the other CDC agents led the scientist and Shaun Taylor out of the hangar to a nondescript brick building further down the tarmac. Trang unlocked the door and ushered them inside. Walker crossed the room and opened another door, revealing a staircase. They descended one flight of stairs, then accessed an elevator that took them even deeper underground to a secure bunker containing a command and control room, guest quarters, a dining room, and several offices.

Andrews Air Force Base was one of the very few military bases still functioning on the east coast. Zombies had overrun most of the others and some large criminal gangs had inflicted heavy losses on additional bases. When the virus was unleashed in Washington, D.C., the President had been removed to Camp David. The Vice-President was transported to Andrews. He was subsequently relocated to an underground bunker outside of DC.

The headquarters for the Federal Bureau of Investigation was located in the heart of the nation's capital. The car bomb and suicide bomber both detonated just blocks from the J. Edgar Hoover Building, forcing the FBI's operations to be evacuated to Andrews, as well.

The FBI as a law enforcement organization, however, was reeling. The President had fired the Attorney General, the FBI

Director and most of the assistant directors. The reputation of the agency was tainted and what was once the premier law enforcement organization in the country had lost the confidence of the President and his administration.

They had given him poor intelligence and bad advice, to go along with the traitors who had been uncovered inside the agency. These were bad enough but it had also come to the President's attention, with Admiral William's help, that the FBI had been given information on the zombie virus and it's potential as a terrorist weapon over a year before the first bio-terror attacks. The CIA had provided solid, actionable intelligence and nothing had been done. To hedge his bets, the President had signed the executive order creating the CDC Enforcement Unit.

For the time being, he had also signed another executive order, this one allowing the CIA to lead the fight on American soil against the terrorists and the zombies. The FBI was assigned to a supporting role, and it's agents were expected to follow the orders of the CIA director or any of his assistant directors, such as Admiral Williams.

When they exited the elevator, Tu led the way down a corridor and pointed to a room on his right. "Dr. Bae-yong, these are your guest quarters. Mr. Taylor, yours is across the hall. The plan is to be in the air in the morning by 0800 hours. There will be breakfast served in the dining room down this hall and to the right starting at 0700 hours. One of us will be guarding your rooms all night and if you need something, please let us know."

Kim smiled at Tu and nodded at the other agents. "Thank you. I feel very safe with you and I'm glad to hear that you'll be traveling with us. Good night."

# Chapter Six

**Travelers Rest, South Carolina, Saturday, 0730 hours**

Sunlight streaming through the window woke Chuck up. He and
Elizabeth had spent the last two nights in the guest bedroom at the
Foster's residence, while Diya had slept on the couch in the living
room. Beth's back was pressed up against him and he turned towards
his wife, wrapping his arms around her.

McCain could get used to being in a warm house, snuggled under
the blankets with Beth. Today, however, they would hit the road
again. The previous two days, Thursday and Friday, had featured
snow, freezing rain, and freezing temperatures. The Fosters had very
kindly allowed their visitors to stay with them until the weather had
cleared up.

Chuck kissed Elizabeth on the back of the head and slid out of
bed. He slipped on his pants and pulled a green Northeast Georgia
Technical College hoodie over his head. After using the restroom,
McCain followed his nose towards the living room.

Kim smiled at her guest, pouring him a cup of coffee. "Good
morning."

"Thank you so much," McCain said, sipping the hot liquid. "It's been nice getting to know you and Jack."

"We feel the same way about you folks. It was very kind of you to go out of your way to bring us that letter and to let us know our Karen is doing so well."

Mrs. Foster had two cast iron skillets working on top of the wood-burning stove. One contained scrambled eggs, the other held several pieces of frying ham.

"Hopefully, it won't be long and she can visit you herself," Chuck smiled.

"Good morning, Mr. Chuck," Diya said, walking in from the sunroom.

"Hi, Diya. You're looking a lot stronger today," McCain told her. "How are you feeling?"

"I feel very good, sir. Miss Elizabeth and Miss Kim helped me so much." The young girl paused, unsure of herself. "Mr. Chuck, can I please talk to you in private?"

McCain glanced at Kim and saw a slight smile on her face. She knows what's on Diya's mind, he realized.

"Sure," he answered, following the young girl out to the sunroom. What's this about? he wondered. He knew that Diya had wanted to stay with he and Elizabeth as they continued their journey, but that was a recipe for disaster. It was dangerous enough for the two of them. Adding a physically weak girl to the mix just wasn't a good idea.

They sat on opposite ends of the couch, the sunlight pouring in, the brief, late winter storm finally gone. Chuck savored his coffee, letting Diya start the conversation.

"Mr. Chuck, remember when I told you that I wanted to stay with you and Miss Elizabeth?"

The big man nodded.

"Well, I talked with Miss Kim last night and she asked me if I would stay with her and Mr. Jack. After I get stronger, I can help them around here. They have chickens, pigs, and in the summer will have a garden. I think I'd like to stay here, if that is OK with you and Miss Elizabeth?"

"Of course. That's a great idea," McCain smiled. "What made you change your mind?"

"Mr. Jack and Miss Kim are very nice people and I think that I could help them and learn a lot from them. Plus, I know that you and Miss Beth have a tough trip ahead of you and I don't want to be a burden."

After a moment, the young girl continued. "Mr. Chuck," she said softly, lowering her head, "I feel so lost but Miss Beth told me that you and her were Christians. She said that your God told her to come to the jewelry store and save me. I don't understand that but I believe her. I should have died there but she said she thinks that maybe your God has a plan for my life?"

This was not the conversation that McCain had expected. "She's right, Diya. God saved you for a reason. The main reason is that he loves you and wants you to get to know him. It wasn't an accident that we found you and were able to save your life. Can I leave you with a Bible? I'll let you have mine so that you can read and see what God might say to you."

The girl's eyes lit up. "I would love to have a Bible, Mr. Chuck. You and Miss Beth have been very good to me. The jewelry that you took from the shop is worth a lot of money and will help me so much. Maybe I can even help Miss Kim and Mr. Jack one day."

The day before, McCain had given her the jeweler's bag stuffed full of all the gold, silver, and diamond jewelry from the display cases in her father's store. It was the only remaining link that she had to her family but would also provide for the young girl's needs.

"Miss Beth told me how you saved her from some bad men and how the two of you fell in love. She said you've only been married a few days. I have something for you, Mr. Chuck." Diya said, quietly, handing him a small black box. "It's a wedding present."

When he opened the box, he saw a matching set of eighteen carat gold wedding bands. The bigger one was plain, while the smaller ring was encrusted with diamonds.

McCain didn't surprise easily but this gift caught him off-guard. "They're beautiful, Diya, but you don't have to..."

"Mr. Chuck, it's a wedding gift for you and Miss Elizabeth. I thought you might like to surprise her with them sometime. You two have done so much for me, please accept my present."

"Thank you, Diya. She'll be very happy, but wouldn't you like to give Miss Beth her ring?"

"Oh, no, Mr. Chuck. You give it to her. She'll kiss you so much!"

"Hey, you two," Elizabeth said, walking into the sunroom, holding her own mug of coffee.

Chuck palmed the box and slipped it into the pocket of his hoodie before his wife could see it.

"Good morning, sleepyhead," McCain said. "This young lady has just informed me that the Fosters have asked her to stay on with them, and she wants to make sure that its OK with you and me?"

Beth slid an arm around her young friend's shoulders and winked at Chuck. "I think that's a good decision, Diya. Mr. McCain and I don't know what's in front of us and we'll both feel better knowing that you're safe."

After a breakfast of ham, eggs, and more coffee, Elizabeth and Chuck sat around the table with the Fosters looking at the maps Karen had provided.

"My suggestion," said Jack, pointing to the map, "is to use Old Highway 25. It's a winding road through these foothills but it'll keep you off the main highway for a ways. Just stay on it for nine or ten miles and it'll dump you onto Highway 25, which will eventually merge with I-26 and runs through Hendersonville. At that point, y'all won't have any choice. There aren't many other roads to choose from. You're gonna hafta take your chances on the main thoroughfare.

"This is where your daughter's at," Foster continued, now pointing to a spot northeast of Hendersonville. "Those folks planned well. It looks like they have a similar setup to ours. I know that area, Chimney Rock Road. It's beautiful country but there's no easy way to get there. Y'all are going to have to go through part of Hendersonville and you said those troopers told you they had some zombie activity there."

Chuck nodded and stared at the Google satellite page. The map didn't provide street numbers but comparing it with the hand drawn map that Tommy Mitchell had left him seemed to point to a house that was two hundred yards off the road, with a winding driveway, nestled behind some trees.

McCain sensed that this wasn't going to be an easy travel day. He briefly considered asking Beth to stay with the Fosters but knew that she'd never go for it. A knot of fear formed in the big man's stomach and he took a deep breath, saying a silent prayer for protection for his wife and for himself. A Bible verse from deep in his subconscious made it's way to the surface. "Don't worry about anything, but pray about everything."

Chuck checked their equipment and made sure his wife got everything on correctly. Even though he had been working with her and training her, she still wasn't used to wearing body armor and weapons. McCain had also asked her to wear several layers of clothing, not just for warmth, but to protect her in the possibility of a zombie attack.

All the CDC agents had been issued protective, kevlar-lined pants, jackets, and gloves. The kevlar wasn't very thick but it had kept McCain from getting infected on two different occasions. Since

Beth was not so equipped, he made sure she was layered enough so that a hungry Z's teeth wouldn't reach her flesh.

At 1030 hours, it was time to say their goodbyes. McCain pulled his worn New Testament from the backpack and handed it to Diya.

"Oh, Mr. Chuck, this is a very special gift. Thank you so much." She started crying as she tried to wrap her small arms around him.

"You're welcome. Remember what Beth and I told you. God has a special purpose for your life and he loves you very much. Pray and ask him to speak to you as you read that New Testament. I'll be interested to hear what you've learned when I see you the next time."

Kim and Elizabeth embraced as Chuck and Jack shook hands. "Y'all are always welcome here," Mrs. Foster said. "Thank you for coming by to give us the update on Karen. And thank you for bringing Diya. We're going to have a lot of fun together."

Jack Foster rode down to the gate in the armored Toyota Tundra. "I expect y'all will stop by again sometime," Foster called as he closed the gate.

Beth and Chuck waved as they started for what they hoped was the last leg of their journey to find Melanie.

Jack was right about the route he had recommended for the first part of the trip. The rural, two-lane road was empty and the scenery was beautiful.

"They were sweet people," Beth commented. "I'm really glad we did that. Thank you for stopping."

"Yeah, good folks. It worked out well with that storm coming through just as we got there. I know we met in a blizzard but I think I prefer the Foster's warm house to that cold one where we spent three nights. That was a pretty cozy bed, as well."

Beth laughed. "No argument from me, although I didn't get quite as much sleep as I would've preferred. Some big man couldn't keep his hands off of me."

"Get used to that," Chuck smiled.

"Did you really mean it about wanting to have a baby one day?" Elizabeth looked up at him in the rear view mirror.

Chuck saw the uncertainty in her eyes. "Of course," he answered reassuringly. "You'll be an incredible mom. It might be a little weird for Melanie to have a sibling who is twenty-something years younger than her but she really loves kids and it'll all work out."

Beth smiled contentedly. She didn't know what she'd expected when she had broached the subject of children with her husband. She had hesitated to even bring it up, expecting to hear him say 'no.' He already had a daughter, after all, and he was forty-four years old. Chuck was constantly surprising her, she realized.

Elizabeth braked the Toyota Tundra to a stop as they both scanned the area. Just ahead of them, as Jack Foster had said, they merged onto Highway 25. A few miles up the road, Highway 25 would connect them with I-26. Ten miles north from where they currently sat was their exit, Chimney Rock Road. After getting off the interstate and turning right, it was a straight shot to Melanie and her host family, the Mitchells, just another eight miles down the road. Eighteen miles, McCain thought. Only eighteen more miles to my daughter.

They hadn't seen any infected yet, but they could see abandoned vehicles dotting the highway up ahead. That usually meant that Zs were close by. A tractor trailer lay on it's side in their lane several hundred yards in front of them. That doesn't look good, McCain thought.

Chuck had Beth place her Glock under her right leg where she could reach it quickly. Her AR-15 was muzzle down, laying on the passenger seat. McCain was wearing his M4 but he also had his pistol out, under his left leg for easy access.

"Let me climb up in the back of the truck and take look," Chuck said, grabbing his binoculars out of his pack.

From the bed of the pickup, he had a little better view and what he could see through the binos didn't make him feel much better. The southbound lanes didn't appear to contain as many vehicles. Not many people would have headed south if that was where the biggest problem areas were, he thought.

He saw movement around two of the abandoned cars that had been going south. Maybe a half-mile up, two groups of Zs were milling around a Ford pickup and a Honda accord. Chuck didn't see any infected on their side of the highway, northbound, but he couldn't see around the overturned eighteen-wheeler, either. There were a few abandoned vehicles between them and big rig, but the area looked relatively clear.

Even though the tractor-trailer was almost completely lengthwise in the road, there appeared to be just enough room to get by on the right shoulder, between the rear of the trailer and the metal guardrail. He scanned the southbound side again and counted the zombies. Twenty-three that he could see in the two packs. That's not too many, he thought, unless they managed to get their hands on you.

"Well?" Beth asked as he got back into the vehicle.

Chuck told her what he had seen. They had talked about various contingencies, but there was no way to really prepare for large groups of attacking zombies who wanted to rip you apart and eat you.

"Same drill," McCain said. "The only thing different is that I want you to put your windows up and just focus on driving. And don't forget: I love you."

Elizabeth gave a slight smile and nodded, Chuck noticing the fear in her eyes. He watched her take a deep breath, push the button to raise her windows, and start the Tundra rolling forward. She drove around assorted abandoned vehicles as they started north.

When they passed a white Plymouth Voyager, they saw that the side and the driver's doors were open, the bloody remains of several bodies scattered on the asphalt. Beth had to maneuver around the collision of a black Ford Mustang and a gray Mercedes. The Mustang appeared empty but a decaying zombie was still seat-belted in the driver's seat of the Mercedes. What had been a middle-aged businessman reached for the armored pickup as it drove past, his mouth moving.

When they got to the wrecked eighteen-wheeler, Chuck realized that the space for getting by it was much narrower than he had thought. He wasn't sure that they would fit and quickly glanced around. The zombies from the southbound lanes were shuffling towards them, ten of the creatures now on their side of the road, fifty yards behind the Tundra.

"Can we get through there?" Elizabeth wondered, slowing to a stop.

"I think so. Let's keep moving," he answered, watching the Zs getting closer, their growling sending a chill down his spine.

Beth steered the Tundra to the right, still uncertain if it would fit through the small opening. She heard the creatures and saw them through her mirror. As the front end of the pickup cleared the rear of the trailer, a big body suddenly slammed into the left side of the Tundra's engine compartment. It had come from the blind side of the tractor-trailer. Beth screamed but she could only see the head of a large, snarling, black male zombie. One of his eye sockets was just a bloody hole, adding to his ghastly appearance.

Another figure, maybe a Hispanic female wearing a flower-pattern dress ran into the front end of their truck, reaching over the hood towards Elizabeth, her mouth working, a sound like a rabid dog's growling coming from her throat. Beth shoved the accelerator to the floor, the Tundra lurching forward a few feet and then stopped, the sound of metal-on-metal coming from both their left and right.

The passenger side of the Tundra scraped against the metal guardrail, while the driver's side was wedged against the rear of the long trailer. The engine roared as Elizabeth worked the gas pedal, to no avail. They were stuck.

"What do we do?" she asked, a hint of panic in her voice.

The sound of Chuck's rifle startled her as he picked off the closest threats through the open rear window. After dropping six of the Zs, he calmly said, "Turn the steering wheel to the right and give it some gas. Then steer back to the left. I think you can wiggle through."

The two zombies in front of them continued to throw their bodies at the truck. Beth turned the steering wheel clockwise and pressed the accelerator. They started moving forward again, inch-by-inch, continuing to scrape both sides of the armor plating mounted on each side.

McCain continued shooting zombies, their bodies piling up in the middle of the highway. He scanned the area as he reloaded with a full magazine and saw that the second group had been joined by more of their friends. At least thirty more infected were heading their way. He felt the truck slowly starting to come unstuck.

"That's it," he encouraged his wife. "Just a little more."

The Tundra was now far enough forward that Elizabeth could see the big male zombie. He was wearing a light blue shirt with a trucking company's name on the left breast and "Ralph" embroidered on the right. Sorry, Ralph, Beth thought, as the pickup finally jumped free, the side mirror being torn off in the process.

The zombie woman on the front of the truck had just gotten a knee on the bumper and was trying to climb onto the hood. As the vehicle surged forward, however, she lost her balance and fell to the road, the Tundra's tires bouncing over her. Ralph reached for Beth, her closed windows preventing him a handhold, but he did manage to grab the side of Chuck's open window. A 9mm hollow point to the forehead from a distance of two feet sent Ralph spinning to the asphalt.

After getting past the overturned truck, Beth and Chuck could see what was in front of them. Car wrecks and abandoned vehicles continued to litter the interstate. Several groups of five or more infected were coming towards them, drawn to the noise. The good news was that the even though they would have to dodge Zs and abandoned vehicles, the roadway ahead wasn't completely blocked.

"Piece of cake," Chuck said. "These are small groups and they all look like slow-movers."

The pickup started moving again. They were able to avoid the majority of the zombies but the heavy bumper on the pickup took out four in the first mile. Elizabeth continued to steer around both Zs and crashed automobiles. After two miles, the highway in front of them was clear of vehicles and infected.

McCain consulted the satellite maps. "Okay, there's a big interchange up ahead, maybe three more miles. After that, it's only another four miles to Chimney Rock Road where Melanie's at. We're almost there," he said, allowing himself a relieved smile.


**Centers for Disease Control Compound, East of Atlanta, Saturday, 1100 hours**

The sound of rotor blades got everyone's attention and a Blackhawk with no markings was suddenly circling the CDC compound. Eddie and the others watched, seeing a crewman manning a minigun mounted on the door. Several other figures were visible inside the aircraft, peering down at the research site.

After circling the area for five minutes, confirming that the landing zone was clear, the helicopter set down on the driveway, outside the front gate. By this time, every occupant at the CDC compound had gathered outdoors to see what was going on. Besides the National Guard the previous day, it had been months since they'd had visitors, and the unannounced appearance of a helicopter aroused everyone's curiosity.

Dr. Martin had sworn the CDC agents to secrecy about the arrival of Dr. Kim Bae-yong. He hadn't wanted to get his staff's hopes up about the arrival of his friend and colleague without knowing for sure that the CIA was going to be able to deliver her. As the aircraft sat down twenty-five yards away, Andy nodded at Marcel and he opened the gate.

"Jimmy, you and Hollywood hang back and cover me and Andy," Marshall ordered. "Just in case."

By the time Eddie and Andy reached the helicopter, four heavily armed figures had quickly disembarked, scanning the area. An Asian woman then stepped to the ground, assisted by a clean-cut young man in black BDUs wearing a holstered pistol. The new arrivals ducked their heads and approached Fleming and Marshall. Eddie immediately recognized Walker, Trang, and the other two CDC agents from the Washington office.

As soon as they were clear of the rotors, the engines on the helicopter roared and it lifted off, flying west. The young man in BDUs stuck out a hand.

"Agents Marshall and Fleming," he nodded. "I'm Shaun Taylor. I work directly for Admiral Williams, the Director of Operations for the CIA."

Taylor had never met the two Atlanta agents but Williams had required him to study their pictures so that he could recognize them on sight.

"We'll talk more later," Taylor continued, "but Admiral

Williams asked me to convey his compliments and to thank you for the incredible work you and your men have accomplished. I'd like to present Dr. Bae-yong."

The Asian woman smiled and nodded at Eddie and Andy.

"Let's get into the compound," Trang urged.

Shaun let the CDC officers escort them all inside. Dr. Martin and his wife, Eleanor, were waiting at the guard shack. When Kim Bae-yong saw her friends, she started crying and fell into Mrs. Martin's arms. Charles led the two women inside the structure that had been converted into a dormitory.

Eddie introduced Shaun and the four Washington, D.C., officers to Andy, Darrell and Marcel. Marshall, Jones, and Estrada had all worked with the Washington agents in tracking down and apprehending Terrell Hill, the terrorist who had infected pizza slices with the zombie virus at a concession stand inside Stanford Stadium on the University of Georgia campus.

With introductions made and with Dr. Bae-yong being taken care of Shaun leaned in and spoke to Eddie. "Is there someplace we can talk? We've got a lot of things to discuss."

Marshall did not have a lot of experience in dealing with the CIA. As far as he knew, he had exactly none. That's not quite true, he thought. He just had not known that he was working for them until Chuck had required that he and Andy sign a confidentiality waiver a few months back.

McCain had informed the two team leaders that the CDC Enforcement Unit was a legitimate federal law enforcement agency but that it was funded and supported by the CIA. The reason for this was so that the Agency could continue to lead the fight against the terrorists who wanted to spread the bio-terror virus.

"Sure, Mr. Taylor. We'll take you to our new headquarters," Eddie replied with a smile.

Nicole Edwards had come outside with everyone else to see what was happening. When she saw the big men in black tactical clothing get off the helicopter, hope sprung up in her heart again. Maybe he's with them, she thought.

As the armed men filed inside, however, she realized that McCain wasn't with them. Dr. Edwards did, however, recognize Dr. Bae-yong. The two were friends, having worked together, off and on, for over five years. Having her onsite was the best news that Nicole had had in a long time.

Edwards watch the CDC agents huddle up beside the guard shack listening to another man who was only wearing a pistol. After a few minutes, Agent Marshall led them towards the main building where the enforcement unit's small office space was located. As they walked by, all the officers nodded politely at her.

One of the new arrivals, though, was obviously checking her out, she realized. He appeared a touch shorter than Nicole, but was powerfully built with piercing blue eyes. He ran a hand through his short-cropped, light-brown hair as he walked by, his eyes never leaving hers, an engaging smile on his face.

"Hello, ma'am. How are you?"

Nicole managed to nod and say, "I'm fine, thanks for asking."

And then they were gone, Eddie leading the other seven agents inside. Dr. Edwards stuffed her hands into the front two pockets of her lab coat and stared off into the distance. It was clear that something was going on, considering all the visitors who had been showing up lately. Maybe things would soon start getting back to normal.

**South of Hendersonville, North Carolina, Saturday, 1110 hours**

Highway 25 had merged with Interstate 26 and the last few miles had not provided any problems. Beth had kept their speed at around fifty miles an hour unless she had to maneuver around an abandoned vehicle or a group of infected. As Chuck had pointed out, a large interchange loomed just a mile ahead. The exit signs identified it as Upward Road. Other highway signs indicated that the exit was packed with restaurants, gas stations, convenience stores, hotels, and even an RV resort park. All were now perfect breeding grounds for zombies.

Once we clear this big exit, the next one is less than four miles away, Chuck thought. We get off there, take a right and the Mitchell's farm and Melanie will be less than ten miles up on the left. Of course, he had no idea what he'd find there, that uncertainty haunting the big man. Tommy Mitchell's note said that was where they were going but it was also obvious that the Zs had swept through this area, with many still lingering behind.

McCain felt the Tundra slowing. Elizabeth pointed at a major roadblock, a half-mile ahead of them.

"Stop and let me check it with the binoculars," Chuck said.

"Okay, but it looks like the entire interstate is blocked," the driver observed, bringing the pickup to a stop in the middle lane.

His wife was right. A barricade composed of police cars and large Department of Transportation dump trucks were stretched across both the north and southbound lanes of I-26. The roadblock was set up about five hundred yards south of the Upward Road exit. Figures were moving slowly back and forth on the bridge, but the distance was too great to confirm that they were zombies. What else could they be? McCain pondered.

The federal police officer stood in the bed of the pickup, moving the binoculars slowly over the barricade, not seeing any way to get around the vehicles. This stretch of highway had been constructed for safety, with metal guardrails on both the shoulders and the median, preventing anyone from driving across it. Two pickups and six passenger cars were scattered in front of the barricade. It was hard to tell at this distance but he thought that he could see bullet holes in some of the windshields.

The roadblock looked formidable, he realized, continuing to stare through the binos. There! He could see a small opening on the left side, next to the median. A police car sat twenty feet behind the barrier, the driver's door standing open and a body, or what was left of one, lying on the pavement beside the vehicle. It looked to McCain like the officer had been filling a spot in the roadblock but had tried to make a run for it. He didn't get very far before the zombies managed to grab and devour him. I wish I could see behind that row of vehicles, Chuck thought. There's no telling what might be waiting back there.

"There's an opening on the far left, next to the center guardrail," he told her, climbing into the backseat. "Looks like a police officer tried to escape but didn't make it. I can't see anything behind the barricade but there's plenty of movement up on that bridge. As soon as we get through the roadblock, punch it and let's get on down the road."

Elizabeth took a deep, cleansing breath and nodded, putting the truck into drive and giving it some gas. As they got closer to the long line of vehicles, Chuck realized that there was plenty of room for them to get past it. Beth steered to the left, maneuvering around a red Dodge Ram that straddled two lanes, just twenty feet from the barrier. The front of the Ram had been shot up, the windshield shattered, and McCain saw a figure slumped behind the steering wheel.

Beth aimed their truck for the opening in the roadblock, both of the Tundra's two left tires now on the small grassy strip next to the iron guardrail. The police car had been parked next to a yellow DOT dump truck.

Suddenly, a loud hissing erupted from outside, causing Chuck to swing his rifle to the driver's side. The pickup truck shifted and quickly became sluggish.

"What happened?" Beth asked, feeling the truck pulling to the left.

McCain glanced out his open window to the ground and shook his head in disbelief.

"Spike strips. The police put them out to puncture bad guy's tires. They were in the grass and now we've got two flats."

Another sound quickly overshadowed the hissing. The growling of hungry zombies was getting closer and louder. McCain scanned the area but didn't see anything. They have to be on the opposite side of the roadblock, he realized.

"Back up!" he told Elizabeth. "Those Zs are on the other side."

Beth immediately slammed on the brakes, shoved the gearshift lever into reverse, and accelerated. Just as the Tundra started reversing with two flat tires, twenty zombies burst through the hole that they had been about to drive through. A crash jolted both of them as the Toyota slammed into the shot-up Dodge pickup, Beth looking at the oncoming zombies and not watching behind them as she reversed. McCain was thrown into the back of the driver's seat, his backpack knocked onto the floorboard by the impact. He quickly recovered, though, knowing that the menacing figures were marching straight for them.

"Sorry!" Elizabeth said, pulling up slightly and quickly steering wheel to the left so she could get around the other big pickup and put some distance between them and the zombies.

Chuck was already firing on full-auto out the window towards the advancing group. These were so close and moving faster than any he had seen in a while. Normally he would engage in the "Semi-Auto" mode on his rifle. Not now. He needed to take control and fast. He slowly swept the muzzle at head height and fired short bursts, taking down several zombies at a time.

Beth continued backing for another fifty feet before jerking the steering wheel counter-clockwise so she could turn them around and go the other way. A metal-on-metal crunching sound let them know that she had backed into the guardrail. Elizabeth turned back to the right and accelerated. Nothing happened. The fender covering the flat rear tire was hung up on the metal barrier, holding them in place, the tires spinning but not taking them anywhere.

"We're stuck!" Beth yelled, seeing the bloody figures surging towards what they hoped would be an easy meal. "What do we do?"

McCain's accurate fire had taken down sixteen of the tightly packed group before his rifle ran dry. He pushed the door open and exited the pickup, grabbing his pistol.

"Out!" he ordered. "Grab your weapons and your backpack and let's go." He pointed to their right.

He took down the remaining five Zs, only firing seven shots from the Glock. More zombies rushed through the opening in the barricade, drawn to the gunshots. Elizabeth threw on her equipment as Chuck reloaded his rifle and continued dropping the approaching flesh-eaters.

The big man glanced back into the Tundra. His backpack containing extra ammo, food, and water was in the floorboard on the far side. The zombies were just thirty feet away, though, their snarling intensifying as they got closer. He put the pack out of his mind, knowing that their immediate survival was the most important thing.

"Run!" McCain told his wife, pointing to the right.

Elizabeth started sprinting while Chuck paused to give her a head start, firing a long burst into the snarling group before running after her. There were still at least thirty infected following them, most of these shuffling slowly. That's good, McCain thought. He figured that most of the Zs on the interstate had come from the many abandoned vehicles, but now he could also clearly see agitated zombies on the bridge in front of them. Some of their pursuers had probably been up there and had made their way down to the highway, attacking motorists who were trying to escape or the police who had been manning the roadblock. *Now if we can just find another vehicle.*

The police officer paused for a moment, halfway across the interstate, and made a headshot on a muscular zombie who looked like he had just worked out, his muscles bulging under his black tank top and shorts. *He looks and moves like he just got infected,* the CDC agent noted surprisingly. Both arms showed open wounds, and his face was covered with blood. Muscles was just fifteen feet away when a 5.56mm round punched through his left eye and pitching him face-first onto the asphalt.

Chuck started sprinting again, trying to catch up with Elizabeth. She was a real runner, having participated in several half-marathons. The CDC officer pushed himself, glancing over his shoulder as the Zs continued after their prey. Even as a part-time professional MMA fighter, the big man had hated to run in training. At this moment, though, he was wishing that he'd put in a few more miles.

Beth had already climbed over the guardrail and turned to check on him. McCain saw her watching him sprint, her eyes wide with fear, as the large group of infected closed in on the couple. He motioned for her to keep going. Instead, she raised her rifle and started shooting their pursuers, dropping four before he joined her.

Chuck jumped the metal barrier and spun around, raising his M4. He pushed the selector to semi-auto and took down five of the closest creatures before the bolt locked open. He hit the magazine release, dropping the empty and grabbing a fresh one from his plate carrier. His gun was ready to go again but they needed to keep moving and create some distance. There were still at least fifteen zombies closing on them.

Elizabeth fired three more shots, her last bullet sending a heavyset man wearing a jogging suit crashing to the pavement.

Chuck tapped her on the shoulder.

"Let's go," he said, pointing in the direction of Upward Road. "Climb that fence and head towards the main road."

A three-foot high, chain-link fence ran along the top of a small rise, ten yards off the highway, adjacent to their location. On the opposite side, a narrow street ran parallel to the interstate and appeared to dead-end into Upward Road. Chuck sent Elizabeth ahead while he turned to check on the Zs, dropping two that had closed to within fifteen yards. The growls and snarls that filled the air sent a chill down the police officer's spine.

By the time he joined Beth, she had managed to get over the fence. Chuck climbed the obstacle and paused, glancing back at their pursuers. The Zs had been slowed at the guardrail, unable to climb over it. The first few bounced off, while their zombie comrades kept pushing forward, knocking several over the barrier. After these managed to get to their feet, they continued up the hill, towards the fence. Additional Zs had stumbled down the exit ramps from Upward Road, following the sound of the gunshots and growls, moving towards the smell of living flesh.

Elizabeth and Chuck ran up the access road, scanning the area for any new threats. For the moment, they appeared to be in the clear except for those who were behind them. Ahead of them was a Dunkin Donuts and a convenience store, sitting side-by-side on their left at the corner facing out towards Upward Road.

McCain glanced back and saw that the fence had stopped their pursuers for the time being, at least.

"We can slow down," he said, breathing heavily. "It'll be a few before they get over that fence."

Beth turned, seeing what he was talking about and stopped, letting Chuck catch his breath. Most of the new zombies on the interstate were now over the guardrail and were shoving up against the fence or were climbing the small ridge towards it. The way in front of Beth and Chuck appeared clear, but they could only see the rear of the two businesses ahead of them.

McCain looked into his wife's eyes and was pleased with what he saw. She was scared but not panicking.

"What's the plan?" she asked.

"We need to put plenty of distance between us and the ones behind us. They'll eventually get over or through that fence. They'll jam enough bodies against it until it collapses. We need to be long gone by then. Let's get across the main road up there and see if we can find a place to hole up so I can look at our maps. We can get to Mel cross-country but it would be better if we could find some more transport. Go ahead and reload."

Elizabeth removed the partial magazine from her rifle and inserted a full one. It wasn't smooth but she got it done and was becoming more fluid. This time, because an attack could come from any direction, McCain had Beth walking fifteen feet behind him, covering the area to their right.

The Dunkin Donuts was just twenty-five yards ahead now. Everything had gotten quiet again except for the growling coming from behind them. Chuck's rifle was locked into his shoulder, the muzzle slightly lowered so he could see over it. He moved slowly but steadily, stepping, listening, and smelling. A slight breeze brought the odor of death to their nostrils. McCain glanced back, confirming that Beth was covering her sector, just like he had trained her. Her AR-15 was up and ready and she was moving with confidence.

A driveway ran behind the doughnut store for the drive-thru window, the business now just in front of them. Hopefully, they could scoot by, cross Upward Road, and then find a place to pause and study their maps. An entrance was on their side of the building, just up from the drive-thru. Chuck knew that there would also be a front door.

McCain motioned for Beth to stop and walked over. "Let's swing out into that field to your right instead of passing so close to the DD."

When he stepped onto the shoulder of the access road, however, he encountered a steep embankment with a three-foot wide drainage ditch full of stagnant, smelly water. That way was a no-go. They couldn't afford to get wet, not knowing how long it might be before they could get dried off.

"Never mind," he said, shaking his head. "I've got point but let's take it slow."

Beth nodded, keeping five yards between herself and Chuck, just as he had shown her.

A loud slamming sound startled both of them as two infected Indian men and an infected Indian woman, all wearing Dunkin Donuts uniforms, burst out the side door. They rushed towards the couple, just thirty feet away, growling and snapping their teeth together. The lead zombie's throat and face were ripped open, blood covering him. The second man's right arm was missing at the elbow. Behind them was a tiny woman who rushed past her two zombie friends, sprinting at their victims. She had no visible wounds but her face was covered with gore.

A hole appeared in her forehead as McCain fired and she dropped to the ground. The other two Zs never slowed down as they continued past her. Chuck's second shot caught the lead male under the nose, punching into his brain. Elizabeth's AR-15 roared and the third zombie joined his friends on the pavement, her bullet striking him above the right eye.

McCain knew that their shooting would only bring out more of the creatures.

"Come on!" he urged, and started running.

As they passed by the doughnut store, movement caught his eye and he saw what he'd been dreading. Fifteen growling Zs had congregated under the awning of the convenience store's gas pumps. Several abandoned vehicles were parked next to the gasoline dispensers, their drivers already dead and consumed or dead and infected, looking for fresh flesh.

I bet we could find a car with the keys in it and keep going, he thought, but quickly dismissed the idea, seeing how many zombies were shuffling towards the couple. Behind that group, the news got worse as Chuck saw thirty or forty more coming from the direction of the bridge over I-26, just a few hundred feet away. Directly across the street from their location stood a Waffle House and a Zaxby's restaurant. To the right of the Waffle House was a patch of woods.

McCain quickly swung his rifle, tracking what had probably been a young woman in her mid-twenties. Her dark hair was tied back in a ponytail and her white tennis outfit was coated with blood and gore. She hadn't made any noise as she sprinted towards them. The tennis player zombie was focused on Beth and rapidly closing the distance.

Chuck fired twice, missing with the first, his second shot penetrating the infected woman's temple, dropping her at Elizabeth's feet. Chuck's wife screamed involuntarily and jumped backwards. If he had missed, that thing would have gotten me, Beth realized, shaking.

"Run for those woods across the street. I'm right behind you," he said, raising his rifle and shooting the closest fast-movers.

McCain was back to firing short bursts in full-auto mode, trying to thin the group out. Their problems just got worse, he saw, glancing down the access road. The pack of maybe forty or fifty infected had kept pushing and shoving against the chain-link barrier until a section collapsed. Those zombies were hungry, too, and surging up the hill after him. They weren't surrounded yet, he thought, but it was getting close.

It was the strangest set of sensations Elizabeth had ever felt, she realized, as she sprinted across the five-lane road. On the one hand, she was terrified. Just a minute earlier, she had almost become a meal for a hungry flesh-eater. Thank God, her husband could really shoot! She was definitely scared, but on the other hand, the rush of adrenaline flowing through her system was like nothing that she'd ever experienced before. The fear was present, but the skills Chuck had drilled into her were helping to suppress it so that she could function effectively.

Behind her, Chuck's rifle began working again and she glanced over her shoulder to see zombie after zombie fall under his withering fire as he shot while moving backwards, towards her. The main group was close to him, less than fifteen yards away now, their growling, snarling, and clicking teeth becoming louder the closer they got to their prey. She turned her attention back to where she was going, running towards the woods.

Six infected suddenly rounded the corner of the Waffle House, moving to intercept the young woman. They snarled loudly as they closed in on what they perceived to be an easy meal. Out of her peripheral vision, Beth saw the door of the Zaxby's fly open, discharging at least a dozen more zombies drawn to the gunfire and the growls of their friends. The chicken restaurant was fifty yards to the left of the Waffle House so Elizabeth knew that she had to deal with the Zs directly in front of her first.

An older, gray-haired woman in a Waffle House uniform, complete with a brown apron, led the closest group. Her hair was done up in a bun, a ballpoint pen sticking out of it for quick access, her glasses hanging from a chain around her neck. The waitress's left ear was missing, while her left arm and neck sported vicious open wounds.

Beth quickly did the calculations. She knew that she could probably make the wood-line before these got to her but it would be cutting it too close and, worse, they would be between she and Chuck. She made up her mind to take her stand on the far side of the road, the Zs shuffling toward her through the parking lot just thirty feet away. Her rifle came up and she fired. The first shot whizzed past the waitress, but the second 5.56mm round hit her in the middle of the forehead, the ballpoint pen flying out from the impact.

Elizabeth kept shooting, missing a few shots in her haste, but killing the other five Waffle House customers-turned-zombies. She turned back towards her husband, watching him break contact with the zombies on the other side of the street, and conduct another reload while sprinting towards her. Beth climbed the slight embankment and paused at the tree line. She guessed there were still over fifty infected in their general area.

A quick glance back towards the bridge caused her to gasp in shock and surprise. A surging mass of bodies was on the overpass, coming towards them from the other side of I-26. These had been drawn to all the shooting, she supposed. There are hundreds of them! the young woman thought, the sounds of their snarls getting louder by the second.

**Centers for Disease Control Compound, East of Atlanta, Saturday, 1120 hours**

The CDC agents, along with Shaun Taylor, crowded around the small table in the enforcement unit's office. After the officers had stood their weapons against the wall and removed their body armor, Shaun got right to business.

"Gentleman, Admiral Williams asked me to give you a preliminary briefing on an upcoming mission so that you could get some ideas flowing. His plan is to be here later today or tomorrow to get the ball rolling. For those of you who don't know, Admiral Williams is the Director of Operations for the CIA and has been tasked with dealing with the situation that I'm about to brief you on."

Taylor described the Tijuana Cartel's invasion of Atlanta and the need to mount an operation to eliminate the cartel soldiers, secure the gang's supply of the zombie virus, and rescue the hostages. At first, the CIA agent merely reiterated much of what Lieutenant Colonel Clark had told them the day before.

After Clark had passed the intelligence on to Admiral Williams a few days earlier, however, Williams had ordered around the clock drone surveillance of the area since Wednesday night. Things were still not functioning normally and the coverage had not been perfect but the analysts at the CIA now had a pretty good idea of what they were dealing with.

"The initial findings," Taylor continued, "are that the cartel has captured and secured the entire intersection of Peachtree and Piedmont Roads and much of the surrounding area, at least a four or five block radius. I'm not from Atlanta but just looking at the maps, it's clear that these gangsters have established a strong foothold and are continuing to push outward."

"What's the estimate on the number of cartel soldiers?" Hollywood asked.

The CIA agent glanced at his notes. "As best the analysts can estimate, close to two hundred. At this point, she didn't feel comfortable narrowing it down any more than that. The chief analyst did tell me this, though. They're not all Mexican. There appear to be quite a few African-Americans, or possibly very dark Latinos."

Jimmy nodded. "I just had a run-in with some BMF members out near Athens. That's Black Mafia Family. They were wearing National Guard uniforms and started shooting at us. The police officer that I was with got hit. She's OK now, but after we killed the thugs, I saw BMF tats on two of the bodies.

"It makes sense to me that any of the surviving gangs in the city would join forces with the biggest dogs on the block. Right now, those are the Mexicans. It wouldn't surprise me if more than just the black gangs are hooking up with the cartel."

"Like who?" Shaun asked.

"The ATL is full of some really bad Latino and Asian gangs. MS-13 has had a big presence here for years. They're predominantly from El Salvador and them and the Mexicans hate each other but I bet they could figure out a way to work together if the prize was the entire city of Atlanta. The Asians, I don't know. They don't really work and play well with others."

"What else, Shaun?" Andy queried. "What have the drones picked up about weapons, sentries, and where everyone is being housed?"

Taylor nodded. "The admiral will be bringing maps and diagrams. The good news is that it looks like the cartel took over a luxury high rise building on Piedmont just off of Peachtree. At this point, everybody seems to be living under one roof. They run regular motorized patrols and there are always sentries patrolling the outside of their HQ."

Jay Walker glanced around the room and chuckled. "That brings up an interesting point, Shaun. We are eight of the baddest asses on the planet," he said, nodding at the other CDC agents, "and I'm sure you're somewhere in that mix yourself. Now I'll admit I was never very good at math, but I believe that that only gives us a whopping total of nine to go up against a minimum of two hundred cartel soldiers?"

Shaun smiled. "There will be quite a few more people joining us. One of the reasons that the admiral has been delayed in getting down here is that he's currently gathering resources. Human resources. I think you'll all be very pleased with the team he's putting together. Like I said at the beginning, we just want you to start thinking about strategies and options. When the boss gets here, we'll all go into full planning mode."

McCain rushed across the street, zombies pursuing closely. Beth had taken out the group from the Waffle House and now the way was clear for them to get into the cover of the woods. He knew by experience that the infected did not move as well on uneven ground, where both trees and thick undergrowth formed natural obstacles. Chuck knew that the Zs would continue to chase them. The forest, however, would allow the couple to create some distance. He hoped.

The CDC officer saw his wife pause at the edge of the tree line and survey their situation, her rifle at a low ready. Her eyes widened when she looked back towards the interstate. He quickly joined her at the top of the ridge, only to see the hundreds of infected stumbling across the bridge, coming after them.

McCain blew out a big breath. "It's gonna be OK," he said, sounding like he was trying to convince himself of that fact. "Get going and I'll catch up to you."

Three running zombies were inside twenty yards, having just sprinted from Zaxby's; a young, African-American woman in business attire and two chunky, thirty-something white guys wearing light blue work shirts. I wonder if they finished their lunch, McCain thought, putting a shot into each of the men's heads and then the young woman's.

As Chuck ducked into the woods, he instinctively touched his rifle mag pouch mounted on the front of his plate-carrier. Only two left, he realized, the full-auto fire causing him go through ammo at a blistering pace. It's going to be a long day.

Elizabeth was not an outdoors person. She hated bugs, snakes, and pretty much everything that could be found in a forest. Part of the training that Chuck had put her through, thankfully, involved situations exactly like this.

"Why do we have to train in the forest?" she had grumbled, as he had her working on her field craft in the thick woods surrounding the Northeast Georgia Technical College just a couple of weeks earlier.

"We've got to be ready for any contingency," he patiently told her. "It's just going to be the two of us. We might have to abandon our vehicle and a thick forest is a great place for us to hide, but tough for Zs to maneuver through."

The idea of abandoning their truck had not even occurred to her. Fortunately for her, it had occurred to Chuck, she thought, as she ran through the thick undergrowth, still unnerved at the sound of so many growling zombies behind her. She had no idea where she was supposed to go, hoping that she wasn't lost and that her husband would be able to find her. The idea of being separated from him in the thick forest almost sent her into a panic attack.

After sprinting hard for a few minutes, Beth stopped, weapon at the ready, scanning the area around her like Chuck had taught her. The sound of someone running in her direction startled her and she instinctively moved behind a large pine tree for cover, raising her rifle to eye level.

McCain broke into view running hard thirty feet to her left. Elizabeth stepped out from behind the tree and waved, not wanting to yell, for fear of alerting any nearby Zs. Chuck saw her and hurried over, panting. Concern was etched across his face.

"Where do we go now?" Beth asked quietly, a tremor in her voice.

"Let's keep moving," he whispered. "They aren't far behind me. Let's keep running in a straight line for a while and then we'll make a sharp turn, one way or the other, and try to lose them. You've got point, I'm right behind you."

The sound of branches cracking and teeth snapping together reached them simultaneously. These zombies were making good time through the forest, McCain realized, shaking his head.

"Go!" he mouthed, turning to face the Zs closing in on them.

Beth started running deeper into the forest, fear gripping her insides. Several shots rang out from Chuck's rifle causing Elizabeth to run even faster. After several minutes of sprinting, she slowed her stride and began walking, staring at every shadow, waiting for something to jump out at her. The heavy brush, the overhanging trees blocking the light, intensified her terror, not knowing where the next zombie might be hiding. Something moved behind her and she spun around, her finger on the trigger of her rifle. Chuck had caught up, momentary relief sweeping over her.

Almost as soon as Beth had sprinted away, several Zs appeared, coming straight for him. These were recently infected and quick. He didn't want to shoot for fear of giving away their position, providing the zombies a noise to key in on. These were much too close, however, and his Colt came up. Chuck pulled the trigger seven times, dropping six Zs. He didn't wait for any more of their friends, rushing to join Beth.

McCain normally liked to keep ten or fifteen yards between team members on a patrol. When he caught up with Elizabeth, however, he could see that she was nearing her breaking point. She hadn't spent enough time in the woods to understand that the forest could be her friend. The relief was evident on her face when she realized that he was staying close to her while they kept pushing forward through the undergrowth.

The Zs were still pursuing them but the terrain was finally slowing them down. Chuck also hoped that the many smells of the wild would confuse their nostrils. The virus intensified the infected's sense of smell, but hopefully, they would all be dealing with sensory overload.

After a few hundred yards the woods started opening up, the brush not nearly as thick, letting them know they were coming to civilization once again. A long building loomed ahead, visible through the thinning trees. They cautiously approached the edge of the forest, knowing they didn't have long to linger, the growls behind them slowly getting closer.

"It looks like a hotel," Elizabeth whispered.

The U-shaped parking lot in front of them wrapped around the two-story building and was half-full of vehicles. Beth and Chuck were on one end of the long structure. The sign in the parking lot identified it as the "Biltmore Lodge."

Two hundred yards to their left, another building, this one a single-story, sat facing them. A sign on top of that facility identified it as the "Smokey Mountain Inn." A group of figures stood motionless near the front entrance next to a large bus parked directly in front of the inn.

"Yeah, it does," Chuck agreed, raising his rifle and scoping the area with his optics. "'Smokey Mountain Tours' is what's written on the bus and all those Zs are senior citizens. They just went out for a day of sightseeing and ended up as zombies."

The presence of the infected, both in front and behind them, limited their options. McCain had felt a flicker of hope when he'd seen all the cars in the parking lot, thinking they could grab one and keep going. That idea was out with Zs almost surrounding them. The other option would take them to their right, behind the big lodge in front of them. That way was safer, allowing them to use the woods for concealment. The sounds of the pursuers from their rear let them know it was time to move.

"Let's circle around the lodge, using the woods for cover. Maybe there's a car on the far side that we can take. I'll go first," the CDC officer said, softly. "Stay close."

Elizabeth took him literally, staying much closer to Chuck than she was supposed to be. He had trained her to maintain a safe distance between them so that they could protect each other and wouldn't both be targets at the same time. At this point, though, she didn't care. She wasn't letting him out of her sight again.

Running blind through the thick forest had been terrifying and knowing there were so many zombies close behind them motivated her to stay near her husband. He set off, moving quickly, around behind the Biltmore Lodge. They stayed inside the tree line, the growls of the pursuing infected lessening but never ceasing, to her dismay.

Beth wondered if they should try to get inside the lodge. It looked like a beautiful place and maybe they could hide there and figure out what to do next. She was about to tap Chuck and make that suggestion when zombie sounds suddenly rang out, this time from in front of them.

They had just reached a position where they could see the other end of the long building. At least ten vehicles were parked near the side door, one of them a white stretch Hummer limousine. The doors of the limo were standing open and several infected came crawling out, bloody flesh hanging from their mouths. A group of over thirty Zs must have smelled or heard the couple and started shuffling towards Chuck and Beth's position in the tree line.

What made these zombies unique was that they were all dressed for a wedding. The bride's long white dress, now ripped apart and covered with blood, and the groom's gore-coated tux identified them. The others were evidently wedding party members or family and friends. These people had clearly been infected for a while and moved slowly, their dead bodies already well into the decaying process. They growled in unison, moving in the direction of what they hoped was an easy meal.

Suddenly, the zombies pursuing them broke out of the woods where Chuck and Beth had been just a few minutes earlier. They did not appear to have acquired the couple's scent because part of the group went around the front of the lodge while others shuffled around the rear towards where they were hiding.

"Plan B," said McCain. "Come on."

Chuck spun around and started sprinting deeper into the woods, Elizabeth staying right behind him. I didn't even get to ask him what Plan B is, she thought.

# Chapter Seven

**Buckhead, Atlanta, Saturday, 1130 hours**

Jorge Quintero was riding shotgun in the white, full-size GMC van as his driver, Julio, pulled up in front of their headquarters, the Peachtree Summit Luxury Condominiums. The black Ford F-150 pickup and the gray Toyota Tacoma pickup pulled in right behind the GMC, five cartel soldiers climbing out of the bed of the Ford and six exiting the Toyota. The group of Latino and African-American gangsters approached the back doors of the van. They left the boxes of confiscated supplies in the trucks, much more interested in the cargo that was contained in the van.

Quintero exited, holding his captured National Guard M4 rifle. The soldiers waited at the rear of the van until he gave them the nod. Pedro, a cartel member who had been serving a life sentence in a Mexican maximum-security prison for several murders, pulled open the back doors, grinning wickedly at what he saw inside. Their cargo of nine young women sat huddled against the far end of the van, terror etched on their faces.

The body of Mario lay just inside the cargo compartment of the van, blood having pooled around him. Seeing his soldier's corpse sent a wave of anger through Jorge. One of the defenders had managed to get a couple of rounds off before Pedro had shot the old man in the head. Quintero had ordered that the dead soldier be tossed into the back of the van with their prisoners.

Most of the girls were in shock at what they had just witnessed. A few them were crying softly. There were even a few defiant looks, Quintero noticed. Good, he thought. Those were the fun ones. He always enjoyed breaking the spirit of the women who weren't smart enough to know that they were beaten and that they now belonged to him and his men.

"Vamonos!" Jorge ordered, but none of the girls moved.

The assistant cartel leader motioned to his men to climb in and drag the young women out. The captives all resisted, several screaming loudly, as they were pulled forcefully by the arm or hair out of the van. An athletic looking, early-twenties white girl backed into the corner of the vehicle. When one of the soldiers reached for her she launched herself at him, firing finger jabs at his eyes, a knee to his groin, and then ridge hand strikes to his throat.

The Mexican fell to the floor of the van clutching his testicles and his throat, groaning and coughing. The wild-eyed girl jumped over her attacker and rushed towards the open rear doors of the van. Jorge, watching from outside, sighed and shook his head. He raised his rifle and sent a full-auto burst of 5.56mm bullets into the young woman's chest, slamming her back against the inside of the vehicle, blood splattering the white walls of the van.

Quintero motioned to one of the other soldiers to go and help the downed man. The sight of their companion getting bested by a girl had all of the cartel members laughing. One of the black gangsters grabbed the dead woman by the legs and dragged her out of the van, dumping her onto the pavement. Her head bounced with a sickening thud.

Jorge was disappointed that he'd had to kill the young woman. She was one of the prettiest of the group and he had claimed her, planning to rape her as soon as they got back to the base. At the same time, killing the girl accomplished two things. It let the other eight prisoners know that rebellion would not be tolerated. It also eliminated a potential ringleader who might try to organize an escape.

"Get them inside and help them get comfortable," he told his soldiers with a knowing smile. "After you get finished, come back and unload the supplies that we captured."

The gang members laughed lustily and dragged the wailing women inside the high-rise apartment building. Jorge understood that having these fresh prisoners around kept his men motivated and eager to continue their conquest of the city. This morning's foray had targeted a large Methodist church a few miles down the road.

Over twenty people had been barricaded inside the large structure, thinking that their only threats were the zombies still roaming the area. Quintero's men had forced their way into the church and engaged in a short shootout with the defenders. An older black man had fired just as Mario had rushed in. He always wanted to be the first guy in, Jorge remembered. It cost him today, as the church member had put two rounds of .45 ACP hollow points into the Mexican's sternum, the big bullets destroying the soldiers heart and killing him instantly.

Pedro was behind Mario, carrying an M-16. He fired a long burst into the black man and several other armed defenders. Thankfully, none of the other survivors in the church could shoot accurately. Carlos was grazed by a round to his right shoulder, but he had just kept fighting. Quintero knew that nothing except death would keep Carlos from enjoying one of their newest prisoners.

The initial gunfire cut down three men and two women. One of the men and one of the women were still alive as Jorge walked over to them and fired single shots into their heads from his Colt Python. When they searched the educational wing of the church, thirteen females of varying ages were found huddled in a classroom.

Quintero was still furious over the death of Mario and he turned his M4 on the group, cutting down four of the older ladies. The nine younger women began to scream and cry.

Pedro located three teenage boys hiding in a supply closet. Without hesitation, he triggered his M-16, blowing them apart. Jorge had the girls searched and led the weeping prisoners out to the van. The church kitchen was well stocked and the food, along with the defender's weapons, were secured in the back of the Ford pickup.

After the captives were dragged inside their HQ, Quintero got on the elevator to report to Tony the Tiger. All in all, it had been a successful mission. They had captured a large quantity of food and several additional weapons. The new women for the soldiers to play with were always welcome. Losing Mario, however, was a tough blow. Jorge hoped that the reinforcements that Corona had requested arrived soon.

### Centers for Disease Control Compound, East of Atlanta, Saturday, 1155 hours

After their meeting, Eddie gave Shaun Taylor and the DC team the bad news that they didn't have any spare rooms or RVs for them to bunk in. They could, however, sleep on the floor of the CDC's office, storeroom, dining hall, or anywhere else they could find floor space. All of the men were combat veterans and took it in stride, just glad not to be sleeping out in the elements. Dry and reasonably warm was better than cold and wet any day of the week.

While his teammates were getting settled, Jay walked over to the dining room, hoping to find a cup of coffee and maybe something to eat. The food selection was limited but Mexican rice and refried beans sounded pretty good and the coffee was hot. After thanking the young woman behind the counter for his food, Walker turned to look for an open table.

Score! he thought. That good-looking woman he'd seen earlier was sitting by herself. The CDC officer made his way across the room and stopped in front of her table.

"Hi," he said, pleasantly. "Mind if I join you?"

The brunette had been lost in her thoughts and hadn't noticed the muscular man approach her table. Jay's voice startled her.

"I'm sorry. I didn't mean to scare you, Dr. Edwards," Jay read her name off of her white lab coat.

Nicole laughed to cover her embarrassment. "I was just lost in my own little world."

She motioned to the seat across from her. "I'm done with lunch and was about to go back to work but have a seat, Agent...?"

"Walker, Jay Walker," he smiled.

"It's nice to meet you, Agent Walker. I saw that you were on the helicopter with Dr. Bae-yong."

"That's right, but please call me Jay. We were her escort to make sure that she got here safely. We work out of the DC office, but it sounds like we're going to be here for a few days."

"Really? Are you and your men going to be a part of the security force here?"

She is gorgeous, Jay realized. Dr. Edwards was a little taller than him, but who wasn't? She had long, wavy brown hair and a beautiful figure. Her light brown eyes, though, were sad, almost lifeless.

"No, we're working on a special mission with the guys from here." Knowing that he couldn't talk about the assignment he shifted gears. "I'm sorry for being nosy, but is your first name Nicole?"

Edwards gave a surprised smile. "And how did you guess that?"

"You created the solution that all the agents were issued that kills the virus on contact, right?"

Pleased that this stranger was familiar with her research, she nodded enthusiastically. "Well, my team did most of the work, but I was so happy that we were able to contribute something for you guys in the field. I feel protective towards all of our enforcement agents. You and your teammates are the tip of the spear and y'all put your lives on the line every day.

"I only wish we could find a breakthrough for a vaccine or a cure for the virus," she sighed. "Hopefully, now that Dr. Bae-yong is here, we can put our heads together and figure it out."

Jay nodded. "It's nice to be able to thank you in person, Dr. Edwards. We've used your solution a number of times when, well, let's just we've had some up close and personal encounters."

The epidemiologist's face lit up. "You're very welcome and please call me Nicole. How long have you worked for the CDC, Jay?"

"Just a couple of years, since they started the enforcement unit. I was one of the original recruits. I'd been in the Navy and was thinking about retiring after twenty-two years. I wasn't sure what I was getting into when I took this job. I just knew that I was tired of living in the deserts of the Middle East."

"Do you have a family back in Washington?"

Walker shook his head. "The Navy was my family. My parents are both dead. I was married, very briefly, many years ago. What about you?"

Nicole looked away, the sadness returning to her eyes. "I'm from Texas. My parents and my brother live in Dallas. As far as I know, they're OK. I've only been in Georgia for the four years that I've been with the CDC. Have you worked with the agents from our office before? Do you know Chuck McCain?"

Ah, interesting that McCain's name is the one she uses to reference the Atlanta office, he thought. I guess she likes tall guys.

"Yes and yes. Marshall and his team came up to Washington several months back for a case they were working on."

"Was that the one involving the dirty bombs mixed with the zombie virus?" Nicole queried. When she saw the surprised look on

Walker's face, Edwards clarified. "Everything pertaining to the virus crosses my desk. I don't know all the details of that investigation, but the samples of the virus mixed with radioactive waste were fascinating."

"I imagine so," Jay nodded. "The results were like nothing that we'd seen before. Those Zs were stronger, faster, and meaner than any that we'd dealt with previously. But to answer your other question: I met McCain when he flew up during that investigation and briefed us on some other things that we needed to know about. I take it that you and he are friends?"

Nicole glanced at Jay and then looked down. "Kind of. He and his men rescued me after the last attack in Atlanta. I'd gotten trapped inside our HQ with one of the civilian security officers. Darrell and I knew that we were going to die; it was just a matter of when.

"When Chuck and his men showed up, neither of us could believe that it was actually happening. I still don't know how those agents fought their way through all those infected to get to the CDC building, get inside, rescue us, and then fight their way back out. After that, I couldn't go home; my apartment was near downtown. Chuck allowed me to stay with him for a few weeks."

Nicole saw Jay's eyebrow rise slightly and she felt the need to clarify. "There were actually several of us living with him. I shared a room with Emily. Her boyfriend, Scotty Smith, is another agent. Emily's a paramedic and her work partner, Darnell, stayed there, too. Chuck was very generous in opening his home. He'd just lost someone very close to him, though, and kept to himself. He left almost two months ago to try to find his daughter and we haven't heard from him since."

Walker could see that Edwards had feelings for McCain. He is a good-looking man, Jay thought. If I swung that way I might have a crush on him, too.

"I'm sure Chuck's fine, Nicole," Jay said, gently. "From what

I've heard, he's one tough hombre."

Nicole looked into Jay's eyes, realizing that he had seen right through her veneer and discerned her feelings for Chuck. Embarrassed, she stood quickly. "It was nice meeting you, Jay, but I need to get back to work."

Jay stood and extended his hand. "Thanks for letting me sit with you, Nicole. I really enjoyed the chat. Maybe we'll cross paths again before I push off for the next assignment."

**South of Hendersonville, North Carolina, Saturday, 1205 hours**

They ran without stopping for hundreds of yards. Beth wasn't a great judge of distance but she figured they'd pushed hard for over ten minutes. The forest seemed to be opening up again and they could see a road in front of them.

Chuck paused at the edge of the tree line, panting heavily, checking their surroundings. A large, open field lay before them on the opposite side of the street. The wide, treeless area bordered the forest with a dirt drive running along the left side of the field. Back to their right was Upward Road where the group of several hundred Zs had last been seen. We don't want to go that way, Beth thought. In the other direction, the narrow two-lane road ran along the edge of the forest for half a mile before curving sharply out of sight.

After a break of two minutes, Chuck leaned in, speaking softly next to his wife's ear. "Across the street, straight up that dirt drive for fifty yards or so, and then we'll cut to the left into the woods again."

Elizabeth nodded. "You never told me what Plan B was?"

"Run like hell," he answered, with a slight smile. "You first and I'll cover behind us."

The young woman raced across the street, glancing over her

221

shoulder, watching her husband give her a slight head start, and then following. She rushed onto the small driveway, noting that the huge open field to her right looked like someone's massive garden, row after row having been plowed, waiting to be planted in the Spring.

What did Chuck say? she tried to remember. She was having trouble concentrating, the stress starting to catch up with her and the adrenaline beginning to wear off. I think he said go fifty yards and turn into the woods. How far is fifty yards?

Chuck was impressed with Elizabeth's conditioning. She'd barely been breathing hard when they stopped. And here I am, sucking wind and feeling every one of my forty-four years.

He kept glancing behind them as they sprinted up the dirt track. Beth was thirty feet in front of him and they had already covered over fifty yards, his wife setting a blistering pace. They needed to get back into the forest, but he couldn't yell. She finally looked back at him and he motioned towards the trees.

Elizabeth nodded and altered her direction, turning into the thick brush. McCain continued scanning the tree line on the opposite side of the street. Still clear. He didn't see the large, partially buried stone that caught his foot, sending him sprawling. He landed hard, stunning and knocking the breath out of himself on the dirt and gravel drive.

Suddenly, soul-penetrating zombie growls erupted from across the road. Chuck clambered to his feet, trying to suck some air into his lungs, his chin stinging from where it had impacted the ground. Beth paused at the edge of the forest, watching him with concern as the Zs came pouring out of the forest where the two of them had just exited. Most of the group were shufflers, but a few sprinters were mixed in.

"Keep going!" McCain yelled, knowing there was no need for silence now. "I'll be right there."

His M4 came up and he fired at eight infected who were less than sixty feet away, sprinting hard. Instead of running away, however, the loud crack of Elizabeth's AR added to the fray as she also fired into the larger group, less than a hundred yards from them. Several fell to her shots, the pack relentlessly in pursuit of their prey, the sounds of gunfire serving to intensify their desire for fresh meat.

Many of the Zs shuffled into the plowed field, the uneven rows and soft soil sending them stumbling to the ground. Others came straight down the dirt driveway, which funneled them towards the couple. McCain surveyed the scene, realizing that the zombies in the field would eventually get through it, but for the moment, it was allowing him to slow down and make good head shots on the closest ones. The awkward terrain meant the undead were tripping as fast as they managed to get back to their feet. At least thirty shuffled down the drive, three more sprinters breaking out of the pack.

"Just shoot at the ones on the driveway," he ordered, his shots dropping the runners.

The last of the quick-movers, a young man with a mullet hair cut, dropped just fifteen feet away and McCain turned his fire back to the rest of the group being funneled towards them, shooting quickly. The Colt locked open and he performed a quick reload, continuing to thin the herd. After just a few shots, however, the rifle was empty again. Oh, crap, that was the partial magazine from earlier, he realized, slamming his last full mag into the weapon.

Beth had stopped firing, her rifle empty as well, and she fumbled with the magazine release. Chuck grabbed her arm and pulled her into the forest where they began running again, pumping their legs as hard as they could. The infected would not stop their pursuit and the couple needed to create some distance fast. The police officer guessed there were at least fifty Zs still moving on that dirt drive and in the field and he was sure that there were plenty more rushing through the forest on the other side of the street, drawn to the gunfire.

As much as he hated to admit it, McCain was starting to think that this was it. He was no quitter, but the big man knew that they couldn't keep running forever. Chuck had no idea where they were and knew that if they didn't find someplace to hide, they were going to become zombie food.

Elizabeth was nearing panic mode. These nasty creatures just would not stop. She had never been so scared in her life. No, that's not true. A thought suddenly penetrated the cloud of fear and fatigue. When those thugs murdered my friends and kidnapped me, I knew I was dead. There was no way that I was getting out of that one. My only hope then was that I could fight and resist to the point where they would've killed me before gang-raping me.

But somehow, against all odds, she had survived. Chuck McCain had broken in, killed all the bad guys and had saved her life. Her husband didn't look like her savior right now, she thought. He looks like he's going to collapse at any moment. Blood dripped from his chin, the result of that nasty fall a few minutes before, and he was clearly out of gas from their non-stop sprinting.

She instinctively slowed her pace, allowing Chuck to keep up. She reached back and took hold of his left arm, dragging him along. Another memory forced its way into her thoughts as she tried to keep her own legs moving.

Right after she'd been kidnapped, the murderers had thrown her into the backseat of her own Jeep Cherokee for the drive back to their safe house. One of the animals sat on either side of her, reaching under her shirt, laughing and telling her all the things they were going to do to her when they got to the hideout. It was in that moment that she had turned back to Jesus. She had been raised in a Christian home but had walked away from her faith when she went off to college.

Knowing that she was going to be raped and murdered, Elizabeth had made peace with God. She hadn't even asked for deliverance knowing that her predicament was probably too much, even for the Almighty. A few minutes later, though, the door had burst open and Chuck had rescued her.

As they continued their flight through the woods, Beth prayed again, quietly speaking from her heart. "I'm sorry that I only seem to pray when I'm in a crisis. Please help us. Show us what to do and where to go. Thank you for bringing Chuck into my life. And no matter what happens, I'll keep trying to trust you."

"Did you say something?" McCain asked, gasping for air.

"Just praying," she muttered, the pace starting to take its toll on her, as well.

After running in a straight line for five minutes, Chuck pulled Beth to the right, changing directions to make it more difficult for the Zs to track them. The terrain began a gradual descent and they ended up in a hollow, surrounded by hardwood trees. A shallow five-foot wide creek ran through the small valley and the ground rose on the other side, promising a degree of safety if they could get there. Even in his exhausted state, McCain recognized this as an ideal spot for deer hunting. The hardwood trees provided acorns and the little creek provided a water source. He just hoped that he and Beth didn't become a food source for their pursuers.

Without hesitation, the couple plunged into the cold water, thankful that it was only a foot deep where they crossed. They scrambled up the embankment, hoping that the Zs would have difficulty climbing the hill. The high ground would provide a natural defensive position. They weren't going to camp out there, but it was the perfect spot to rest for a few minutes. Chuck collapsed against a large oak tree, Elizabeth plopping down next to him, both of them gasping for air.

Even now, McCain was still working, though. "Let's get you

reloaded," he gasped, trying to control his breathing.

Beth's rifle had locked open back on the dirt driveway and they hadn't stopped running since. Chuck walked her through removing the empty mag and inserting a fresh one. He showed her how to gently release the slide so that it wouldn't slam closed and give the pursuing Zs a noise to key in on.

"Turn around and let me get into your pack," he asked softly, patting her on the shoulder.

She felt him open her backpack and rummage through it as she kept watch down the hill and across the creek, feeling better now that her weapon was loaded again. A moment later, her husband handed her a bottle of water.

"Drink half and let me have the other half."

She hadn't even thought about how thirsty she was, gulping the water greedily and then handing the remainder to Chuck. He had removed two extra rifle magazines from the pack and put them into his mag carrier. For the first time, she saw that all his other pouches were empty. Did he really shoot that much?

"You're bleeding," Beth whispered, reaching for the small first-aid kit attached to her web gear.

Elizabeth pulled out a square gauze bandage and quietly ripped the paper off. She pressed it against his chin, pulling it away after a few seconds.

"It's not very deep. I think it's more of a scrape than anything else. Do you want me to try to clean it now or wait?"

McCain poured a few drops of the precious water onto the gauze and let her work on his chin. Chuck's breathing was finally coming back under control as she wiped the dirt from her husband's wound. He then stuffed the used bandage in one of his cargo pockets, not wanting to leave behind something containing their scent.

Elizabeth was still thirsty but understood that they had to carefully guard what was left. Beth knew she'd had four half liter bottles in her pack. Now she had three. Both of their backpacks had contained similar loads. Food, water, extra ammo, and a few clothes. With the loss of Chuck's pack in their abandoned vehicle, they'd lost half of their supplies. Really, more than that because they also had extra food and water in the vehicle along with a shotgun. All left behind.

McCain took one of the partially full rifle mags off of Beth's web gear, leaving her with two full and one partial, along with the thirty-rounder in her weapon. They had both gone through a lot of ammo and didn't have very much left to hold off a horde of flesh-eating zombies. Beth hadn't fired any rounds from her pistol, however, and Chuck had only cranked off a few from his Glock so they both still had a quantity of 9mm ammo.

The woods were still quiet but they knew that it was time to get going again. Chuck climbed to his feet, looking surprisingly refreshed after the brief respite. The big man scoped the woods across the creek, not seeing any signs of their pursuers. They turned and plunged deeper into the forest.

The couple slowed their pace slightly, moving at a brisk walk, conserving their energy since they weren't in contact with the trailing zombies. Chuck was leading with absolutely no idea where they were heading, just hoping that they would eventually come across a house or business where they could seek shelter. Twenty minutes later, the forest started opening up again and they found themselves standing on the edge of yet another country road.

Directly across from them was a large mobile home park. From what they could see, it was composed primarily of single-wides, with a few double-wides thrown in.

"Watch behind us," the police officer told his companion, raising his rifle and scoping the trailer park, looking for any signs of activity.

He could only see one section of the trailer community, a line of trees hiding the rest from his view. He knew the layout, though. They were all the same. Narrow streets containing rundown trailers. No yards to speak of. No real privacy, the mobile homes packed in tightly.

He had a quick déjà vu moment: as a young police officer who often worked the rural area of his county, he had spent many Friday and Saturday nights breaking up fights and mediating domestic situations in similar trailer parks early in his career. The lack of privacy and close proximity sometimes led to neighbor-on-neighbor clashes.

When McCain had first become a cop, a backup unit was a luxury. You were expected to be able to take care of yourself because the officer in an adjoining sector was at least fifteen minutes away. One memorable night, he'd been dispatched to a large brawl in the street of one of the trailer parks.

As the rookie officer pulled his cruiser into the neighborhood, he saw a scene right out of the WWE, with at least twenty people, both men and women, slugging it out. This was redneckery at it's finest, he had thought, adrenaline pumping through his system. Chuck had been on the force for less than a year and didn't know that no one in the department would have ever held it against him if he had waited for backup on an altercation of this magnitude. Twenty-to-one odds were never good to bet against.

As a newbie, McCain just assumed he was supposed to put a stop to the riot, and waded in with his nightstick and metal flashlight flailing. The combatants all quickly turned on him and Officer McCain realized that he had probably made a tactical error. Chuck was a fighter, though, and went into full combat mode.

When the next two police cars arrived twelve minutes later, they found the bloody and bruised officer holding his own against a large group of intoxicated trailer dwellers. Four of the biggest males and one of the females were sprawled unconscious around him. A fifth man, who was clearly inebriated, was lying off to the side, screaming in pain that his leg was broken. Chuck hadn't even been able to handcuff anyone yet, still just fighting for survival.

The three officers had ended up arresting twelve suspects, nine of whom required a stop at the hospital emergency room first, courtesy of McCain's fists, elbows, feet, nightstick, or flashlight. That incident had also solidified Chuck's reputation with his fellow officers.

Now, looking out over the mobile home park in front of them, he wondered what adventures this one would hold?

Chuck leaned over and whispered some instructions. "Let's go all the way down that main street and see if we can find an empty double-wide to hide in. A trailer isn't the best safe house but we don't have many options. If we're on the far side of the complex and get compromised, we can duck back into the forest over there."

He led the way across the blacktop, the distant sound of the pursuing zombies just now reaching their ears. Beth wondered how they had been able to track them, but then remembered Chuck describing how strong their sense of smell was.

The run-down community looked quiet but they both had their rifles up and ready, moving cautiously. The road leading into the park had mobile homes on both sides of the street, most of them single-wides. The trailers were all older and hadn't been cared for, even before the zombie apocalypse.

A car was in one driveway and a pickup truck in another. McCain checked them to see if the keys were in the ignition, but they weren't that lucky. Other than those two, there were no other vehicles to be seen. Nothing was moving and there were no signs of life.

The main road that they were on circled the trailer park. Three side streets ran to the left off of the main drag, cutting the complex into thirds. They peered down the first street as they passed by it, not seeing anything of interest. McCain stopped suddenly, however, when they got to the second intersection. Elizabeth was walking backwards, scanning the area behind them, and bumped into her husband.

"Oh, sorry!" she whispered. "What is it?"

Chuck motioned for her to look. About halfway down the street, a gray SUV sat with all four doors standing open. Other than the vehicle, the street was empty. They both strained their ears, not hearing anything. The smell of death was in the air, though, the scent of decomposing flesh all around them. There are more Zs here, McCain thought, it's just a question of where are they hiding?

"What do you think?" Beth asked softly.

"I think we need to go check to see if the keys are in it. If they are, that's our ride out of here."

Noise behind them caused the couple to spin around. Zombies were pouring out of the woods where they had just been, over two hundred yards away. Sensing that they were finally closing in on their prey, the group began snarling, with many of them snapping their teeth open and closed.

"Don't they know that they're dead?" McCain quipped. "Come on, let's check this car."

They rushed down the street to the SUV, a Chevrolet Blazer. As they got close, they could see the dark splotches of dried blood all around the vehicle. Chuck swung out wide, pointing his rifle into the open SUV.

"The remains of a body in the backseat," he said, continuing forward to check the front.

It was empty and he leaned in to check the ignition. Nothing. He checked the floor mat and around the driver's seat but there were no keys to be found. Elizabeth was scanning the area but glanced into the Blazer, quickly wishing that she hadn't. The badly mangled body of what had probably been a child lay on the rear seat, a bloody leg hanging out of the open door.

A loud growl to their rear let them know that they had company. A young, professional, black male zombie in an expensive suit turned onto their street off the main drive, sprinting towards them just fifty yards away.

Beth heard more growls from the other end of the street, as well. Chuck's rifle barked and the infected businessman's head snapped back, dark blood spurting from the wound between his eyes as he fell to the pavement. Elizabeth turned quickly to cover their flank. Two obese women, one white, one black, both clearly infected, were shuffling towards them from the opposite end of the short street.

"Let's cut between those trailers," the CDC agent ordered, pointing towards two brown mobile homes across the street before breaking into a sprint.

As they got to the next street over, the sounds of growling and snarling were coming from all around them now, echoing around the circular neighborhood, accompanying the stench of death that became stronger with every step the couple took. They could both hear and smell them, but other than those two fat Zs and the one that Chuck had shot, the streets right around them were still empty. As they approached the last section of the main roadway that wrapped around the complex, they finally saw where all the residents of the trailer park had been hiding. They were having a feeding frenzy in the front yard of a double-wide trailer just down on their left.

The remains of several bodies were scattered over the small front yard and street in front of the residence. There wasn't much left and many of the bones had been picked clean. A mixed group of at least thirty white, black, and Latino zombies turned towards their new victims and began growling in unison, shuffling in their direction. Two doors to the right of where Beth and Chuck stood, another pack of twenty were on their knees in front of a rundown single wide, ripping apart what had probably been a large dog.

The snarls of the pursuing group were getting closer and Beth suddenly saw eight Zs come stumbling out of a trailer across the street. They all tumbled down the three wooden steps that led to the front door, landing in a pile in the front yard. In seconds, however, the infected were climbing to their feet.

"They're everywhere!" Elizabeth exclaimed.

McCain grabbed her arm as she started to raise her rifle and pulled her onto the small wooden front porch of the trailer next to them. Zombies were now less than thirty feet away. Now we're surrounded, he realized.

"Up! We're gonna get up on the roof," he ordered.

Elizabeth had no idea what he was talking about. How were they going to climb to the top of the single-wide mobile home?

He bent over and cupped his hands in front of her. "Hurry! Gimme your foot and I'll hoist you up."

The zombies were almost to them. Beth did what she was told and found herself being propelled upward, over the side of the trailer, landing on the flat roof. She quickly turned to check on her husband. Once he saw that she was up, he swung his leg up onto the top of the wooden rail that encircled the porch. From that vantage point, he was tall enough to reach over the small ledge to the top of the single-wide.

As Chuck tried to pull himself up, however, the black nylon sling on his rifle caught on the side of the trailer. The infected were just a few feet away from the man she loved. Elizabeth scrambled to her feet and started firing at the closest ones. In her panic she rushed her shots and missed four times before hitting any of them.

McCain suddenly gasped as a balding middle-aged Z with a large beer gut managed to sink it's teeth into his left calf. Beth saw the thing holding him with both hands, biting his leg, and Chuck struggling to shake it off. She leaned down and with trembling hands fired into Beer Gut's head, terrified that she would hit her husband.

The bullet ripped open the back of the zombie's skull and McCain was able to pull his aching leg free and swing it over the side of the trailer. Elizabeth tried to help pull him up, her lack of upper body strength making it difficult. He finally wiggled his rifle loose and pulled himself onto the roof where he lay panting. Disappointed Zs snarled just below them, their arms extended towards the top of the trailer.

Wide-eyed with fear, Beth knelt next to Chuck, tears pouring down her face, clasping his hand. The single-wide was quickly surrounded by at least a hundred infected, their growls making it difficult to hear each other.

The young woman pressed her mouth against the big man's ear. "Did you get bit?" Terror made her voice quiver. Her husband had been infected and would turn into a zombie. He startled her with a kiss.

"I don't think so," he answered, pulling himself to a sitting position and removing a small plastic bottle from a pouch on his vest.

He squirted some liquid from the container onto his pants where the zombie's teeth had just been. McCain had explained to her previously that the bottle contained a solution, created by a team of CDC scientists, which killed the virus on contact. It wouldn't help you if you'd been bitten, but it was perfect for someone who'd had contact with infected bodily fluids and had gotten them on their clothes or skin.

Chuck pulled up his kevlar-lined cargo pants and then his thermal underwear. He was wearing thick, calf-length socks under his combat boots. He pulled the sock down to reveal a large purple bruise in the shape of a bite mark, but the skin wasn't broken. The kevlar pants had saved his life once again.

Elizabeth fell into his arms sobbing. "I thought I was going to lose you."

The stress of the day and their current predicament, coupled with Chuck's close call, unleashed a torrent of tears. McCain held her, letting her cry it out, the sounds of the infected getting louder as the crowd around the trailer grew. They were safe for the moment, the Zs unable to climb onto the roof, but their situation was dire.

As her sobs finally subsided, Beth took several deep breaths to get her emotions under control. She looked around at the zombies in various states of decay and decomposition gathered below them and shuddered. The smell and sounds of death surrounded them.

After a few minutes, Beth yelled into Chuck's ear, "What are we going to do now?"

"I need a nap," the CDC officer answered, lying back down the roof of the mobile home.

"We're just a few feet away from getting ripped apart and eaten and you want to take a nap?" she snapped, angrily.

McCain laughed. "I'm just kidding, but all that running did wear me out. Why don't you come lay down here with me and I'll tell you what I'm thinking?"

### Centers for Disease Control Compound, East of Atlanta, Saturday, 1315 hours

Jimmy opened the door to the pop-up trailer that he and Grace were sharing. He was carrying a styrofoam plate of food for the young woman. Grace had barely left the camper since they had arrived on Thursday. Of course, she needed to catch up on her rest, and she was also still recovering from her gunshot wounds.

There was more to it, however. Jones was no shrink but it was clear that Cunningham was dealing with depression and probably PTSD after all that she had been through. The problem was, he had no idea how to help her. He really cared about her, though, and was willing to give her the time and space she needed to work through it.

One of his goals was to get Grace to go to the dining hall with him. So far, she had only gone once when they had arrived on Thursday. After that, she had stayed inside and asked Jimmy to bring her back some food. Jones would keep asking but wouldn't put any pressure on her. He knew that it would be good for her to meet some of the CDC people. Most of them had lost family and friends and Grace needed to know that she wasn't the only one who was hurting.

Jones put the food down on the small table and sat down on the edge of the double bed. Cunningham was on her side, facing away from him, a blanket pulled up around her shoulders. He touched her shoulder but got no response.

The bed was small and Jimmy was thrilled to be sharing it with Grace. There was no doubt in his mind that he was in love and he thought that, maybe, she felt the same way. The loss of her family, however, was a devastating blow that she was struggling to overcome.

They hadn't been intimate yet but they had kissed several times. The campus police officer had apologized and asked him to be patient with her. The CDC officer was a patient man. His concern, however, was that her depression only seemed to be getting deeper.

"I sure wish you would talk to me," he whispered.

After a moment, she rolled over onto her back. Her face was streaked with tears. He felt a stab of pain and helplessness as he realized that she had been crying again. He lay down next to her and held her tightly.

"I'm sorry, Grace. I wish I knew what to say. It breaks my heart to see you like this."

She took a deep breath. "You don't have anything to be sorry for. You've been so good to me. I just feel like I've got this black cloud hanging over my head that I can't shake and that it's never gonna leave. I've always been a positive person until all this happened. Now, for the first time in my life, I've actually had suicidal thoughts."

"No, Gracie, please don't say that. I can't imagine how bad you're hurting. When my mother died, I struggled with all kinds of emotions, but I eventually came out the other side. Is there anything I can do to help you? I…I'm in love with you and I'll do anything to help you get better."

Oh, crap, Jones thought. I just told her I loved her. There's no going back now, but it's true. I really do love her.

Grace didn't say anything and Jimmy thought he might have overplayed his hand.

"I love you, too," she finally said, softly. "And don't worry. I'm not going to hurt myself. My daddy was a pastor and I know that suicide is never the answer. Plus, you risked your life to save me. We've already been through a lot together, haven't we?"

Jimmy chuckled. "We sure have. That was the journey of a lifetime. And I don't know if I've told you this or not, but you are one tough warrior. I'd fight next to you any day of the week. Of course, right now, I'm enjoying sleeping next to you."

Cunningham laughed. "That's sweet. I don't think I've ever thought of myself as a warrior before."

They lay there, holding each other for several minutes. "What do you think happened to Chuck?" Grace finally asked.

"I don't know. We know how tough it is out there. I only had to get to Athens. He was going all the way to North Carolina, but now you got my curiosity up. Have you got a thing for Chuck? I saw the look on your face when Eddie told us he hadn't been heard from."

She looked into his eyes, giving him a sad smile. "No, I just told you that I love you. I don't even know Chuck. We only talked a little bit that day in Athens but I watched him holding that woman, Rebecca, right? I saw him holding her after she'd been shot, but then

I saw him later in the day fighting for everything he was worth to save some innocent people he didn't even know. I guess I admire that and I wanted to talk to him about how he overcame his grief and kept functioning."

"I don't think he ever overcame it," Jimmy answered. "If anything, he just compartmentalized it and kept going. We ran so many missions after Rebecca was killed, and Chuck had gotten promoted to run the entire Atlanta CDC enforcement operation.

"We all knew that he was dying inside, but he also was a serious badass who just kept operating at a high level. After his promotion, he could've stayed in the office but that's not how Chuck works. He always led from the front. In my heart of hearts, I figure he's fine and we'll eventually see him driving up and taking charge again."

### South of Hendersonville, North Carolina, Saturday, 1425 hours

Elizabeth had grown numb to the sounds of the infected surrounding them. There had to be over two hundred zombies shoving against the sides of the mobile home. The stench was overpowering and she had pulled her scarf up to cover her nose and mouth. She had asked Chuck why he hadn't tried to get inside a trailer rather than climbing on top. He had shrugged and said that they would've been trapped if they had done that and the Zs would eventually been able to force their way in.

"But we're trapped up here on top now," she said, trying to stay calm, the realization that they were going to die in that mobile home park taking center stage in her mind.

They wouldn't be able to reconnect with Melanie. She and Chuck would never get the chance to grow old together. They wouldn't have the opportunity to have a baby. The young woman tried to suppress her tears, knowing that it wouldn't help anything, wiping her wet eyes on her sleeve.

Since they had stopped running, Beth found herself shivering, her sweat now causing her body temperature to drop. The outside temps were probably in the high forties or low fifties but would plummet once the sun went down. Both of them had wet feet from their run through the creek earlier. One of the first things Chuck had made her do on the roof was take off her wet socks, replacing them with one of the two dry pairs in her pack. Of course, McCain's pack and his extra socks had been left behind and he was starting to shiver, as well.

The big man sat next to her calmly studying the satellite maps of the area. When Karen Foster had requested the couple visit her parents, Chuck had asked her to check the technical college's library for maps of the entire area between Hartwell, Georgia, and Hendersonville, North Carolina. The federal police officer leaned towards Elizabeth, holding the maps where she could see them.

"Okay, this is where we are," pointing out the mobile home park. "The woods over there only go for about a quarter of a mile. Then we'll come to that neighborhood," he said, his finger resting on a large residential area. "If we've gotten some distance between us and these nasties we'll look for a house to bed down in. If we're still in contact, we keep running."

He pointed to another area on the map. "The forest behind that subdivision ends after a few hundred yards and then we'll come out near this big church. There's a lot of homes around it so we should be able to find a safe place to rest for the night."

Beth looked at her husband like he was crazy. "But how do we get away from here?" she asked, pointing at the zombies below them. "We're surrounded!"

Chuck grinned at her. "Yeah, that part of the plan is a little shaky."

He reached into his cargo pocket and withdrew a cylindrical

object. "This is a flash bang grenade. It's really loud. When we're ready to go, I'll toss it as far as I can behind us. Hopefully, they'll be drawn to the explosion and we can slip away."

Chuck touched her arm and looked into her eyes. "Look, we've got to try and get away from here. There's no way we can survive the elements up here over night. I'll throw the grenade. We'll wait a couple of minutes for the Zs to get moving that way. I'll climb down and then help you down and we go back into Plan B mode."

Elizabeth finally nodded. She trusted Chuck with her life but was still terrified at being pursued by such a large group of zombies. What if the Zs didn't rush towards the explosion? What if she or Chuck fell down while they were being pursued?

He was right, though. They had to try. They would freeze to death if they couldn't find shelter. McCain checked her rifle, as well as his own equipment. He told her that the goal was to not shoot any more than they had to.

After a few minutes, Chuck leaned over and kissed her gently on the lips. "I love you so much," he said, and then stood, pulling his pretty wife to her feet.

The noise of the infected got even louder as they could see their prey, just out of reach. McCain held the flash bang in his left hand, his strong hand, and prepared to pull the pin with his right. Suddenly, another sound got the CDC officer's attention. He scanned the sky, quickly looking around him.

Elizabeth felt her heart pounding inside of her, waiting for the explosion. Rather than throwing the grenade, however, Chuck was staring up at the sky. Something had gotten his attention. After a few seconds, she heard it, too. What was that? A large black helicopter suddenly appeared above them, hovering low enough for Beth to observe several figures crowded inside. A huge man wearing a black helmet leaned out the side door, holding what she thought was a sniper rifle, his bushy beard waving in the wind.

She looked back at Chuck and saw a look of disbelief on his face that turned into a smile. He shoved the grenade back into his pocket as the helicopter dropped even lower. They're going to land right on top of us! she thought. The bearded man saluted Chuck and motioned for the two of them to duck.

The aircraft, a Blackhawk, her husband told her later, continued it's descent. McCain pulled her down and they crawled towards the far end of the roof. The wind generated by the rotor blades threatened to blow the petite young woman off the top of the trailer but Chuck had a firm grip on her backpack.

The Blackhawk came to a hover just inches off the roof of the mobile home. McCain crouch walked the last several feet, pulling Beth with him. The bearded sniper and a young black man in dark BDUs pulled the two of them into the helicopter and helped them get strapped in. The smaller man handed each of them a headset.

Still not sure if this was actually happening, Elizabeth glanced around the passenger compartment and saw two more large, heavily armed bearded men, and a smiling young woman wearing jeans and a camo jacket with a black shotgun standing between her legs. An elderly man, also wearing BDUs and a holstered pistol, watched her and Chuck with interest. McCain took off his helmet and slipped the headset on, Beth following his lead.

"That was good timing, Admiral," Chuck's voice came over the intercom as he looked at the older man.

"Take us up, Colonel," the older man nodded at McCain and then looked up front towards the pilot, "and then bring us around for a gun pass. Sergeant Harris, can you take out that big group of infected?"

"Yes, sir, Admiral!" the door gunner responded with enthusiasm, settling in behind some kind of machine gun.

Elizabeth watched Chuck, still smiling, reach over and pat the sniper on the back. "Good to see you, Scotty! What took you so long?"

Her husband nodded at the young woman sitting on the other side of Elizabeth in the back of the helicopter. "Nice to see you, Emily. Thanks for taking care of Scotty."

Scotty? McCain had described each of his teammates to her. Was this Scotty Smith? Chuck had told her that Smith's girlfriend was named Emily. How did they find us?

Scotty was a giant of a man. Grinning, he leaned over to Chuck and pulled the headphones back from his boss' ear and said something that only McCain could hear. Chuck repeated the process, sliding Smith's headphone aside and answered, speaking directly into his ear. The huge man's eyes got big, a shocked look on his face as he turned to stare at Beth.

The pilot's voice came over the intercom. "I'm going to hover off here to the side and let you do your thing, Harris. Whenever you're ready."

"Yes, sir. Engaging now."

They all glanced down as the machine gun cut loose, the barrels spinning, spitting out thousands of bullets into the swarm of zombies below them. The gunner fired short bursts, sweeping the gun at head height cutting them down by the dozens. Heads exploded, the red mist hanging in the air, and bodies were blown apart. In less than a minute, half of the group had been eliminated.

The pilot took them up and made a big circle, putting Sergeant Harris in position to take out the rest of the Zs. After they circled the area for a few minutes looking for more targets, Elizabeth felt her stomach in her mouth as the helicopter quickly ascended, their speed increasing. This was her first helicopter ride, but at the moment, she was still trying to process the fact that she and Chuck were alive.

"Mr. McCain, it looks like you and your companion were in a little bit of a predicament," the elderly man said, a twinkle in his eye. "Is this Melanie?"

Chuck had a confused look on his face. Elizabeth gave an embarrassed laugh when McCain didn't answer, giving her husband an elbow in the side.

"Oh, no, sir," McCain finally answered. "This is Elizabeth, my wife. We got married last Monday."

The admiral, Emily, and the other two armed men looked on in surprise. Emily leaned close to Elizabeth and put an arm around her shoulders, a huge smile on her face.

"Well, congratulations on your wedding," Admiral Williams said, over the intercom, looking at Beth. "I'm sure there's quite a story there." He looked back at Chuck. "Agent McCain, we need to get back to Georgia. We have a very serious situation and I need your expertise."

"Respectfully, sir," McCain said, "not yet. I've been trying to get to my daughter for two months and now we're less than ten minutes away by air. I'm not going back to Georgia without seeing her."

Elizabeth sensed the mood in the helicopter instantly shift from joyous to tense. The two bearded bookends glared at Chuck, slowly easing their rifles around. They had never heard anyone tell the admiral "no" before. Scotty saw this, shifting his body so that he was facing them, his rifle across his knees. He's making sure they don't try anything stupid, Beth realized, still not quite sure what was happening.

The machine gunner turned so that he was facing McCain, his hand drifting towards a pistol on his belt. Smith made eye contact with the young man and gave a slight shake of his head. The young sergeant swallowed, keeping his hands away from his gun.

Admiral Williams saw everything and spoke over the intercom. "It's OK, gentleman. Mr. McCain and I just need to have a chat. Colonel, can you find us a safe spot to land?"

"Yes, sir. Give me a moment."

Two minutes later, the pilot's voice came over the intercom.

"Admiral, I'm going to put down on a two-lane road. It's a long, straight stretch and there are large fields on either side. I circled the area and it looks clear but I don't want to be on the ground any longer than ten minutes."

"That's fine, Colonel. Thank you."

The Blackhawk touched down and the pilot cut the power, shutting down the engines. Chuck leaned over to Beth and said, "I'll be right back."

McCain unbuckled his harness and started to leave but turned back, remembering something. He looked at Emily. "Em, this is my wife, Elizabeth. Beth, this is Emily. She's an amazing person and I'm really glad you get to meet her."

The two young women smiled as Chuck climbed out of the aircraft. The two bodyguards started to get out, as well, but the admiral waved them back. McCain turned and offered a hand to the older man, helping him down to the ground.

The two men walked out into an empty field, away from the aircraft. "Who are Tweedledee and Tweedledum?" McCain asked.

Williams chuckled. "Those are my bodyguards. You met them a while back. They came and took custody of that FBI mole that you and Agent Fleming captured. I was promoted a few months back from Assistant Director of Operations to Director of Operations. My former boss decided that the end of the world was a good time to retire so I was appointed to take his place. Of course, I'm fifteen years older than he is and you don't hear me talking of retiring.

"Anyway, the Director of the CIA insisted that I have security and those two are very good at what they do. Tim was former Delta Force and Tom came from SEAL Team Six."

"Congratulations on the promotion, sir. It's definitely well deserved. How did you find us?" McCain asked. "I knew the CIA was good but this takes the cake."

The older man laughed again. "It's pretty simple. Your rifles all have a GPS transmitter inside of them. That was how I located Agent Smith and then you."

"That's brilliant! What about the rest of my team in Atlanta?"

By now, they were out of earshot of anyone at the helicopter and the admiral stopped, turning to his companion, but ignoring his last question. "Chuck, I want to hear about the last two months and especially about your pretty wife. Unfortunately, that'll have to wait. Let me tell you what we're dealing with."

McCain knew the admiral well enough to know that when he called him by his first name, it was serious. Chuck both liked and respected the admiral and truly hoped that they could reach an agreement to continue working together.

"Does this have anything to do with a Mexican cartel in Atlanta?" McCain asked.

Williams nodded, clearly impressed that Chuck had heard about the crisis. "It has everything to do with a Mexican cartel."

He gave his subordinate a rundown on the situation. McCain listened intently as the admiral described some of the atrocities that the gang had committed. The clincher for Chuck was when Williams pulled out his satellite smart phone and pushed play on a video.

"I just received this video on the flight over to find you. It was taken this morning."

The footage had obviously come from a drone, the image sharp and clear. Two pickups and a van were driving down a deserted main thoroughfare, stopping in front of a tall building. Armed men climbed out of the back of the pickups and approached the rear of the van. The obvious leader of the group paused at the doors of the van, speaking to the others.

When the back doors were opened, the cartel soldiers climbed inside, dragging a group of women out a few moments later. Suddenly, the gang leader lifted his rifle, firing into the back of the van. One of the other soldiers reached inside and dragging the lifeless body of a woman out by her leg, dropping her onto the street.

Chuck felt anger rising up inside of him as he watched the men pulling the remaining women inside the large building.

"Where's this at?"

"The cartel has taken over a high-rise apartment building in Buckhead as their headquarters. They've got thirty or forty women locked up inside, and they're being used as sex slaves. The gang has secured several of the surrounding blocks and don't show any sign of leaving. Obviously, they've taken advantage of the terrorist attacks in Atlanta to establish a foothold. We've got to stop them before they get too entrenched."

"How many gang members are we talking about?"

Williams shrugged. "We're not sure. Probably close to two hundred. But there's something else you need to know. They have a quantity of the virus. The President has ordered me to personally put together an operation to eliminate the cartel presence on American soil, secure the virus, and free the hostages.

"My assistant, Shaun, is at the CDC site and has briefed your agents there. I also took the liberty of sending four officers from the DC office to Georgia to be a part of this. There'll be quite a few other assets in play and we'll work out other details and issues as we plan. I'll have overall command of the mission but once we launch, you'll have tactical command of the entire operation."

The admiral saw the shocked look on McCain's face and wanted to tell him more but the helicopter pilot was motioning for them to return to the aircraft.

Chuck was surprised at the admiral's confidence. McCain had been a police officer for twenty years, most of that time as a SWAT officer and a team leader. His two years of being embedded with the Army Green Berets as a police liaison had helped hone his fighting skills to a high level. Planning and leading an operation to take down a couple hundred bad guys, however, was something else entirely. He wanted to help but his own family came first.

"Admiral Williams, my daughter is less then ten minutes from here. I haven't seen her in months and I need to know that she's OK. As far as I know it's a secure location and the satellite maps show a landing zone near the house. Take me there and let me see her. We can all spend the night on the farm and tomorrow I'll go with you back to Georgia."

The older man shook his head and sighed. "Mr. McCain, there aren't many man who negotiate with an admiral. Most people just say, 'Yes, sir,' and snap to it. Not you. I guess that's one of the reasons I like you so much."

Williams stuck out his hand. "You've got a deal. And I'll even go a step farther. After we eliminate this problem in Atlanta, I'll let you use the helicopter to come back and spend some more time with Melanie."


Tim, Tom, and Scotty stood around the outside of the Blackhawk, weapons at the ready, watching for threats. Emily and Elizabeth chatted briefly, with Beth trying to keep an eye on Chuck. The two men were engrossed in their conversation. A few minutes later, McCain was staring at something on a screen and she saw that expression on his face. She had only seen that look a couple of times, usually right before he went into combat mode.

Emily had observed the hundreds of zombies surrounding Chuck and Beth on top of the mobile home. When Elizabeth told her new friend what the two of them had gone through that morning, Emily could sense how stressful it had been and put a comforting arm around her shoulders.

Beth sighed with relief when she saw Chuck and the older man, the Admiral, they had called him, shake hands. He seems like a nice man, she thought. It was obvious that her husband liked him and that was good enough for her.

"I'm sorry, I'm so tired, Emily. I really want to talk to you," Elizabeth said, yawning, weariness suddenly engulfing her.

"Don't worry about it. We can chat later."

For some reason, Beth felt her eyelids getting heavy and she closed them, finally feeling secure for the first time in hours.

When they got back to the helicopter, McCain saw that Elizabeth was asleep, leaning on Emily. He nodded and smiled at Em, mouthing, "thank you." Chuck pulled the satellite maps out of his pocket and showed them to the pilot, Colonel Michael Doran, and co-pilot, Major Juanita Custodio. Admiral Williams spoke to his bodyguards and Scotty, letting them know of the change of plans.

As Colonel Doran started the engines again and readied the aircraft for takeoff, Major Custodio compared McCain's maps to her own, plugging the coordinates into the Blackhawk's GPS.

"I've got the location programmed, Colonel," the co-pilot said. "It's just under seven miles. We'll call it an ETA of five minutes."

"Roger," the pilot acknowledged, lifting the helicopter into the air.

# Chapter Eight

**Hendersonville, North Carolina, Saturday, 1535 hours**

The pilot circled around and came in from the rear of what they hoped was the Mitchell farm. Beautiful, Chuck thought, surveying the property below him. What a great location to ride out the zombie apocalypse. The main residence was at least five hundred feet off of the roadway, hidden behind a thick copse of trees. Another smaller house was located a hundred feet behind the other. A well-kept barn sat off to the right of the first two structures. A fence surrounded the property, a combination of chain-link and wood.

Several large, open fields surrounded the home. McCain spotted four cows, a chicken coop, and a pigpen located around the property. Colonel Doran brought the helicopter around so they could view the front of the farm. Sergeant Harris peered over the sights of his mini-gun, looking for threats, while Scotty Smith looked out the other side, the sniper rifle cradled in his massive arms.

Three pickup trucks, two SUVs, and a passenger car were parked next to the main house. Chuck recognized Brian's white Honda CRV in the middle of the group. Or at least one like Brian's, the big man told himself. They still hadn't seen any signs of life.

"I've got three, make it four armed males coming out a side door," Sergeant Harris said, covering the men until they could verify who they were.

McCain had only met Brian once, and had never met the rest of his family, just talking to his father, Tommy, on the phone. The men kept their long guns pointed at the ground, watching the circling helicopter with curiosity. Suddenly, a familiar form was standing with the men.

"That's Melanie!" Chuck yelled over the intercom.

He leaned out next to Sergeant Harris and waved. After a moment, he saw her jump into the air, grab the man next to her by the arm and shake him, and then wave both arms at the Blackhawk.

"Colonel, can you put us down in that field behind the house?" the admiral asked, softly, watching the excited young woman below.

"Yes, sir."

McCain stuck his arm outside and pointed to the rear of the house and then moved back to where Beth was still napping. Emily grinned at him as he leaned in and gently kissed his wife. She woke up, disoriented, looking around with uncertainty in her eyes.

Chuck pulled the headphone back from her head and put his mouth next to her ear. "We're here. I just saw Melanie and we're about to land."

With relief evident on her face, Elizabeth sat up and put her arms around him as the aircraft descended, making a soft landing behind what Chuck thought of as the guesthouse. McCain had his and Beth's harnesses unsnapped before they had settled onto the ground, quickly jumping out of the Blackhawk. He held his wife's hand and motioned for her to crouch, the two of them running clear of the spinning rotors into the waiting arms of his daughter.

"Daddy!" Melanie squealed, holding him tight, crying for joy. Brian stood just behind her, cradling an AR-15, smiling broadly.

After several minutes, Chuck said, "I've been so worried about you." He held Melanie's face in his hands and just looked at her, tears running down his face. A University of Georgia cap sat on her head, her light brown hair just touching her shoulders. Freckles were sprinkled across her nose and face.

"And I've been so worried about you," she said, kissing him on the cheek and hugging him tightly again. She finally looked up at him and laughed. "That was quite an entrance!"

"If you only knew," he said, smiling.

Colonel Doran shut down the engines on the helicopter and they didn't have to shout anymore. The rest of the passengers disembarked slowly, allowing Chuck, Melanie, and Elizabeth to have their moment. McCain finally pulled free and nodded at Beth.

"We have a lot to talk about but I want to introduce you to Elizabeth. We got married this past week," Chuck said.

Melanie's mouth dropped open and she stared at the pretty young woman, not much older than herself. After a moment she regained her composure and put her arms around Beth, not knowing what else to do. As they were hugging, McCain stepped over to Brian and embraced the young man.

"Thanks, Brian. I asked you to take care of my daughter and you did."

"Yes, sir," he said. "We've been praying for you."

"Can you introduce me to your family?"

"Of course," he answered, wiping his eyes on his sleeve.

Brian's dad, Tommy, was short, stocky, and grinned easily. The two men shook hands and McCain quickly found himself in a bear hug as Tommy embraced him.

"It's great to finally meet you, Chuck. This is my wife, Terri."

A smiling, petite woman took Chuck's hand. "We've heard so much about you that I feel like I know you already," she said. "And we love Melanie. Oh, this is our other son, Barry."

A teenager built like Tommy was holding an AK-47 with a Glock on his waist. McCain stuck out his hand. "Nice to meet you, Barry."

"You, too, sir."

"Chuck, these are my parents," Tommy said. "This is Claude and Betsy and this is their farm."

The federal police officer shook hands with the elderly couple. Claude appeared to be in his eighties but moved well and had an M1 Garand slung over his shoulder and a bandolier of clips around his waist. A belt holster held a cocked and locked Colt Government Model .45. His wife, Betsy, was a plump, gray-headed matron with a happy demeanor.

McCain smiled at them. "I'm sorry to invade your farm like this but I've been trying to get to my daughter for over two months."

Betsy dismissed the comment with a wave. "We love Melanie and we're glad to meet you. Let's all go inside and have some coffee. I don't get to entertain guests very often."

As they were walking to the house Chuck saw that Beth and Melanie were walking together, talking quietly. He sidled up to Tommy.

"Please let your parents know that we don't want to be a burden. We've got MREs in the helicopter if they'll just let us sleep here for the night. We'll be leaving tomorrow."

"Don't worry about it, Chuck. We're set pretty well for food and my mom would love nothing better than to cook for y'all. But why do you have to leave so soon?"

"Orders. We've got a bad situation in Atlanta that needs to be dealt with as soon as we can."

"Worse than an invasion of zombies?" Mitchell asked incredulously.

"Surprisingly, yes. Thanks so much for taking care of Melanie. Oh, and I met your buddy, Ben Thompson, and his family. Actually, I also met your other neighbors, Leroy and Anthony. Good people."

"That's great! Did you stay in our house?"

"We did. Beth and I got married Monday night in Ben's living room and we spent the next two nights in your beautiful home. Thank you for your hospitality."

"Ben did your wedding? This week? Wow, Chuck! Congratulations!"

"Thanks. Sorry to change the subject but how secure are you guys here? We ran into hundreds of Zs down around the Upward Road exit. That's not that far from here."

Tommy took a deep breath. "We're blessed. There's a campus of the North Carolina Justice Academy less than half a mile away. They were running an academy when the zombies were seen heading this way. Over twenty of the recruits went and got their families and moved them into the dorms there. They've got a roadblock that they man 24/7. We're on good terms with them and my mom will occasionally cook up some food and take it down there."

McCain nodded. "There was a huge roadblock down on I-26 at Upward Road that got overrun. We had to abandon our vehicle there. It looked like they lost some police officers."

Mitchell shrugged. "I don't know. We've only had a few zombies out this way, thank God. We're almost ten miles from the interstate. Those police recruits, well, they're real cops now, they've had a couple of groups attack their barricade, but they've killed them all."

When they arrived at the house, Chuck saw Colonel Doran say something to Sergeant Harris. The young non-com nodded, turned, and headed back for the helicopter. Smart, McCain realized. Doran is probably keeping someone on security to guard the Blackhawk. That's our ride out of here and we can't be too careful with it.

Claude Mitchell held the door open, welcoming all of his guests. Chuck waited for the two most important women in his life to catch up with him. They each took one of his arms and went into the beautiful farmhouse.

Most of the passengers from the Blackhawk sat around the living room or kitchen table, sipping coffee or tea and munching on the fresh oatmeal raisin cookies that Betsy had baked. Claude sat engrossed in a conversation with the admiral, Scotty, Tim, and Tom, and Colonel Doran. The elder Mitchell had been an Army Ranger in the Korean conflict. When he found out that Smith had been a Ranger, as had Tim, a bond was immediately formed. The admiral's and Tom's Navy SEAL backgrounds had the five men sharing stories of their individual conflicts spanning over seven decades. Tommy, Brian, and Barry Mitchell listened as the warriors talked, envying the camaraderie that the men had already developed.

The short nap and a cup of coffee had perked Beth back up and she sat talking with Emily, Terri, Betsy, and Juanita Custodio. After a few minutes, however, the admiral poked his head into the kitchen and asked the women to join them in the living room.

"Now, Mrs. McCain, I don't want to put you on the spot, but your husband told me that you might want to tell us all how the two of you met."

It took a minute to register in Beth's mind that he was talking to her. "Oh, you're talking to me! I'm sorry, Admiral. I've never been called 'Mrs. McCain' before. Please just call me 'Elizabeth' or 'Beth.' So Chuck told you that, huh?"

"He did, right before he and Melanie slipped out to take a walk."

Elizabeth had never been shy in front of a crowd. And if her husband wanted her to tell these people their story, she would.

Chuck and Melanie walked hand-in-hand out behind the guesthouse. He and Beth had both taken hot showers, courtesy of the Mitchell's generator. Melanie had loaned Beth a pair of jeans and a black UGA hoodie. McCain had on a fresh 'Army Proud' t-shirt and sweatshirt which Scotty had handed him after hearing that his friend had lost his backpack. Chuck had left his body armor and rifle inside and was just wearing his pistol belt.

The big man noted with approval that Mel had on Rebecca Johnson's 9mm Glock 19 pistol. He had given it to her that fateful day on the UGA campus after Rebecca had been killed. McCain had told Brian to get Melanie somewhere safe. The virus was spreading so fast that they couldn't even go back to their dorms for any of their possessions. Chuck had given Mel the pistol and several magazines of ammo.

As McCain and his daughter strolled across the pasture, a memory popped into his mind. When she was a little girl, just three or four, one of their favorite pastimes was going by McDonald's, getting their lunch-to-go and visiting a local park. They always ate next to the lake and Mel had squealed with delight when the hungry geese would come begging for bread.

"We've got a lot to catch up on, but I need to tell you something important," Melanie said, her voice nervous. "Brian and I got married two months ago."

Chuck squeezed her hand. "I'm glad. He's a good man and I'm happy to hear it. Did Tommy do the ceremony?"

His daughter nodded, exhaling with relief. Tommy and Terri Mitchell had been lay pastors in their church back in Hartwell before fleeing to the safety of Tommy's parent's farm.

"You're not mad? I'd always dreamed of you walking me down the aisle."

McCain pulled her close and wrapped his arm around her. "How could I be mad at you? These are crazy days that we're living in. And you had no idea if I'd ever show up."

"Yeah, what happened? I expected you months ago." Melanie hung her head, sounding disappointed. "When you never came, I...I thought the worst."

Mel led him across a field and into a clump of trees. A well-worn path stopped in front of a half-acre pond. A picnic table stood next to the body of water and they sat down, side-by-side.

"This is where I would come everyday to pray. I knew you were in the middle of fighting the zombies, terrorists, and who-knows-what. I'd sit here and pray for you and the other guys, not knowing if you were already dead or not. I wondered some days if God was even listening."

"He was listening, all right," her father said. "I left over two months ago, heading to Hartwell, hoping that you or Tommy had left me a note or a map as to where you were going. It turned into quite an ordeal."

"Two months! What happened?"

He shrugged. "I kept running into people who wanted to kill me."

McCain told Melanie about his journey. He normally would have glossed over most of the dangerous aspects, but this afternoon he wanted her to know how hard he had tried to reach her. Chuck especially wanted her know how he and Beth had met. McCain gave more details than even he felt comfortable sharing but he needed Mel to understand how they had connected and why it had taken him so long to finally reach his daughter.

Mel's eyes registered shock and then started watering as he related how Elizabeth's friends had been murdered and she'd been kidnapped. He told his daughter how he'd been able to save the young woman, getting shot in the process, and then of their three days in an abandoned house, waiting out a winter storm.

"I can't explain it, but trapped in that freezing house, we fell in love," he admitted.

Mel squeezed his arm as he spoke of getting shot again during an attack on the Northeast Georgia Technical College campus. McCain smiled as he related how Beth had stayed by his side for the next month, helping Karen nurse him back to health.

He didn't tell Melanie about every ambush or zombie incident that they had had but he did tell her about the day that he and Beth had had. Chuck admitted that he had believed they were going to die earlier, running to the point of exhaustion, the hoard of hundreds of zombies relentlessly pursuing them. Trapped on the roof of a trailer in a mobile home park, his main goal was to allow Elizabeth to get away safely, even if he perished in the process.

Melanie held her father's hand tightly as he shared how close they had come to dying just hours earlier. She took a deep breath, calming herself, but grateful that God had, indeed, answered her prayers.

"You're going to stay with us, right? You and Elizabeth?"

He shook his head. "I have to leave tomorrow."

The disappointment was immediate on Mel's face. "Tomorrow?" she exclaimed. "But you just got here!"

"I know but I have a mission that the admiral needs my help on back in Atlanta. He promised me, though, that once we take care of this situation, he'll fly me back up here for some R&R. My plan, though, is to leave Beth with you guys, if that's OK?"

"Of course. I'm still not sure what I feel about you being married, but it's fine. I want to get to know her. She seems really sweet, but I'm not calling her 'Mom,' though."

Chuck laughed. "I don't think she'd let you. Why don't we head back inside? It's getting cold out here."

They stood but Melanie hesitated, looking up at her father. "There's something else. The only other person who knows this is Brian. I was waiting before I told his parents, but you're here and I've got to tell you. I'm pregnant! I just took the test yesterday and it was positive."

McCain had been punched in the face by two hundred and sixty-five pound heavyweights during his professional MMA career.

Those shots were nothing compared to the stunned surprise that he felt at this moment. He grabbed his daughter and hugged her, feeling his own eyes watering.

"Congratulations, Sweetheart! You're going to be a mommy and I'm going to be a grandfather!"

Father and daughter let themselves into the house through the kitchen and quietly made their way to the living room, where they could hear Elizabeth talking. McCain realized she was telling her attentive audience about their wedding ceremony the previous Monday.

"So, then I realized everyone in the room was looking at me. Chuck had gotten up and was standing with Pastor Ben by the fireplace and he said, 'If you don't have anything better to do tonight, would you marry me?' And I did."

Her listeners burst out in applause as McCain glanced around the room. Emily wiped her eyes with a Kleenex, staring intently at Scotty. The bearded man stuck his hand out and she handed him the tissue so he could dab his own tears. Tim, the burly former Delta operative, was standing against the back wall next to Chuck, blinking and then turning away.

When he saw Chuck looking at him, Tim shrugged and said, "It's dusty in here. Dust always makes my eyes water."

Beth saw that her husband had slipped into the back of the room with Melanie and said, "Here he is now. Mr. Romantic."

This brought a laugh from everyone. McCain slid over next to his wife's chair, put an arm around her and looked at the all of the Mitchells.

"I can't tell you how thankful I am for how you've all looked after Melanie. And she told me the good news that she and Brian got married. I wish I could've been here, but at least we get to celebrate tonight!"

It was a wonderful celebration and Chuck's heart was full. Betsy Mitchell had served a simple dinner of scrambled eggs, bacon, and hash brown potatoes. Everyone agreed it was one of the best meals that they'd ever eaten. McCain watched Tom, the former SEAL Team Six member, eat quickly and then slip out to relieve Harris at the helicopter. A few minutes later, the young crewman was inside and devouring his dinner, as well.

After dinner, Admiral Williams went outside holding his satellite phone. The inside of the Mitchell seniors' spacious home was lit by candles, the windows all covered with blackout shades. As Emily, Melanie, and Elizabeth sat talking in one corner of the room, Chuck pulled Scotty aside to catch up with him.

The two men shared some of their experiences from the previous two months. After the last big attacks in Atlanta, neither Scotty nor Emily had been able to return to their apartments so Chuck had let them stay with him. When he had left on his journey to find Melanie, he knew that the couple was planning to drive to Gatlinburg, Tennessee, where Emily's brother lived with his family. Her parents had fled there, as well.

"I saw you had my Remington 700 and Em had my Benelli."

Smith smiled. "You told us to make ourselves at home and you were kind enough to leave your gun safe open. She loves that shotgun, plus she's also wearing your little Glock 26. I found some fifteen round Glock 19 mags and that's what she's been carrying. I really like that rifle. It's a good shooter and 30.06 puts Zs and people down hard."

McCain nodded. "I killed a lot of deer with it. I'm glad you've gotten some use out of it. So what all did the admiral tell you about what's going on?"

Scotty's eyes got big. "Did you know that we've been working for the CIA all along? He told me that he's the Director of

Operations and that our CDC Unit was created to let the spooks stay in the middle of the fight against the terrorists and the zombies."

Chuck was surprised. What Smith had just shared was classified. After McCain had put all the pieces of the puzzle together many months earlier, Rebecca Johnson had sworn him to secrecy. If the media had gotten ahold of that information, the firestorm would have shut them down. Now I guess it doesn't matter, he thought.

"Yeah, I figured it out early on but Rebecca made promise to keep my mouth shut."

Smith shrugged, taking it all in stride. "Anyway, he told me something about a group of Mexican gang members trying to take over a section of Atlanta. He said we'd all get a full briefing later. What have you heard?"

"The pastor who performed our wedding has a ham radio," McCain answered. "He told me that he'd heard people chatting about it. Then, a couple of days ago, we talked to some South Carolina State Troopers who said they'd heard the same stuff over their radio. The trooper said it was a Mexican Cartel.

"Admiral Williams showed me a video a drone took this morning of maybe ten armed gang members dragging eight young women out of the back of a van. I guess one of the girls tried to put up a fight because some bastard shot her and they threw her body onto the street. The admiral said this cartel has taken over several blocks of Buckhead and that these scumbags have maybe forty women being held as slaves."

"Oh, man! That sucks!" Scotty said, shaking his head angrily. "Sounds like they want us to go in there and arrest them? Any idea how many there are?"

Chuck grunted. "He told me maybe two hundred, but that's not all. Somehow, these bastards have gotten their hands on some of the virus. I don't know how much arresting we'll be doing. The boss' exact words were, 'eliminate the cartel presence on U.S. soil, secure the virus, and free the hostages.'"

Smith smiled grimly. "I like eliminating better than arresting."

Laughter erupted from where the young women were sitting on the other side of the room, all three of them staring at Scotty. Suddenly self-conscious, he stood and walked over, standing next to Emily.

"What's so funny?"

"Nothing, Scotty. Nothing at all," his girlfriend said, trying to keep a straight face, but bursting into laughter again.

"She just told us how you two met," Melanie said, a big grin on her face, "and the terrible pickup lines you used to get her number."

The muscular man smiled broadly. "I thought I was pretty smooth. And those lines must not have been too bad because she gave it to me," he said, proudly.

The door opened and Admiral Williams slipped back in. He made eye contact with Chuck and motioned with his head to the other side of the room. McCain could see the weariness in the elderly man's eyes, but knew that his boss was a warrior.

"Everything OK, sir?"

"I've been on the phone," the CIA man said, "trying to get some more assets for this operation in Atlanta. Things are slowly coming back to normal. The President has even authorized using military units to eliminate the infected up and down the east coast. So many of the local police departments have been gutted and so much of our military is committed to other things. I'm asking for a few spec ops units from the west coast to be assigned to our mission but I'm still waiting to hear back on that."

"What about other feds?" McCain asked. "If we can't get military units, maybe we could get some FBI, ATF, or even DEA agents to help us take down this cartel?"

Williams paused before answering. "You know how badly the FBI let us down. They had a terrorist mole assigned to one of their deputy directors. And that mole had dirt on his boss and blackmailed him to do his bidding. Several other traitors were identified and removed from the Bureau. The President doesn't trust them. He's cleaned house and fired the Attorney General, as well as the FBI Director.

"Believe it or not, he's directed the CIA to oversee the elimination of the zombies and the coordination with local law enforcement in regards to cleanup. The director is a good man but he's a political appointee. He's smart enough to know that he's in over his head and is letting me run the show, for the time being, anyway. The FBI has been ordered to cooperate with us in every way possible, but I don't see them having a large role in this mission.

"The President wants the situation in Atlanta resolved ASAP, so that's why I'm here. I don't want to send you in until we've got all the pieces in place, but we have to eliminate the cartel's presence, recover the virus, and those poor women must be rescued. The President was very clear in his terminology. This is more of a military operation than a police operation so I'm not sure how other federal police officers would respond to those orders. You'll probably be working with a mixed bag of special operators, but I'm confident in your abilities to accomplish the mission."

The admiral handed McCain his satellite phone. "I just got another video that you'll be interested in. One of our drones followed two of the cartel's vehicles out of Atlanta. They left on Thursday morning and we intercepted them yesterday outside of El Paso before they could get into Mexico. I was able to borrow a SEAL team from Coronado to stop them."

Chuck suddenly remembered something, his finger poised over the video play button on his boss' phone. "I'm sorry, sir, but I've been meaning to ask you about the rest of my men. If our weapons have GPS trackers in them, where's everybody else? Rogers and

Matthews were the only ones unaccounted for when I left, but Jimmy Jones told me he would be leaving, as well, to try and locate a young woman, a police officer in Athens."

The CIA man sighed. "I'm sorry, but it looks like Agents Rogers and Matthews didn't make it. Were they traveling together?"

Chuck nodded. "Both of their families were on the west side of Atlanta, out I-20. When I released everyone to take care of their own, they left together. How can you tell that they might be…dead?" He hated to even vocalize the possibility.

"The trackers allow us to pinpoint where the weapon is. Both of their rifles are over near I-285 and I-20 and haven't moved for weeks. I'll give you the coordinates to check after we deal with the cartel. It's possible that they both lost their M4s and kept going, but that doesn't strike me as likely."

Williams let those words hang in the air before continuing. "On the other hand, Agent Jones lost his rifle in Athens but Shaun told me that he and the police officer he went to rescue are back at the CDC site."

"That's really good news, but I hate to hear that about Chris and Terrence," Chuck said, shaking his head.

McCain turned his attention back to the admiral's satellite smart phone and pressed play. A SUV and a full-sized van came into view on a deserted stretch of highway. Both vehicles suddenly veered off onto the shoulder, slowing down just as they came to an overpass. Armed figures appeared from concealed positions beside the interstate. Chuck watched several SEALs firing into the SUV while others focused on the second vehicle, quickly eliminating the driver and passenger.

The commandos cautiously approached the rear of the van. Moments later, the ten kidnapped women were standing with the SEALs on the side of the road as the two vehicles were searched. One of the victims appeared to be injured, and one of the operators tended to her. Two minutes after it started, a Navy Seahawk helicopter touched down on the roadway and the freed hostages were placed aboard.

Three minutes after that, with the scene secured, the vehicles having been searched, a second Navy helicopter touched down, allowing the SEALs to board. Start to finish, the operation had taken seven minutes and twelve seconds. Chuck handed the admiral's phone back.

"Very impressive. What's the story?"

"The SEALs used stop stick sticks to flatten their tires. They gave them a chance to surrender so that we could interrogate them but those silly men thought they could win in a firefight with the best of the best. Six dead cartel members and they rescued ten women who were being shipped back to Tijuana. One of the hostages was slightly wounded during the shootout. A spent round hit her in the head. It took a couple of stitches to fix her up.

"Another of the girls was Puerto Rican and bilingual. She heard some of the soldiers talking as they were loading them into the van. Thanks to her, we know who we're dealing with now. Antonio Corona, aka, Tony the Tiger, is calling the shots in Buckhead. He was the lieutenant for his uncle, Jose "Pepe" Corona, the head of the Tijuana Cartel. Antonio was sending the girls to his uncle as a gift and was asking for more soldiers. We recovered a letter from one of the bodies that confirms what the girl overheard.

"But it gets even better. The SEALs found two vials of liquid wrapped with bubble wrap, in a small box. The letter said that they contained the zombie virus and Tony the Tiger was giving his uncle a 'very special weapon.' As you can see, this is really turning into something serious. Those vials will be delivered to us at the CDC in a couple of days for evaluation, but thank God we intercepted and stopped those bastards."

Chuck sat back taking it all in. The last thing that they needed was to have the bio-terror weapon in the hands of one of the largest Mexican criminal gangs. It was bad enough that the invaders in Atlanta had the weapon, but the CDC agents and some of their friends would be paying the gangsters a visit very soon.

By 2200hrs, McCain was ready for bed. Terri Mitchell had prepared a guest room in the small house for he and Beth. Terri tried to give the admiral the other open guest room but he had deferred, giving it to Emily and Scotty. Williams chose the couch in the main house. Tim, Tom, and the Blackhawk crew rolled out sleeping bags on the living room floor. Colonel Doran set a watch schedule, making sure the helicopter was guarded all night.

Beth had moved to the small table in the kitchen, she and Melanie still engrossed in conversation. That made Chuck happy. He had been concerned about how that relationship was going to work out. He need not have worried as the two young women were clearly enjoying getting to know each other. He kissed Melanie on top of the head, Elizabeth on the lips, and went to bed, falling asleep as soon as his head touched the pillow.

An hour later, his wife crawled into bed, sliding right up next to him. Always a light-sleeper, Chuck's eyes popped open.

"Are you awake?" she asked, excitedly.

"I am now," he yawned. "I was sleeping good, too!"

"Sorry, but I had to tell you congratulations. Melanie told me! You're going to be a grandfather!"

"Thanks! And you're going to be a grandmother."

Beth had clearly not considered the ramifications of her husband's daughter's pregnancy. "Wait a minute! I'm way too young to be a grandmother."

"You'll be a good one," he went on. "I wonder what they'll call you? Granny Beth? Grandma Beth?"

The young woman swatted his chest softly and laughed. "That's not very nice!"

Chuck wrapped his arms tightly around Elizabeth. "I'm really glad you guys got to hang out. I've got to leave tomorrow but Mel said they'd love to have you stay here with them. I should be..."

"No!" she answered emphatically, pushing herself up and looking into his face. "I'm not leaving you again. I'm going with you."

"Sweetie, I don't know how safe it's going to be where I'm going. I've got a big mission to plan and execute and..."

"I'm not staying here," she said, in a tone that Chuck hadn't heard before. "I love Melanie and the Mitchells are beautiful people but I'm going with you. I'll stay out of your way while you work, I promise. I'm a pretty good administrator and you might even find a job for me."

She paused for a minute and then continued. "And please don't talk to me about danger. Nothing I do for the rest of my life will be as dangerous as the day we had today, or the last two months, for that matter."

McCain shook his head and was silent for several minutes. It was hard to argue with her logic, he thought. He finally sighed and said, "Okay. I'd rather bunk with you than Scotty any day."


**Centers for Disease Control Compound, East of Atlanta, Sunday, 1220 hours**

The Blackhawk circled the compound, the sound of the rotors carrying inside the buildings where the scientists were hard at work. Dr. Nicole Edwards clicked "save" on the file she had open on her computer, and rushed outside, hope rising inside of her. The helicopter's side doors were open and she could see several people crammed into the passenger compartment as the aircraft circled the location.

Some of the CDC agents had grouped near the gate, smiling and talking quietly. She got the feeling that they were expecting someone. Maybe it was him, she thought, hanging back in the shadows of the main building, where the labs were located. Nicole heard footsteps and glanced around to see Jay Walker and the Asian agent heading towards the front entrance.

Jay slowed as he came even with the epidemiologist, nodding and smiling at her. "Hi, Nicole. You working Sundays, too?"

"Seven days a week until we can solve the riddle," she answered wearily.

"We need to get over there where all the excitement's at but let me introduce you to my boss. Tu Trang Donaldson, this is Dr. Nicole Edwards. She's the brilliant mind behind that solution that kills the virus on contact and if I was betting man, I'd bet that she'll have a vaccine developed before long."

"Nice to meet you, Ma'am," Tu greeted her warmly. "Thanks for all your hard work. These can't be easy conditions to work in."

Edwards blushed at Walker's kind words. She also found herself surprised that the powerful looking Asian man spoke English with a slight Southern drawl.

"Very good to meet you, Agent Donaldson. Thank you both, but I think your job is much harder than mine! Do y'all have any idea who's on the helicopter."

"Just call me 'Tu.' We're not sure; we were just told to expect some guests."

Walker gave a slight tip of the head to the woman and shrugged. "Could be," he said, softly, as if reading her thoughts.

Nicole looked away as Jay looked into her eyes. Then the two agents were gone, off to join the others as the aircraft touched down just outside the gate on the driveway. Agent Walker was a very interesting man. He was confident but not cocky. In a lot of ways he reminded her of Chuck, just a smaller version, she thought, smiling to herself. Jay was clearly interested in getting to know her. He had gone out of his way to sit with her the previous day in the dining room and she'd been impressed that he had been familiar with her work. Jay was a pleasant man and they'd had a nice chat.

When she had mentioned Chuck during their conversation, however, she had felt a slight shift in his demeanor. And he had read her like a book. Am I really that transparent? Nicole wondered with a sigh.

The passengers were still inside the aircraft as the pilot shut the engines down. Edwards found herself walking towards the gate. A white-jacketed figure was suddenly strolling beside her.

"Hi, Nicole," Dr. Martin greeted her. "Sorry, no more world-class scientists today. Agent Marshall informed me that there's a big operation being planned and some of the key players are on board. We've also got a paramedic joining us. We've been lucky that no one has needed a doctor, but with Mrs. Marshall's pregnancy, it'll be good to have someone with medical training on-site."

"Where are they all going to sleep? We don't have that much space here."

Martin sighed. "I know. We'll figure something out. I'll talk to Admiral Williams and see what we can do."

"Admiral Williams? Who's he and how did the Navy get involved with what we're doing?" Edwards asked with a smile.

Her question was left unanswered as the passengers started to disembark from the helicopter. Two large bearded men holding rifles were off first. One of them helped an elderly man climb out. The next person off the aircraft was Agent Scotty Smith. The scientist had gotten to know him and his girlfriend, Emily, during the time that they had all stayed at Chuck's house. And there's Emily now, Nicole noted with a smile, as Smith helped her to the ground.

Several of the CDC agents pointed at Scotty, a ripple of excitement running through the crowd as Smith waved to his friends. Another figure was climbing out, a smile on his face. Oh, my God! It's him! He actually made it back. Edwards realized that she'd been holding her breath and let it out, her heart pounding inside of her chest. Chuck assisted a young woman to the ground and the group made their way towards the compound. Is that his daughter? What was her name? I think it was Melanie, Nicole remembered.

When the Atlanta CDC agents recognized McCain, it was all they could do to contain their excitement. Everyone knew that yelling might draw infected to the location but these men were thrilled to see their boss, giving each other high fives and slapping one other on the back. Grace, the female police officer, stood quietly next to Agent Jones, holding his hand as tears streamed down her cheeks, trying to smile even as she cried.

When the group got inside, everyone wanted to shake McCain's hand and hug him, the federal officers all talking at once. Edwards saw that the young woman let Chuck have his moment, standing off to the side, smiling broadly. Dr. Martin and the older man walked towards the dining room, talking as if they had known each other for a while. I wonder if that's the admiral? Nicole pondered.

Edwards watched McCain turn, looking for his young companion, and then motioning for her to join him. She did, stepping forward with a shy look on her face as Chuck introduced her to the group, his big arm around her shoulders. Scotty Smith saw Edwards standing back from the circle of CDC officers and broke into a big grin.

"Hey, Nicole!" He greeted her and covered the distance in two strides wrapping her in his massive arms.

Emily joined them, embracing the scientist warmly. She and Nicole had shared a bed in Chuck's guest room for over two weeks before the rural CDC location was up and running. Scotty had been relegated to the living room couch. The women had become close, and after living under the same roof for a couple of weeks, Scotty considered Nicole a part of the team.

"I'm so glad to see you!" Edwards finally said, grinning. "It's been too long. You guys look great."

A deep voice came from beside her. "Hi, Nicole! It's good to see you," Chuck said, hugging his friend, the woman's heart suddenly flooding with emotions.

After a moment, he pulled away and motioned at the pretty young lady beside him. "Nicole, I want you to meet someone. This is my wife, Elizabeth. We got married last week."

Edwards was already extending her hand, expecting McCain to say, "This is my daughter." When she heard the word "wife" she almost withdrew her hand. Chuck saw the stunned expression on Nicole's face and interpreted it as surprise.

"Yeah, it surprised me, too," he said, slipping an arm around Beth's waist. "We met a couple of months ago and got married this past Monday. Beth, Dr. Edwards is one of the leading epidemiologists in the world. She and her team are working night and day to find a cure for the virus."

"It's nice to meet you, Dr. Edwards."

Nicole could only force a smile and nod at Elizabeth. She had so many questions. The group started moving towards the dining room, sweeping them all along. The scientist's stomach had been growling just a few minutes before, letting her know it was lunch time. Now, however, she wasn't sure if she'd be able to eat.

As everyone moved in the direction of the dining room, Chuck and Elizabeth found themselves being swept along, everyone wanting to speak with McCain. The big man felt a strong hand grab his right arm and a gravelly voice spoke so that only he could hear it.

"Don't you ever pull a stunt like that again! You had everyone here worried to death about you."

Chuck turned and looked into the unsmiling eyes of Andy Fleming and immediately understood that when he spoke of "everyone" being worried, he really meant himself. Fleming was a man of few words but had become one of McCain's best friends.

"Hey, buddy, good to see you, too."

"I'm serious, Chuck. If you ever decide to go on another cross-country trek, let me know and I'll go with you," Andy said, finally smiling.

"Oh, no," McCain answered. "Then I'd have to answer to your wife and I've heard that Marine wives are the toughest women on the planet."

Fleming laughed. "She is that and then some. I'm really glad you're OK, boss. It sounds like we've got a big adventure in front of us."

"Yes, we do," he nodded, gently guiding Beth to where he could introduce her. "Andy, I want you to meet my wife, Elizabeth. We just got married a week ago. Beth, this is Andy Fleming. He's one of my team leaders, but more importantly, he's also one of my best friends."

The former Marine shook the pretty young woman's hand and laughed. "See, this is just what I'm talking about. I leave you alone for a couple of months and you come back married. It's very nice to meet you, ma'am. I hope this guy hasn't corrupted you too much. I'll introduce you to my wife, Amy, later. She can offer you some tips on how to handle knuckle draggers like us."

Beth looped her arm through Chuck's and smiled, enjoying the banter between the two friends. "That would be nice. I'd love to meet her."

**Centers for Disease Control Compound, East of Atlanta, Sunday, 1630 hours**

After lunch, Admiral Williams briefed all the CDC agents on the nature of the mission that lay before them. He played the two drone videos that he had shown Chuck the day before. This time, though, the drama was played out on the large screen TV in the team's small office. The resolve of the agents was solidified even more as they watched body of the dead woman was dragged out of the back of the van and dropped onto the pavement, her head bouncing as it struck the surface, and as the laughing cartel soldiers herded the other women into the high-rise building.

Williams made it clear to the agents that McCain was in charge and would immediately begin planning the mission. The admiral also let them know he was going to be bringing in more shooters than the ten CDC agents that they had on hand. For the time being, the officers would begin studying maps and brainstorming. Although the President wanted a mission executed ASAP, Williams had told him that with all the moving pieces it might take as long as two weeks before they would be ready to go.

The Director of Operations for the CIA concluded, "I realize that these are not optimal living conditions here and you'll need a better location more conducive to planning an operation. Agent McCain and I will be flying over to Dobbins Air Force Base in the morning and lining up accommodations, equipment, and logistical support for you."

Andy Fleming's hand went up. "Sorry to interrupt, sir, but weren't they overrun a few days after those thousands of Zs swept north out of Atlanta?"

"That was correct, Mr. Fleming. However, in the last month the base has been retaken by a mixture of National Guard and active

duty troops, mostly Marine Corps personnel," he added, nodding at
Andy, Jimmy, and LeMarcus, "as well as some police officers. Air
Force and Marine air units have been running multiple sorties
everyday, shredding packs of infected. They've killed thousands of
zombies and have resecured the air base.

"At any rate, we'll meet with the major in charge and make sure
that Dobbins will suffice as a staging and planning area. And, yes, I
said, 'major.' They suffered a lot of losses and Major Singleton is
the ranking officer."

"Admiral, what about this location?" Eddie asked. "Our families
and some very hardworking scientists are here. We haven't had any
zombie activity to speak of but we can't leave this site undefended."

"We're working on that, as well, Mr. Marshall. You are correct.
We will not leave this location without security. I'm just not sure yet
what that security will look like."

Chuck was feeling a bit overwhelmed as he walked out of the
meeting. He had been off the grid for the previous two months,
trying to get to Melanie, rescuing Elizabeth, helping defend the
technical college that she had worked at, getting shot twice, getting
married, and not having any contact with his teammates during that
time. Now, he was not only being thrown back into the fray, but he
was also being asked to plan the biggest operation he had ever been
involved in.

Thankfully, McCain had great people on his team and he
intended to utilize their expertise. Andy had been a MARSOC
Marine and was an elite, world-class operator. Walker and Trang
from the D.C. CDC office had both been in special operations, Jay in
SEAL Team Six and Tu as a Green Beret. Each of the other CDC
agents had extensive military or law enforcement backgrounds, or
both. This would be a team effort as they put the op together.

All of the living quarters were occupied and he had no idea

where he and Beth would sleep. Probably on the floor of one of the offices, he guessed. She had insisted on coming. Now she was going to find out what it was like to live as a grunt. Still deep in thought, he almost ran into the figure that materialized in front of him on the sidewalk.

"Hi, Agent McCain," Grace Cunningham greeted him.

"Grace! I didn't get a chance to say 'hello' earlier," he said, embracing the campus police officer. "I haven't had a chance to catch up with Jimmy, either. I just asked him how he'd managed to get to you and get back here in one piece. He just shook his head and said it was the trip of a lifetime."

Cunningham hung her head. "Yeah, I guess that's what it was," she said, quietly. "Could I talk to you for a few minutes?"

Chuck started to say "no" and see if they could set it up for another time, but there was something in the her eyes that told him this was important.

"Sure, you want to walk and talk?"

She nodded, sticking her hands in her pockets as they started around the perimeter of the location.

After a few moments, Grace blurted out, "I had to do something really bad and it's eating me up on the inside. I was hoping maybe you could help me."

We've all had to do some really bad things, he thought. That's the nature of living in a society where zombies roam the landscape and law, order, and decency have broken down.

"I had to shoot my parents," she continued. "I tried to get them to leave town but my daddy was a pastor in Athens for over twenty years. Plus, he was stubborn," she smiled bitterly. "He was a good man but he was stubborn. Somehow, he or my mom got infected. I had to kill both of them. My sister, Hope, was already dead. Mama and Daddy had..."

Cunningham stopped and took a deep breath. There were no

tears now, just a deep sadness in her heart.

"I'm so sorry, Grace," Chuck said, shaking his head and putting a comforting hand on her shoulder. "What an awful world we live in where you would have to do something like that."

Grace looked into the big man's eyes, hoping that he would somehow understand what she was feeling. "I wanted to talk to you because I know that you lost someone you cared about. I was there when it happened, but I didn't know everything until later and Jimmy told me the whole story. I know it's different but how did you get over it? I feel so sad all the time. I told Jimmy I was even having suicidal thoughts for a while."

Chuck nodded. "I understand. When Rebecca got killed I blamed myself. I relived that shootout everyday, and was having nightmares every night. I just couldn't forgive myself. I hadn't been able to protect her and I thought I was going to carry that pain around forever."

Grace nodded, having experienced the same emotions. "What happened? You don't act like you're sad now. How were you able to move on with your life?"

McCain took a deep breath, remembering that day in a cold, abandoned house when he and Beth had opened their hearts to each other. "Did you meet Elizabeth?"

She shook her head. "Not yet. She looked a little overwhelmed with everyone wanting to shake her hand. Jimmy told me that you guys got married last week?"

"That's right. It's a crazy story, but I never thought I'd ever be able to love again. Then I met Elizabeth and, well, we did fall in love."

Chuck paused, looking into the young woman's eyes. "Can I ask you for a favor? I'm going to be very busy over the next couple of weeks with an assignment. Jimmy and the rest of the guys, we're all going to be working on this. Would you make a point of getting to know Beth? I'd feel better knowing that she's got some friends.

"She and Emily met yesterday and seemed to hit it off, but she still doesn't know anyone else here. And, I think it would help you to hear a little of what she's been through. I'll let her give you all the details but Beth had to kill her mother after she got infected. Then, her dad turned, as well, and tried to eat her. She watched the police shoot him. That sent her spiraling into a really deep depression."

Grace's eyes grew large at the revelation that she wasn't the only one who'd had to take out infected family members.

"Are you sure she wouldn't mind talking to me?"

"Not at all. She's a good person and I'm blessed to have found her. Part of her healing and my healing was finding each other. I don't want to pry or get into your business but I know a guy who's crazy about you. I'm sure he's frustrated because he doesn't know how to help you."

The young woman looked down, thinking about what the big man had just told her. "You're right. Thanks for talking to me, Chuck. I'll get to know Elizabeth and look after her. And I'll try to let Jimmy into my world. I love him, too, but this black cloud makes it hard to even think about having a relationship."

They had gotten back to where they had started their walk. "One more thing, Grace. I know you said your dad was a pastor, but we all have to sort out our own relationship with Jesus. After Rebecca died, I prayed and read my Bible but I felt so far away from God. I couldn't understand why he had allowed her to die, or why we're having to deal with the zombie virus. I had so many questions and no answers."

Cunningham nodded slowly as Chuck articulated exactly what she had been feeling. Before Jimmy had come for her, she'd spent hours reading the Scriptures and trying to pray, only to feel that the Lord wasn't anywhere to be found.

"I've felt the same way," she admitted quietly.

McCain gave her an understanding smile. "I still don't have all the answers and there's still a lot of things that I wish God would make clear. But, one of the things that I do understand now is that the Lord often heals us through the love of the people he has put around us. For me, it was Elizabeth, and some of the goofballs that I work with. For you, it might be Jimmy, maybe Beth, and even some of the other people onsite here who have had to deal with tragedy. But then, after you get healed, God is going to use you to help others, as well."

Chuck's words resonated with the young woman and she nodded. "I've never looked at like that. I guess I've just been focused on my own grief, but you're right. There are a lot of hurting people in the world right now. You've really given me some things to think about."

Grace gave him a quick hug and then turned towards her camper. Chuck headed for the dining room, looking for the woman who had helped him climb out of his own dark hole.

McCain found Beth seated at a table with Emily and Andy's wife, Amy, who stood and embraced her husband's boss. Mrs. Fleming's shoulder length brown hair was pulled back into a ponytail, her green eyes sparkling as she greeted him.

"Welcome back! And congratulations on getting married!"

"Thanks, Amy. It's good to be back. I heard that Tyler has become an unofficial member of the security team."

"You know it. He's so much like his father, it's scary," Amy smiled.

"I guess that's good and bad," Chuck laughed. "I'm just glad you guys are here and are safe."

"Well, we're glad you're back where you belong. We were all worried about you, but I could tell that it was really eating away at Andy. And I can't wait to get to know Elizabeth," Amy said, smiling at the younger woman.

McCain spoke to several people in the dining room and then offered to show Beth around the compound. The couple walked hand-in-hand around the perimeter, enjoying a peaceful few minutes together, knowing that things were about to get hectic for Chuck and his team.

He told her about his conversation with Grace and saw the understanding his wife's eyes. "Would you mind talking with her?" he asked. "I think you'd be able to help her and y'all might end up becoming good friends."

"Sure. I was just wondering if maybe God was going to somehow use what I went through to help others."

"That's usually the way that it works," her husband said. "God takes some trial or tragedy that we've dealt with and helps us get through it. We're then able to bring that same healing to other people."

They walked in silence for several minutes before Elizabeth spoke up. "What's the deal with Dr. Edwards?"

He glanced over, a puzzled expression on his face. "I don't know. What do you mean?"

"Did you two ever date or anything?"

"Me and Nicole? No. I don't think I'd ever even had a conversation with her until the day we rescued her. She and one of our security officers had gotten trapped in the CDC Headquarters so we went in and got them out.

"After that, she stayed at my house for a couple of weeks. Her apartment was in Buckhead and there was no way that she could go home. She and Emily shared my guest room, Scotty slept on the couch, and Darnell slept in my recliner. He was Emily's paramedic partner.

"We talked a little during the time she was there, but I probably wasn't the best host. I was still reeling from Rebecca's death. Plus, we started running daily rescue missions in the city until the power and communication grids broke down. Me and the guys would brief early in the morning in my living room and then we'd leave. We'd get back after dark and I'd eat and go to bed."

Beth nodded thoughtfully. "Okay."

"Okay?" he echoed. "There's got to be more to that question about us dating than just 'OK.'"

"You really don't know, do you?" she said, with a slight smile, amusement evident in her eyes.

"Know what?" he answered, starting to feel annoyed.

"That woman is in love with you. When you introduced me as your wife, I saw it on her face. She was devastated. I saw her a little while ago in the dining room. She wouldn't even make eye contact with me and looked like her world was coming to an end."

That revelation sent the big man back on his heels and he immediately went back through his interactions and conversations with Nicole, looking for clues. He also wondered if there was anything that he might have said or done to lead her on.

He finally shook his head, realizing that he had never picked up any signs from the beautiful scientist. "It's the zombie apocalypse and I'm living in the Days of Our Lives."

Elizabeth stepped in putting her arm around his waist. "You're cute," she said. "Dense, but cute."

**Over Atlanta, 1500 feet, Monday, 1000 hours**

The Blackhawk cruised across the overrun city at one hundred and fifty miles an hour. Admiral Williams, Chuck, Tim, Tom, and Scotty gazed out the open doors as the ground rushed past them. Scotty was along as an extra gun just in case they had to make a forced landing or if they encountered any unexpected problems.

McCain had instructed the CDC agents who had remained

behind to begin studying the satellite maps of Buckhead which the admiral had provided them. Although everyone would be able to offer their input as they planned, Chuck specifically needed Andy, Tu, and Jay's spec ops expertise and asked them to start sketching out the operation.

Chuck's goal was to have a working plan by the end of the week. That would leave them another week to train and prepare. Hopefully, by that time, the other assets whom the admiral had spoken of would have arrived.

When they were a mile out, co-pilot Major Custodio radioed the tower at Dobbins Air Force and requested permission to land. It was immediately granted, Chuck figuring there weren't a lot of flights going in and out of the large air base. They were directed to land adjacent to a large building just northwest of the control tower.

Major Singleton was a stocky woman with short, black hair. Her olive green flight uniform was clean and pressed, as were the fatigues of the tall, lean Marine Gunnery Sergeant and the two heavily armed airmen who accompanied them. McCain suddenly felt self-conscious at his own black BDUs, which hadn't been washed in weeks, and his unshaven face.

The major waited as the visitors ducked under the still-spinning rotors and approached her and her escort. A Beretta 9mm hung from a shoulder holster under the officer's right armpit. The African-American Marine cradled an M-16 rifle to go along with the cocked and locked .45 ACP pistol hanging from his waist. McCain watched the two of them scrutinizing the newcomers as Admiral Williams approached the woman with his hand out and a smile on his face. Singleton shook his hand, nodded at the others and motioned towards the two-story building behind her.

The front door opened into a lobby of an administration building. Once inside, they could speak without having to yell. The major introduced herself and Gunnery Sergeant Eric Gray.

"Thank you for receiving us on short notice, Major. My name is Jonathan Williams. I was an admiral in the greatest Navy on the planet, but my current position is that of Director of Operations for the Central Intelligence Agency." Williams nodded at his companion. "This is Chuck McCain, the Officer-in-Charge of the Atlanta office of the CDC Enforcement Unit."

When the admiral mentioned his previous rank, both the major and the gunnery sergeant stood up a little straighter.

"Why don't we go into the conference room, sir" the major said, pointing at a large room behind her. "When the Chief of Staff called me yesterday on my sat phone, he didn't give me a lot of information about your visit. He just said that a CIA official would be visiting and that we should cooperate in every way possible."

Singleton directed them to a large oval table where they seated themselves. McCain removed his body armor, standing it and his rifle against the wall. As Chuck got comfortable in the padded leather chair, Gray leaned over to him.

"Agent McCain, I heard a rumor that a friend of mine works with you. He and I were on a team together."

Chuck glanced at the Marine's uniform, noticing the gold jump wings with the gold MARSOC eagle pinned above them.

"Might be," the CDC officer answered. "What's his name?"

"Fleming. Andy Fleming. He the left the Corps for personal reasons but then I heard a while later that he'd signed on with CDC Enforcement."

McCain smiled. "Andy's one of my team leaders. We were lucky to get him."

The Marine nodded but Chuck could see the question in his eyes. If a world-class operator like Fleming was just a team leader, who are you, Mr. McCain?

One of the major's security detail brought in bottles of water for each of them and then stepped out, closing the door behind him.

Chuck glimpsed Scotty, Tim, and Tom talking to the two young airmen, probably probing them for information on the amenities and the security of the base. McCain examined the major. A pair of flight wings were sewn on the left side and her name was on the right of her flight suit. The only other markings were the cloth gold leaf clusters signifying her rank attached to her shoulders. Singleton's eyes were intelligent and, while respectful, she didn't appear overawed by the appearance of a retired admiral who now held a high position in the CIA.

"So, Admiral, how can we help you?"

"Major, what I'm going to tell you is not classified but I would ask for yours and the gunnery sergeant's discretion about who you share the information with. We've got a Mexican cartel that's moved in and established a foothold in Buckhead. They used the governmental breakdown that we've experienced to slide in and take over a five or six block radius, although that seems to be increasing every week. With the power and communications grids down, not many people know what's happening."

Williams gave them all the information he had. While the major's face remained impassive, the Marine was clearly skeptical. Two hundred cartel soldiers on American soil? Taking over a large chunk of one of Atlanta's nicest areas? McCain could see that Gray wasn't buying. Not yet, anyway.

The admiral pulled out his phone and showed the two videos, narrating as Singleton and Gray watched. "One of those girls the SEALs rescued spoke Spanish and confirmed what was in a letter that we recovered from one of the dead gangsters. They were driving to Mexico to get reinforcements. What you also need to know is that this gang has also somehow managed to get their hands on a quantity of the zombie virus. That's why Agent McCain and his men will have a leading role in this mission.

"The President has ordered me to execute an operation to

eliminate the cartel presence on American soil, recover the zombie virus, and rescue the women who are being held as sex slaves." Williams locked eyes with the major and the gunnery sergeant. "Notice that I didn't say 'arrest.'

"The President views this as a foreign invasion. He's not prepared to call it an act of war yet because he believes that the cartel is acting on their own and doesn't represent the government of Mexico. However, he wants to send a strong message to the other cartels, the Mexican government, and anyone else who might want to take advantage of us that that would be a very bad idea."

The Marine's eyes hardened as he watched the videos, Chuck noticed. Whatever doubts he had harbored were gone and the gunnery sergeant appeared ready to do what Marines do best: go to war.

The major's expression remained neutral but she nodded and placed her hands flat on the table. "So what do you need from us, Admiral?"

# Chapter Nine

**Buckhead, Atlanta, Monday, 1730 hours**

Antonio Corona stood on the sidewalk in front of his building, waiting for Jorge and the patrol to return. His security team stood off to the side, smoking and talking quietly. Corona was leaning towards calling the high-rise El Palacio de Corona. That just sounded good, the way that it rolled off of the tongue. This was a luxury apartment building, better than anything in Mexico, and he liked the idea of having his name on it. Of course, he would also eventually rename this section of the city, as well. Maybe East Tijuana?

His thoughts were interrupted as the three-vehicle caravan passed through the roadblock on the corner and drove towards him, stopping in the street. His soldiers in the back of the pickups were subdued. Quintero was riding shotgun in the van and his expression showed that it had not been an easy mission. Jorge's door was open before the vehicle stopped and he slowly approached the cartel leader.

"We lost more men, señor. Boxer and one of the black gangsters were killed. I never got his name. Lobo is wounded and I don't think he's going to make it."

Tony the Tiger felt his anger rising. They had lost almost fifteen men in the last week. Their eight-man patrol was killed the past Wednesday when the traitorous maintenance man had tried to flee. They had lost Mario on Saturday when they had attacked the church. On a scavenging raid Sunday, Gordo had taken a bullet to the head, killing him instantly. Jose had also been wounded on that mission, dying later in the day.

If his math was correct, his force was down to one hundred and seventy-two. Minus the six who were away seeking reinforcements from his uncle, there were a hundred and sixty-six soldiers. He couldn't afford to keep losing men but that was the cost of taking new territory.

Corona had ordered Quintero to start pushing their patrols further out. They needed food and supplies, but more importantly, he wanted to establish a larger foothold in the city. On the plus side, his teams were consistently finding quantities of goods in the neighborhoods surrounding Buckhead. The downside was that many of those neighborhoods contained pockets of armed survivors who were not afraid to use their firearms.

"What happened?" Antonio asked, trying to keep his voice under control.

His lieutenant sighed. "We found a really nice neighborhood just a few miles from here, Jefe. The place where rich people live. The houses are huge, mansions. We had to kill some zombies but we found a lot of food, good booze, expensive jewelry, and some guns.

"In the middle of the neighborhood was this big building, like a country club. It's where the swimming pool and tennis courts are. They had boarded up the windows and there were some cars parked outside. When we went to break in, the people inside started shooting at us. They had holes cut in the walls to fire out of. Lobo got hit in the leg and went down. Boxer ran to grab him and got shot in the face.

"We all started shooting at the building and the people inside quit firing. A few of the guys managed to get to Boxer and Lobo and drag them back to the vehicles. One of the black guys was giving covering fire, but somebody inside shot him in the chest."

Antonio was furious, cursing loudly and kicking the passenger door of the van. "What did you do to the scum inside? Did you kill them all?"

Quintero hesitated before answering. "Señor, we started our raid with ten men. After the shooting we were down to seven. I don't know how many people are inside that country club but we're fortunate to only lose three. I knew you wouldn't want me to lose any more of our soldiers so I gave the order to leave."

Corona kicked the door of the van again and then again, leaving a large dent in the metal. The gang members paused from unloading the bodies of their comrades and the supplies that they had stolen, listening to the confrontation between the two top cartel leaders. Turning back to his lieutenant, Antonio said, loud enough so that all the raiders could hear him, "Take as many men as you need and kill them all! Everyone! Burn that building to the ground if you have to, but I want them all dead! Is that clear?"

Jorge smiled grimly. "Si, señor. Do you want us to go now or first thing tomorrow? It'll be dark soon and it might be good to let the men unwind a little tonight."

Tony the Tiger nodded, looking around at the dejected and angry gang members. "Of course. They worked hard today. Tonight, let them drink and enjoy our lady guests, but tomorrow, go make an example of those gringos."

### Centers for Disease Control Compound, East of Atlanta, Monday, 2300 hours

Beth and Chuck were lying on the floor of the CDC's office, their breathing slowly returning to normal. They didn't have a bed but they had been given a room to themselves. An unzipped sleeping bag was spread out on the floor and another covered them.

Thirty minutes earlier, McCain had presented his wife with the wedding band that Diya had given him for Beth. The set had been one of the few things that he had not lost when he left his backpack behind, the small box tucked into one of the agent's cargo pockets. The young woman's eyes had gotten large with surprise, she had squealed, and thrown herself into his arms. He gently placed the diamond-encrusted ring on her finger and allowed Elizabeth to place the plain gold band on his. She had then pushed her husband to the floor and showed him how much she appreciated the beautiful gift.

"When are you leaving?" Elizabeth asked softly, her head resting against his chest.

"If the other security team coming to guard this place gets here Wednesday morning like they're supposed to, we'll fly out after lunch. We'll finalize our plan out at Dobbins, train for a week, and then execute the mission. I don't foresee being gone any longer than two weeks."

McCain could sense his wife's unease at their upcoming separation. "Are you sure I can't come with you?" she asked softly, her fingers touching his face gently.

"No, I really need you here. In fact, what would you think about me assigning you to the security team on a part-time basis?"

"Really?" she asked, surprise in her voice.

"Sure, if you'd be up for it. You were quite the warrior princess on our fun run through the forest with hundreds of Zs chasing us. Even though the admiral has some people coming to keep this place safe, every gun counts in a crisis and you'll do fine.

"I also spoke to Dr. Martin. He's in charge of the facility as well as the scientists and could use some help in the office. The CDC has lost so many of their support staff and I know you have a background in admin work. Didn't you tell me that one of your jobs was assistant to the president of the technical college?"

"Yes and I enjoyed it, but I don't know anything about diseases or scientific research. Do you really think I'll be able to help?"

"When I mentioned it to the good doctor, his eyes lit up and he couldn't say 'yes' fast enough. If you're willing to dive in, working with Dr. Martin would be your primary job, but you'd pull a few security shifts, as well."

"I see what you're doing, Mr. McCain." Her fingers were now touching the various scars on his face. "You're trying to keep me busy so I won't worry about you."

He smiled. "No fooling you. But, everybody here does have to work. That's the only way this place can continue to function. According to the admiral, though, things are starting to get back to normal in a lot of areas. After we deal with this situation in Buckhead, my guys and I will go back to eliminating the infected. The boss estimates another three months and the infrastructure should be up and running so people can go back home and start acting normal again. We can move into our house and try to figure out what normal means."

"That'll be nice and I can't wait to set up house with you. I'll be happy to help out here wherever they need me. What's this scar?" she asked, her hand rubbing an old injury inside his hairline.

"That was from my very first pro fight," he chuckled. "Big Bubba Brown."

"Wait, Bubba? That was his name?"

"That's what he called himself. I never got his first name. He looked liked a Bubba, too. He was six foot four, two hundred and sixty-five pounds, had a beer gut, a shaved head, and he loved to fight. His primary job was as a bouncer at a biker bar, so that tells you how tough he was. He'd already had four pro fights but had only won two of them.

"He outweighed me by almost thirty pounds and he'd never been knocked out. When the referee said 'fight,' we both rushed out and immediately clashed heads. Bubba's mainly a standup fighter, like me, and real aggressive. Both of our heads busted open and we were bleeding like stuck pigs. Twenty seconds after the fight started, the ref called in the doctor to check both of us.

"Thankfully, the doc was easily intimidated and Bubba and I both threatened to beat him up if he stopped the fight. I could only see out of my left eye, with the blood flowing down into my right one. The great thing about Bubba, though, was that he was right in front of me. The bad thing was that he had a jaw like granite. I hit him with bomb after bomb and he just smiled at me.

"He was landing some pretty good shots of his own and the crowd was loving it. Two big, bloody heavyweights slugging it out. Between rounds my trainer told me to quit hitting him in the head. 'All you're gonna do is break your hands. Hit him in the body and you'll stop this guy next round.'

"So that's what I did. I threw a few jabs to get his guard up and then started ripping into his body. A few kicks, some knees, a lot of hooks and uppercuts, and three minutes later, Bubba went down and the referee waved it off. We both ended up at the same hospital later to get sewn up, and then we went out for a few beers."

"I'll never understand that," Beth said, shaking her head. "You guys try to kill each other and then go have a drink later?"

"That's the fight game. Some fighters took it personally. For me it was just an outlet for my martial arts and I earned some extra money."

"Are you going to fight any more, when things do get back to normal?"

"I doubt it. It's a young man's game and I haven't been able to train for months. I'll keep working out, maybe do some sparring in the gym, maybe coach a little."

After a moment, Elizabeth spoke again, her voice hesitant. "If I'm working with Dr. Martin, does that mean I'm going to be around Dr. Edwards?"

"Probably. Nicole has a team of researchers that she supervises and she reports to Dr. Martin. Why?"

"I saw her earlier as I was walking around. I smiled and nodded at her but she turned away and pretended like she didn't see me."

McCain chuckled. "I can't believe I didn't pick up the vibe that she had a crush on me. I guess I should feel flattered."

"Well, don't feel too flattered, Mr. McCain. I guess it's good that I'm always armed now. At least I can protect myself if she tries to stab me in the back."

### Buckhead, Atlanta, Tuesday, 1100 hours

A van and two SUVs parked one street over from the clubhouse in the Chastain Country Club Community. Twenty soldiers exited the vehicles, four of them carrying gas cans. The smart thing would have been to attack the survivors before the sun came up, but that thought had never even occurred to Jorge Quintero.

He'd had several shots of tequila and a few beers the previous night before forcing himself on one of their female "guests." She had resisted as he raped her, so he had beaten her in a drunken rage, transferring his anger over the deaths of his men earlier in the day onto her. The woman's cries only intensified his violence and a minute later, her nude, bloody, lifeless body lay at his feet. Jorge had given the corpse a final kick, gotten dressed, and left the ninth floor prison, ordering two of his men to dispose of the dead girl.

Still slightly hung over, Quintero led the cartel soldiers towards the rear of the large white clubhouse, built to look like a southern plantation home. As they circled behind another mansion, abandoned like the rest of the rich neighborhood, they could see their target. The swimming pool and tennis courts were behind the clubhouse, creating obstacles the gangsters would have to go around to get into position to exact their vengeance.

The group of thugs paused, bunched together as they surveyed the scene. They had no concept of noise discipline, but their voices carrying across the still morning. Movement on the roof of the building got Quintero's attention. A man and a woman, both with long guns across their legs, were seated in folding chairs on a small section of the flat roof. The chairs were back-to-back so the couple could survey the entire area around them.

The slim white man turned towards the gang's position, saying something to the woman. Everything began to come unraveled as the female sentry ran to a spot on the roof and shouted an alarm. The male sentry quickly knelt, bringing up a scoped, bolt-action rifle.

"¡Vamonos! Mátalos!" Jorge ordered. "Let's go! Kill them all!"

A shot rang out from the roof and a gangster from MS-13 collapsed next to Jorge, a large red spot spreading over the center of the man's white t-shirt. The criminals started sprinting towards the clubhouse, firing from the hip. The man's next shot missed, but his third pull of the trigger dropped a Mexican, the bullet hitting the skinny gang member just above the belt, doubling him over as he fell onto his face.

Quintero fired a long burst at the gunman's position, most of the rounds missing, but one managing to find the male sentry's head, killing him instantly. The cartel members were running, shooting, and screaming profanities in Spanish and English, the latter by the four black American gang members, wanting revenge for their friend's death from the previous day.

Return fire quickly came from the defenders inside the clubhouse, bullets coming through the gun slits that had been cut in the walls or the plywood that covered the windows. The woman on the roof stood in the open, firing an AK-47. Another cartel soldier, Chi Chi, screamed as a round hit him in the right shoulder, spinning him around and dropping him to the asphalt. A Black Mafia Family member, T-Man, Jorge remembered, grunted as an AK round found his sternum, taking him out of the fight and out of this world.

A shotgun blast caught the defender center-mass, the 00 buckshot spreading enough to cover the female sentry's abdomen, chest, and throat. A rifle round also found her leg and she collapsed next to her dead friend. The return fire from the cartel had finally caused the defenders on the inside to duck their heads and the criminals reached the exterior walls.

"You know what to do," Quintero ordered the four men carrying gasoline. "Hurry up!"

The survivors were unable to aim their weapons down from inside the building, the firing slits only designed to engage attackers approaching them. The gang members were safe for the moment and within minutes gasoline was being applied to all of the boarded up entrances, as well as the exterior near the ground floor windows. Two of the men had five-gallon cans, while the others had two-gallon cans.

They didn't have enough gasoline to cover the entire house so Jorge had ordered them to douse the areas that the survivors would try to escape out of. This was a large structure and the cartel lieutenant knew it would take a while for the fire to really get going. The gang members began taunting those inside, telling them what was about to happen to them. I wonder if any of the gringos speak Spanish? the gangster leader wondered.

As soon as his men had poured out the contents of their containers, each was to strike a match, light the gas, and then try to escape without getting shot in the back. Shouts told Quintero that the fires had been ignited and he saw the flames slowly licking up the side of the clubhouse. Panicked voices could now be heard inside as the Americans realized that they were about to be burned to death.

The General Atomics MQ-1 Predator was on-station, circling the area at fifteen thousand feet. Admiral Williams had one of the armed drones and its crew transferred to Dobbins Air Force Base. Having the unmanned aerial vehicle operated so close to the action allowed it to remain overhead much longer.

The drone had followed the convoy as it departed from the cartel's HQ that morning. The video feed was being monitored by the one man, one woman crew in a special room at the Air Force base. The drone's pilot, First Lieutenant Jim Cox, and the sensor operator, Senior Airman Heather Cook, watched the scene unfold in the country club neighborhood in Buckhead. As the cartel members set the building ablaze, they both felt helpless, knowing that innocent lives were about to be lost.

"Call the major," Cox ordered. "We need her in her now!"

Even though the normal phone system was down, one of the technical sergeants had rigged up a field telephone system covering most of the base. In less than a minute, Cook had gotten Major Singleton on the phone and asked her to join them in the drone command center. Four minutes later, the major and Admiral Williams strode into the small room.

"What've you got, Lieutenant?" the major asked.

Cox quickly recounted what they were seeing in real time as well as the events of the previous ten minutes. Singleton and Williams both watched the seventy-two inch video monitor in horror as fire began to spread along the outside of the clubhouse. The remaining cartel members had split into two groups, managing to flee to opposite corners of the burning structure, leaving behind six bodies of their comrades, two of whom had been shot fleeing after setting the building on fire. The gangsters found cover behind trees, cars, or even a large green utility box, watching and waiting for anyone inside to try and break out.

"Do we know that there are people inside that building?" the major asked.

Cox glanced at Cook. Her job was to monitor the video feed and interpret it. The senior airman nodded. "There were two sentries on the roof, ma'am. They engaged the attackers, killing several. We watched one of them walk over to an opening in the roof and it looked like she was yelling down into the building. Both sentries went down during the initial firefight."

While she was talking the sensor operator zoomed in on hole that had been cut through the roof. A head suddenly popped up, and a middle-aged white man crawled through and then reached back inside, pulling a teenage girl and then a middle-aged woman onto the roof with him. Over the next five minutes, twelve other survivors climbed onto the roof. Six of them were armed and cautiously approached the sides of the building, looking for a way out.

One of the armed survivors jerked and fell. Everyone on the roof dropped flat onto their faces to get out of the path of additional bullets. The video showed two of the defenders shooting blindly over the edge, before pulling back. The flames continued to envelope the clubhouse, spreading faster, fire reaching upwards towards the flat area of the roof where the group was trapped.

"Admiral, this is your show," the major acknowledged. "What do you want to do?"

"What's the weapons package on the drone, Lieutenant?" he asked.

"Two Hellfires, sir," Cox answered.

Williams looked at the screen closely, noting the positions of the cartel soldiers, estimating distances.

"Lieutenant, can you put a missile on either side of that structure in the middle of those two groups of attackers?"

"Sir, that's danger close to those victims."

"Son, those people will die if we don't do something. They might die even if we do do something. Take out those killers and let's see if we can give those poor people a chance. I'll accept responsibility for the order, Lieutenant. Major, can you launch a Search and Rescue mission to go pick up any survivors?"

"Yes, sir," she said, grabbing the phone, making a call, and issuing orders.

Thirty seconds later, the pilot nodded at the CIA man and his commanding officer. "Weapons free. Targets are acquired. Launch one, launch two. I've got two good launches, standby for impact."

Quintero watched with satisfaction as the building crackled, the flames starting to engulf it. He still expected those people on the roof to try to make a break for it. That's what he would do. There was no way that he would allow himself to be burned alive.

Directly across from the clubhouse, another mansion sat up on a hill. Jorge tapped Carlos on the back and nodded to the hill adjacent to their position. "Let's go over there. Maybe we can get high enough to see the gringos and shoot them."

Carlos was a good soldier and nodded at his boss. Quintero told the others in his group, "Me and Carlos are going over there," pointing to their destination. "Keep a close watch for those gringos to try and make a break for it."

The other cartel members smiled and grinned, occasionally yelling to the people trapped on the roof to come down and that they would be spared. Jorge and Carlos started running, covering almost a hundred meters, getting halfway up the incline from which they could engage the survivors.

A buzzing sound suddenly came from overhead and Quintero glanced back towards the ever-growing fire. The group of soldiers on the far side of the building were in a small patch of woods. A flash and the clap of an explosion sent a concussion sweeping across the street, knocking Jorge onto the grass, Carlos falling on top of him.

Jorge's ears picked up another buzzing sound, this one even closer, like it was dropping right on top of him. There was another roar as the missile exploded, disintegrating the men whom Quintero had just been with. The second concussion sucked the air out of the cartel lieutenant's lungs, picked him up and slammed him down onto the hard ground, and sending him into the darkness.

He awoke with incredible pain all over his body and a ringing in his ears, unsure how long he had been unconscious. A heavy weight pressed his face into the ground. It took all of his strength to roll over, shoving Carlos' dead body off of him, the left side of his face aching. A loud vibrating noise cut through the air and Quintero looked up to see a gray helicopter circling the scene. He also saw that the middle of the clubhouse was now completely engulfed in flames, a section of the roof having collapsed inward.

Jorge struggled to get to his feet and stumbled towards the mansion that he and Carlos had been running for before the explosions. A glance over his shoulder revealed that the aircraft was descending towards the large parking lot across from his position. Had they seen him? Were they coming after him? He ducked behind the house, looking for an opening, a place where he could hide for a few minutes and assess his injuries.

The gangster suddenly realized that he had lost his rifle, but he couldn't risk going back to the front to look for it. Thankfully, the reassuring weight of the Colt Python .357 Magnum revolver still hung from his waist. The double French doors of the large house were locked. Quintero used the barrel of the gun to smash out the pane of glass closest to the door handle, reaching through to unlock it. Stupid Americans, he thought.

As he stumbled inside, the smell of decaying flesh hit him in the face. If his ears weren't damaged and the sound of the helicopter wasn't already so loud, he would have also heard the growls coming from down the hallway. Suddenly, a black man and woman were in the living room, rushing towards the Mexican. Gold chains jangled around the man's neck, just below where his flesh had been ripped open. The woman's dreadlocks hung from her head, blood covering her face.

The loud explosions of the .357 Magnum barely registered in Jorge's ears. His first shot caught the man in the face and sent him to the floor. He missed with his second shot, the round smashing into the far wall, but the third hollow-point bullet hit the woman under the right eye, snapping her head back, and dropping her to the carpet, as well.

After waiting for a moment, no other zombies had appeared, and Quintero moved to the other side of the house, peering out the windows. The helicopter was down in the parking lot, a hundred yards from where he watched, soldiers advancing on the positions where his men had been. They moved quickly, weapons up and ready.

Moments later, additional figures came from behind the house, being escorted by the armed men. One of the soldiers was actually carrying an injured women, another was supporting a wounded man. Jorge counted nine people being loaded into the helicopter. Two of the eight soldiers climbed in with them and in seconds, the helicopter lifted off. A second aircraft that Jorge had not even known was in the area touched down, allowing the last six troops to board. It was quickly airborne, as well, disappearing out of sight.

After the sound of the two aircraft receded, the ringing returned to his ears. Quintero found a small bathroom next to the massive kitchen and examined himself in a mirror. His vision was blurry but he saw that his left eye was swollen and there were several small cuts on his face, with blood coming out of both ears. His head throbbed, his back was pulsing with pain, and a wave of dizziness forced him to grab the sink for balance. Pretty much every part of his body hurt, he realized.

Jorge needed to get back to their secure area in Buckhead, but to do that he would have to retrace his route to where they had left their vehicles. The dizziness passed and he staggered out the rear door. For some reason, his balance was unsteady, like he'd had a lot to drink, he realized. He glanced around the yard for his rifle but didn't see it. Carlos' Benelli shotgun was near his body, though, so Quintero picked it up.

Corona isn't going to be happy, Quintero thought, as he tried to maneuver back down the steep driveway. The dizziness suddenly returned and the gangster lost his footing, slamming down hard onto the concrete and rolling twenty feet down the hill, coming to a rest at the edge of the roadway. He groaned, feeling the blood dripping from his face and his hands, scraped from trying to stop his roll.

He'd lost the shotgun when he stumbled, but could see it laying near the top of the driveway. Jorge briefly considered trying to retrieve the weapon, but knew that he'd never make it. I just need to get back to mi familia, the cartel, he thought.

After a minute, he managed to push himself to his feet again, stumbling across the street towards the clubhouse, where the fire continued to rage, the building appearing to be ready to collapse in on itself. He paused briefly to look at the crater where his men had been. Where he would have been if he had stayed there a minute longer? Most of the bodies were completely destroyed. A direct hit, he realized.

Quintero glanced around the area for another weapon but didn't see anything. He did see several gringo bodies lying at the rear of the house, the flames licking their bodies. They must have tried to jump off of the roof, he thought. A few minutes later, he had made it back to their vehicles. He managed to climb into one of the SUVs to drive back to tell Antonio Corona the bad news.

## Centers for Disease Control Compound, East of Atlanta, Wednesday, 0930 hours

McCain and a few of his team stood near the front gate, waiting. Fleming, Walker, and Trang were in the office mapping out their plan of attack. Grace stood next to Jimmy, smiling at something that he'd said. It's good to see her smile, Chuck thought. Elizabeth was meeting with Dr. Martin, discussing how she might be able to help him and the researchers that he oversaw.

Admiral Williams and Shaun Taylor had flown back to Dobbins the previous day to make the final arrangements for housing and equipping his men for the upcoming operation. Williams had given Chuck a satellite smart phone and the two men had talked three times on Tuesday and twice already on Wednesday. The CDC Supervisory Agent now had a much better idea of the assets that would be participating in the raid.

The eight CDC agents would be joined by eight National Guard troops and their commander, Lieutenant Colonel Kevin Clark. Williams had pushed hard for Clark's entire team of thirteen men and women but the former Ranger was adamant that he could not leave their families unprotected. The SOP that he had been using had worked, always leaving four soldiers and one of their armed humvees behind to guard their compound.

The admiral had also been able to secure fifteen Marine reservists from the air force base. None of their officers had survived and their ranking NCO, Gunnery Sergeant Gray, would be joining them on the operation to bump the number of Marines to sixteen. Williams told McCain that Major Singleton wasn't happy at all about Gray participating in the high-risk mission. They'd had a heated conversation in the admiral's presence, the major telling the marine that she relied on him for every detail of the base's security.

"With all due respect, Major, I'm a senior Marine NCO. I'm not going to put my men in harm's way and sit behind a fence here waiting to hear the outcome of this mission. And if I'm not mistaken, ma'am, you feel the same way because you've been flying multiple combat missions a week yourself, killing Zs. You also believe in leading from the front."

At that, the Air Force officer had turned away, the truth of his words silencing her. She was already planning on being a part of the raid, too, her HH-60 Pave Hawk helicopter serving as McCain's command ship. Even with those Marines being temporarily loaned out, there was still a force of almost forty security personnel on the large base, a mixture of Marines, Air Force Security, and several civilian police officers who had been allowed to bring their families into the perimeter in exchange for the officers' help in keeping the facility secure.

Williams had also procured half of a SEAL Team platoon from the west coast to participate in the mission. Along with these eight naval warriors, the admiral told Chuck that he was allowing his own two-man security detail, Tim and Tom, to participate. Major Singleton would be arranging for infiltration, air cover, medevac, and exfiltration if they were forced to pull out before the mission was accomplished.

Normally, forty-three against so many bad guys would not be the kind of odds that Chuck would want to tackle. Being heavily outnumbered by violent gang members was not the ideal situation, especially when he remembered that any zombies in the area would be drawn to the sounds of the attack. And McCain anticipated a lot of gunfire.

On the plus side, there was a lot of experience on the team, even if they hadn't worked together before. And they would have air cover above them. What concerned McCain the most was the timeframe. The plan would be finalized by Friday and his task force would train together for a week at the Dobbins Air Force Base indoor firing range, conducting both dry and live fire rehearsals.

The big man's thoughts were interrupted by two marked police cars driving up the access road towards the front gate. He had been told to expect some guests who would provide security for the CDC location while he and his men were away. Chuck was constantly amazed at the admiral's influence. He made things happen in the most difficult of circumstances.

The police cruisers stopped near the gate and a familiar figure got out of the lead vehicle. Sergeant Josh Matthews had been McCain's assistant squad leader on the SWAT team when Josh was a corporal and Chuck was a sergeant. Their history went back even further than that, though. Corporal McCain had been Matthews' field training officer when the young recruit graduated from the police academy.

Months earlier, their paths had crossed again at Peachtree Meadow High School. Terrorists had unleashed the zombie virus on the sprawling suburban high school, killing and infecting hundreds of students, faculty, and parents. Over twenty police officers had also been killed while trying to rescue victims hiding inside the school. Sadly, a SWAT Team had also been overrun by zombies.

Josh had led his eight-man team inside in an attempt to locate the first SWAT assault group which had entered the school. They had not been heard from in over fifteen minutes. Just as Josh's men had gotten inside the high school, however, a large group of infected students and teachers attacked them. Matthews had lost four of his teammates, the other four just barely managing to escape the same fate.

When the CDC officers showed up to render aid, Sergeant Matthews and his three remaining SWAT assault team members fought alongside the federal police officers, killing hundreds of zombies and rescuing many survivors. The two men had not seen each other since that difficult day.

Matthews smiled and waved at his former boss. McCain waved back and the gates were opened allowing the police cars to pull inside. A total of six officers exited the vehicles, looking around at the busy compound. Josh and Chuck shook hands and embraced. The SWAT officer was a solid five foot ten inches tall with a face that looked much younger than his thirty-eight years.

"Good to see you, Josh. What a nice surprise. I had no idea who was going to show up."

Matthews chuckled. "I don't know who your boss is, but he certainly has some pull. The department is almost back up to half strength. Officers are slowly trickling back in as this thing seems to be winding down. There don't appear to be as many fresh Zs. Assistant Chief Hughes is in charge after Chief Anderson got infected."

"Oh, I hadn't heard that. That's too bad," Chuck said.

"He was a good guy, but he should've left when he had the chance. His wife wouldn't leave without him and when some zombies got loose in their neighborhood, it got ugly fast. The chief and his entire family, gone. One of our rookies actually had to put a bullet into Anderson's head after he got infected."

McCain shook his head. "What about Lisa and your kids?"

Josh shrugged and looked away, the pain evident on his face. "I've got no idea where they're at. Since the divorce, she's done everything she can to keep me from seeing them. She changes her phone number every few months and I'm not even sure what state they're in. The last I heard, she was in Alabama, near some of her family. She's in violation of pretty much every point on our divorce paperwork, but with the zombie apocalypse, there aren't many courts in session to get a hearing."

Chuck put a hand on his friend's shoulder. "Sorry, man. That sucks, but if she's in Alabama, the kids are probably fine. They didn't get hit nearly as bad over there."

Wanting to change the subject, McCain nodded at the other officers. "Who do you have with you?"

"Remember the three SWAT guys who went into the school with us? I've got them and two other solid officers you can count on. The chief said this Admiral Williams told him that there are also a few civvy security types here, as well?"

Chuck nodded. "And another cop. That girl standing over there with the shotgun was with Athens Campus Police. Grace Cunningham. She was inside Sanford Stadium when the university got infected. I've seen her in action, and she's tough as nails. The older black guy over there is Darrell Parker. He's a retired City of Baltimore PD sergeant and the young guy with him is Marcel. He was Air Force Security Forces. We've got a few others that will fill in as needed, including my wife. Come on, I'll show..."

"Your wife?" Josh repeated. "Since when do you have a wife? I remember your first one and hearing you swear off ever getting married again after your divorce."

"I did, didn't I?" McCain laughed. "Well, that was a long time ago. Beth and I just got married last week. We haven't even had a honeymoon yet. Come on, let me show you around."

### Centers for Disease Control Compound, East of Atlanta, Wednesday, 1230 hours

The gray Air Force Pave Hawk helicopter circled and then landed near the front entrance. The pilot shut the engines down and Marcel opened the gates. The admiral's assistant, Shaun, was the first one off of the helicopter, cautiously carrying a small red plastic box.

Several of the CDC agents and police officers ducked under the still turning rotors and grabbed the cardboard boxes one of the crewmen pushed towards the open door. The last time Chuck had spoken to the admiral, he asked if he would check with Major Singleton to see if they had any food to spare. The CDC facility was running low on groceries and with the enforcement agents leaving for a couple of weeks, there was no one to go looking for supplies. The major had sent two week's worth of food and the boxes were quickly carried inside.

Admiral Williams' assistant, Shaun Taylor, located McCain in the CDC office, sitting at the table talking with Fleming, Trang, and Walker, satellite maps scattered in front of them. "Hey, Shaun," Jay greeted him. "You got our ride outside?"

"They should be about done unloading some food that the Air Force sent over, so let's try to be airborne in the next thirty minutes? Chuck, can you take this to whichever scientist should get it?"

He handed McCain the container, glad to be rid of it. The federal police officer carefully opened it and peered inside at the two glass vials, wrapped tightly in bubble wrap and then double-bagged.

"Is this what the SEALs found on those dead cartel members?"

"That's it. The admiral was hoping we could get a confirmation that it really is the virus before we leave. Even if we have to head out little later, let's see what we can find out."

"Sure, I'll take care of it," Chuck answered.

He considered asking one of the other agents to handle the task, but instead, stood and picked up the plastic box.

"Guys, grab your gear and let's be ready to go ASAP. I'll get this over to Dr. Edwards and see what she can tell us."

The two laboratories where the researchers worked were spartan compared with their labs at the Centers for Disease Control in Atlanta. Hopefully, they could be back there in a few months. For now, however, they were making do in the much smaller facility. Dr. Bae-yong oversaw a team of epidemiologists in one of the labs and Dr. Edwards supervised a second team in the other.

McCain saw Edwards on the other side of the room, peering into a microscope. She was wearing elbow length rubber gloves, protective glasses, and a protective mask for her nose and mouth. There was no room for error when dealing with the deadly bio-terror virus. Eight other white-coated researchers were working at different stations around the lab.

He saw her eyes get big as he approached, surprise etched on her pretty face. She stepped back from the microscope, removed her gloves and goggles, and pulled her mask down.

"Hey, Nicole. Sorry to bother you, but I've got something that you'll be interested in."

The scientist forced a smile and Chuck saw it: the hurt in her eyes that she tried to cover up. How could I have missed that? he wondered.

"No bother at all, Chuck. I haven't gotten a chance to congratulate you on getting married. She seems like a very nice girl," she said, a slight emphasis on 'girl.'

"Thank you and you're right. She's a wonderful person and I was blessed to find her."

There was a moment of awkward silence but Edwards spoke first. "So, what's that?" she asked, nodding at the red container.

"Two vials of the virus," he answered, handing the box to her. "Some Mexican cartel members were transporting it back to Tijuana. There's a big group of the gang that have taken up residence down in your neck of the woods, Buckhead, and they're supposed to have some more of this. Can you please check and verify what's in these test tubes?"

Nicole put her protective equipment back on and removed the double plastic bag, laying it on her table. She picked up an xacto knife and carefully sliced the two bags open, gently removing the bubble wrapped test tubes. Another cut with the razor-sharp knife and the writing on the glass vials became visible.

She gasped and stepped backwards, startling the police officer. "Chuck, these are mine. These are from the ones that I lost. That's my writing on the tubes."

"What? How did you lose them?" he asked, confused.

"Remember when you came and rescued Darrell and I? I told you that I'd lost two bags when he had tried to escort me out to my car, hours after the bombs went off in Atlanta. When we walked out onto the parking deck there were a group of infected out there. He was helping me carry my stuff because I knew I wouldn't be back in the lab anytime soon.

"When the zombies rushed us, Darrell had to drop everything and start shooting. Then my keycard wouldn't work because the power had gone out. Thankfully, he had a real key but we just barely made it back inside. My laptop satchel and a padded bag containing ten vials of the virus and experimental vaccines got left outside.

"When you and your guys got there, I asked you to check the parking deck for my bags but they were gone. Somehow, that cartel has gotten their hands on them."

Chuck digested the information. "I do remember that. Did all ten contain the same thing? I know you were experimenting and trying different things."

The scientist nodded. "We still are. Those ten vials are deadly and they all contain some form of the virus. The only difference is that in probably half of them, the person will take longer before they turn. My assistant, Kumar, and I had been able to alter the molecular structure of the virus slightly and had been testing it on the lab mice. That was how Kumar got infected. One of the mice got loose and bit him on the ankle."

"Can you confirm that's what's still in the test tubes?"

"Sure, give me half an hour." She paused, looking down. "I've felt so guilty about losing those test tubes, not knowing who had picked up them up. If you could recover the rest, that would be incredible."

"That's the plan. We're leaving today for Dobbins Air Force base on the other side of town. We'll stage there and go in next week sometime. It's good to know the source of these vials and that there shouldn't be any more floating around. I'll feel a lot better knowing that all ten are back in your capable hands."

"How big is this cartel? You just said a big group."

McCain sighed. "As best we can figure, probably around two hundred."

"That many? In Atlanta? Is it just you and the CDC teams that are taking them on?"

"We'll have some other people helping us. I'd appreciate it if you wouldn't share any of this yet. It's not classified, but people have enough to worry about right now. This is really more of an invasion. These scumbags have captured at least a six-block radius around Peachtree and Piedmont Road. And they have over forty women that they're keeping as sex slaves."

"Oh, my God!" Edwards exclaimed. "That's terrible and I live very close to there. I know you're going after the virus, but what about those women?"

Chuck nodded. "They're part of our mission. Eliminate the cartel, recover the virus, and rescue the prisoners."

"Please be careful," she said, the concern evident in her voice. After a pause, she took a deep breath and continued, "And I really meant it. Congratulations, Chuck. I hope you and your wife are very happy together."

He saw the sincerity in her eyes and somehow understood she was letting go. "Thanks, Nicole. This mission just got even more important if I'm going to liberate your neighborhood," he said, with a grin.

She smiled and turned back to her microscope. "I'll come find you when I know something for sure."

Forty minutes later, the CDC agents carried their weapons and packs to the guard hut. They would wait there until McCain gave them the order to board the helicopter. Eddie and Candice stood with Jimmy, Grace, Scotty, and Emily. Candice's morning sickness wasn't as bad now and she was able to laugh at something Scotty said.

Andy, Amy, and Tyler chatted quietly with Hollywood and LeMarcus. Tu, Jay, Shaun, and Terry were engrossed in their own conversation. Chuck and Beth had taken a few steps to the side so they could say their goodbyes, as well. They were just waiting for the lab results before they left.

A few minutes later, Dr. Edwards exited the lab building and strode towards the entrance. When she saw Chuck and Beth together, she slowed her stride. Forcing a smile onto her face, however, she stopped in front of the couple and made eye contact with Elizabeth.

"Congratulations on getting married, Elizabeth. I hope you and Chuck are very happy together."

Beth gave her sweetest smile. "Thank you, Dr. Edwards."

The scientist looked at McCain and her tone became serious. "The results are confirmed. Both of those vials contain the virus. I ran both compounds through the computer and confirmed that, without a doubt, they were part of the ones that I lost."

Chuck nodded. "That's what I needed to know. Thanks for putting a rush on that, Nicole. Now, we get to go recover the other eight vials."

The big man turned towards the rest of his agents and raised his voice. "Okay, guys, say your goodbyes and let's load up."

Nicole was still standing there as McCain reached to embrace his wife. The scientist turned to go to give them a moment of privacy. "Good luck, Chuck. Be careful."

Chuck grinned at her. "Will do. Hopefully, when you see me

again, your neighborhood will be free of invaders."

Edwards nodded and headed back towards her building, not wanting to see Chuck and Elizabeth kissing. She was trying to turn the page, but it would take her a little time. Footsteps sounded behind her.

"Nicole?"

She looked over her shoulder to see Agent Walker approaching.

"Hi, Jay. You ready for this?" she asked, forcing another smile onto her face.

"Oh, yeah," he answered enthusiastically. "This is going to be great, but I wanted to say 'goodbye,' and ask you for something."

"Oh?" she answered, surprise in her voice. "What do you want to ask me?"

The Navy-SEAL-turned-CDC-agent looked into her eyes. "I'd like to have dinner with you when we finish this mission. What I'd really like to do is take you out to a fancy restaurant, but the dining hall here will have to do for the time being."

That's so sweet, she thought. He seems like a really nice man and he's obviously interested in me. Why not? After a moment, she realized that he was waiting for an answer.

"Yes. I'd like that," she nodded. "Are you going to be staying on here after the mission or will you have to go back to D.C.?"

"We'll probably get a few days of down time here after we wrap this up and then I'll have to leave. Maybe you might even have a few meals with me?" he said, with a grin.

Nicole found herself nodding at him, a genuine smile forming on her face. "We could probably arrange that."

Tu's voice rang out from the front gate. "Come on, Jay, we're loading up."

The sound of the Blackhawk's rotors starting to turn echoed around the compound and Walker started to go, but stopped to look into Edward's eyes again. "As you can see, Dr. Edwards, I'd really like to get to know you, and I'm looking forward to spending some time with you."

Nicole's eyes got big. He's certainly not afraid to speak his mind, she thought. "Thanks, Jay, that's very sweet," she said, softly. "Please be careful and I'll talk to you when you get back."

Five minutes later the helicopter had disappeared, heading west. The scientist continued to stare into the sky, trying to process the emotions that were flowing through her when someone bumped into her shoulder.

"I'm so sorry, Dr. Edwards. I wasn't watching where I was going. I…"

Elizabeth McCain had waited until her husband left before she had started crying. Her eyes were filled with tears and she'd walked blindly into Nicole. The scientist instinctively put her arms around the young woman and let her cry. I could probably use a good cry myself, Edwards thought.

After a moment, Beth wiped her eyes and regained her composure, apologizing again. "Sorry about that and thanks for the hug," she said, with a sad smile. "I haven't had to send him off to battle before."

Nicole understood. "No problem at all. He's very good at what he does and he has a great team."

The young woman nodded and took a deep breath. "I know and I'll be OK."

"Can I ask you something? Dr. Martin told me that you were going to be doing some of our admin work," Nicole said, steering the conversation to less stressful subjects. "Aren't you a police officer?"

Elizabeth gave a slight laugh. "No. I was a career counselor at a technical college, but I also served as the administrative aide to the president of the school. I'd never had any experience with guns to speak of until I met Chuck and he saved my life."

Edwards stared at her, surprised to hear that Beth wasn't a cop and at the revelation McCain had rescued her from something life-threatening. The young woman carried herself like a police officer and certainly looked like she knew what she was doing when holding a weapon. Nicole's curiosity was now fully aroused. After a moment, the epidemiologist slid an arm around her shoulder and guided Beth into the lab building. "Well, since we're going to be working together, I look forward to hearing all about how you two met."

Nicole wanted to dislike Elizabeth. She wanted to be able to find some character flaw in the young woman as an excuse to keep her at arms length. As they started working together, however, Edwards found herself really enjoying Beth's company.

Chuck's wife was unpretentious, humble, and treated everyone with kindness and respect. Instead of disliking Elizabeth McCain, Dr. Edwards found that Chuck was right. His wife really was a special person.

# Chapter Ten

**Dobbins Air Force Base, Marietta, Georgia, Wednesday, 1630 hours**

The camo-pattern C-130 Hercules flew low over the main runway and the buildings surrounding it. The pilot had been given clearance to land and assured that the base was secure. With so many zombies still roaming the east coast, however, this west coast aviator wasn't taking any chances. The four powerful engines roared as the big aircraft leveled off, circling to make a final approach.

The pieces are coming together, McCain thought. He and the other eight CDC agents had gotten settled into their quarters, Major Singleton giving him a room of his own. Lieutenant Colonel Clark, eight of his troops, and three of their heavily armed hummers had arrived earlier in the day. The fifteen Marines and Gunnery Sergeant Gray were already on-site.

Just as he had hoped, Andy, Jay, and Tu had created the operational plan that they would be using. McCain had made a few minor tweaks, but he was pleased with what they had developed on such short notice. With the arrival of the SEALS, training would commence at hyper-speed so that they could execute the mission as soon as possible. Chuck still wished he had some more shooters, but at least they would have solid air support.

Admiral Williams and Colonel Clark joined the CDC agent on the tarmac to greet the newcomers. Major Singleton would have been there, but she was flying a hunting mission enroute to intercept a group of thirty zombies, spotted by the drone a few miles away. Earlier that morning, Williams had played the video of the attack on the survivors in the country club for McCain, Clark, and Gray. The warriors were already locked in, but this latest attack on innocents only served to solidify their resolve.

The pilot made a perfect landing and the C-130 taxied towards the welcoming committee, turning so that the aircraft was pointed out for a quick getaway, if needed. The ramp descended and eight heavily armed men moved purposefully towards Williams, Clark, and McCain.

A moment later, four more figures descended the ramp. These were also dressed for battle, but their uniforms were different, the camouflage pattern of the woodland variety. The sand-colored berets that each of the men wore, however, carried the distinctive patch of the British Special Air Service.

As Chuck pondered the presence of the SAS on American soil, the SEALs approached. The Navy commandos carried themselves with confidence, evaluating him, Clark, and the admiral. The tallest of the group spoke to the three men.

"I'm Chief Petty Officer Chris Norris. We were ordered to report to a Director Williams of the CIA."

The chief's tone wasn't insubordinate, but it was clear that he wasn't excited to be reporting to someone with the Agency. The SEALs, like others in the special operations community, were often tasked with performing missions for the CIA. The working relationship between the intelligence organization and those called upon to do its dirty work was often strained.

"That would be me, Chief. I'm Admiral Jonathan Williams, retired, now the Direction of Operations for the CIA."

At the mention of his rank, the Navy warriors all came to attention. "Please, gentleman, at ease. I also had the privilege of graduating from BUD/S Class 42, doing two tours in Southeast Asia. Unfortunately, I caught an AK round in the leg that knocked me out of your esteemed fraternity. After that, it was either go back into the civilian world or stay in the traditional Navy. I chose the Navy."

Chuck suppressed a smile. The admiral was a master at connecting with people. Under normal circumstances, Williams would have never talked about his background. When dealing with a group of Navy SEALs, however, he established common ground and had them hooked.

McCain could see the immediate respect in the warriors' eyes. The old man in front of them might not look like much now, but he was an elder statesman, a tribal leader, a respected warrior who had cut a trail for them to follow. He might work for the CIA, but he was one of them.

The SAS commandos joined the group, the same confident demeanor present in every step that they took. Chief Norris nodded at them.

"Admiral, I'd like to present Sergeant Billy Ryan and his squad from the Special Air Service. We were training together when the request for help came and I didn't think you'd mind having a few of our cousins along for the scrap."

Williams smiled warmly at the newcomers. "Good initiative, Chief. Welcome, Sergeant." He nodded at each of the beret-clad troopers.

"Sergeant, we're going to have a full briefing in a just a few minutes, but did the chief tell you what this was all about?"

Ryan popped to attention. "Not really, sir," he answered enthusiastically, the heavy Cockney accent sounding out of place in the heart of the southern United States. "He just said there was gonna be a bit of a barney, and, with your permission, sir, we'd like to offer our services."

"By all means, Sergeant. We're glad to have you. Thank you for volunteering and, yes, there is going to be a bit of a fight."

Speaking to both the SEALs and the SAS troops, Williams said, "Please, let me introduce you to these other two gentleman," nodding at Clark and Chuck. "First of all, this is Lieutenant Colonel Kevin Clark. He has a highly trained group of National Guard soldiers who have been fighting zombies and criminal gangs in Atlanta since the collapse. He was an Army Ranger before retiring and accepting a new commission in the Georgia National Guard.

"Standing next to him is Chuck McCain. Agent McCain is the Supervisory Agent in Charge of the CDC Enforcement Unit of the Atlanta Office. He has been involved in the bio-terror attacks from the very beginning. Agent McCain and his men have not only killed thousands of infected, they also tracked down and eliminated or arrested most of the key terrorists involved.

"Mr. McCain and his agents are the experts on the zombie virus and he will be in tactical command of this operation. I'm in overall command, but I have designated Agent McCain to run the show."

As Williams finished the introductions, Shaun Taylor joined the group. "This is my assistant, Agent Taylor. He'll escort you to your quarters and let you store your weapons and gear. This base is a secure location, but I would recommend always wearing at least a sidearm, just in case an infected were to slip through a hole somewhere. After you get your gear squared away, we'll meet in the building behind us for our first briefing."

As Taylor led the newcomers to their quarters, Chuck spoke up, "Admiral, I need to talk to you about something before we head inside."

Williams stopped walking. Clark said, "I'll see you in a few," and kept moving towards the administration building.

"Colonel, it would be good for you to stay. I'd like your input on this, as well. Admiral, I think every person on this operation needs a signed Presidential Pardon, preferably before we conduct the operation. Can you arrange that for us?"

The admiral was surprised by the request. "Mr. McCain, why do you feel a need for that? Don't you trust me? This mission has the full backing of the President. I've spoken to him directly twice, and to his staff multiple times, confirming his orders in regards to this operation."

"I trust you completely, Admiral, but I also understand that political winds change. You won't be the Director of Ops forever. We'll have a new President in a couple of years. That new President will likely appoint a new Attorney General."

Kevin nodded slowly, understanding in his eyes. "He's got a good point, Admiral. We're all happy to go kill some gangsters, but I don't want to get arrested a few years down the road because some liberal AG reviewed the operation and decided that we used excessive force."

"Exactly," Chuck said. "With the breakdown of law and order over the last several months, law enforcement and prosecution of criminals has become non-existent. When order is restored, I could see some local and federal prosecutors trying to make names for themselves by retroactively prosecuting citizens and cops who may not have followed due process while protecting themselves or their families.

"Boss, we're ready to go kick some ass," McCain continued. "I just want to know that we've done everything we can to protect our people after the mission is over."

Williams was silent, turning away and staring across the runway. After a few moments, he sighed and turned back to the other two men.

"As usual, Mr. McCain, you're thinking ahead. This is

something that I hadn't even thought of," he admitted, "but you're exactly right. We do need to protect our people from prosecution. Get me a list of everyone involved. Shooters, pilots, crew members, even the drone operators, and I'll get to work on it. I can't promise you that I'll have the pardons before you execute, but I give you my word that I'll make it happen."

"That's good enough for me, sir," Chuck nodded.

"Thanks, Chuck," Kevin said, as they continued towards the briefing room. "When I think back on all the shootouts we've been in with gangs of criminals since this mess started, it's never even occurred to me that one day, someone may decide to review our actions and see if what we did was justified or not."

While the new arrivals got settled, former Marine Staff Sergeant Andy Fleming sat with current Gunnery Sergeant Eric Gray in the dining facility, catching up over a cup of coffee. The two men had served together on one of the elite MARSOC teams for a year before Andy had left the Corps because of a family crisis. During the time that they had been teammates, they had fought side-by-side during a six-month deployment in Iraq, their friendship being forged in the heat of battle.

After they had discussed former teammates, close calls, and the role that each had played in the current bio-terror crisis, Fleming noticed that his friend had avoided mentioning his girlfriend, Felicia, and their son, Jamal. Andy knew that they had lived just across the bridge from Manhattan in Brooklyn, New York. The Islamic suicide bomber who had detonated himself near NYPD headquarters had also parked his explosive-laden vehicle near the 911 Memorial, not far from the Brooklyn Bridge.

When the two bombs exploded, the bio-terror virus was blasted outward in two densely populated areas. Within a few hours, Manhattan, Brooklyn, and Queens had groups of zombies sweeping through, killing and infecting thousands of innocent people. Fleming decided against asking about Gray's family, not wanting to rip open a fresh wound.

After a comfortable silence, Eric spoke up. "So what's the deal with this McCain guy? They've got a cop leading a military operation? I'm surprised they didn't tap that light colonel, you, or even that SEAL guy, Walker, to run this show."

Fleming nodded, understanding the question. He, too, had had doubts at the beginning about Chuck being the right man to lead a group made up of mostly former special operators. Those misgivings had quickly vanished when he saw the big man in action. Now, Andy would follow his friend into Hell with a water pistol.

"He was a local cop for twenty years, most of that time on SWAT. When he took early retirement, he did two one-year tours with the green beanies in Afghanistan as their police liaison. He doesn't talk about it much, but it sounds like he saw a lot of action there.

"I was Chuck's assistant for over a year when they started up CDC Enforcement. When he got promoted to run the Atlanta office, I got bumped up to team lead. Trust me on this, Eric, you've got nothing to worry about with McCain. He's as good an operator as any I've ever worked with and he's by far the best leader I've served under. He's just pissed that he's going to be in a helicopter directing the action, rather than on the ground executing it."

### Buckhead, Atlanta, Friday, 1300 hours

The cartel leader came by the injured man's room on the forty-ninth floor to check on him again. The gangster had visited his friend several times since Jorge had somehow managed to drive himself back to the base, collapsing as he climbed out of his vehicle, blood pouring out of his many wounds. The twenty-seven year old

African-American woman acting as Quintero's nurse shuddered every time Corona came into the apartment, watching him closely, but knowing there was nothing she could do if he wanted to rape her.

The boss had been the first one to violate her after she was captured weeks earlier, and she could never forget his disgusting body odor, his greasy hair, his bad breath, or the pain that he had caused her. Now, the Mexican just leered at her as she treated Jorge Quintero's wounds. Her biggest fear at the moment, however, was that she would throw up or pass out as she applied fresh bandages.

Janelle Washington had discovered early on in the Emergency Medical Technician program that she did not have the stomach for blood and gore, changing majors at the vocational school to Business Administration. After graduating she had gotten a job at a nearby architectural firm as a receptionist. It wasn't her dream job, but it was a real corporate position, as opposed to her years of working as a waitress, and would look good on her resume later.

Now, Washington wasn't sure that there would even be a later. She and several of her workmates had taken refuge in their offices, as zombies roamed the streets. Many of her colleagues had tried to flee that afternoon when the bombs had gone off. Knowing what she knew now, Janelle realized that her friends most likely never got out of Atlanta.

Janelle had considered fleeing, as well, but lived in Forest Park, a suburb just south of the gridlocked city. As they watched events unfold on the television in their break room, the remaining architects and support staff of the New South Studio weren't sure what to do. The local news anchors reported that traffic was shut down throughout the city and that the zombie virus had been released on a large scale near the heart of the downtown area.

The reporters were encouraging people to stay in place, assuring them that the authorities would have the situation under control in a matter of hours. Aerial views from news helicopters contradicted what the anchors said during their broadcast, though, showing that the entire interstate system and most of the surface streets were packed with stopped cars, trucks, SUVs, and tractor-trailers. It didn't look like the mess was going to be unraveled any time soon. Groups of Zs moved outward from ground zero where they had been infected and attacked hundreds, maybe thousands, of people who were trapped in their vehicles. Nothing was moving and no one was getting in or out of the city by car.

The days had turned into a week in which Janelle and her workmates tried to survive. That week led to additional weeks of living in their office building. They had found food in the lobby cafe and the small convenience store located inside their building.

Every day, Washington and her co-workers watched out the windows, hoping that something had changed over night. Peachtree Road in front of their office building, however, had been a war zone as the infected preyed upon those foolish enough to try and make a run for it. The main thoroughfare was packed with abandoned vehicles, the remains of corpses, and roving packs of zombies.

Several of her friends started to crack after being stuck in the cold offices for close to a month, their meager food and water supplies almost gone. Finally it was just Janelle, Tina, and Jerry who were left inside the New South Studio. Earlier that day, the three of them had watched from the lobby as one of the senior architects, Dale, had been jumped by zombies while he made a mad dash for his Black BMW M4 convertible. Dale had reassured his co-workers that he knew he could make it to his car and he would get the Zs to follow him as he raced out of the parking lot.

This would create an opening for everyone else to sprint for their own vehicles, Dale had told them confidently. He had not made it halfway across the parking deck before a group of eight Zs ran him down, tackled him, and ripped him apart. The dying man's screams drew in another twenty-five of the killers and soon, there was nothing left of the architect but a few bones and some scraps of clothing.

Washington and the two others retreated back upstairs to their fourth floor offices. They had seen other survivors in their building, but they had either fled, or were staying locked behind their own doors. Janelle, Tina, and Jerry had sat in stunned silence after watching Dale die. For almost an hour, no one said anything. Each of them had come to the same conclusion. They were all going to die there, probably by starvation.

Suddenly, gunshots rang out from the street below them. They had been hearing gunfire much more regularly over the last week, but none of it had been close. The three co-workers jumped up and rushed for the windows, observing a large group of armed men cutting down the infected in front of their building.

"Those are military vehicles," Jerry noted, pointing at the two tan humvees. A gunner stood in the hatch of each of the hummers firing machine guns into the hoard of rushing zombies. Two full-size pickups pulled to a stop behind the humvees, their beds full of men with guns, all of them firing into the packs of infected.

The loud gunfire only served to draw more Zs towards them. Soon, a large multitude was converging on the band of attackers. After shooting continuously for over five minutes, all four vehicles roared away, leaving several hundred dead infected behind. The streets were still packed with Zs, however, and it looked like the armed men were fleeing before they were overrun.

As the vehicles had raced away, the survivors began banging on the windows and yelling. In seconds, the only sounds to be heard were the growling zombies below them.

"Why did they leave?" Tina asked, angrily.

No one had an answer. The three only hoped that the people with guns would be back soon. They began to hear more gunfire coming from different directions over the next several hours. The following day, the same four vehicles returned, stopping in the middle of Peachtree Road again, cutting down over a hundred more Zs before leaving.

This pattern was repeated for two more days, the survivors moving downstairs to watch from the windows of the lobby as the heavily armed group decimated the ranks of infected. Finally, the survivors' banging on the glass doors attracted the attention of the armed men. A Hispanic looking man stood in the passenger door of one of the military vehicles, the tattoos visible on his arms and shaved skull. He raised his rifle towards the two women and the lone male, waving them outside. The only visible zombies were the hundreds that had been shot and were now sprawled motionless around the area.

Without hesitation, the survivors rushed towards their heavily armed saviors, Washington now noting for the first time the Mexican flags fluttering from the military vehicles. The Hispanic and black men in the vehicles stared at Janelle and Tina, licking their lips, their intentions slowly becoming clear. Janelle considered turning to run back toward the building but a line of guns were now pointed at them.

"Come! Come here, now!" the man with the tattooed head shouted, his English slow and halting. This man was clearly the leader and he turned and said something to the others in Spanish.

Janelle was almost fluent in the language, the only good thing to come out of dating a Puerto Rican for two years. That relationship and her four years of high school Spanish had developed both her understanding and conversational skills. She gasped as she heard what his orders were.

"Don't touch the black girl. The boss will like her. The white girl is mine first and I'll take care of the guy."

Neither of her friends understood what was said, but they had almost reached the humvees. Before Washington could shout a warning to her friends, the leader's rifle came up and a loud shot startled her. Jerry screamed and fell to the pavement clutching his chest. The two women instinctively turned to run but strong arms grabbed them, dragging them towards the pickups.

Their captors spun them around and forced the two women to watch as the man with the tattoos walked over to Jerry and fired a shot into his head. Tina screamed, Janelle cried, the gang members laughed as the leader walked towards them, smoke still curling out of the end of his rifle.

He took his time letting his eyes rove over both of his captives' bodies. "You run, you fight, we kill you. You belong to cartel now. Comprende?"

Both of the girls managed to nod their heads and were each dragged into the back of separate pickups. The criminals had orders not to hurt or rape either woman, their commander designating the white girl for himself and the black one for the big boss. That didn't keep the gangsters from ripping their shirts open and groping them as they made their way back to their headquarters.

Janelle lost count of how many times she had been violated and abused since their capture. The greasy cartel leader had forced himself on her that afternoon, keeping her locked in his apartment for over a week, raping her repeatedly. When he had tired of her, he had sent her to the "pool" where the rest of the captive women were kept on the ninth and tenth floors.

After being sent to join the other sex slaves, she had been used and abused several times a week. The captives were there for the cartel soldiers' use and those animals used them a lot. Janelle had finally grown immune to the sounds of the other girl's cries or screams. She had only tried to fight back once when one of the scumbags pulled her into a bedroom and began molesting her. He had beaten her and then held a knife to her as he raped her, threatening to cut her throat. In hindsight, Janelle wished that she had kept resisting so that he would have killed her.

Washington had become friends with several of the other captives, their common plight creating bonds of dependence. The girl whom she had grown the closest to, however, Melissa, had been beaten to death several nights earlier by the man she was supposed to be treating. She had learned his name: Jorge Quintero, the second-in-command.

He had shown up drunk, like most of their captors did, and dragged Missy, as she was known to her friends, into one of the bedrooms. A few minutes later her screams shattered the night and the sound of fists striking flesh lodged in the pit of Janelle's stomach. She had rushed out of the room she shared with five other women, knowing it was useless, but feeling that she had to try to do something.

The Rat, the nickname the girls had given one of the guards assigned to them, stood outside the bedroom door where the sounds of the beating intensified. Washington and two other girls approached but the Rat looked at them, shaking his head, and raising his weapon. When the three women didn't leave, the guard racked a round into the shotgun and leveled it at them.

Janelle felt completely impotent, angry tears streaming down her face. She clenched her hands into fists so tightly she could feel the fingernails digging into her palms. Her friend was being brutalized and there was nothing that she or anyone else could do to stop it. This wasn't the time to make a stand, but it was the moment in which she vowed that she would kill Quintero and as many of the others as she could before they killed her. When she found out later that Missy was dead, Washington cried herself to sleep.

Late the next afternoon, one of the few guards with any English, Pedro, asked if any of the prisoners had medical training. The women merely stared at the floor, none wanting to help their captors in any way. Behind his back, the women called him Snake because of his beady eyes.

The guard left but returned twenty minutes later. This time, he asked for anyone with medical training, promising them extra food and that no one would have sex with them or hurt them while they treated a patient. Washington's hand went up.

"I have some medical training."

Several of the other girls looked at her with surprise. Why would she offer to work with the men who had caused them such pain?

"Bueno," Snake said, motioning towards the door.

Pedro got into the elevator with her, pushing the button for the forty-ninth floor. The young woman had no idea what she was volunteering for, but she hoped that it might provide her with an opportunity to strike back. She was led into an apartment where four other Mexicans sat drinking beer in the large living room, their rifles laying beside them.

Snake nodded at one of the bedrooms, sudden fear filling the woman's heart. Maybe it was a trick, Janelle thought. She quickly put that out of her mind. If they wanted her, they could have raped her downstairs, just like all the times before. Snake had forced himself on Washington twice before, not that she was keeping count.

Antonio Corona sat in a chair beside the bed, staring at a motionless figured covered by bloodstained white sheets. His eyes recognized Janelle as Snake led her into the room.

"She said she has medical training, Jefe," he said in Spanish.

Corona nodded, staring into Janelle's eyes. "You nurse?" he asked in halting English.

"No, I was in school to be an EMT, an emergency medical technician."

The cartel leader didn't understand so Washington rephrased her answer.

"I was training to work on an ambulance."

"Ah, bueno. Jorge hurt very bad. You check him?"

Janelle had to swallow her revulsion and forced herself to answer calmly. "Of course. How was he injured?"

"No sé. He in big fight. Maybe grenade or bomb."

She nodded. In reality, she could care less how the animal had been hurt, but she needed to play her part well. God or fate or luck had given her this opportunity. One way or another, she would kill Quintero, and if the opportunity presented itself, she would take out Corona and as many others as she could before they managed to kill her. She had to bide her time for a few days and get them to let their guard down.

"I need to examine him," Janelle said, walking towards the bed.

Antonio stood up and grabbed her by the left arm, putting his face close to hers. "We watch you. If you hurt Jorge, your death will be long and slow. Entiende?"

It took every ounce of self-control not to try and scratch out the animal's eyes. Not yet, she told herself. Make your death count. Take some of them with you.

"I understand," she answered, looking down and trying to appear subservient.

The cartel leader released her arm and watched as she pulled the sheet back, exposing a sleeping or unconscious Jorge. He was on his stomach, clad only in his boxers, several open wounds visible on his back. Blood oozed out of two of the most serious ones, dried blood surrounding the others, and she noted injuries to the back of his head.

Washington took a deep breath, forcing herself not to gag. There were cuts and scrapes on the Mexican's shoulders and elbows. Corona had Snake help her turn Jorge over so she could check his front side, also. His left eye was swollen and dried blood covered his face and ears, plus both of his knees were gashed open.

She pulled one of the eyelids open, unable to see the pupil in the unlit room. "I need some light to check his eyes."

Antonio handed Janelle a small flashlight. The generator was now only being operated a few hours a day to conserve fuel. When she shone the light into the injured gangster's eyes, she saw that the pupils were dilated and didn't react to the light. Those were two of the primary identifiers for a concussion, she remembered from one of her courses before she had dropped out. She also noted the dried blood around Quintero's ears.

Washington handed the flashlight back to the cartel leader. "He's got a brain injury, but I can't do anything about that. He may wake up today, tomorrow, or next week. I don't know. All I can do is clean and bandage his wounds so that they don't get infected. It also looks like his eardrums have burst. He may have lost his hearing, temporarily or permanently. We won't know until he wakes up."

The words "brain injury" had the desired affect on Corona, stunning him into momentary silence.

"Is he going to die?" he asked quietly.

I sure hope so, the young woman thought. I just hope I'm the one to kill him, and if I'm lucky, you along with him.

"I don't know. I can monitor his condition, but I need a first-aid kit if I'm going to take care of his wounds."

Corona yelled to one of his guards in the other room to go and find a first-aid kit. This was followed by the sound of a door opening and closing. He stared at Janelle for several minutes.

"You stay here, in other bedroom, close to Jorge. Pedro will sleep on couch in living room," he said, nodding at Snake. "No one will hurt you, but you take care of him," pointing at Quintero.

Two of the holes on the wounded man's back were deep and needed stitches. Washington didn't trust herself to sew him up. It was all she could do to keep from throwing up every time she changed his bandages. She suspected that there was possibly something inside his back. What was the word she had heard in class? Shrapnel? Metal fragments, maybe? Janelle was no surgeon and didn't intend to learn on this scumbag.

Jorge had regained consciousness the night before, but his brain had really been scrambled. He babbled incoherently in Spanish, calling for Antonio. Pedro aka Snake, had alerted the guard stationed outside the door to go get the boss. A few minutes later Corona arrived, a concerned look on his face.

The cartel leader tried to talk to his lieutenant, but Quintero mumbled about helicopters, bombs, explosions, and zombies. After a few minutes, the wounded man fell back into unconsciousness.

Tony the Tiger turned to Washington. "He say something to you?"

She shook her head. "I don't understand Spanish," she lied. "It just sounded like he was calling for you."

The gangster sat with his friend a while longer and Janelle went back to bed. She actually found herself smiling at something she had heard Quintero say before the boss had gotten there.

"The American military is coming. They're going to kill us all."

That thought actually gave the young woman a sense of hope for the first time in months.

### Dobbins Air Force Base, Marietta, Georgia, Tuesday, 1030 hours

Chuck walked out of the indoor firing range, happy with what he was seeing. The SEALs were up at the moment, working through some room clearing drills, clearly the right ones for the job that McCain had in mind for them. The range had been set up like a shoot house, allowing the Marine range officer to change up the scenarios each time a team went through.

The ops plan left the individual units intact and allowed them to focus on their strengths. The CDC agents were tasked with recovering the virus and taking out any cartel members who got in their way. One of the women who had been rescued by the SEALs in El Paso, the one who understood Spanish, told them that she thought all the extra weapons were stored on the twenty-fifth floor. Chuck was hoping that the vials containing the bio-terror weapon would be there as well.

She also knew that the two cartel leaders occupied the forty-ninth and fiftieth floors. The rescued hostage couldn't be any more specific than that. The CDC team would just have to start at the top and work their way down until they found the cartel's armory.

The SEALs and SAS would be inserted by helicopter a few blocks away. The Navy commandos had been given the job of locating and securing the hostages on the ninth and tenth floors. After the women were safe, the SEALs would consolidate them all to one floor.

A few of the warriors would stay to protect them, letting the others go to continue searching the building and engaging cartel members. They would be working their way up, searching the building for hostiles. The SAS would enter the building with the SEALs, but would start at the bottom, working their way up floor-by-floor, hunting for bad guys.

The National Guard troops would eliminate the gangsters guarding the vehicle depot at the corner of Peachtree Road and Piedmont Street. After the parking lot was under their control, they would leave one of the hummers and three soldiers there and would tactically deploy their other two vehicles on the back side of the cartel's HQ.

Drone footage had shown a two-vehicle patrol of cartel soldiers always cruising the area. Plan A called for the patrol to be taken out by the unmanned aircraft. If that wasn't practical, Plan B involved the National Guard troops or the Marines engaging the gangsters when they tried to get into the fight. Lieutenant Colonel Clark would also be the assistant mission commander, ready to take charge if something happened to McCain.

The Marines would deploy in two Light Armored Vehicles to the front side of the high-rise building. The LAVs were armed with a 25mm cannon and an M249 machine gun, and the three person crews for the LAVs had jumped at the chance to be part of the operation. The goal of the National Guard and the Marines was to form a loose perimeter around the cartel's headquarters, preventing any of the gang members from escaping.

For the last five days, the training had been intense. They had started at 0800 hours with one group in the range, the other groups practicing helicopter or vehicle insertions, or doing walk-throughs in one of the large aircraft hangars. After lunch, they met as a group, studying satellite maps, discussing strategy and contingencies, and looking for ways to reduce any chance of friendly fire.

After that, the individual units split off and went over their own part in the operation. Redundancy is the best way to prevent mistakes and they went over the plan again and again, making sure each operator knew their role, as well as their teammates'. As the mission commander, McCain led the group meetings. When the smaller groups met, he wandered around listening, learning, and answering questions.

The two CDC elements would infiltrate together, Tu leading the men from Washington, D.C., and Andy leading those from Atlanta. Chuck would be in Major Singleton's Pave Hawk directing the action and monitoring radio traffic. Two additional helicopters would be overhead providing support to the operators on the ground. A fourth Pave Hawk would be in the area, acting as the medevac in case anyone was wounded. The Air Force reserve crewmembers were paramedics in their civilian jobs and had also received extensive combat first-aid training.

Admiral Williams' bodyguards, Tim and Tom, would drive in with the Marines. They would be the only troops that McCain had in reserve. The former Delta operator and the former SEAL Team Six member would stay with the Marines in front of the building, available to deploy wherever they might be needed.

McCain glanced down at the ops plan in his hand, amazed at the amount of experience and skill they were taking into this mission. We might just pull this off, he thought, pulling open the door to the administration building.


Chuck found Admiral Williams seated behind a desk, his head against his chest, napping in the small office he had been provided in the air base's admin building.

"Hey, Boss, you got a minute?"

The older man jerked awake, looking up at McCain, embarrassed that he'd been caught sleeping.

"Of course. I'm sorry. I must've fallen asleep reading these reports."

"No problem, sir," Chuck said, with a smile. "If anyone deserves a nap, it's you. I just wanted to let you know that I think we're ready."

The admiral yawned and nodded. "That's good news. I watched some of the training yesterday and I was impressed. Everybody looks sharp. When do you want to go?"

"What about tonight? Let's get it over with. Cancel the afternoon training and let everybody get a nap. I think 0400 hours is a good time to hit these bastards. Send the hummers and the LAVs out at 0300 and have them in position. Launch the birds at 0330, and start killing bad guys at 0400."

Williams grunted. "If you think the group is ready, you have my permission to proceed."

"Thank you, sir."

He started to turn but something occurred to him. "Admiral, one more question. Why did you pick me to lead this operation? Colonel Clark has much more experience with these types of missions. Even several of our CDC agents have much more spec ops experience than me."

The admiral stared at the younger man for several moments before answering. "After the mission, Mr. McCain. Ask me that question after we wrap this up and I'll give you the answer."

Chuck nodded and went to let the men know that it was game on.

### Dobbins Air Force Base, Marietta, Georgia, Tuesday, 1330 hours

McCain strode to the front of the room, conversations slowly coming to a halt as the warriors waited to go over the operation plan again.

"Gentleman, this will be our last meeting," he said, letting the words hang in the air for a moment. "We're going in tonight. We're as ready as we're gonna be. I just came from the drone operations center and the cartel is up to something. They've beefed up their patrols and added a few extra guards around their HQ. Maybe having twenty of their guys killed by Hellfires got their attention.

"We'll go over the ops plan again and then you'll have the afternoon to clean weapons, check your equipment, and get some sleep. 0200 hours will be our wakeup time, the hummers and LAVs will be out the gate at 0300. The helicopters will launch at 0330 and we'll commence the assault at 0400 hours.

"Before we go back and review everyone's responsibilities for the hundredth time, let me mention a couple of things that we haven't talked about. First of all, the admiral has assured me that each assault team member and support team member will be given a full Presidential Pardon. Hopefully, we'll never need them, but I've been a cop for a long time and I've seen too many officers hung out to dry for doing their job."

From across the room, SEAL Chief Petty Officer Chris Norris spoke up, "That's a good idea. I never even thought of that."

Several of the other commandos nodded their heads. "Even though we have the full authority of the White House behind us," Chuck continued, "political climates change and I don't want any of us to have to worry about anything but executing this mission.

"That brings me to the second issue that we haven't really discussed: rules of engagement. Our mission calls for us to 'eliminate the cartel's presence on US soil.' We aren't going in to arrest these bastards. At the same time, you're going to have to use your best judgment if they start trying to surrender. Our ROEs are like most of the ones you've encountered before on the battlefield: self-defense of yourself or someone else. Any armed bad guys or gang members displaying aggressive behavior should be taken out.

"We'll be giving you some flex cuffs to take with you to secure prisoners. Admiral Williams has assured me that they will find room at Guantanamo Bay for any that we take into custody. They will be treated as enemy combatants and not as arrestees.

"You guys know the score, however, and we're going to be outnumbered at least four to one. Don't get hurt trying to arrest these guys. The most important part of our mission is recovering the zombie virus. We can't get distracted from that and the fewer of these scumbags we have to process later, the better."

"Sounds like my kind of ROEs," Scotty quipped. "Kill 'em all and let God sort 'em out."

This got a laugh from everyone. The warriors seated in the room liked what they were hearing. They were being allowed to go and do what they did best without having their hands tied behind their backs by restrictive rules of engagement or politics. And the idea of being outnumbered only motivated them. These men and women knew that they were better trained than their opponents and there was no question in their minds that they would prevail.

An hour and a half later, they were done. Everyone knew their job and they had all memorized the area around the cartel HQ. McCain would be overhead directing traffic as needed. His goal was to let each team leader do their thing with minimal interference from him.

### Buckhead, Atlanta, Tuesday, 1930 hours

Janelle knew that she was going to have to make her move soon. The wounded gangster was slowly starting to recover his strength. The lingering effects of the concussion and his burst eardrums, however, still had Jorge feeling dizzy when he stood, the thug needing someone to help him walk to the restroom.

Even though Quintero was getting stronger, the young woman also suspected that the wounds on his back were becoming infected. She had told Corona, and then Jorge himself, that he needed to have the shrapnel removed. At first, Antonio had ordered her to do the surgery.

Washington felt a wave of nausea at the suggestion. She'd come close to fainting every time she changed his bandages, a combination of her repulsion for the man and her own weak stomach. Janelle could not begin to imagine performing any type of surgery on anyone.

"Sir," she appealed to Antonio, putting a subservient tone in her voice. "I don't have the surgical instruments and I'm not a surgeon. I didn't even finish the EMT school. He needs a real doctor or at least someone with more knowledge than me."

Corona finally relented, realizing that the woman might do more harm than good. Washington heard him telling one of his bodyguards to plan a looting trip for Wednesday morning to find a doctor or a nurse.

The man had made the mistake of asking his boss where they were supposed to find a doctor in the middle of an abandoned city during a zombie apocalypse.

Antonio had screamed at his subordinate, "I don't know and I don't care! Find a hospital and check there. Find a clinic, a doctor's office. Anything. Just find me somebody who can get those pieces of metal out of Jorge's back!"

Washington saw that the cartel leader was much more on edge than normal. A couple of days earlier, she had overheard him telling one of his other bodyguards to increase the number of sentries around the building and add extra soldiers to their mobile patrols. He'd lowered his voice but she heard him saying that he thought they were going to be attacked any day now.

That was good news, she thought, but Janelle also knew that if Corona's looting team found a doctor, she would be sent back with the rest of the women, to be abused and violated once again. There was no way she was going to let that happen again. The tension was building inside of her, but Janelle had decided she would rather die than go back to being a sex slave for these animals.

After checking her patient and finding him napping, Washington went into her bedroom. Snake sat on the couch in the living room, leering at her as she came out of Quintero's room. One of the plusses of being Jorge's nurse was that she had her own room for the first time in weeks and no one had hurt her in several days. Guilt quickly rose up inside of her, though. I've got a private room, but all those other girls are down there being pawed over, raped, and forced to do all kinds of things.

She would kill Jorge, and if she was lucky maybe she could take out Snake, as well. If God smiled on her, Janelle thought, she might even be able to go after Tony the Tiger before his bodyguards shot her. Of course, God hadn't cared about how she or the other women had suffered for the last couple of months. He sure didn't seem to care when Quintero raped Missy and beat her to death. Something deep inside of Janelle, however, still wanted to believe.

A phrase popped into her mind. "I will never leave you nor forsake you." What is that? she wondered. That sounds like a Bible verse from when Mama took me to church as a child. Obviously, that wasn't true. If God was real, he sure hung me and all these other girls out to dry. I don't think the good Lord's even in my same zip code right now.

As she sat on the edge of her bed, Washington resolved that the next morning, she would act. The previous day, she had found a metal letter opener in the back of a drawer in the small desk in her bedroom. Janelle had slipped it under her pillow, the little blade giving her the means to get her revenge.

The small knife wasn't much, but it should be enough to kill the man who had captured and enslaved her and murdered one of her friends. She had seen Jorge's pistol sticking out from under a pillow on his bed. If I can take Señor Scumbag out, maybe I can grab his gun before Snake or anyone else knows what's going on, she thought.

The fact that she was contemplating her own death so nonchalantly had to be because of how much she had suffered. Her thoughts drifted to her family, wondering if they were even still alive. Her mother and grandmother lived together, just outside of the city limits of Atlanta. Her brother and his family also lived in the area. A tear dripped down her face as Washington realized she would never see them again, celebrate any birthdays or holidays together, or even have her own family one day.

From deep inside of her, something prompted her talk to God about her situation. The young woman hadn't prayed in years and really didn't want to start now. Why should she pray to a God who clearly had better things to do than take care of a group of defenseless women while a gang of evil men abused them?

She wrestled with her emotions for a few minutes and then sighed, the words coming out in a whisper.

"Look, I don't know if you're there or not. I don't know why you're letting all this bad stuff happen. I thought you were all about love. But if you're even listening, I could use some help.

"I know there's something in your book about revenge being a bad thing, but these are really evil people. Would you help me in the morning? Help me to be brave and to kill that bastard in the other room. I'd love to kill Corona, too, and anybody else that I could. Maybe help me get Snake as well?

"I know I'm asking for a lot, but somebody has got to do something to stop these animals. And...well, I don't want to die, but if there's a Heaven and a Hell, I'd like to be with you in Heaven tomorrow."

# Chapter Eleven

**Buckhead, Atlanta, Wednesday, 0407 hours**

The sound of rotors beating the air startled Corona out of his sleep. This was soon followed by automatic gunfire from the direction where their fleet of stolen vehicles was parked. Moments later, diesel engines roared down the street, coming to stop near the front entrance of the Peachtree Summit building, gunfire now coming from all around the cartel's headquarters, the sounds of an intense gun battle shattering the night.

A minute later, one of his bodyguards knocked and then entered his bedroom. "Jefe, we need to go. The gringos are attacking us, just like you said. We need to get you out of here."

Antonio threw on his clothes and stepped over to the window, carefully pulling the curtains back, trying to see who was assaulting them. He had been sleeping in this safe house for the last few nights, a two-story residence located on a quiet side street across from the captured condominium building. Tony the Tiger had had a feeling, a premonition that they were coming.

The bombs or missiles that had killed his men and wounded Jorge let the cartel leader know that the Americans had gotten serious. He had never expected the gringos to use that kind of firepower on their own soil. Now that they had, however, he sensed

**337**

that his headquarters would be their next target.

Martina Drive and the surrounding streets were part of a large community on the opposite side of Piedmont Road. His men had cleaned the neighborhood out of people and supplies, three of the cartel's women coming from homes in which the residents had chosen not to flee when the zombies came through. Of course their husbands or boyfriends had received a shot to the head as the captives were forced to watch.

Antonio had chosen one of these homes as his fallback location. It was less than two hundred yards from their high-rise building, but it looked like their attackers were only concentrating on the tall structure. The cartel leader had also spread his soldiers out, hoping to create a surprise for any gringo federales or soldiers that came for him, putting groups in structures on either side of the HQ. An office building and a smaller, three-story apartment location housed some of his best gangsters.

The residence that Tony the Tiger was using wasn't a mansion but it was a nice, American-style home. The hefty cartel leader had also liked having another sleeping option if their generator went out again and he didn't feel like climbing fifty floors of stairs. The home's garage was spacious enough to store his personal humvee in case he ever needed to make his escape. Like now.

At 0401 hours, the three National Guard hummers had roared towards the corner of Peachtree and Piedmont. The three Mexicans guarding the parking lot with the pool of stolen vehicles were slumped in their chairs, sleeping soundly, an empty Tequila bottle sitting the middle of their folding table. The diesel engines jarred the squad leader, Julio, awake.

Julio tried to sit up, not wanting to get caught sleeping. He assumed the approaching vehicles belonged to the cartel's patrol, returning from making their rounds. Judging the sound of the powerful motors, he could tell the vehicles were almost upon them.

"Wake up, amigos. The patrol is coming back."

One of the other two men started snoring, the other reached blindly for the table, grabbing the empty bottle and putting it to his mouth. The squad leader saw two of the big humvees continue by the intersection, the third one stopping near his position. A sudden realization rushed into his brain, panic stabbing him in the gut. *We don't have any more of the American hummers.* The gangster groped for his M-16, laying just in front of him on the table.

Corporal Corey Whitmer was standing in the open hatch of the military vehicle. He fired a two-round burst from the Browning M2 .50 caliber machine gun, both of the six hundred and fifty-five grain bullets catching Julio in the chest. The thug was knocked backwards out of his chair, his left shoulder and arm severed and sent flying by the force of the rounds. Whitmer swung the muzzle of the Browning and blasted the other two gang members before they could wake up and reach for their own weapons, their bodies similarly destroyed.

"November Golf One to all units," Lieutenant Colonel Clark transmitted, "intersection secure."

Clark's driver, Private Joe Thompson, maneuvered the humvee to provide covering fire to the units three hundred yards down Piedmont Road at the cartel's HQ, as well as to keep an eye on the area around the large intersection. With their parking lot full of stolen vehicles now in American hands, the cartel members would only be able to flee on foot. The other two National Guard hummers continued down Peachtree Road, turning left onto Maple Drive, which ran parallel with Piedmont Road, behind the cartel HQ.

Sergeant Thomas Jackson positioned his hummer, armed with the M249 light machine gun, on the backside of the fifty-floor building. First Sergeant Ricardo Gonzalez had his driver, Private Lawrence Long, continue down another five hundred feet to the intersection of East Paces Ferry Road where his gunner, Private Dan

Merchant, could bring his Mk 19 Grenade Launcher to bear on the side of the high-rise and cover the Marines in the front.

McCain couldn't hear the gunfire over the Pave Hawk's engines but he could see the muzzle flashes below him as the assault force engaged the cartel soldiers around their captured HQ. The night vision goggles on Chuck's helmet illuminated gang members trickling out of the front entrance of the Peachtree Summit, being cut down by the accurate fire of the Marines, SEALS, and SAS commandos positioned nearby.

As the return fire slackened a few minutes later, the SAS and the SEALs broke for the entrance to begin their mission. Chief Norris tossed a fragmentation grenade into the lobby, the warriors ducking below the level of the five steps that led into the building. The explosion blew out most of the windows, forcing every one else in close proximity to take momentary cover behind the light armored vehicles.

The commandos swarmed inside the tall building, firing bullets into the heads of those criminals who had been shot or who had been injured in the blast. Confident that the lobby was secure after a thorough sweep, Norris waved the combined American and British team towards the stairwell.

"SEAL One to CDC One, lobby secure, we're proceeding upstairs for mission objectives."

"CDC One clear," McCain acknowledged.

Another of the Air Force's helicopters darted in, hovering fifteen feet over the top of the high-rise building. The flight engineer and the gunner tossed ropes out of both of the open side doors. Andy and Tu each grabbed one and fast-roped to the roof, taking up cover positions until the rest of their teammates were down and ready to go to work. Fleming let McCain know that they were starting their mission at the top of the structure and moved for the door on the other side of the roof, giving them access to the high-rise.

Three minutes after making entry into the penthouse suite on the top floor, Andy called his boss again. "CDC Two to CDC One."

"CDC One," Chuck answered.

"This top floor belongs to Corona, but he's not here, " Andy Fleming reported. "Two of the girls were locked in one of the bedrooms. They said he was here earlier in the evening, and he, well,…this guy's an animal, boss. He keeps two of the prisoners at a time, using and abusing them until he gets tired of them. Then he'll grab two more. They have no idea where he's at, just that he's slept somewhere else the last few nights. They also confirmed that the rest of the prisoners are on the ninth and tenth floors."

"CDC One clear. See what other info you can get from the women and then continue your search for the virus."

Chuck felt the anger rising inside of him towards Antonio Corona and his gang of criminals. Unfortunately, he was circling at fifteen hundred feet, watching and listening to the events play out below him. Hopefully, one of his shooters would get the cartel leader's head in their sights.

On the ground below, the gunfire coming from cartel members began to pick up in its intensity. Corona's men who were housed in smaller buildings on either side of the skyscraper were firing from the windows and doors of their hideouts. McCain could see that the cartel forces were trying to get organized so they could get back into the fight. They didn't have the training of the American forces, but the gangsters understood that they were fighting desperately for their survival. "

Marine One to CDC One." Gunnery Sergeant Eric Gray's voice was calm, but Chuck could hear the rattle of gunfire as he transmitted.

"Go ahead, Marine One."

"We've got heavy fire coming from these two structures on

either side of the target location. There appear to be at least twenty or thirty guys in each one. Did we have any intel about hostiles using additional buildings? Any chance there might be hostages anywhere other than the main structure?"

"Negative, Marine One. CDC Two advises they've had contact with two hostages on the top floor. Those ladies confirmed that the main group of captives are housed inside the high-rise, the ninth and tenth floors."

"Roger, CDC One. In that case, I'm going to light these scumbags up!"

The gunnery sergeant directed the gunners of his two light armored vehicles to turn their M242 Bushmaster 25mm chain guns loose on the gangsters. The high explosive rounds ripped through the windows, doors, and walls of the structures, decimating the cartel soldiers inside. In a matter of seconds, over fifty of the Tijuana Cartel had been killed or severely wounded.

The gunfire from around the outside of the Peachtree Summit slacked off to nothing. Now it would be up to the warriors on the inside to complete their mission objectives.

As the SEALs rushed up the stairs, bypassing uncleared levels, to get to where the hostages were located and as the SAS started clearing the first floor, a group of cartel fighters huddled just above them on the second floor. The twelve Mexicans and four African-Americans could hear the gunfire from outside and from below them inside the building, interspersed with an occasional shout or scream as bullets struck home. They knew that in moments they would be fighting for their lives as well.

A muscular black man, Shamar, had told his floor-mates when the attack started that they all needed to leave. Shamar had enlisted in the army right out of high school. He had only lasted a year, however, before being arrested, serving two years in a military prison, and then given a dishonorable discharge, for setting up a drug distribution network on his base. His limited time in the military, however, let him know that the Tijuana Cartel and the Black Mafia Family members did not have a chance against the forces that were attacking them.

The BMF gangster pulled a rope ladder out from under his bed, and rushed out onto his balcony. It was on the side of the building, blocked from view by the smaller apartment building next to the high-rise. In moments, Shamar was climbing down the side of the building, his M-16 strapped across his back.

The rest of the group quickly descended as gunfire echoed all around them. The sound of several helicopters circling above let the gang members know that their chances of escape were minimal. When everyone was on the ground, Shamar led the way behind the neighboring apartments, heading towards the lot where the cartel's vehicles were stored. If they could get there undetected, and if they could grab a few vehicles, maybe, they had a chance.

The American criminal considered trying to escape on foot. He felt confident that they could get by their attackers and slip away into the night. The problem with that was that Shamar and his companions would be on foot and there were still plenty of zombies in Atlanta. No, better to try and get some transportation.

"Air One to November Golf One," drone pilot First Lieutenant Tim Cox called Colonel Clark, "hostiles heading your way on foot. I'm counting sixteen bad guys. Right now they're behind that shopping center to the right of the high-rise."

"November Golf One is clear. Keep me updated."

Five minutes later, the drone pilot spoke again. "Air One to November Golf One, looks like they're getting ready to charge out from behind the shopping center."

Corporal Whitmer stood in the turret of the big .50 caliber

machine gun, scanning the area in front of him through his night vision goggles. Driver Joe Thompson stood next to his door, rifle up and ready. Colonel Clark adopted the same posture behind the passenger door.

"Wait until I shoot," Clark ordered quietly.

Suddenly, the three soldiers saw the group through their NVGs, crouching and running towards their position. The colonel waited until they were out in the open, their closest cover now fifty yards away, before he pulled the trigger. Shamar was leading the way, sprinting hard towards the parking lot.

The crack of Clark's rifle loosed the fire of his two companions. The first two shots from Kevin's rifle caught Shamar in the chest. The thug stumbled, but ran another fifteen feet before collapsing to the pavement. Thompson quickly dropped two more of the gangsters.

Whitmer's machine gun ripped through the ranks of the criminals blowing their bodies apart, a single bullet punching through one man to kill the man behind him, as well. The three soldiers fired for another ten seconds, and then realized that they had no more targets. They were all down, none of them moving.

### Buckhead, Atlanta, Wednesday, 0415 hours

Janelle Washington awoke to the crackling of gunfire. The Mexicans were fond of shooting into the air at all hours of the night, especially after they had been drinking, but this sounded different. Within seconds, there was a steady barrage of automatic weapons firing in street below, along with the thumping of helicopter rotors circling overhead. Her bedroom was on the backside of the building and she would have to go into the living room to peer out those windows to see what was happening.

The young woman reached under her pillow, withdrawing the

letter opener and slipping it into the left sleeve of her sweatshirt. She quietly eased the bedroom door open and saw Snake standing by the large window, clutching his shotgun, peering around the curtains and down onto the street, forty-nine floors below. A single candle provided minimal light for the large room. Hearing the door, the guard turned towards the captive, fear evident on his face, even in the barely-lit room. The unmistakable smell of marijuana smoke filled the living room letting the young woman know how Pedro had been entertaining himself.

"You stay there!" he ordered, pointing back at the bedroom.

"I need to check on Jorge and make sure he's OK."

"No!" Snake ordered. "Go back to room."

Janelle shrugged and pointed at the cartel lieutenant's door. "Okay, but if Jorge has a panic attack because of all the shooting, I'll have to tell el Jefe that you wouldn't let me help his friend. Jorge has a neurological injury and I need to make sure he stays calm."

Pedro didn't understand most of what the African-American woman said, but even stoned and with his limited English he understood enough to know that she was threatening to tell Tony the Tiger that he wouldn't let her do her job as Quintero's nurse. He wasn't sure what he should do. He could see the fighting raging below, but felt that the machismo of the cartel fighters would thwart any attack by the weak Americans.

Before the guard could answer, Washington took a couple of steps forward and lowered her voice. She grabbed the bottom of her sweatshirt, pulling it up a few inches, exposing her stomach.

"Let me check on Jorge and then you could come tuck me into bed? It's lonely in there by myself. What do you think?" She eased closer to one of the men who had hurt her and so many other women.

Snake's eyes got large and he unconsciously licked his lips. He closed the gap and stood in front of the black woman.

"Okay! You check Jorge and then…" he said, grabbing his crotch, and grinning broadly.

"Oh, yeah, Pedro. You and me."

Janelle reached out, touching Snake's face seductively with her left hand. Her right hand suddenly shot forward with the letter opener, stabbing him just below the solar plexus, shoving the blade in as deep as she could, thrusting upward. Warm blood spurted out over her hand as the guard tried to grab her arm, gasping loudly. He sunk to his knees, his heart punctured, the shotgun slipping from his grasp to the carpet with a thump.

The dying man's eyes bulged with surprise as Janelle said, in perfect Spanish, "Enjoy Hell, you piece of…"

"Pedro!" A loud shout came from Quintero's bedroom, startling the woman back to the reality of her situation. She had killed one of her tormenters, but her primary target still needed to be dealt with.

Washington tried to pull the blade out of Snake, but her hand slipped off, the letter opener slick with blood. She snatched up the shotgun from the floor, spinning around just as Jorge's door opened. The gangster stood in the doorway, his left hand holding onto the frame for balance, the Colt Python in his right hand, dangling at his side.

As Quintero's eyes focused on the scene in front of him in the flickering candlelight the gangster snarled, bringing the .357 Magnum revolver up, the muzzle tracking towards her midsection. Janelle quickly pointed the .12 gauge shotgun and pulled the trigger a split-second before Jorge fired the revolver. Something whizzed by her as the gangster dropped his gun and crumpled to the floor, a groan coming from deep inside of him.

The young woman stepped forward, sighting in on the Mexican's prone figure and pulled the trigger again. Nothing happened. Janelle had a very limited knowledge of guns and had no idea how to make the pump shotgun shoot again. No matter how hard she pulled the trigger, it wouldn't fire at the figure lying on the floor a few feet away.

Washington had to make sure the rapist and murderer was really dead, cautiously approaching the doorway. She turned the shotgun around, planning to use it to club him to death since she couldn't get it to fire. In the candlelight, she saw the pool of blood forming around his waist.

The cartel thug lay on his left side, his head tantalizingly close, a low moan coming from his lips. Janelle raised the long gun over her head, bringing down the stock towards his skull. Jorge's left arm suddenly shot out grabbing her right ankle, jerking her to the floor.

Washington dropped the shotgun as she fell, screaming as the wounded man pulled her towards him, and then using her leg to pull himself towards her. She kicked him in the face with her free left foot, eliciting a grunt of pain from the criminal. His grip, however, was strong as he dragged his victim closer. Quintero's right hand was suddenly grasping her throat and squeezing.

Janelle tried to scream again but nothing would come out, blackness starting to overtake her. She grabbed at the hand that was choking her, trying to pull it off but his grip was too tight. Janelle felt hair and then the animal's face with her right hand, and she drove her thumb into Quintero's left eye socket. Washington heard him squeal in pain as a loud crashing noise came from the other side of the room. For the woman, however, everything had gone dark.

The two CDC teams moved together down the stairwell to the forty-ninth floor. The captives on the top floor had told them that Jorge Quintero occupied the floor below Corona and Fleming chose to keep all the agents together as they prepared to confront the cartel leader's lieutenant. The women weren't sure where the armory was, although one of the girls had heard two of the guards talking about storing some supplies on the twenty-fifth level.

Each floor contained four luxury apartments. Jimmy Jones cautiously opened the stairwell door, scanning the dark corridor with his night vision goggles. Clear. That was good news, but the federal officers had no idea which door to start with.

Andy motioned to the first door on the right, his team stacking outside as big Scotty Smith prepared to kick their way in. Tu's team would stay in the hallway providing rear security and to prevent anyone from escaping from the other three doors.

Suddenly, the sound of a struggle came from across the corridor, the sound of someone grunting in pain carrying into the hallway. Smith paused, his foot in the air, and the agents listened, trying to hear what was happening. A man's voice and then two gunshots rang out, and the CDC officers quickly moved as one man, lining up outside the new apartment.

Andy nodded at Scotty and the former Army Ranger drove his foot into door, shattering the frame. Fleming was the first one in, moving to the right, his rifle up and ready. Eddie, Jimmy, Hollywood, and then Scotty followed, alternating going left and right.

A body was lying in the middle of the room, a blade protruding from it's abdomen. Fleming kept moving to the right, seeing a struggle taking place on the floor, in an open doorway on the far side of the room. A black woman was on her back, Jorge Quintero choking her with one hand, his other hand covering his left eye, blood seeping out between his fingers.

Andy recognized the gangster's face from the photos that the admiral had provided. Actually, at the moment, the officer couldn't recognize Quintero's bloody face, but the shaved head covered with tattoos was a clue. The former MARSOC Marine operator fired two quick rounds from his suppressed M4 into the Mexican's face, snapping his head back, killing him instantly.

"Bad guy down. Clear the rest of the apartment, guys. Scotty, we've got a woman that needs to be checked after the apartment is secure," Fleming said. Smith also functioned as the team's medic, and Scotty and Andy covered their teammates as they quickly, but thoroughly, made sure there were no other threats in the condominium.

Two minutes later, Eddie gave the all clear and Scotty knelt beside the woman, feeling for a pulse. Smith noted Quintero's bloody corpse, the shotgun blast having caught him in the crotch.

"Hey, guys, she did a number on this dirt bag. It looks like she shot his balls off."

As he touched the girl's neck, her eyes flew open, her hands shooting towards the bearded man's face. Smith calmly caught both of her arms with his left hand.

"Hi, I'm Scotty and you're safe now. We're police officers and are here to rescue you. I'm also a paramedic; are you hurt anywhere?"

Janelle tried to answer, her voice coming out as a croak after being choked unconscious. "I...I don't think so. My throat hurts. Is he dead?"

"Very. Remind me not to piss you off. You took out his privates and my buddy, Andy, over there, put a couple of bullets in his head. Who's the other dead guy? What's your name, by the way?"

"I'm Janelle. Janelle Washington."

She sat up, sliding back against the wall so that she could get a look at her rescuers. Washington wasn't able to see much, the light in the room so dim. Big men, dark clothing, helmets, guns. They really had come to rescue them. Janelle had long since given up hope, but here they were.

"That was Snake," she said, pointing at the man with the letter opener sticking out of him. "That's what we called him. His real name was Pedro. He was my guard. He...," she looked down, embarrassed. "He hurt me and some of the other girls." Janelle pointed at Jorge's body. "He was the worst, though. I'm glad he's dead."

Andy knelt beside Janelle. "Like Scotty said, you're safe now and we're here to get you and the other girls out of here. Do you have any idea where Antonio Corona is?"

Washington shook her head, pointing at Quintero. "No, Corona's been coming by regularly to check on him. He got injured last week and they had me taking care of him. I was waiting for my chance to kill Jorge, maybe even kill both of them. Antonio's apartment is upstairs."

Fleming nodded. "Yeah, we just came from there. There were two other girls in the apartment, but no Corona. We're going to take you up there while we clear the rest of the building."

Tu Trang and his team covered each of the other four doors in the hallway. Three of them led to other condominiums, which would be searched shortly, and the fourth led to the stairwell. Trang peeked back into the open door after hearing Andy's suppressed M4 and saw that everything was under control. Each of his men knelt in the corridor, making themselves smaller targets and focusing on protecting Andy's team. Jay Walker was responsible for the stairwell door.

A few minutes later, the sound of footsteps climbing the stairwell could be heard. Walker had the best angle on the door and he waited, his muzzle pointed in that direction, the former SEAL peering through his NVGs over the top of his rifle. The door burst open and three cartel soldiers, all carrying rifles, rushed into the hallway, breathing loudly from their exertion.

Jay triggered a burst at head height that connected with all the gangsters before the Mexicans even realized that they were under attack. The three thugs collapsed in the doorway, their dead bodies propping the door open. The CDC agents waited, expecting to see more of the criminals show up, but silence prevailed.

LeMarcus Wade whispered loudly across the corridor, "Come on, Jay, sharing is caring, man. You got to let us kill some of the bad guys, too."

Inside the apartment, Janelle flinched at the gunshots from outside the doorway. Jimmy and Hollywood cautiously took a look, checking on the other CDC agents. A minute later, Jones walked over to Andy and reported in.

"All good. They just took out some bad guys who were probably coming to see Señor No Balls."

"Cool. Let's get Janelle upstairs and then we can kill some more, too. Grab those guns and we'll leave them with the ladies."

Ten minutes later, Washington had been delivered to Antonio Corona's apartment with assurances that someone will be back for them after they were finished eliminating the cartel.

### Buckhead, Atlanta, Wednesday, 0425 hours

Corona had watched the shootout for several minutes at his window before complying with his security team's wishes. His concern now was whether or not they could actually get away. The gringos had helicopters circling overhead and he knew that he couldn't outrun them or their weapons. They had also brought some kind of tanks and his humvee would not be a match for them if he stayed and fought.

Tony the Tiger had noticed that the armored vehicles had tires, though, four on each side. Maybe he could use that to his advantage. The cartel leader would try to escape, but he was no coward and would punch the gringos in the nose first. And if they killed him, he would die fighting living up to his name.

His four-man protection detail led the way into the garage. They had already packed some supplies in the back of the hummer. Antonio seated himself in the front passenger seat, clutching an M-16, stolen body armor strapped uncomfortably around his chest, his fat gut sticking out from underneath. Carlos, the leader of his bodyguards, carefully eased open the garage door, and motioned for the others to get into the vehicle with their boss.

Carlos climbed into the driver's seat. Tico stood in the turret, manning the light machine gun. Corona gave quick orders to his team, the concern evident in their eyes. They clearly all wanted to get away to fight another day, but the gangster knew that he needed to hurt the Americans before he fled and possibly even slow their pursuit of him.

The driver slowly pulled out of the garage, keeping the headlights off, easing towards the end of the street, where Martina Drive intersected with Piedmont Road. Looking down to their left, less than the length of a soccer field away was the closest armored vehicle. The silhouette of the second LAV was evident further down the road, at least a hundred feet of space between the two.

Antonio saw the soldiers or police officers, whatever they were, crouching behind the menacing-looking vehicle, firing at his men who were shooting at them from the widows of the high-rise.

"Tico, put a burst into the soldiers and then take out the tires on that tank. Carlos, be ready to turn around and get us out of here."

"Air One to CDC One." The drone was flying high over the action, providing a video feed for Admiral Williams back at Dobbins Air Force Base.

"CDC One," McCain answered.

"A vehicle, it looks like a humvee, just came out of the garage of a house across the street from the front of the high-rise. There's a side street just up from the LAVs and the vehicle is approaching the corner without any headlights."

"Roger," Chuck acknowledged. Before he could take any other action, screams erupted over the radio.

"Marine One to November Golf One! We're taking heavy fire from a hummer at our three o'clock. I've got men down. Is that your units firing in our direction?"

"Negative," Colonel Clark answered immediately. "I see the vehicle but I can't engage without shooting at you, Marine One."

"Marine One clear. The shooting just stopped, but I've got four Marines down. I'm going to need a medic and a medevac ASAP."

"Air One to CDC One, that hummer just did a U-turn and is tearing off down the street."

The medevac helicopter was circling the scene, hoping not to be needed. The pilot had heard the radio traffic, though, and called the Marine commander on the ground.

"Medevac to Marine One. I'll meet you at the designated pickup location immediately. Can you get the wounded there?"

The designated pickup point had been decided ahead of time. It was a large grocery store parking lot four blocks away, out of sight of the gunfight.

The gunnery sergeant hesitated. "Marine One to Medevac. One of the LAVs is damaged. I need to keep the other one on station. Do we have a humvee that can transport the wounded?"

Lieutenant Colonel Clark jumped into the conversation. "November Golf One to November Golf Two."

"We're already rolling," First Sergeant Gonzalez answered.

"CDC One to November Golf One," McCain called Clark. "I need you to take command. We're going after that fleeing humvee."

"November Golf One is clear and assuming command."

Chuck flipped over to the intercom system in the helicopter. "Major? We need to follow the hummer that's trying to get away."

The Air Force pilot had been monitoring the conversation and swung the Pave Hawk in that direction. "I'm clear. Don't worry. He won't get away. We can take them out with the miniguns."

"Sounds good. If possible, though, I'd prefer not to kill them all. I'd like to interrogate at least one of them. If Corona is in that humvee, he's better off alive than dead. At least, until I can have a chat with him."

There was a long pause. "Are you saying you want me to land after we disable that vehicle?"

"Yes, ma'am, if at all possible. Even if you can't get close, I'm sure you can find a place to set down and let me go in on foot. It's that important. Those bastards might even have the virus with them in their vehicle."

Singleton didn't say anything else, focusing on flying, trying to catch up with the fleeing vehicle.

"Air One to CDC One, they just turned right onto Peachtree Road and are hauling ass north."

Less than a minute later, they saw the stolen military vehicle ahead of them, racing up the mostly deserted five-lane road. Suddenly, tracers arced up from the hummer directly at the helicopter. Multiple combat deployments had sharpened Singleton's reflexes and she immediately jerked the collective back so that the bullets flew under them. The Air Force officer then pushed the controls to the side, putting the right door gunner in position to bring his machine gun to bear.

"Weapons free, Tommy!" Major Singleton told Sergeant Thomas.

The young crewman didn't have to be told twice, sending a burst of return fire at the speeding vehicle. His first target was the gunner firing the M249 light machine gun at them. Something slammed into the side of the Pave Hawk, just as Thomas' tracer rounds walked into the cartel gunner. He jerked and disappeared from view.

"I got him!" the young sergeant exclaimed. "Now, let's take out the driver."

The six barrels of the minigun spun as it fired, capable of firing over two thousand rounds a minute. Sergeant Thomas raked the side of the vehicle with minimal effect.

"It must be one of the armored humvees," he observed over the intercom. "I'll take out the tires."

McCain recognized the area they were flying over as they approached a large intersection. They had just passed Lenox Mall to the right and were coming up on Phipps Plaza on their left. Both of the large shopping malls were considered the most high-end shopping in all of Atlanta. Of course, now, they sat empty or held decaying zombies who had not yet been dealt with.

Moments later, the humvee veered to the left, turning onto Wieuca Road, just as Thomas' next burst took out both of the tires on the driver's side. The speeding vehicle was already going too fast to make the turn. With two tires now destroyed, Carlos was unable to control the hummer, and the military vehicle jumped the curb and slammed into a utility pole, snapping it in half. The speed of the hummer kept it moving forward to strike a large oak tree, coming to a sudden, jarring stop. Steam rose from the smashed front end of the vehicle.

The Air Force helicopter hovered over the scene, waiting for the occupants to exit. After a minute, however, it didn't appear that anyone was getting out. Chuck searched the ground below through his NVGs. An enormous church was just a couple of hundred yards north of their location.

"There!" Chuck pointed at the large open parking area. "Could you put down in that church parking lot? It won't take long, but I've got to check that humvee."

The major didn't answer, but he felt the Pave Hawk start to descend. She ordered her co-pilot and the two crew members to watch for power lines as she looked for the best place to set down.

"Can I take Sergeant Thomas with me?" McCain asked the pilot as they touched down.

The major turned around, clearly not happy with being on the ground. "Tommy, go with Agent McCain and make sure he doesn't get hurt."

"Yes, ma'am." The crewman unsnapped his harness and grabbed an M4 rifle.

The second crewman, Corporal Jarvis Baker, retrieved his own rifle to keep watch over the helicopter and his teammates. McCain and Thomas exited the aircraft, ducked under the spinning rotors, and trotted towards the wrecked vehicle. Both men glanced around as they ran, knowing that there were infected in the area. Chuck realized that he had not let Clark know where they were.

"CDC One to November Golf One, status report?"

"November Golf One to CDC One. The casualties are in the air, heading towards the air force base. Marine One was hit, as well, but he didn't report it. My medic is patching him up at the scene and he'll be back in the fight in a few minutes.

"Units inside the building are still searching floor-by-floor. Oh, and that cartel mobile patrol finally showed up. When November Golf Two was transporting the wounded to the medevac point, the gangbangers tried to ambush them. Private Merchant finally got to fire his grenade launcher and blasted all three vehicles into little pieces. What about you?"

"I'm on foot," McCain answered, "approaching the humvee. The gunner on the Pave Hawk took them out and they crashed. Now, we're gonna check and see if anyone is still alive and search the vehicle. We're on Wieuca Road, just off Peachtree in case we need you."

"November Golf One clear. Be careful, McCain."

The smoking humvee was just in front of them now, Chuck

moving slowly up on the driver's side, the stock of his rifle pressed into his left shoulder. Sergeant Thomas was positioned behind a nearby tree to cover his approach and to make sure no infected snuck up on them. The back door of the hummer was slightly open and McCain silently pushed the selector on his suppressed rifle to "Auto."

The door suddenly flew open and a bloody cartel soldier stumbled out, attempting to raise an M-16. The police officer triggered a short burst, catching the gangster in the chest with three 5.56mm rounds, knocking him back against the open door. Chuck put a second burst into the gunman's head, making sure that he stayed dead.

Through the opening, McCain could see the unmoving driver slumped over the steering wheel, but there didn't appear to be anyone else in the front passenger seat. The machine gunner's shattered body lay in the rear floorboard, blood pooled around him from multiple hits.

A groan came from inside the hummer. Maybe the driver was still alive? he wondered. Chuck moved around to the passenger side. He held his rifle up, activating the attached flashlight, illuminating a figure in the front passenger floorboard. McCain jerked the door open with his right hand, prepared to fire with his left.

The crumpled form groaned again, but another noise, the too-familiar sound of multiple growling zombies came from back behind the CDC agent.

"Keep an out for those zombies, Tommy," Chuck quietly called over to Air Force sergeant, keeping his own weapon pointed at the two figures in the front compartment. "When you see them, let me know how close they are."

McCain couldn't see the passenger's hands, but the driver's right moved slowly towards a holstered pistol on his hip. Chuck fired a single shot into the side of his head, blood and brains splattering the side window. The federal officer then reached in with his right arm and grabbed the passenger by the collar and jerked him roughly out of the vehicle, prepared to shoot him, too. The Mexican cried out in pain as he was forcefully removed from the humvee, a gold-plated Beretta, clattering against the door and falling to the ground. A rifle was slung across the man's chest.

Chuck recognized Antonio Corona from the pictures that they had been provided. He threw the cartel leader face down and dropped a knee into his back, eliciting an agonized grunt from the gangster. McCain tossed the thug's M-16 aside and patted him down for any additional weapons. Antonio's left hand was hidden underneath him and Chuck roughly grabbed his elbow, pulling it slowly backwards to expose a hand holding a long blade.

Corona fought to free his arm, but McCain's strength prevailed, the Rambo style knife visible through his NVGs. Tony the Tiger struggled to turn over onto his back, a position from which he might be able to bring the sharp weapon into play. Instead, the CDC officer put his left knee on the back of Corona's arm and extended it out to the side. Chuck still controlled the hand holding the blade and jerked it backwards, his knee pinning his elbow to the ground. There was an audible snap as McCain broke Corona's arm, an agonized cry escaping the criminal's mouth. The federal agent tossed the knife away.

The growling and snarling was getting closer, coming from the direction of Phipps Plaza on the opposite side of the street from them.

"Agent McCain, I've got two groups heading our way. A group of around twenty-five and another of maybe twenty. They're inside a hundred yards."

"Okay, I'll be done here in a minute."

Chuck roughly rolled the cartel leader onto his back and straddled him, the criminal clearly in lot of pain. McCain saw that his right arm hung at an odd angle, his shoulder appearing to be shattered, probably from slamming into the dashboard when they crashed. Two broken arms, Chuck thought. Sucks to be him, but in a few minutes it won't matter.

"Where's the virus, Corona?"

The Mexican managed a smile, displaying the bravado that he was known for. "American federale, eh? You arrest me? You read me my rights? I need hospital, gringo policía. I'm going to sue you, puerco! Then, I'll track you down and rape your wife while you watch and kill your whole family!"

"Arrest you?" Chuck answered with his own grim smile. "The most you can hope for from me is a quick death and you just lost that by threatening my family."

The gangster launched a wad of spit and mucus towards McCain's face. It didn't make it quite that far, landing on the agent's body armor. A lightning-fast, straight left punch caught Corona flush in the face and knocked him unconscious, his head thudding into the hard ground.

Chuck stood, eyeing the coming zombies. These all appeared to be slow-movers, decay having taken it's toll on their bodies. They were still dangerous, but none of the Zs were runners.

"How good are you with that rifle, Tommy?"

"I qualified as a Marksman, sir."

"Well, go ahead and start shooting. Go for the closest ones, semi-auto, head shots only. I need another minute."

Sergeant Thomas began cutting down the infected, the crack of his M4 echoing around the intersection. Chuck glanced down, noting that Antonio was still out. McCain pulled the flashlight off his belt, quickly searching the interior of the hummer. The front and rear passenger compartments were empty.

He pulled open the back hatch of the military vehicle and saw four backpacks, several gallon jugs of water, and two large cardboard boxes of food. McCain saw another bag hidden behind the backpacks. A black canvas bag. The CDC agent carefully opened it, shining the flashlight inside. The eight test tubes were there, still intact, the padded case having protected them, even when the humvee had slammed into a power pole and a tree. A tag hung from the handle of the bag, identifying the owner as "Dr. Nicole Edwards, CDC Epidemiologist." A wave of relief swept over the police officer.

Cursing came from the cartel leader as he regained his consciousness. Chuck left the bag and grabbed Corona, jerking him to his feet by his injured arms. McCain pulled the velcro straps loose from Antonio's body armor, snatching it off of him and tossing it aside, the criminal's broken bones causing him to cry out again. Corona was a fighter, though, and tried to pull free from the officer's grasp. The federal agent slammed the cartel leader face-first into the side of the hummer, stunning him again and knocking the breath out of him.

"How many, Tommy?"

"I've shot maybe twenty, sir. There are more coming from across Peachtree Road. We need to get out of here."

"Take off. I'll be right behind you. I'm almost done."

"I don't want to leave without you, Agent McCain."

"Go! I'll be right there."

Sergeant Thomas turned and began trotting towards the helicopter. The closest zombies were inside fifty yards converging on Chuck's position. McCain let his rifle hang from it's sling and began walking towards the Zs dragging Tony the Tiger with him, one hand holding the back of his collar, the other hand grasping the back of the criminal's pants.

Corona quickly surmised what was happening, hearing the growls of the approaching infected. He struggled to get free but was no match for the CDC agent. Chuck walked out into the street and hurled the Mexican across the concrete median that ran down the center of Wieuca Road. The injured man landed on his face, busting his nose open on the asphalt. The clicking of zombie teeth intensified as the smell of fresh blood filled the air.

The cartel boss managed to push himself to his feet, his desire for survival suppressing all of the pain that he was feeling. He began running blindly towards Peachtree Road, not realizing that he was running directly towards one of the approaching groups of flesh-eaters. Suddenly, Antonio Corona's fat body spun around as one of his legs collapsed, sending him back to the asphalt.

Chuck's shot had struck the running man in the back of his left leg, shattering the femur. Tony the Tiger tried to get his leg to work to no avail, screaming curses at McCain in Spanish and English. The zombies from Phipps Plaza turned their attention towards the meal that was making the most noise to go along with the strong scent of blood. McCain saw another large group of infected crossing Peachtree Road, focused on the hefty man who was now trying to crawl away.

The CDC agent rushed back to the humvee, grabbed the padded bag, and sprinted towards the waiting Pave Hawk. Ahead of him, Tommy's rifle fired several times, letting him know that they weren't out of the woods yet. Suddenly, a piercing scream filled the night air as dead hands and teeth grabbed Antonio Corona, ripping him apart, and devouring the gangster.

Chuck could hear the shots and see the muzzle flashes up ahead of him as the young sergeant fired into a group of Zs closing on him. The non-commissioned officer was wisely shooting and slowly retreating, the decaying zombies shuffling after him, only thirty yards away. McCain continued to run, wanting to get back to the helicopter as quickly as possible. He was almost to Thomas, when a running figure burst towards them, a freshly infected Z, coming from the backside of Phipps Plaza.

The fast-moving zombie was making a straight line towards the sergeant, just twenty-five yards away. Chuck stopped and raised his rifle, out of breath and his heart pounding. He led the runner, sighting just ahead of him as he ran, and squeezed the trigger. Miss. McCain fired again. Another miss. Chuck fired a third time, this round slamming into the right cheek of the sprinter, sending him to the pavement at the sergeant's feet.

Major Singleton had the rotors spinning as the two men dove inside the aircraft. Another group of Zs was slowing crossing the church parking lot, their growls and groans being drowned out by the noise of the helicopter. In seconds, the Pave Hawk was high over the scene back enroute to the still-raging gun battle.

### Buckhead, Atlanta, Wednesday, 0450 hours

"CDC One to November Golf One, I'm back on station, assuming command."

It had taken less than five minutes to return to their orbit around the Peachtree Summit Luxury Condominiums. It looked like the gun battle outside the building had completely stopped, although an occasional muzzle flash came from one of the high-rise's windows. Each time, it was met by blistering, accurate return fire.

"November Golf One is clear. CDC One is in command."

"CDC One to CDC Two."

"CDC Two," Fleming answered.

"Corona's dead and I have the virus. He had all eight of the vials with him. Change your mission objectives to clearing floors until you meet up with the SEALs and the others."

"Roger, CDC Two is clear."

Now that the fighting had ended outside, McCain released his reserve force, Tim and Tom, to clear the two smaller buildings that the cartel had been using. The former Delta and SEAL operators quickly mopped up the few gang members who still had any fight left in them. The 25mm chain guns on the LAVs had devastated most of those who had tried to make a stand there. An occasional shot rang out as the two men dealt with wounded criminals.

After those structures were cleared, Tim's voice came over the radio, "Reserve to CDC One, exterior buildings are secure. Request permission to assist units in the high-rise."

Chuck smiled to himself. He knew that the warriors wanted to be in the middle of the fighting and was surprised that they had waited this long to ask to go in. It was a testimony to their understanding of the tactical situation. Tim and Tom understood the importance of having a force held in reserve in case other units ran into trouble and needed backup.

"CDC One to Reserve. Permission granted. Make contact with SEAL One when you get inside and find out where you can be put to work."

"Reserve is clear."

It took over three more hours before the scene was declared secure. Floor-by-floor, apartment-by-apartment, room-by-room, the warriors worked through the tall building. Many of the floors were unoccupied, but they still had to be carefully searched. Most of the cartel members inside their headquarters chose to shoot it out with the SEALs, SAS commandos, or the CDC Agents. The results were the same, their bullet-riddled bodies now lying in living rooms, doorways, corridors, and stairwells.

The mixed force of military and federal law enforcement completely overwhelmed the cartel soldiers. The Americans owned the darkness as each member of the attacking force wore night vision goggles. The gangsters had no such luxury and were forced to fire blindly, hoping to hit something.

Two of the SEALs received minor wounds as bullets struck their body armor. One of the CDC Agents from Washington, D.C., LeMarcus Wade took a round to the head, his ballistic helmet saving his life. Wade was knocked to the ground and was unconscious for a few seconds, but quickly climbed to his feet and continued fighting, even though he was still slightly groggy.

Only twenty-eight of the Latino gangsters and six of the African-Americans surrendered of their own volition. These were secured with flex-cuffs and duct tape, then blindfolded and gagged. They were left scattered up and down the tall building, the team leaders recording in a notebook where they had been left.

The sky over Atlanta began to lighten, the sun slowly making it's climb in the eastern sky. By 0750 hours, it was daylight, and at 0820 hours, Andy's voice came over the radio, "CDC Two to CDC One, we've linked up with SEAL One. The building is secure. How do you want us to proceed with getting the hostages and the prisoners out?"

"Have Reserve escort the victims down and the rest of the you figure out a way to get the prisoners down to the lobby. Maybe we can find the generator and crank it up so you can use the elevator? Those clowns were using it a lot."

"Marine One to CDC One, one of my Marines is an engineer. I can have him attempt to locate and get the generator going."

"CDC One clear. I'll be on the ground in a few. Well done, gentlemen."


Major Singleton dropped McCain off at the medevac point, and then lifted off again to provide air support for the ground units. A humvee was waiting for him, Kevin Clark seated behind the wheel. The colonel nodded at Chuck as he got into the passenger seat.

"I left Thompson and Whitmer at the intersection. I figured you deserved a ride. Good work getting Corona. Were you able to interrogate him?"

McCain glanced over at the former Army Ranger and shrugged. "Not really. I tried but he wasn't very talkative. It didn't matter because he had the virus with him in the humvee."

Chuck had left the padded bag in Major Singleton's helicopter for safekeeping. The CDC agent didn't elaborate any further on his time with the cartel leader and Clark didn't press it. Corona was dead and as far as Kevin was concerned, he didn't care if McCain had executed the bastard on the side of the road. The bio-terror weapon was back in the hands of the good guys, another of their primary objectives having been met.

Kevin dropped Chuck off in front of the building, next to the undamaged LAV. Gunnery Sergeant Gray had dried blood on his face. The right sleeve of his fatigue jacket had been cut open, bloody gauze wrapped around his bicep. Gray was clearly in pain, but he continued to cover the front of the building, his M-16 braced against the side of the armored vehicle.

McCain held his hand out to the Marine. "I'm sorry about your men, Gunny. You guys fought like hell, and I'm not sure we could've done this without you."

Gray took the offered hand and nodded at the men around him. "Thanks. They're good Marines. Have you heard anything from the base hospital?"

"No, but I'll give them a call on the SAT phone in a few. How bad were they hurt?"

"Four wounded. The two most serious were a round to the head and another guy took one to the throat. I doubt they'll make it. The others both caught rounds in their legs."

"What about you?" Chuck asked, nodding at the Marine's bandaged arm.

The Marine looked offended that McCain would even mention such a minor gunshot wound. "This is nothing. I've hurt myself worse in training. What about the guys who shot my Marines? Did you get them?"

"There were four of them in that humvee, including the cartel leader, Antonio Corona. They're all very dead."

The Marine non-com looked into Chuck's face and gave a slight smile. "Well, that's good to hear."

"Air One to CDC One." The drone pilot's voice sounded excited and McCain got the feeling that he wasn't going to like what he had to say.

"CDC One, go ahead."

CDC One, you've got several groups of infected converging on your location."

"How many and which direction are they coming from?"

There was a pause. "Sir, they're coming from every direction. I'm estimating close to a thousand. They're moving pretty slow but they're coming your way. I'm guessing all the gunfire got their attention."

Chuck had three quick pictures flash through his mind. The first was from his and Elizabeth's recent sprint through the forest being pursued by hundreds of Zs, the feeling that they were going to die still vivid in his memory. A second image popped up, this one of McCain, the CDC agents and a small group of law enforcement officers being overrun by a pack of several thousand Zs near the Atlanta Braves stadium. One of his men, Luis García, had been killed along with so many others.

The third picture was of that terrible day on the University of Georgia campus when Rebecca Johnson had been mortally wounded. Afterwards, the CDC agents had killed as many of the zombies as they could, even entering the stadium where thousands of infected were feasting on fresh victims. Chuck had barely survived that day, as well.

Gray heard the radio traffic and saw the dark shadow pass over

McCain's face. Then just as quickly as it came, it was gone and the big man took charge.

"CDC One to Air One. Distance and ETA?"

"The closest group is coming from the north, down Peachtree Road. They're a mile out. I'm estimating three to four hundred, all coming from the Lenox Mall area where you were earlier. Plan on them arriving in thirty minutes.

"The others are similar sized groups, most a couple of miles away. The second closest group is a couple of hundred. I'd say you've got forty-minutes to an hour before they show up."

"CDC One to November Golf One and Alpha Foxtrot One, are you both clear on that radio traffic?"

"Roger, what are your orders?" Colonel Clark asked.

"I'm clear," Major Singleton answered.

"Alpha Foxtrot One, you and the other two air support units are weapons free. Air One will guide you to the packs of Zs and I want you to kill them all. Minimize property damage as much as you can, but eliminate those Zs."

"Alpha Foxtrot One, roger."

"November Golf One, we've got your three hummers and one mobile LAV. The first group is coming right at you. Hold your position but let's use the vehicles to take out any stragglers that manage to sneak past Alpha Foxtrot One's guns."

"Roger, we're on it," Clark acknowledged.

"CDC One to all units. Secure the prisoners in the lobby and leave two guards with them. If anybody tries to escape, shoot them. Put the hostages wherever you think is safe. Leave them a few weapons, just in case. Everyone else, reload and let's get ready to kill some zombies!"

McCain stepped off to the side and pulled out his satellite phone and dialed Admiral Williams.

"Hello, Mr. McCain, it's good to hear from you."

"I'm assuming you're watching the video feed from the drone and have been monitoring our radio traffic?"

"That's correct. You and your men have done an excellent job. Something happened with the video, though, when you were trying to take Antonio Corona into custody. There's a big chunk of footage that we don't have. I'm assuming he is no longer with us?"

"Yes, sir," Chuck smiled, realizing that Williams had probably had the drone crew delete the footage of him feeding the cartel leader to the zombies. "He was shot trying to escape, but, as you heard, I did recover the virus."

"Outstanding work! What do you need now?"

"More transport. We've got the forty-three women we rescued and thirty-four prisoners. As soon as we deal with the zombies that have us surrounded, we'll be ready to pull out. Also, one of the Marine LAVs is damaged and we'll need to make arrangements to get it back to the air base."

"Let me know when you want the transport enroute. I've got a Chinook waiting on the tarmac just outside. There are twelve FBI agents and eighteen army Rangers in the helicopter. They'll be relieving you and cleaning up the scene. We should be able to get all of your people out of there in two trips, plus Colonel Clark's vehicles and the operable LAV will be driving out."

"Yes, sir," Chuck said, wondering to himself where the additional personnel had come from. The admiral had told him that there were no other troops or law enforcement available for their operation. He would definitely ask him about that later.

"One more thing, Admiral, can I get a status report on those casualties that were brought in?"

McCain heard Williams sigh. "I'm sorry. One of the Marines was DOA and another died in surgery. The other two are in stable condition."

"Thanks for letting me know, sir. I'll pass it on to Gunny Gray."

**Buckhead, Atlanta, Wednesday, 0910 hours**

As it turned out, air superiority won the day. The drone pilot guided Major Singleton and the other two Pave Hawks to the closest pack of zombies, the group shuffling south on Peachtree Road on a collision course with the recently liberated Buckhead neighborhood. The major maneuvered into position, hovering at five hundred feet, this time allowing Corporal Baker to go first. The crewman triggered a short burst at the lead Zs, making sure the gun was operating correctly.

The 7.62mm rounds ripped the first several zombies apart. Every fifth round was a tracer, allowing Baker to see exactly were his bullets were impacting. The corporal began firing longer bursts, starting at the front of the large group of infected and working towards the rear. The Zs were spread across the five-lane road as they meandered south, and Baker moved the muzzle slightly as he fired, mowing them down.

Soon, the barrels of the minigun were spinning empty, the two thousand rounds of ammo used up, over half of the zombies eliminated. Singleton swung the helicopter around so that Sergeant Thomas could bring his minigun into play. In two minutes, the rest of the Zs had been blown apart by the sergeant's accurate fire.

The drone crew gave the coordinates for the next closest group and the second Air Force helicopter made quick work of them. The process was repeated for the next forty minutes. Air One then had the Pave Hawks circle around to each area once more, eliminating stragglers.

At 1005hrs, the area was pronounced clear and everyone breathed a sigh of relief. Chuck called Admiral Williams and requested that the Chinook head their way. He then ordered his men to prepare the hostages and their prisoners to leave.

The Rangers were the first ones off the big helicopter where a squad of Marines waited to escort them and the FBI agents from the grocery store parking lot to the scene of the battle. A burly Ranger captain looked McCain over as they shook hands in front of what had been the cartel HQ. Chuck introduced him to Andy and Scotty, letting them walk the soldiers and federal agents through the area of the shootout.

The agents from the Federal Bureau of Investigation were clearly unhappy with being dumped into the middle of Atlanta to serve as a cleanup squad for a much less prestigious federal agency such as the CDC Enforcement Division. One of the newcomers, however, had a mission of her own. Special Agent Maria Sanchez's camera hung from a strap next to the M4 rifle across her chest. She was designated to take photos of the bodies and the scene as she and her teammates cleaned it up.

What none of her colleagues suspected, however, was that she also planned to snap a few photos of the shooters who were responsible for this massacre. She knew that the Tijuana Cartel would want revenge and this was one way that she could repay the debt that she owed them. Maria saw bodies scattered all around the high-rise building and her team had been told that almost a hundred and fifty dead gang members were both inside and outside the tall edifice, as well as the two smaller structures on either side, and other locations within a two-block radius.

A tall, muscular figure wearing black was having a conversation with one of the Rangers with whom she had flown in with. Two other men, one even taller and bigger with a bushy beard, the other shorter and wiry, flanked the first man. They were similarly dressed in black BDUs, the words "Police" stitched across their backs. Those must be some of the CDC agents, Sanchez realized. The others clearly deferred to the muscular man.

Maria raised her camera to take a picture of the front of the Peachtree Summit Luxury Condominiums. She shifted her angle slightly and snapped several photos of the CDC officers. Uncle Pepe will be able to find out who they are, she thought. His influence goes very deep.

The soldiers and the feds were tasked with bagging bodies and securing all the weapons on the scene. The body bags, the recovered firearms, along with the soldiers and FBI agents, would be removed the next day. A repair team would be sent from Dobbins for the damaged LAV, along with a Marine security element. They would arrive later in the day on Wednesday.

By 1120 hours, McCain had released Clark's National Guard humvees and the operational LAV. The rescued women were already at Dobbins Air Force Base, being checked and treated by the medical staff. The Chinook had returned to Buckhead and was just lifting into the air with the prisoners and several Marines to guard them. The two Pave Hawks touched down and took on the SEALS, the SAS, and Tim and Tom.

Major Singleton's helicopter was the last ride out. When she landed, McCain let the CDC team board ahead of him. The big police officer took a final look around, making sure they hadn't left anyone behind before climbing into the helicopter with his men.

"Is that it, Agent McCain?" Singleton asked.

"Yes, ma'am, mission accomplished. Do you have any beer at the base? I think this calls for a drink."

"As a matter of fact, we do. Beer and maybe even something stronger."

"Well, then, let's get back to Dobbins!" Chuck said, with a smile.

# Chapter Twelve

**Dobbins Air Force Base, Marietta, Georgia, Thursday, 0850 hours**

The shooters and their support team had been allowed to eat, rest, and clean their weapons Wednesday afternoon and evening. Thursday morning, the debriefing would begin at 0900hrs. McCain was hoping to be back with Beth, and to have his team back with their loved ones, by Thursday afternoon. The warriors had finished breakfast and were moving towards one of the empty hangars to start their meeting.

Chuck held his coffee cup under the spout of the large urn in the front of the base dining hall. Scotty Smith walked up behind him, also holding an empty mug.

"Hey, Scotty," Chuck greeted his friend. "I haven't gotten to talk to you and Andy and the rest of the guys, but great work yesterday."

Smith nodded his thanks, more subdued than normal.

McCain turned and started to go, but something was off in the big former Army Ranger.

"You OK, Scotty?"

"I don't know, Chuck. I've got a lot of stuff whirling around in my head."

"What kind of stuff?" McCain asked, sipping his coffee.

Smith took a deep breath, held it, and then let it out. The bearded man glanced over at his boss and shrugged. "Like I'm wondering if I should ask Emily to marry me."

Chuck nodded and gave a slight smile. "So, killing a bunch of bad guys and rescuing a big group of hostages has got you thinking about marriage?"

Scotty laughed. "I know it sounds strange, but no one's ever accused me of being normal. When we were with Melanie's in-laws a couple of weeks ago, and Elizabeth told us how you guys met and fell in love, I saw Emily keep looking over at me, like she was hoping I'd take the hint or something.

"Man, I was impressed with you breaking in and killing those four kidnappers, especially the part where you had to beat that one guy to death. Good stuff! But, Em was more into the whole love story part of the rescue.

"I've been thinking about it and what impressed me the most was the fact that you were brave enough to ask Elizabeth to marry you. I mean, these are crazy times that we're living in, but you still went for it. I really love Emily and think I need to follow your lead."

McCain smiled at his friend again and slapped him on the shoulder. "I think you should. Emily's a keeper and she really loves you."

"You know, Andy predicted this," Smith grinned, shaking his head. "Right before that mess in downtown Atlanta, he saw the handwriting on the wall and he claimed Best Man status. I told him it wasn't going to happen anytime soon, but it looks like he was right and asked be my Best Man. If she says 'yes' do you think maybe you'd be one of those guys that stands next to the poor sap getting married?"

"You mean the groomsmen?"

"Yeah, would you be one of them? I bet Em would also want Elizabeth to be one of the chicks that stands next to her."

"Those are the brides maids and yeah, buddy, I'd be honored to stand next to you."

"Thanks. As you can see, there's a lot of stuff I don't know.

Maybe you can kind of guide me a little? I've never asked a girl to marry me before. I sure don't want to screw this up."

McCain slapped the bigger man on the shoulder again and laughed. "Sure, I'd be happy to help. Let's go get this debriefing done so we can get back to our women. We'll talk later about the best way to ask her."

Smith breathed a sigh of relief. "Thanks, Chuck. I knew I could count on you."

Chuck stopped by the restroom and Scotty continued on to the hangar, feeling like a weight had been lifted off of his shoulders. As he walked in, he saw the SEALs, the SAS, and several of the Marines gathered around one of the Air Force Pave Hawk crewman, a sergeant, the CDC agent noticed.

Sergeant Thomas was animatedly telling of his time on the ground with Agent McCain. "One of those gangsters jumped out of the humvee with an M-16 and McCain blasted him. A minute later, the driver tried to draw on him and he put a round into his head. McCain then jerked the cartel leader out of the vehicle and slammed him down on the ground.

"Agent McCain tried to interrogate him and asked where the virus was. They were on the other side of the hummer from me and I couldn't see anything, but I could hear everything. The Mexican said something about suing him and then said he was going to rape McCain's wife while he watched and kill his whole family.

"Man, that was the wrong thing to say! McCain told him, 'The most you could hope for from me was a quick death and you just lost that by threatening my family.' We had two groups of Zs coming towards us and a few minutes later McCain dragged this guy to his feet, picked him up, and threw him out into the street, in front of the zombies.

"He'd already told me to head back to the helicopter and that he'd be right behind me. I started but turned back in time to see that cartel leader get up from where he'd landed and start running. McCain shot him in the leg and then took off after me. Those two groups of Zs grabbed that scumbag and ripped him apart. I doubt there was anything left of that bastard.

"And then, just a minute later, Agent McCain saved my life. Most of the zombies were slow-movers but this one sprinter came charging me. I was focusing on the ones right in front of me and didn't even see him, but that CDC agent put a round in the runner's head, dropping him right in front of me."

The warriors all nodded appreciatively at Sergeant Thomas' story. There would be no sympathy from them for someone who had invaded their country, murdering, enslaving, and brutalizing so many people.

Scotty Smith spoke up. "Chuck's been my boss for almost two years now. I'm only scared of two people on the planet: my girlfriend and Chuck McCain. I've seen a lot of combat but if I could only pick one guy to stand beside me, it would be him. Trust me, let's just be glad he's on our side."

McCain and Admiral Williams walked to the front of the room, ready to start the debriefing. The admiral congratulated everyone for a successful mission and they had a moment of silence for those who had lost their lives. The final tally was one hundred and forty-six dead gang members. There were thirty-four prisoners who would soon be on their way to Guantanamo Bay. The assault force lost two dead, two wounded with serious injuries, and six with minor wounds.

The debrief took almost six hours and Major Singleton had the dining staff bring food into the hangar so that they could eat while they worked. Everyone was ready to get back to their families.

Finally, Chuck gave the CDC agents the order to board Admiral

Williams' Blackhawk for the ride back to the Centers for Disease Control location. The warriors all shook hands with their new friends, the camaraderie born out of fighting beside someone creating a lifelong bond. Williams approached McCain, making no effort to get on the aircraft.

"You're not coming with us, sir?"

"Not today," the elderly man answered, extending his hand to Chuck. "I have a few more loose ends to tie up, but I'll fly out and see you in the next couple of days. You and I have some things to talk about. For now, enjoy being with Elizabeth. She's a lovely lady and I'm very happy for the two of you. Rest up a bit and I'll see you soon. And congratulations, Chuck. That mission could not have been executed any better. You and your men did an exceptional job."

### Centers for Disease Control Compound, East of Atlanta, Thursday, 1615 hours

The reunion with Elizabeth had been sweet. She had put on some makeup and fixed herself up nicely, McCain thought as he wrapped his arms around her. He couldn't help but notice, however, that Nicole Edwards had dolled herself up as well, standing with Beth, Emily, Grace, Amy Fleming, Candice Marshall, and others as the helicopter touched down. Jay Walker had walked right up to the scientist and had embraced her, the two of them walking away together, talking quietly.

Chuck motioned with his head towards the couple. "I guess there's a story waiting to be told."

Elizabeth giggled, wrapping her arms around her husband again. "Oh, yeah. I'll fill you in later. I also want to hear about the mission, at least whatever you can tell me, but you look kind of tired. Maybe you need a little nap before dinner?"

The big man noticed that his wife was leading him towards their makeshift bedroom and he let her lead the way.

Later, in the evening they patrolled the perimeter, catching up on the last week that they had been apart. Chuck discussed their attack on the gang's base, leaving out the gory details, but letting her know that over forty captive women had been rescued, the cartel presence eliminated, and the bio-terror weapon recaptured. McCain mentioned the two dead and the two wounded Marines, a costly sacrifice for their victory, but not as bad as it could have been.

Elizabeth described how, over a couple of days, she and Nicole had become friends. They had sat at the scientist's desk as Nicole helped Elizabeth get familiar with their database of experiments and their current workflow. The goal was for Beth to figure out ways to take some of the pressure off of the researchers by handling their data entry and keeping it organized.

As they worked, Edwards had asked her how she and Chuck had met. Beth never got tired of bragging on how her husband had rescued her, just in the nick-of-time. Nicole had hung on every word as Elizabeth told the story, the databases forgotten.

They had eaten together in the dining hall that evening, continuing their conversation, moving on talk about their backgrounds and families. The epidemiologist had asked Beth about her family, but had seen the look of sadness cross the young woman's face. Elizabeth shared how her parents had gotten infected and how she had been forced to kill her mother and then watched the police shoot her zombie father before he could infect anyone else.

Edwards had apologized profusely for bringing up such a sensitive topic. Elizabeth had given a slight smile and told her that it was Chuck who had helped her get over the guilt and, and ultimately the depression, that she had carried over the death of her mom and dad.

The two women had ended up back at Nicole's small room,

sharing a bottle of wine, and talking into the early hours of the morning. The scientist had not had a close woman friend in years, and she felt surprisingly comfortable with Elizabeth. After several glasses of wine, Nicole had described how Chuck and his men had rescued her in the zombie overrun CDC headquarters. Dr. Edwards finally admitted to Beth that she had had a crush on her husband, expecting the other woman to be angry. Elizabeth smiled, patting her new friend's arm.

"It's OK. I understand."

"You're not mad?" Edwards asked.

"Of course not," Beth smiled. "Remember, he saved my life, too. We haven't been together very long, and I'm still not sure what he sees in me sometimes."

Edwards draped her arm across the younger woman's shoulders. "Oh, I understand what he sees in you. You're beautiful, for sure, but you have a kind heart. You are a good person, Elizabeth, and Chuck McCain is one lucky man."

Over the next couple of days, Nicole opened up about her feelings for Jay Walker. As she described their conversations, Beth got excited for her.

"This guy really likes you, Nicole."

"You think so? I'm not sure what to think."

"I'm probably not the best one to be giving relationship advice," Elizabeth said, with a smile, "but this Walker guy has laid it all on the table. It's up to you now. When he gets back, he's going to be looking for some hint that you're interested. Eventually, they're going to send him back to Washington, D.C., but he seems like the type who will do whatever it takes to be with you, if you want him to. Do you like him or not?"

Edwards looked at the younger woman and sighed. "I think so. I've always been focused on my career and really haven't taken the time to date. I'll take any relationship advice you can give."

Elizabeth also told Chuck that Dr. Martin had been so impressed with her work that he had offered her a permanent position whenever they were able to get human resources back up-and-running. Not only was she working with the scientists, she was also helping organize Martin's life. As the acting director for the CDC, he had to follow many different protocols and keep detailed records of everything that they were currently doing for the time when things would be back to normal.

Within two days, Beth had gotten her head wrapped around what he did. Two days after that, she began taking tasks off of his plate and handling them. Martin was amazed at how quickly Elizabeth had figured out a way to make his life easier.

"I wanted to talk with you before I accepted his job offer," she told her husband.

"Do you want the job? Obviously, there's a need and everyone likes you and your work."

"You wouldn't mind me working at the same place as you? I really like what I'm doing. I know it's just administrative stuff, but I feel like I'm a part of something important."

Chuck smiled. "Take it. I want you to be happy, plus we can commute to the office together."

The next day, McCain strolled into the lab carrying a black canvas bag with Dr. Nicole Edwards' name on it. The epidemiologist was in a deep conversation with an Asian woman, both of the scientists wearing white lab coats. Beth sat at Nicole's desk, typing data into a spreadsheet. She winked at her husband, but kept working. Nicole saw the big man walk in and smiled, motioning him over.

"Welcome back, Chuck. I heard that it was a successful mission and that my neighborhood is secure again."

McCain nodded. "Except for the occasional zombie sighting,

that's true. Hopefully, in a couple of months, you'll be able to return home."

"Wow! That's good news! I'd like to introduce you to someone," she said, nodding at the other woman. "Chuck McCain, this is Dr. Kim Bae-yong, the leading epidemiologist in the world."

"It's an honor to meet you, ma'am," Chuck said, as they shook hands.

"And it's very nice to meet you, Agent McCain. I've heard so much about you and your teams' work in combating the terrorists, as well as all you're doing to eliminate the infected."

Chuck smiled. "I have something here that will, hopefully, help you and your teams in finding a vaccine for this virus."

He handed Nicole the bag, watching her eyes light up. The scientist put on her protective equipment and carefully opened the bag, relieved to see all eight vials of the bio-terror weapon in place. She glanced back at McCain to see if he was holding anything else.

"Sorry, but I don't have your computer with me. It was a long, tough fight, and I forgot about it. There are some other people cleaning up the scene and I've asked them to look for it. If they find your laptop, I'll have it delivered here."

Edwards smiled and said, "Thank you. These experimental vaccines will help us so much with our current research. On another note, I've really enjoyed getting to know Elizabeth. You were right. She's a wonderful person and I'm happy she's going to keep working with us."

**Centers for Disease Control Compound, East of Atlanta, Saturday, 1330 hours**

The Blackhawk had landed at 1300hrs. Admiral Williams, Shaun, Tim, and Tom had gotten off with the admiral's assistant recruiting a few volunteers to offload another week of supplies provided by Major Singleton. Williams had greeted McCain warmly, asking for him to be available after he met with Dr. Martin. The scientist and the older man disappeared into Martin's workspace.

When the admiral and the acting director of the CDC walked out twenty minutes later, they were both smiling. Williams nodded at Chuck.

"Is your wife around, Mr. McCain? I think it would be good for her to join us as we talk. Dr. Martin has very kindly offered the use of his office for the next hour or two."

That's interesting, Chuck thought. Admiral Williams was definitely not your stereotypical CIA type, wanting to keep a lot of secrets. He was security conscious, to be sure, but he was also glad to share as much information with his subordinates as he could. It was unusual, however, to have a spouse sit in on a work-related meeting, especially when one worked for the Central Intelligence Agency.

"Yes, sir. Give me just a minute to find her."

Five minutes later, Chuck and Elizabeth sat across from the Director of Operations for the Central Intelligence Agency.

"I'm going to get right to the point, Chuck. I'm replacing you as the director of the Atlanta office for CDC enforcement."

McCain felt Beth stiffen as she heard her husband being fired. Chuck saw a twinkle in the admiral's eye, though, and he was curious as to where this conversation would go. Chuck nodded, not saying anything. He reached over and gave Elizabeth's hand a reassuring squeeze. McCain hadn't been looking for a job when Rebecca Johnson had recruited him to the new agency. Of course, he didn't like the idea of being fired, but Chuck knew the admiral well enough by now to know that he had something else up his sleeve.

Williams stared over the desk for a minute before he spoke again. "We'll talk about your future in just a moment, but I'd like to ask for your recommendation on who should take your place? Is there someone on your current team, whom you feel could fill the very large shoes that you'll be leaving?"

Without hesitating, McCain said, "Eddie Marshall is your guy, Admiral. He's a proven leader, with an extensive background in both local and federal law enforcement. He'll do a fantastic job, plus he's got two great team leaders in Andy and Jimmy. For that matter, Scotty and Hollywood could easily lead their own teams, as well."

"That's good to hear," the admiral said. "He was my pick, as well, but I wanted to hear it from you after having served together as team leaders, and then as his boss."

"Eddie will make a great director, sir. I've got to admit, though," McCain smiled, "I've never been fired and then asked to name my successor."

Elizabeth still wasn't sure what was going on, but her husband didn't seem too concerned about losing his job. Then again, the only time that she'd ever seen him truly rattled was when he proposed to her, she thought, suppressing a smile.

"Oh, I didn't say I was firing you. I just said I was replacing you. I have another job for a man of your skills and expertise, if you'll take it. The reason I had you direct that op against the cartel was that I needed to see you in action. You had the challenge of leading a diverse group of special operators, conventional troops, federal agents, and even some citizen soldiers with the National Guard.

"Of course, you couldn't leave well enough alone," the admiral said, with a grin, "and you had to get Major Singleton to land so that you could get into the fight, as well. But, truth be told, I would've done the same thing. And you were in the right place at the right time to recover the virus and to deal with a very evil cartel leader."

McCain glanced at Beth and saw the questions in her eyes. There are some questions that will never be answered, Sweetheart, he thought.

Williams continued, "I purposefully withheld some resources

from you, but you still led your men to victory. I would have sent those Rangers and FBI agents in immediately if you'd needed them but you managed with the assets you were given, and even though significantly outnumbered, our mission objectives were met."

"I didn't have to do a whole lot of leading, Admiral," McCain answered quietly. "Those men and women are warriors and just needed to be pointed in the right direction."

Williams shrugged. "Don't be so modest. You and a couple of your agents developed the ops plan, you oversaw their training, and you executed the mission." He locked eyes with McCain for just an instant as he said, "executed."

Beth's eyes beamed with pride as Admiral Williams spoke of Chuck's leadership ability. She was feeling much better about the direction that this meeting was moving. What was he going to ask Chuck to do? she wondered.

"So, my proposal is this: I need you in Washington. I'm adding two new assistant directors of operations. One of them will be filled by Lieutenant Colonel, soon to be full Colonel, Kevin Clark. He'll be focusing on clandestine para-military operations abroad, and whatever else I need him to do in that realm.

"You would be my second assistant director. Your focus would be on the east coast here, coordinating with local and federal law enforcement in the elimination of the remaining infected and the removal of the dead. On paper, you'll be under the umbrella of the Department of Homeland Security, but you'll report to me. We just won't publicize that. Representing DHS will get you more cooperation in local LE circles than representing the CIA.

"I wish I could offer you more specifics about this new position, but you'll be making it up as you go. We've never had to clean up after a bio-terror attack of this magnitude before, but you're a very resourceful man and I have full confidence in you. If you take this job, you'll need to have the beginnings of a staff. I can authorize you to take of two of your current agents with you."

"Scotty and Andy," Chuck answered immediately, realizing that in his mind, he had already said "yes."

The admiral nodded. "Good choices, although Agent Smith does seem to be a bit of a loose canon."

McCain laughed. "He is that, but he's also one of the best shooters that I've ever worked with. He and Andy are both excellent leaders and are great at connecting with local cops."

"Very good, you know them better than I do. Now, let me turn my attention to the lovely Mrs. McCain."

Beth blushed at the compliment and smiled brightly.

"I understand that you have already become a popular member of the team here. Dr. Martin was singing your praises earlier. He told me that he's never had a personal assistant who learned their position so fast. You've evidently got him and the researchers organized so that they can focus doing what they do best."

"I'm glad I'm able to play a part," she answered, appreciative of the kind words. "It's an honor to be a part of their team."

Williams smiled and continued, "And he told me that he's offered you a full-time job?"

"Yes, sir."

"Well, that's wonderful. I'm glad that you've found you're place here so quickly. If you take that job, and if your husband decides to accept my offer, we'll have to work something out. Chuck's new position will require him to be based in Washington, D.C., and there will be some travel involved. I took the liberty of discussing the situation with Dr. Martin and he sees no problem at all with you working remotely and just coming to the office in Atlanta a couple of times a month. Would you be willing to work in that capacity?"

"Of course," Elizabeth answered quickly, excited at the possibilities that were in front of them.

The admiral turned his gazed back to Chuck. "So, Mr. McCain, what do you think?"

"If I took this position, when would I start?"

"Well, let's see. I promised you that I'd get you back to North Carolina to have a longer visit with your daughter. There was something else as well…oh, that's right! You two haven't had a honeymoon yet. International travel is still being severely restricted for fear that individuals might be carrying the virus. I could, however, make arrangements for the two of you to fly to California. How does a couple of weeks in San Diego or Los Angeles sound? Chuck, what if we say that you would start in six weeks? Four weeks for the two of you to travel and then two weeks to get settled in DC?"

Elizabeth had never been to California or Washington, D.C., before and her face lit up. Chuck couldn't help but smile at the surprised look on Beth's face. How could he say 'no' to that?

"Admiral, I accept your offer. Thank you for your confidence in me and I'll work hard not to let you down. One question, though. This seems like the kind of position where we'll work ourselves out of a job in a year or two. Eventually, all the zombies will be eliminated and things will be back to normal. What then?"

"Mr. McCain, a man with your skills and mindset will always have a job. When it gets to that point, I'm sure I can find something else that will challenge you."

Williams' next meeting was with Eddie and Chuck. Marshall was clearly surprised to be offered the promotion, but he gratefully accepted and congratulated McCain on his new position.

"Mr. Marshall, I know that you're going to do an excellent job. Mr. McCain will be asking Agents Fleming and Smith to join him on his staff so you'll have to do some recruiting. I'd suggest that before the DC team heads north, you might see if one of them is interested in moving to Atlanta. Of course, being a former SEAL myself I'm a little biased, but if it was me, I'd be going after Agent Walker.

"Supervisory Agent Trang is going to be going through the same rebuilding process as you. His pool of potential recruits is a little bigger in the Washington-Metro area so I would let you have one of his men."

"Thanks, Admiral. I'll check with Jay and see if he would be interested in transferring. He and I worked together on capturing Terrell Hill and I would love to have him as one of my team leaders."

**Centers for Disease Control Compound, East of Atlanta, Saturday, 2030 hours**

Later in the evening, all of the CDC agents and their wives or girlfriends had sat together in the dining hall as they enjoyed their meal of fettuccine Alfredo and canned vegetables, courtesy of the Air Force. Jay had asked Nicole to join them, and she sat between he and Elizabeth. Jimmy Jones and Scotty Smith kept the table laughing with one funny story after another.

Everyone had heard the news that Chuck would be leaving for another position and that Eddie would be their new leader as they began the process of rebuilding the Atlanta operation and continuing their mission. Both Fleming and Smith had accepted the offer to join McCain's staff without hesitation. For the two remaining Atlanta agents, Jimmy Jones and Hollywood Estrada, they were disappointed to see their friends go but knew that they would continue to cross paths in the war on terror.

Leadership transitions always have the potential to create tension and uncertainty among those whom it affects. With Marshall being chosen to replace McCain, though, Jones and Estrada breathed a sigh of relief knowing that they were in good hands. They trusted Eddie completely and knew that this would be a seamless transition.

As the meal was winding down, Scotty stood up and asked for the table's attention.

"Before everyone gets finished and heads to bed, I'd like to say something."

"Man, you ain't never lacking for anything to say," Jones quipped. "Except that time Chuck knocked you out. You were kinda quiet then."

Those who knew what Jimmy was talking about laughed and Smith smiled, instinctively rubbing his jaw. "Hey, Jimmy, why don't you go a couple of rounds with him and see how long you last!"

Jimmy laughed. "No, man, I'm good. I'll pass on that one. When Chuck hits people they fall down and don't move for a while. But thanks for the offer."

When the laughing subsided, Scotty took a deep breath. "We've all been through a lot together and I consider everybody at this table my family. Some of us are going to be moving away and leaving behind people that we really love."

Emily listened to her boyfriend talk with a sense of uncertainty. They had been dating for over six months and had fallen in love. At the same time, she wasn't sure how Scotty moving to Washington, D.C., was going to affect their relationship. He'd mentioned his new job to her as they were walking to the dining room, but had not had much time to elaborate.

Over dinner, she tried to stay engaged in the conversations around her but was preoccupied with her own thoughts. Maybe later, she and Scotty could talk it out. That was one of the reasons why she loved him so much. He always had his own unique way of making her feel better.

She was surprised when he stood up at the end of the meal and started talking. What did he just say about "leaving behind people that we love." Her heart sank at the thought of him living so far away in a society where travel was so difficult.

But then Emily heard his voice get softer, a little less sure of itself. "But there's someone here that I'm not planning on leaving behind."

The young woman realized that her boyfriend was now staring down at her from his full height of six foot five inches. "Emily, you're everything that I ever wanted in a woman and I can't imagine not having you with me." He paused taking a deep breath. "What I was wanting to ask you was if you…"

A voice cleared loudly across the table. Smith paused and looked over at McCain who was motioning down with his hand.

"Oh, yeah. Thanks, Chuck."

Scotty dropped to one knee in front of his girlfriend. Even kneeling he was still slightly taller than the diminutive young woman.

Something clicked inside of Emily and her mouth dropped open.

"Em, what I was wanting to ask is if you'll marry me?"

There was a collective gasp around the table at what they were witnessing. Emily sat frozen in her chair, but then reached over and wrapped her arms around Scotty's neck and hugged him tightly, tears running down her face.

"I'd love to marry you, Scotty," she answered quietly.

"You will?" he answered, sounding surprised.

The muscular man hugged her back and stood up, easily lifting the young woman into the air. After a moment he turned to all his friends, his trademark grin plastered across his face.

"She said 'yes!' Can you guys believe it? She really said 'yes.'"

The room erupted in applause as even the other diners around the room picked up what was going on at the enforcement unit's table. Scotty eventually set his new fiancée back on her feet. He held her face in his massive hands, kissing her with a gentleness that even his friends didn't know that he was capable of. When he finally came up for air, Smith looked across the table at McCain and mouthed, "thanks for the help."

As the group started to disperse, Jay asked Nicole to take a walk. They had been able to share a few meals together since his return, but the CDC agent was still getting mixed signals from the beautiful scientist. She had certainly looked gorgeous when he had gotten off of the Blackhawk a couple of days before and she hadn't pushed him away when he had hugged her. Other than the hug, though, there hadn't been any other physical contact.

Edwards had, however, been more open and they'd had several great conversations getting to know each other. She was warming up to him, but what was she really looking for? Walker was tired of being single and found himself very attracted to Nicole. She was a beautiful woman, but it was more than that. She was also very smart, but it went even deeper than that. He liked talking with her. He loved the sound of her laugh. He enjoyed just being with her. Have I fallen in love? he wondered.

Nicole hadn't said much during dinner, but had laughed at Scotty's and Jimmy's stories and cheered along with everyone else as Smith had proposed to Emily. She seemed to have enjoyed herself and Walker was intrigued to see how close Edwards and Chuck's new wife had become. At one point Nicole had leaned over to Jay, putting her hand on his arm and thanking him for inviting her to dinner with his friends, telling him how much fun she was having.

Now, they were walking together under the light of a full moon, the forest around them quiet and tranquil. "Can I ask for your opinion on something?" Jay asked.

"Sure, what is it?"

"You know, they're getting ready to send us home in a couple of days."

"Yeah, I heard that," she answered, quietly.

"Well, I've got a big decision to make. Eddie Marshall is the new boss here with McCain taking a new job and moving to Washington. Eddie asked me if I'd be interested in transferring down here and being one of his team leaders."

"He did?" Nicole responded excitedly. She hadn't known what to expect when Jay went back home. Washington was a long way from Atlanta.

"Yep. Now, I need a little help. Like I said, this is a big decision for me. I like working with Tu and the guys, but I also have a lot of respect for Eddie and his team. What do you think I should do?

"I told you before that I want to get to know you. It's been nice the last couple of days hanging out, but I guess I'm wondering if you see any kind of serious relationship in your future, in our future. If you're not interested, I'll head back to DC. But, if you thought this old Navy guy had a chance, I'd…"

Jay never completed his sentence as Nicole wrapped her arms around his neck and kissed him long and hard. When they came up for air, they just held each other.

"Please stay," Nicole whispered. "I don't even know what a serious relationship looks like. I've never had one, but I'm willing to learn."

Walker kissed her again and whispered in her ear, "Let's learn together."

I hope you enjoyed *Climbing Out of the Ruins* as much as I enjoyed writing it! If you did, would you consider leaving me a review on Amazon? Reader reviews mean so much to authors.

And don't forget to tell your friends about the Zombie Terror War Series. If by chance, you are jumping in with book five, make sure you go back and read the other volumes. You'll be glad you did!

Stayed tuned for more with Chuck, Elizabeth, and the entire team coming in 2019. There is still more work to be done!

Made in United States
North Haven, CT
03 September 2022

23595273R00236